D0251173

Like a River Glorious

Greenwillow Books
An Imprint of HarperCollins*Publishers*

This book is a work of fiction. References to real people, events, establishments, organizations, or locales are intended only to provide a sense of authenticity, and are used to advance the fictional narrative. All other characters, and all incidents and dialogue, are drawn from the author's imagination and are not to be construed as real.

 Printed in the United States of America. For information address HarperCollins Children's Books, a division of HarperCollins Publishers, 195 Broadway, New York, NY 10007.
www.epicreads.com

The text of this book is set in 11-point Hoefler.
Book design by Paul Zakris

Library of Congress Cataloging-in-Publication Data is available.
ISBN 978-0-06-224294-5 (trade ed.)

16 17 18 19 20 21 PC/RRDH 10 9 8 7 6 5 4 3 2 1
First Edition

 Greenwillow Books

For Sheila & Dave Yarbrough,
who were my "breath of heaven" when I needed it most

Dramatis Personae

In Glory, California:

Leah "Lee" Westfall, a sixteen-year-old orphan girl

Jefferson McCauley, Lee's best friend

The Joyners

Rebekah Joyner, a widow from Tennessee

Olive Joyner, her seven-year-old daughter

Andrew Joyner Jr., her four-year-old son

Unnamed baby girl, her infant daughter

"Major" Wally Craven, former wagon train leader

Hampton Bledsoe, an escaped slave

The Illinois College Men

Jasper Clapp, studied medicine

Thomas Bigler, studied law

Henry Meek, studied literature

The Hoffmans

Herman Hoffman, a farmer from Germany

Helma Hoffman, his wife

Martin, their fourteen-year-old son

Luther, their twelve-year-old son

Otto, their ten-year-old son

Carl, their nine-year-old son

Doreen, their six-year-old daughter

At Hiram's Gulch:

Hiram Westfall, Lee's uncle

Frank Dilley, hired gun and former wagon guide

Jonas Waters, Dilley's second-in-command

Abel Topper, mine foreman

Muskrat, local leader

Mary, Chinese immigrant

Wilhelm, hired gun

Reverend Ernest Lowrey, widower and traveling preacher

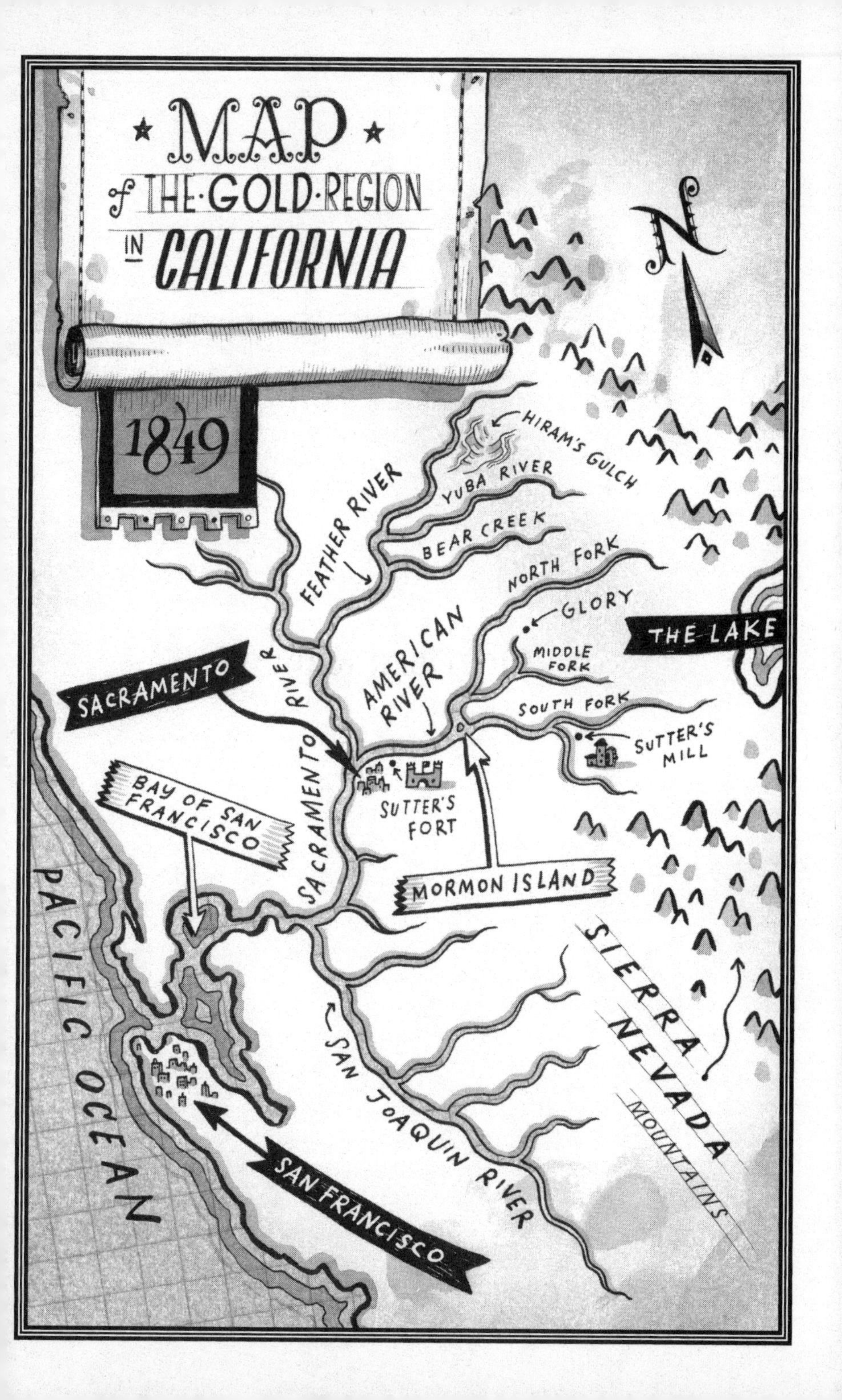
MAP
of THE·GOLD·REGION
IN CALIFORNIA
1849
N
HIRAM'S GULCH
YUBA RIVER
FEATHER RIVER
BEAR CREEK
NORTH FORK
GLORY
THE LAKE
AMERICAN RIVER
MIDDLE FORK
SOUTH FORK
SUTTER'S MILL
SACRAMENTO
SACRAMENTO RIVER
SUTTER'S FORT
BAY OF SAN FRANCISCO
MORMON ISLAND
PACIFIC OCEAN
SIERRA NEVADA
MOUNTAINS
SAN JOAQUIN RIVER
SAN FRANCISCO

October 1849

Chapter One

Sunrise comes late to California. Even when golden light washes the sky, and the snow-tipped peaks of the Sierra Nevada glow pink as winter roses, we remain in shadow for a spell, dwarfed by the slope of the land. Inevitably, a spark sears a crease in the mountains. Within moments, it becomes a flood of light, too bright to look on. The shadows are brow-beaten away, and our camp is swathed in color—tall green pines and waving yellow grass along the blue rapids of the twisting American River.

I stand facing east, my hand shading my eyes. At my back are the sounds of our waking camp: tin pans clanking, breakfast fire crackling, dogs splashing through the shallows.

"Morning," comes a voice at my ear, and I jump. It's Jefferson McCauley Kingfisher, bleary faced and yawning, suspenders hanging at his sides. His black hair is badly mussed, like a family of mice nested there during the night. "What's got you so tickled?" he grumbles in response to my smile.

"You have Andrew Jackson hair."

Jefferson frowns like he just bit into a sour persimmon. "He's the last fellow I care to resemble. You know what he did."

I wince. "I was just thinking about the picture they had at school and . . . I mean, I'm sorry."

He runs his fingers through his hair. "Well, so long as I don't have Andrew Jackson eyebrows, I'm still the finest-looking fellow for at least"—he glances back at our distant camp, toward Becky Joyner at the griddle, the Hoffman boys helping their father check the wagon, Henry Meek grooming his scant beard—"a hundred feet."

I harrumph at that. Jefferson is the finest-looking young man for a hundred *miles*, but I'd never say so aloud. Wouldn't want it to go to his mussy-haired head.

"A whole month in California," he muses, "and you've never missed a sunrise."

"Course not. It's the finest thing I ever saw." I gaze east again. That's where we came from, the lot of us. We started off a company of almost fifty wagons and three times that many people, but some went their separate ways. Some died. Now all that're left are eighteen souls and a single wagon between us.

"There are finer things," he says softly. My cheeks warm, from sunshine and the sure knowledge that Jefferson is studying my face.

I'm saved having to reply when Becky Joyner calls out, "Breakfast is ready!"

"I smell eggs," Jefferson says quickly. "Can you believe it? Eggs! For a while I thought I'd eat nothing but quick bread and prickly pear for the rest of my short life."

"Burned eggs," I clarify. Becky never saw a breakfast she couldn't improve with a liberal charring.

"Well, I'm glad for them, burned or not. C'mon, let's wash up." We head toward the river's edge and crouch to wet our hands.

Jefferson rolls up his sleeves and scrubs at his forearms. "Once we find a good claim spot, I'll head back down to Mormon Island to get some chickens. If we have enough gold, I'll look around for a good milk cow, too."

"We'll have enough," I assure him, and we share a small, secret grin.

At Mormon Island, we talked to a family who'd had a rough time of the crossing and were already giving up and going home. It's a shame, because my gold sense is buzzing like it always does in these hills, soft and smooth like a cat's purr. There's plenty of gold for everyone here, at least for now.

As I reach forward to splash water onto my face, the buzzing intensifies, becomes almost unpleasant—like bees swirling a hive.

Jefferson's hands go still above the water. "Lee?" he whispers, with a quick glance behind to make sure no one is listening. "Your eyes are doing that thing again."

According to him, my eyes turn more golden than brown when I'm near a find, like tiger's-eye gemstones, he says.

"There's something nearby," I whisper back. "A nugget, I think. Not that big, or I'd be near senseless."

"Well, let's find her!"

"I . . . okay, sure." It feels peculiar to stretch out with my gold sense while his eyes are so intent on me. He watches me all the time now. Sometimes he glances away when I catch him at it, but sometimes he doesn't. Just stares like a man with nothing to hide, which always gives my belly a tumble.

"So how does it work, exactly?" he says. "You just close your eyes and—"

"Breakfast is nearly done for," Becky calls out. "You miss it, you fend for yourself."

I shoot to my feet, a little relieved. "Breakfast first," I say. "Nugget later."

Jefferson frowns. "All right." He grabs my upper arm as I'm turning away. "No, wait."

His hand feels huge and strong now. A man's hand. When he gazes down at me, he looks just like the boy I grew up with. But he's changed so much this last year, it's like a stitch in my side. Like I've lost part of him. We've changed together, I reckon. We're still best friends, for sure and certain, but there are parts of Jefferson McCauley and Leah Westfall that are long gone, dropped like so much baggage in the land we left behind, or maybe scattered like seeds across the continent.

"Lee, there's something I need to ask you." He looks down at his boots, that frown still tugging his lips, and suddenly my heart is like buffalo stampeding in my chest.

I yank my arm from his grip. Whatever he has to say, I'm not ready to hear it. I know I'm not, and I open my mouth to tell him I'm in no mood for another no-good, fool-headed proposal, but the words can't seem to find their way out.

"We've been friends our whole lives," he says. "Best friends. And I'm not sure how to get past that to . . ." He pauses. All of a sudden his gaze snaps to mine, his face filled with determination. "To what I want."

My heart curls in on itself. *No, Jefferson, not now. Not yet.*

"I'm not sure it's what *you* want," he continues. "But a man ought to make his intentions clear, and my intentions are to—"

A rifle booms, too close.

Jefferson lurches forward, eyes flying wide.

I reach to catch him as another gun sounds—a pistol this time, closer to camp.

Mrs. Hoffman screams as Jefferson sags into my arms.

"Lee?" Jefferson whispers, his eyes glazing. "I think I'm shot."

I have to find cover. I have to get him somewhere safe. A shot zings past my ear. The horses neigh in panic. I drag Jefferson back toward the line of pines, his heels digging furrows in the damp earth.

"Everyone, get behind the wagon!" the Major yells.

Gunpowder scent fills my nose as more shots ring out.

We reach the trees. I spot the thickest trunk and yank Jefferson behind it. He settles gingerly to a sitting position. "It's not that bad," he says, but his dark Cherokee complexion has gone white like curdled cream.

I crouch beside him. I itch to grab my gun, to run and make

sure the little ones are hidden away. But not until I know Jefferson is safe. "Show me," I demand.

He shifts to reveal his right flank. His shirt is in tatters and soaked in blood.

"The bullet's not in me," he says, and I'm glad to hear the strength in his voice. "It burns a fair bit, but I'll be fit in no time."

I yank my kerchief from under my collar and untie it. "Here." I thrust it toward him. "Wad it up and press it against the wound. I'll be right back."

Crouching to make myself small, I creep through the trees toward our wagon and the campsite.

"You be careful, Leah Westfall," Jefferson whispers at my back.

Through a break in the pine branches, I see the wheels of our wagon. More gunshots rip the air, and I dare to hope some of my people are firing back. I'm desperate to lay eyes on them, to make sure everyone is all right. But until I figure out who is attacking and where they're coming from, I have to be patient. I have to be a ghost.

I inch forward on silent feet.

There, tucked behind one of the wagon wheels. Little Olive and Andy Joyner are huddled tight, like a ball made of limbs. Olive's face is streaked with dust and tears, but when she catches my eye and sees me put a finger to my lips, she gives me a quick, brave nod.

The younger Hoffman boys are crouched behind the opposite wheel, their tiny sister, Doreen, sheltered between them.

Otto holds his daddy's pistol clumsily in one hand, like it's a snake that might bite. I can't see Mr. Hoffman, but I know he's nearby; I know it because he carries my mama's locket now. But not even the sweet siren call of gold can tell me whether he's alive or dead.

Beside the wagon is the Major's triangle tent. It's caved in a bit, and a tiny flag of fabric waves in the breeze near the top—a bullet hole. I hope to God no one is inside.

There's no sign of Becky Joyner and the baby, the older Hoffmans, the three college men, or Hampton. We left the horses tied up in a nearby meadow, including my precious Peony, but there's no way to know how she's doing. I'm not the praying type, but I can't help slipping a little something heavenward: *Please, please let everyone be all right.*

More shots crack the air—two from across the river, one due south. Just three people shooting at us, far as I can tell, and only the one rifle between them. The revolvers aren't much of a menace at this distance, but I need my own rifle and powder horn if I'm to take care of the fellow who winged Jefferson. They're in the holster of Peony's saddle, which is laid out across a log on the other side of our still-smoking campfire. Out in the open.

A cry pierces the air. The Joyner baby. It's followed by shushing and murmuring, which does absolutely nothing to quiet the tiny girl but fills me with so much relief I'm suddenly a little unsteady. Becky and the baby. Both alive.

The guns go silent all at once. The birds have fled, and my companions are as quiet as the grave in their hiding spots, so it's just Baby Girl Joyner, wailing her little head off to the open sky.

A man's voice rings out. "Didn't realize y'all had a baby!"

Only the daft and the desperate attack a camp full of people without scouting it first.

From somewhere to my right, Tom Bigler shouts, "We have six children under the age of ten and some womenfolk besides!" Tom studied law at Illinois College, and he's been speaking on our behalf more and more since we arrived in California Territory.

"You Mormons?" the strange man calls out. "We don't hold with Mormons."

"No, sir," Tom says. After a pause . . . "Is that why you're shooting at us?"

I hold my breath. We've heard a lot of grumbling about the Mormons since we got here, though as far as I can tell they're just regular folks who don't make any trouble. I'd hate to hear we were attacked because someone thought we were Mormons.

But I'd hate it even more to learn they're my uncle's men, looking for *me*. Because that would mean this is all my fault. We haven't seen Uncle Hiram since that day at Sutter's Fort, but I've been expecting him to come calling, and not in a friendly way.

"This here a good spot for color?" the man hollers. "Found anything?"

Tom doesn't respond at first, and I know he's considering his answer. The man's voice came from the south. Maybe I can creep around our camp and come up behind him. I'll have to be very slow and careful, like I'm hunting a deer.

I start to creep back, away from the wagon, but Tom's voice stills me. "This is a very good spot," he lies.

Our group has been waiting on word from Jefferson and me that we've reached a promising location. This stretch of river does have some gold. But not a lot. Not enough to stake claims here. The others think we've got an eye for prospecting, us being born and raised in Georgia gold-mining country. But the truth is, I've got witchy powers that lead me to gold as sure as the west leads the sun.

"Well, maybe we want this spot for ourselves," the man says.

Not my uncle's men, then. Just a few cussed claim jumpers.

"We haven't staked claims yet," Tom says. "Got here last night. Already found a bit of dust without even trying. But if you let us pack up and be on our way, we'll find ourselves another spot, and you can have this one with our blessing."

A long pause follows, interspersed with mutterings. They can't get away with this so easily. Not after they shot Jefferson. I'll be glad to get everyone safe, sure, but I'd almost give up Daddy's boots to mark their faces. I want to know trouble when it comes at me next.

"You got ten minutes," the man calls out. "If any of you start loading guns, we start shooting."

"That's a deal," Tom says. "We'll be away before you know it."

I can hardly believe my eyes when Becky Joyner pops up from behind a large boulder, baby over her shoulder. She boldly hastens to the campfire and, using her free hand, starts chucking things into the back of the wagon—the still-hot griddle, the water bucket, the baby's blanket. Though the air is crisp, sweat sheens her face, and short strands of blond hair have curled wet against her neck.

When no one shoots at Becky, Hampton appears from behind a large tree trunk. "I'll fetch the oxen and hook them up," he says.

"I'll help," says Otto, crawling out from under the wagon.

Major Craven hobbles out with his crutch from behind the same boulder Becky used for cover and hurries toward his tent to pack it up. I've no time to mark the others, because I'm already dashing back into the trees to fetch Jefferson.

Jeff has pulled himself to his feet. He leans against the tree trunk, and his breaths are fast and shallow. The bloodstain has spread down the side of his trousers.

"Don't think I can ride," he gasps as I wrap one of his arms around my shoulders to bolster him. "Just get me into the wagon."

We stumble through the trees. He's so tall now, and heavy enough that my thighs burn. When did he get so big?

"Jasper!" I holler as we near the wagon. "Jeff's been hurt!" Everyone is scurrying around, working fast. The sides of the canvas bonnet are rolled up for easy loading, and the bed is already nearly full. "Jasper!"

The young doctor comes running, along with several others. He waves them off. "No, no, keep working," he says. First thing in the morning, and Jasper is in a starched white shirt, as clean as a groom at his wedding. He's got some odd notions about dirt for a miner, but maybe not so odd for a doctor. He insists that keeping himself clean saves lives.

Jasper's eyes are narrowed, assessing, even before he reaches us. Together we lower Jefferson to the ground and roll him onto his side. Olive Joyner stands over us, rag doll clutched in one hand. "I'll get your kit," she says, calm as a woman grown, and she dashes away.

"Bullet's not in me, Doc," Jefferson pants out.

"I'm no doctor," Jasper says as he peels the shirt away from the wound. "Just studying to be one." His voice is calm and soothing, like bullets haven't just been flying willy-nilly.

"You're all the doc we need," the Major says. He taps his wooden leg against a rock. Jasper amputated the Major's leg to save his life on our journey west.

The strange man's voice rings out from the trees. "Didn't mean to hurt nobody! It were an accident!"

"Well, you shouldn't be shooting at stuff if you're so cussed bad at it!" I holler back, and Jasper gives me a dark glance that looks so much like Mama's stop-antagonizing-people-or-else face that it puts a lump in my chest.

Jefferson hisses as Jasper starts poking around. I refuse to look at the wound, focusing instead on Jeff's pale face. "You're going to be fine," I tell him, though I've no idea if it's true.

"Course I am," he says through clenched teeth, but he reaches for my hand. I grab it and squeeze tight.

Olive hurries back, blond braids swinging, Jasper's medicine chest banging against her knees. The chest is nearly half the size of the girl, and it's a wonder she lugged it here so fast.

Jasper pours water from his canteen over Jefferson's flank. Though I've never had a stomach for injuries, I can't help glancing at the wound. It's a jagged tear in the skin, still bleeding freely, but it's small. Jefferson was right. The bullet just grazed him, taking a chunk of skin with it.

"You *are* going to be just fine," I say in relieved wonder.

"Told you so," Jefferson says.

Jasper follows the water with a liberal dose of Hawe's Healing Extract, but I turn away when he pulls out a wicked needle and some thread.

Olive, on the other hand, stares transfixed. "That's how I sewed Dolly's pinafore," she says.

"Skin feels a little different than calico under the needle," Jasper says to her. "But if you can sew a pinafore, you can stitch a wound."

Jefferson's fingers squeeze the bones of my hand together as the needle pierces his skin.

"I could do that," Olive says.

Jasper ties a knot and snips the leftover thread. "Tell you what. Next time Lee or Jefferson bags a rabbit, we'll practice some stitches on the bullet hole."

"Okay, Jasper!"

I stare at the girl. Such a quiet little thing, who gets teary-eyed at the slightest provocation. But I guess everyone is brave about something.

"All right, Jefferson," Jasper says as he ties off the wrapping. "It bled a good bit, so I want you to ride in the wagon until I know that wound is sealing properly. But you should be fine."

Jeff winces as we help him to his feet. "Thanks, Doc," he says.

The strange man's voice hollers out, "I reckon it's all right if you need a few more minutes, given that you have an injury."

Our camp is already packed up. We've had to move fast before, and everyone knows exactly what to do. Major Craven is near the wagon tongue, checking the oxen harnesses. "At least they don't seem keen to murder us all," he grumbles.

"Stupid men can be just as dangerous as murderous ones," I tell him.

"More dangerous, often as not," he says, and he helps us shove Jefferson onto the wagon bench.

Hampton approaches, Peony and Sorry saddled up and trailing behind him, and I'm so relieved to see them both. I grab Peony's reins and plant a kiss on her pretty white nose. "Just a bunch of fuss and noise, girl," I tell her, and true to form, she tosses her blond mane, more annoyed than frightened.

"The sorrel's got a small gash on her foreleg," Hampton says. "Must have panicked when the guns went off. I think she's fine, though."

"Can't ride her, anyway," Jefferson says.

"I'll lead her instead of tying her to the back of the wagon," Hampton says. "Otherwise that gash will fill with dust."

"Thanks, Hampton."

Jefferson's sorrel mare looks as sorry as ever, with her head drooping and her tail limp like it's the worst day of her life, but that's just her way, ever since she was a filly, so I'm not worried.

"Roll out!" Mr. Hoffman says in his big, booming voice.

The Major whips his stick over the oxen's heads, and the wagon lurches away. The rest of us follow, me on Peony, Jefferson on the wagon bench, the rest on foot. Mrs. Hoffman carries the Joyner baby to give Becky a break, and Martin Hoffman hefts his tiny sister, Doreen, onto his shoulders, much to her delight. Tom Bigler and Henry Meeks slap Jasper on the back for another job well done.

I let everyone get ahead so I can watch them all and ponder a bit in solitude. I think of the nugget I sensed, still hiding in the riverbank. I hope she stays there, bright and shining and perfectly forgotten until the end of days.

"The place is all yours!" I call out to the trees. "Good luck with it."

"Good luck to you, too," a voice calls back. "Sorry about your friend."

The hair on my neck stands on end. I can't mark the man's face, so I mark his voice—deep and gravelly, landing hard on his words.

Once I'm certain we're out of sight, I grab my rifle and my powder horn and start loading.

Chapter Two

We head east along the American River, passing several promising camping sites, but no one suggests we stop. Can't blame everyone for wanting to put some distance between ourselves and those cussed claim jumpers.

The sun is getting low, and trees fill our path with dapple shade as we come to a swift tributary creek. Mr. Hoffman wades in to check the depth and figure the best ford for the wagon. "It's shallow," he says, knee deep in icy water. "We can roll right through."

Jefferson flicks the reins of the oxen and hollers them forward.

"Wait!" I call out. "Stop."

Everyone turns to look at me.

My gold sense is humming, strong and pure. "This is a good area. For claims, I mean. Maybe up the creek a ways."

The Major twists on the wagon bench to face me. "You sure, Lee? Why here?"

My face warms as my companions stare. It's innocent staring; no one except Jefferson knows what I can do. Still, I feel like a deer in their sights. Especially when I notice how keen the Major is on my face, or maybe my eyes, which probably look like gemstones right now.

"I . . . er . . . well, it's the rocks. And the high bank." I gesture toward the creek. "See how smooth they are? And how deep the bank cuts through the land? This creek floods big every spring. And flooding means gold." I allow myself a steadying breath. Nothing about that was a lie.

It's just not the whole truth. The surface gold will be gone after a season. But here, gold runs deep too. I feel it pulsing way down in the earth, like a toothache in the root of my jaw. Back in Georgia, after the surface gold played out, everyone took to the mines, and them that own the mines make the money. There's going to be a mine here someday, for sure and certain.

"I agree with Lee," Jefferson says, with a knowing look that no one else would understand.

"Well, okay!" the Major says. "Let's start looking for a campsite. Any objections?"

"Their word is good enough for me," Becky says.

"For me too," Mr. Hoffman says.

Jefferson and the Major turn the oxen upstream along the creek bank. The older Hoffman boys, Martin and Luther, scout ahead to clear branches from the wagon's path. Gold continues to sing, loud and sweet.

Becky's voice echoes in my head: *Their word is good enough for me.*

I have to tell them. I have to tell them all, and I have to do it tonight.

We agreed to stick together, at least until we found a nice amount of gold. We've been through too much, Mr. Hoffman said, to give up on one another. Besides that, Jefferson pointed out, people you can trust with your life are hard to come by out here in the West. "We're family now," Becky Joyner concurred. So after reaching Sutter's Fort, we headed into the hills to find a prospecting spot that would allow us to stake adjacent claims.

I almost told them the truth then. But keeping secrets is such a habit. Especially when your mama and daddy died for them.

My new family has a right to decide whether to throw in their lot with a witchy girl like me who could get them all killed. We got lucky with those claim jumpers. If they'd been working for my uncle, we wouldn't have gotten away with a single bullet graze.

I glance at Jefferson, riding on the wagon bench. His hand grips the edge to brace against bumps. Everything about that hand is so familiar. The shape of his knuckles, the exact color of his skin. My eyes start to sting, and I have to blink fast to keep the tears back, because if anyone else got killed over my secret, it would break my heart into a million pieces.

"Whoa!" the Major calls, and the wagon jerks to a stop. He sets the wheel brake and hops down. I knee Peony forward to see what's halted us.

The creek is dammed by a warren of branches and mud.

Above the dam, the creek widens into the prettiest pond I ever saw, teeming with cattails and buzzing dragonflies. The pond's headwater is a stair-stepped rapids, frothing white. There, a huge blue heron stands sentry like a statue, eye on the surface, waiting for his next meal to wriggle by. A lone grassy hill overlooks it all, well above the flood line, big enough to pitch a whole mess of tents.

"Glory be," Becky Joyner whispers, staring agape.

Jefferson's big yellow dog, Nugget, gives a delighted yip and rushes forward, scattering a whole mess of sparrows.

"Beaver," I tell Becky. "They always pick the nicest spots."

"Beaver dam means fish," Major Craven says, with a fever in his eyes, same as my daddy always got when he talked of gold.

Mr. Hoffman ambles over, frowning. "You sure there's enough distance between us and those claim jumpers?"

"This is California Territory," Tom says. "Can't set up camp without taking a risk."

"But if we make camp on that hill," I say, pointing, "we can see folks coming at us. And we'll set a watch, just like when we were with the wagon train."

No one protests. "Let's get to work," the Major says.

We skirt the pond and head uphill, where we unload the wagon, let the animals out to graze, and start ringing a fire pit. We move fast and with sure hands; we've all done it a hundred times before.

Hampton whistles jauntily, and Henry shares a joke and a laugh with the other college men. I'm the only one who sets about the work with heavy hands and a frown.

⬩ ⬩ ⬩

We're well enough into the mountains that some of the oaks have given way to conifers, and our evening fire smells sharp of pine wood. The dogs, Nugget and Coney, are exhausted from exploring, and they curl up together as near to the fire as they dare. The Major caught a whole mess of trout, and he showed Becky how to roll them in flour batter and fry them up, which makes for the most delicious meal we've had in months—especially since the Major had a hand in cooking it.

I'm licking my greasy fingers clean when Jefferson says to everyone gathered around the fire, "Plenty of timber to be had. And this hill is sound."

"The boys and I could have some shanties built in days," Mr. Hoffman agrees. "Like the ones we saw along the river. Maybe even a cabin before winter."

"I'd dearly like a cabin for the little ones," Becky says. Her baby daughter sits in her lap, facing us all. The baby kicks her chubby legs out at irregular intervals, babbling at nothing in particular. "We're well enough into the mountains to get a little snow."

"A cabin would keep our goods a lot drier than a shanty," Jasper says.

"It's settled, then," Mr. Hoffman says. "Tomorrow morning, my boys and I will lay out a foundation. Lee and Jefferson can help everyone else stake claims, all adjacent like we planned."

Jasper lifts his tin mug as if it's full of ale instead of pine-needle tea and says, "Here's to finding our winter home."

"What are we going to call it?" Henry asks.

"Call it?" Mr. Hoffman says.

"If it's a settlement, it needs a name."

Luther brightens. "We could call it Good Diggins."

Martin, his older brother, snorts and cuffs him on the shoulder. "Numbskull."

"Don't call your brother names!" Mrs. Hoffman says from some distance away. When it comes to her children, that woman has the ears of a bat.

"But we passed too many other Diggins already!" Martin protests. "Smith's Diggins, Missouri Diggins, Negro Diggins . . ."

"How about Prosperity?" the Major says. "That's what it's going to bring us."

Becky frowns. "Shouldn't count our chickens before they hatch, or weigh our gold before it's shining. That's just asking for the Lord to humble you."

"You've a fair point there, ma'am," the Major says. "What about Hope? Because if there's one thing I already have a whole mess of, it's hope."

Maybe it's a trick of the firelight, but Becky's gaze on the Major turns soft. "I suppose that'll work," she says.

Jefferson speaks to everyone, but his eyes are on me. "Hope is too uncertain. I mean, hopes can be fulfilled, but hopes can be disappointed."

I've got to change the subject, because I know he's not referring to gold and I'm not ready for that conversation. "All that matters right now is we've got a glorious place to start."

Mrs. Hoffman comes to sit beside her husband. She leans

a head on his shoulder and smiles softly. "Glory be to God," she says.

"All ehr und lob sol Gottes sein." Mr. Hoffman nods solemnly.

Jasper lifts his mug again. "To Glory, California."

"Hear! Hear!" someone mutters. Everyone raises a mug or a spoon or something in salute, except me.

"Wait!" I say. "Please. I have to tell you something first."

Everyone hushes. The fire pops. Something splashes into the pond below.

"I . . . You need to know . . ."

Jefferson's eyebrows lift in surprise, but then he gives me an encouraging nod. He has wanted nothing but the truth from me since the beginning.

Locking gazes with him emboldens me to say, "My uncle is still after me. He didn't expect to find me surrounded by friends. But he'll regroup. He'll try again."

"Well, he's not getting you," Jasper says, and the others murmur agreement.

"And I appreciate that. I do. But you all need to know why. Before you decide to . . . whether or not I can stay with you."

"What are you talking about, Lee?" Becky says.

"Bah!" says the baby.

I screw up my courage and blurt: "I can find gold! Not like normal folks. Like . . . a witch."

The Major frowns, and the expression is so out of place on him that it turns my throat sour. "Never took you for a teller of tall tales," he says.

Jefferson clambers to his feet, favoring his injured side. "I think a demonstration is in order. Herr Hoffman, you still have that bauble?"

Mr. Hoffman's brows are furrowed deep enough for planting corn. But he reaches into his pocket and pulls out the heart-shaped locket my mama wore until the day she died. It's changed hands a few times, but I'm glad that something of hers made it all the way across the continent.

Jefferson takes it from him. It dangles from his fingers, sparking in the firelight. "This locket is made of nearly pure gold. Lee, turn around."

I do as he asks, guessing what he has in mind. While I face the dark, everyone shuffles around and exchanges muted whispers.

"Okay, we're ready."

I turn back around, and I pause a moment, memorizing my companion's faces. They're about to know everything about me. No going back after this. But I will do anything, *anything*, to keep my new family safe. Even if it means being alone all over again.

Solemnly Jefferson says, "Where's the locket, Lee?"

It's a lump of sweetness in my chest, calling as soft and clear as a whippoorwill.

"Beside the fire, in Becky's Dutch oven."

Mrs. Hoffman gasps.

"Fancy trick," says Henry. "You've got keen hearing, I'll give you that."

Jefferson's eyes narrow. "We'll do it again. Turn around, Lee."

I do so without complaint, happy to let him take charge. He's not doing it to boss me; he knows how hard it is for me to tell the truth, and he's easing my burden.

More murmurings and shufflings.

"Okay, Lee."

It's farther away this time, and I have to close my eyes and focus. It tugs me southward, to the edge of the pond at the bottom of the hill. No, that's something different. Something bigger.

I rise to my feet and head downhill.

"Where's she going?" Mrs. Hoffman says.

"Hah!" says her husband. "She got it wrong this time."

I pay them no mind. I'm already on my knees, digging in mud that's damp but gritty—so different from the mud back home in Georgia. My fingertips know gold the moment they touch it, and I can hardly control how fast they scrape and dig to get at it.

Finally I can hook a finger around it and pry it from the mud.

"Whatcha got there, Lee?" says little Andy, and I jump. I turn to find that everyone has followed us down the hill. The half-moon gives just enough light for me to make out their faces. Jasper's eyes are bright. Becky is calm and cool as an early fall morning. But Mr. Hoffman glowers, and in the dark, his form is hulking and monstrous.

I wipe the nugget on my trousers and hold it up for everyone to see. "It's gold," I say. "Very pure. Worth about eighty dollars."

"You already knew it was there," says Henry.

"The locket is in your pocket, Henry Meek," I tell him.

Silence greets me. After a moment, he fishes it out and hands it back to Mr. Hoffman without a word. Everybody stares at me like I might bite, or maybe cast a hex.

"There's more in the pond," I say to fill the awful quiet. "But there's even more on the east bank. A vein, I think. Close enough to the surface to get to, if you're handy with a pickax. Lots of dust in the rapids for the little ones to pan. It's a good spot. The best we've come across."

Major Craven worries at the fabric padding his crutch with his thumb. "That's why your uncle sailed all the way around the world to find you," he muses in a voice barely audible above the sound of the running creek.

Jefferson jumps in with, "Remember how she found Andy, that time he got lost on the prairie? He was carrying that locket."

Becky's eyes are wide with understanding. "That's why Mr. Westfall killed your ma and pa," she says. "That's why he wants you so badly. You have . . ."—I expect her to say "a burden" or "a curse"—"a gift from the Lord."

"I . . . Yes, I suppose so."

The Major straightens. "Well, Hiram Westfall can't have you."

My relief is short-lived, because Mr. Hoffman says, "You're saying he might kill us, too?"

I promised myself I would be truthful. "Yes."

"I can't lose another child," Mrs. Hoffman says, her voice wavering. "I *can't*."

And I can't blame her. I miss Therese more than I've let on to anyone, even Jefferson.

Mr. Hoffman's face falls into his hands. His silhouette becomes a huge lump against the sky, like the weight of all of California is stooping him low. "We never should have come here. It's the worst decision I ever made, and . . . I'm sorry, Helma. *Bitte, vergib mir.*"

His wife pulls his head down to her shoulder.

I force the words out: "I'll pack up my gear. Peony and I will be gone by morning."

"No!" Jasper shouts. He's as excited as I've ever seen him, taken with the fever, same as my uncle.

"Anyone who sticks with me is going to get rich, for sure and certain," I tell him. "But they might get dead, too."

"I'm going with Lee," Jefferson says. "No matter what."

"Me too," Jasper says.

Hampton steps forward and places a hand on Jefferson's shoulder. "I'm already a dead man," he says, "if those slave catchers ever find me. Might as well be with friends."

I swallow against a sudden sting in my throat. "I didn't want . . . I mean, you shouldn't all separate on my account. I'll just go. I'll point you in the right direction so you can all get to prospecting, and I'll leave you in peace."

"No," says Mr. Hoffman. He has straightened, and his voice has steadied. "You stay, Lee. We'll go."

"Where?" Tom asks. "You've got no experience. You need Lee and Jefferson to—"

"Home. Back to Ohio."

"Vater, no!" Martin cries.

His father winces but says nothing.

Mrs. Hoffman reaches over and grasps her husband's hand so that they face us united. He squeezes back and says, "We're not the first to give up and go home; talked to a few folks at Sutter's Fort and Mormon Island who were already making plans to leave California. I thought crossing the desert would be like crossing the ocean, and there would be a better life waiting for us on the other side. But gold isn't worth our lives. We'll go by ship this time, arrive home a lot poorer, but grateful not to lose anyone else."

We are silent for a long moment. I expect others to announce their own departure, but no one does.

I offer the nugget to Mr. Hoffman. "Here."

He takes it from my hand.

"And this, too." I reach into my pocket and pull out another. "I found it two days ago. Worth about fifty dollars."

"I can't—"

"You can and you will." I shove it into his hand. "I have a leather pouch in my saddlebag filled with smaller ones. They're all yours. They can buy passage for your family."

He shakes his head. "I still have a candlestick left. Once I sell it—"

"Use it to give yourself a new start back in Ohio. Take it as a gift. In Therese's memory, because she was my friend."

"I . . ." Concern for his family's welfare overcomes his pride. "All right. Thank you, Leah Westfall." He rummages in his pocket and pulls out my mother's locket. "I should be returning this to you."

With a nod, I take it from him and slip it around my neck. I breathe deep as the heart-shaped piece settles against my chest, setting my magic to buzzing, welcoming it home where it belongs.

Together, we all trudge back up the hill. Martin Hoffman hangs his head and kicks at the ground with each step. Once we reach the wagon and tents, he dashes off into the darkness. Mr. Hoffman starts to go after him, but Mrs. Hoffman grabs his arm. "Give the boy some time."

I grab my rifle from Peony's saddle holster. "I'll take first watch."

"Wake me in a few hours," Jefferson says.

But I'm still sitting on the hilltop, wide awake, rifle across my lap, when morning blushes the sky.

A condor soars high above. It's a giant of a bird, bigger even than an eagle, with magnificent black-and-white wings. Like everything else in this territory, it's both familiar and odd, and it makes my old home in Georgia seem like a very small, distant place.

After breakfast, we split up our gear. The Hoffmans agree to let us keep all the tents, the mining gear we bought at Mormon Island, and Mr. Hoffman's gray gelding. In exchange, they'll keep the wagon and half the oxen, which they'll take to San Francisco and sell.

Everyone says their good-byes. The four Hoffman boys are stone-faced as they hitch up the oxen, except Otto, whose lower lip quivers. Martin goes about the work with jerky, slapdash movements, yanking on the hitch so hard that an ox lows in protest.

Mrs. Hoffman hugs Becky fiercely.

"I'd dearly love a letter from you, Helma," Becky says.

Mrs. Hoffman promises to write. "Take care of that baby girl," she admonishes. "And *you* must write *me* when you've finally settled on her name!"

As the wagon rolls away, Olive Joyner runs after it, doll swinging at her side. "Doreen!"

My heart stops as the Hoffman girl leaps from the back of the wagon and tumbles to the ground. But she jumps nimbly to her feet and runs toward Olive, bonnet whipping at her back. The two little girls throw themselves into each other's arms.

Olive pulls away. She shoves her rag doll into Doreen's arms. Without another word, she turns and dashes into the nearest tent.

Martin Hoffman strides back toward us to fetch his little sister. Doreen doesn't protest when he swings her up, but tears stream down her cheeks, and she's still staring at us over her brother's shoulder, Olive's rag doll dangling from her tiny hand, when the Hoffman family disappears into the trees.

Chapter Three

Becky wipes at her cheek and smooths her blond hair. "Well," she says, checking a hair pin. "The cure for a heavy heart is *industry*." With that, she turns toward the fire and begins scraping the breakfast dishes.

No one else moves for a moment. I look around at all the folks who are willing to risk their lives to stay with me: Jefferson and Hampton; Jasper, Tom, and Henry; Widow Joyner, with her two little ones; and Major Craven. I swallow the lump in my throat. "So, who wants to learn how to pan for gold?"

"Me!" Andy shouts, raising his hand like he's in a schoolroom.

"And me," Jasper says, a bit sheepishly. For all that he's a doctor and wants to help people, he's caught the fever like everyone else and wants to feel the weight of heavy pockets.

"I'll go with Jefferson and stake all our claims," Hampton says.

"There's nothing to it," Jefferson says, nodding. "Folks at

Sutter's Fort said to pace it out, pound some stakes into the ground, and connect them with string."

Tom rubs at his chin. "Doesn't seem right, having everything so informal."

Henry cuffs him on the shoulder. "Not everything in the world is a law written in stone."

"Well, it should be! Especially with California destined for statehood. We need the law more than ever in tumultuous times. What if—"

"What if you come and help me lay out the foundation for our cabin?" Henry interrupts gently, to everyone's relief. Once Tom gets on a tear, there's no stopping him.

"Possession is nine-tenths of the law," Tom says. "Putting up cabins seems like a much more secure way to make our claim than stakes and strings."

"Won't do us any harm to do both," Major Craven says. He waves his crutch at us. "I'm not much for heavy lifting or hammering or digging these days, but I'll tend to the animals and then stand watch."

"Watching the widow," Jefferson whispers at my side, and I hit him with an elbow.

"Olive, go with Lee," Becky orders her daughter. "Later, you'll teach me what you learned about panning for gold."

Olive has crept out of the tent, and though tears still streak her cheeks, she stands stoically, hands clasped against her pinafore. "Yes, Ma."

"Don't sound so disappointed," Jasper says. "We'll have fun."

He pats her head, and she jerks away. She doesn't care for that any more than I would.

I stare for just a moment toward the trees that swallowed up the Hoffman family; then I grab a wide, shallow pan, a bucket, and my hat. "All right, Andy and Olive. Are you ready to get soaking wet?"

"Yes, ma'am!" Andy says, while Olive regards my pan suspiciously.

"I've got the shovels," Jasper says.

"Then let's go."

If we were back in Georgia, trying to pan for gold in those played-out creeks, we could be at it all morning and not have anything to show for it but sunburned necks, blistered hands, and a few flakes of shiny dust. Here in California, my gold sense is humming all the time, like my school bell has been pulled, and there's ringing in my ears that won't go away.

Jasper convinces the children to stand quiet long enough for me to concentrate, and I pick us a prime spot. It's a wide, flat place in the creek, shallow enough for Andy and Olive, with a tinkling like chimes bouncing up through the ripples.

As expected, the gold comes easy. Mostly I supervise and explain what to do. Jasper shovels the gravel and black sand, and he and Olive take turns shaking the pans in water until the heavy pieces sink to the bottom. Olive hums as she works, some old hymn. It's her favorite tune—I've heard her humming it while she helps her mother.

"Slow down," I tell Olive. "You have to let the gold settle. Do you see it?"

"Where?" she asks.

All I mean to do is point, but it seems as though the flake lifts out of the water and sticks to my finger, just as if I called it. It's the strangest feeling, like a static shock when it touches my skin.

"Did you do that on purpose?" Jasper asks.

"Do what on purpose?" I say. "Give me your hand." I brush the tiny speck of gold into his palm. "You hold on to what we find. Now both of you, get back to work. This gold isn't going to pan itself."

My students do well. Jasper has a good touch, Olive has a good eye, and Andy has a good time. He splashes in the water and chases fish and cheers every time his sister or the doctor announces another find.

Jefferson and Hampton are exploring along the creek, trailed by the dogs, marking off claims for everybody in our group, and of course they want my advice. So I leave Jasper and Olive to pan, and Andy runs up and down the bank with me while we pick out good spots. I try to listen not just for the gold song coming from the water, but also for the deeper hum stretching back into the banks. I help Hampton choose the richest spot for his border of string—he's got freedom to buy and family to reclaim from down south.

We're tying off string at the edge of Hampton's claim when I notice Jefferson staring at me. "You don't have to watch my eyes," I grumble. "When I sense gold, I'll tell you straight."

"That's not why I'm looking," he replies, and Hampton fails to keep the grin from his face.

I hightail it out of there and return to Jasper, who has two hands full of tiny nuggets. He's staring at them, eyes wide.

"A few ounces," I say. "Not bad for half a morning's work."

He holds out both hands. "Pick one—it's your half."

"Keep it all," I say. "Jefferson and Hampton say this stretch is going to be your claim. That's Tom and Henry's claims, right adjacent, so you can work them all together. I was supposed to be teaching you, and it seems like you've been taught."

"Are you sure?"

"Are your feet wet?"

Jasper laughs and pours all the gold into one hand. He picks out the largest nugget and calls to Olive. "Here you go, partner. For your all your hard work."

She takes it reverently and holds it like it's a hummingbird's fragile egg.

"Where's mine?" Andy says. "I helped, too."

"I've got yours right here," Jasper says, and he gives me a wink as he hands another tiny stone to the boy.

For a moment, I am happy, maybe the happiest I've been since Uncle Hiram murdered my parents and stole my life from me. I have sunlight on my face, and the siren call of gold singing under my skin. I'm with family again, my real family now, whatever the law says, and I'm doing something I'm good at.

"I'm cold," says Olive.

"Let's get you back to your ma and dried off," I say. Jasper gathers our tools and whistles a tune as we head downstream. When we come within sight of camp, Andy takes off running.

"Ma! We found gold!" he hollers. His trousers are soaked through, his right leg slathered in mud up to his knee.

Becky jumps up from the table, the one that made it here all the way from Chattanooga. Her red-checked tablecloth is spread across it just so, the corners perfectly aligned, and a vase full of purple alpine rises from the center. It's like God dropped a tiny tavern right into the middle of the wilderness.

Sitting at the table is a stranger.

My hand flies to the five-shooter at my hip. The man sits across from Becky, scooping up half-burned flapjacks like they're manna from heaven. Crumbs cling to his wild gray beard. Becky holds the fussing baby to her chest like a shield.

"Hush, Andy," I whisper. "Say no more about the gold."

"Okay, Lee," Andy whispers back. Olive slips her hand into mine. I glance around for the Major, who was supposed to be keeping watch.

"This gentleman is Mr. Tuggle," Becky says smoothly, though I know her well enough to note the wariness in her eyes and the carefulness of her speech. "He paid me two dollars for a plate of flapjacks."

"And a mighty fine breakfast it was, ma'am!" he exclaims. "The best flapjacks I ever had."

Olive and I exchange a baffled glance. The bearded man is either daft or deceitful, because Becky Joyner is the worst cook in the whole wide West.

He wipes his mouth with one of Becky's embroidered napkins, then rises from the table and stretches out his hand to shake. "Just call me Old Tug," he says. "And your name, mister?"

"It's . . ." I almost say my last name, Westfall, but I don't want to make it any easier for folks to connect me with my uncle. "Lee. *Miss* Lee."

His gaze darts down to my trousers, then up to my chin-length hair. "Pleased to meet you, *Miss* Lee. You'll have to forgive me. We don't much get the pleasure of gentler company in these parts." His skin is craggy and weathered, his nose peeling from the sun. His riotous gray beard nearly covers a smile only half full of brownish teeth.

I'm about to retort that my company is anything but gentle when I sense someone at my shoulder. I turn and am relieved to see Jasper. "This is Jasper Clapp," I tell Old Tug. "He's our doctor. Most of our other menfolk are about their chores, but I expect them back any moment."

"I see." Which I hope means Old Tug got the message; we are not alone and helpless out here.

"Where are you headed, Old Tug?" I ask.

"Not sure yet. Looking for a place to stake a good claim."

"If you head back to the river and point your boots east, you'll see plenty of good prospecting land."

"I was thinking this might be a good place."

Major Craven materializes at the tree line, swinging forward on his crutch and cradling an armful of Becky's dishes. He must have taken them to the creek to wash. "Sorry, sir," he calls out cheerfully. "But every parcel within view has been claimed already."

Old Tug frowns, his eyes narrowing. "You don't say." His voice does not match the one I heard when Jefferson was shot, but he could easily be one of the silent claim jumpers who shot through the trees.

The Major stacks the dishes beside the fire pit. "We wouldn't mind having some good neighbors, though. Be happy to show you a few promising spots that haven't been claimed yet."

I stare at him. Has he gone mad?

Becky bends over to clear away Old Tug's dishes. "Indeed, sir," she says with her sweetest smile. "We could do with some company on occasion. Wouldn't be right to let go the finer tenets of civilization just because we're out in the wilderness."

Old Tug stands from the table, revealing a ragged hole in the knee of his trousers. "I couldn't agree more, ma'am." He flips his hat onto his head. "Mind if I come back tomorrow morn? Might bring another fellow or two."

This seems to take Becky aback, and my grip on the five-shooter tightens. "I . . . I suppose that would be all right," she says.

"Would you accept gold dust for payment?" he asks.

Her eyes widen. "You mean you want to bring me paying customers?"

"Lots of gentlemen in these parts with gold to spare would pay to have such a fine breakfast," he says.

Becky's face is transformed with wonder, and Lord help every man within a thousand miles, because it makes her one of the prettiest women I ever saw. "Why, certainly, Mr. Tuggle. Bring as many friends as you'd like."

Tug turns to the Major. "Mind showing me to one of those promising spots?"

Craven grins. "Not at all, sir, not at all." He grabs his Colt.

Jasper steps forward, hoisting his rifle, too. "I'm coming with you."

I give Jasper a grateful nod. There's no way we're leaving our friend all alone with this strange man.

As Jasper, Major Craven, and Old Tug skirt the pond toward the beaver dam, Becky says to me, "I must be a better cook than I thought!"

I blink. "It must be from all the practice." I step forward to grab the table, just like I've done hundreds of times, but I stop short, laughing.

"What's so funny?" Becky asks.

"I was about to put the table away in the wagon. Then I remembered we don't have a wagon anymore."

She grins.

"Becky, I have to ask. Why were you so blasted *friendly* to that man? You practically invited him to join us."

She puts her hands on her hips and stares me down. "And what would have happened if I'd bullied him away? He'd have become suspicious, that's what. He would have realized that we're sitting on the best gold claims in the Sierra Nevada."

"Oh."

"And then he would have jumped our claims or gotten close enough to learn our real secret."

Our real secret. Tears prick at my eyes. "Oh."

"So we're going to be friendly. Like it or not, we'll encounter plenty of folks here in California. More are pouring in every day. Might as well establish some good neighbors."

I scuff my boots in the dirt. "You're right, of course. Sorry."

"I'm not daft, you know. We'll set a double watch tonight. Just in case."

I groan, thinking of lost sleep, as Becky flips the dishrag over her shoulder, signaling an end to it all. She crouches to tend to Andy and Olive and make appropriate exclamations over the gold they found.

All the chores are done, so I mosey back up the creek to find Jefferson standing ankle-deep in ice-cold water, trousers and sleeves rolled up, leaning on a shovel.

"Glad you're here," he says. "I wanted to ask you if this is a good spot."

I give him my best glare. "Jasper say you're fit to work yet? You're supposed to be staking claims, not heaving dirt."

A smile tugs at his lips. "Worried about me, are you?"

"You're going to tear your stitches, and then you'll be useless for two more weeks."

He digs into the bank and comes up with a shovelful of mud and gravel, which he tosses into his broad pan. "Claims are done. And I'm hale enough to dig my way from here to Sacramento."

He looks it, too. His forearms are corded with muscle, his skin burnished by the sun, his black eyes bright. He catches me staring, and his tiny smile turns into a full-blown grin that makes my toes feel funny.

I snatch the shovel from his hand. "If you're so hale, you won't mind when I dunk you in the creek."

Quicker than a blink, he steps so close that my nose nearly touches the hollow of his throat. "Try it," he whispers. "I dare you."

"I . . ." I can't stop thinking about his lips. "When did you get so blasted tall?" I blurt.

His hand comes near to my ear, and he gently runs his thumb and forefinger against a lock of my hair. "It's growing out," he says. "I'm glad. You always had the prettiest hair."

I'm not sure what to say about that, so I change the subject. "A stranger came into our camp," I say.

His hand drops. "What? Who?"

"Man by the name of Tug. Paid Becky two dollars for a plate of flapjacks."

"Poor fellow." Jefferson steps away and squats to grab his pan full of mud.

The air around me suddenly feels cold and empty. "He thought I was a boy."

He snorts. "Anyone who thinks you're a boy needs spectacles." He dips the pan into the creek and lets a ripple of water wash over its contents. Mud loosens from the gravel and swirls away.

"Maybe it's because I'm wearing trousers today."

"You look like a girl *especially* in trousers," he says, and that tiny grin is back, making me feel funny all over again.

"Well, anyway, he said he'd come back in the morning for more flapjacks. With friends. Becky suggested we set a double watch tonight. Just in case he comes early."

"Good idea." He dips and swishes the pan once more. "We can stay up together. Watch the stars. Like old times."

And just like that, a double watch doesn't sound so bad. "Just like old times," I agree.

He flicks some larger stones out of the pan, plopping them into the creek. "So, witchy girl, am I going to find any gold in this here pan?"

"A little. Enough to be worth your time."

He flashes that wide, bright smile I never tire of seeing. "That's what I like to hear."

Hours later we head back to camp with a small pouch full of tiny gold nuggets and flecks, worth at least thirty dollars. Henry and Tom have marked out a large rectangle on the hill-top and begun clearing it of brush and rock. Becky has bol-stered the fire pit with stones, and her cook pot hangs over it from an iron spit. Hampton has set up a tying post for the horses and is now busy with his ax; the pile of firewood beside him is already thigh high. Major Craven and little Andy are working on a lean-to made of pine branches, which is a good thing, given that the rains will start long before we get that cabin finished.

Warmth and pride fill my chest. It's only been a day, but Glory, California, already has a sense of permanence about it. Of home.

The next morning, Old Tug shows up with two other men in tow. They're as filthy and unkempt as he is, and just as appreciative of Becky's flapjacks, which are crisp on the outside and mushy in the middle.

My mama would have smacked my knuckles with a wooden spoon if I'd shown the table manners of these men. They shove food down their gullets like it's the last meal of their lives, letting crumbs and gobs of butter stick to their beards. All the while, they look back and forth between Becky and me, with an occasional glance at Olive. It makes me twitchy, the way they stare. Like they're starving animals, and I don't mean for food.

Major Craven and Jefferson stick close by the whole time, rifles within easy and noticeable reach.

The men leave Becky with two dollars and a couple of pinches of gold dust.

"We need to send someone back to Mormon Island," she says cheerfully as she clears the table. "I'll need more flour, salt, and coffee. Eggs, too. And bacon, maybe? If they're paying me two dollars for flapjacks, think what I can get for eggs and bacon!"

Runny eggs and burned bacon, she means, but I hold my tongue.

"It would be better to get a milk cow and some chickens," she continues happily. "I guess I have to learn how to raise chickens and . . ." She frowns, looking up at me. "Lee?" her voice is suddenly shy. "Do you think Tom or Henry could teach me how to make butter? They made the most delightful butter, back when Athena the cow was still with us."

I hide my smile. Mrs. Rebekah Joyner was a fine lady back

in Chattanooga, and I reckon she didn't work a day in her life before hitting the trail. "If they don't, I will," I tell her. "And anything else you want to learn. I should warn you that I never was much for cooking. The Major would be a better teacher on that count. But I can show you all you need to know about raising chickens and keeping dairy cows."

Her relieved smile flutters away as she stares at me. No, she's staring beyond me. I turn, dread coiling in my gut.

A man walks toward us, hat brim low, a saddlebag thrown across one shoulder. Something about that walk is familiar, and for a split second I'm certain my uncle has found me, that it's one of his men bearing down on us. I'm about to dash for my rifle when Becky exclaims, "Martin!"

I peer closer. It *is* Martin Hoffman, weary and faltering, tall and skinny as a pine. His sister Therese appeared just like this, that day she hiked through the desert to get help for her family. She stumbled the same way, held her chin with the same determination, the same blazing sun on her shoulders. I sprint toward him.

"Martin! Is everything all right? Your family . . ."

He looks up and grins.

Jefferson's boots pound up behind me. "Martin?"

"They let me come back," Martin says.

"They're all right?" I persist.

"Last I checked. We parted ways."

Becky and the Major have caught up to us, along with little Andy.

"Martin, your ma must be beside herself!" Becky exclaims.

The boy straightens. "I'm almost fifteen years old. She said I'm a man now. That she can't keep me from trying for my fortune here in California." He pats his hip, where a shiny new Colt revolver hangs from a leather holster. "Vater lent me his gun, on the condition that if I haven't made something of myself in a year, I'd go back home to Ohio."

The Major leans on his crutch and claps the young man on the shoulder with his free hand. "Son, we're happy to have you back."

Jefferson is grinning fit to burst, and it occurs to me that he and Martin probably became good friends, and I didn't even notice on account of trying so hard not to see how much Jefferson liked Martin's sister, Therese. "There's room for you in my lean-to," Jefferson says. "You can help me convert it into a shanty. And I'll show you where I staked my claim so you can—"

"Give the boy a rest," Becky says sternly. "Come along, Martin. I'll fix you some coffee and flapjacks. Plenty of time to set up later."

Andy runs forward and throws his arms around Martin's thighs. Martin reaches down and sweeps him up, and Andy hides his face in Martin's neck so we can't see his glad tears. Everybody is looking at Martin, and that's why they can't see mine. It feels like my family is whole again.

Chapter Four

During the next week, we keep busy making a home. Hampton marks out a decent pasture and starts putting up fence posts; he was a shepherd before his owner died and he ran off to join us. The Major and Jefferson spend most of their time digging a foundation and felling trees to build a log cabin. The college men, Jasper and Tom and Henry, leave on a supply run for Becky, armed with the most perfectly penned and beautiful grocery list I've ever seen.

Andy and Olive pan in the creek, accompanied by splashing dogs, under Martin's watchful eye when he isn't off hunting.

I spend the days sifting through everyone's claims, casting out with my sense for easy gold. Anything I find goes to the claimant. That's the rule, and I stick to it. By the end of the week, everyone is at least a hundred dollars richer. But Becky is richer still. On top of her claim findings, she makes an additional seventy-five dollars selling breakfasts to hardened miners, meals that would pucker the tongues of lesser men.

When the number of morning guests reaches five, the Major vows to make Becky more furniture. We don't have the tools to make good lumber, and the nearest mill is more than a day away. So he splits a few logs in half, turns them flat side up, and starts rigging a rough table and chairs.

On the seventh day after Martin's return, Old Tug finishes his breakfast, smears the food on his beard around with one of Becky's napkins, and stands from his chair, adjusting his suspenders. I'm sitting on one of the Major's log benches, working polish into the leather of Peony's saddle, when Old Tug starts toward me. He holds his hat in his hand and grins like a boy at Christmas.

He's lost a fair number of teeth, with one standing like a sentinel front and center on the bottom row. He's probably Daddy's age, if my daddy were still alive, and he hasn't washed his shirt or trousers in weeks. He's tried to mat his hair down with grease, but his beard sticks out like a wire brush covered with gray ash. His breath reeks of Becky's coffee and unscraped teeth.

"Found somethin'," he says, eyes twinkling.

"You don't say."

He reaches into his pocket, but I already know what he's fishing for—a gold nugget the size of a juicy ripe strawberry, niggling at me like an itch under my skin.

"Take a gander at this," he says. "Found it on my claim yesterday. And it's just the beginning. Lot more where this came from."

"Congratulations, Tug," I say, trying to sound surprised.

"I'm real happy for you. Now, if you don't mind, I need to tend my horse." I haven't given Peony nearly enough attention lately, so I plan on taking her for a ride and then giving her the best rubdown of her life.

I stand, hefting the saddle over my shoulder, and I start to head up the hill, but he blocks my way. "I wanna talk to you first," he says.

I take a step back. "Sure, Tug. What about?"

"Seeing as how I made my stake and all, I was thinking I could give this to you, like a ring or whatnot, and you and me could get hitched."

I blink up at him as the words sink in. "Tug, are you—"

"I'm asking you to marry me," he says, his grin bigger than ever. "As of this morning, I'm the most eligible bachelor in the area, and you're the most eligible girl. Only makes sense we end up together."

"No, sir, that doesn't make sense at all."

"Course it does." His laughter has an ugly quality. "Imagine how jealous the fellows will be, me being the only one who snagged a wife, and a young one to boot!"

I think of my daddy's boots, still on my too-small feet because I refuse to take them off. Specifically, I think of their steel tips and the damage they could do.

I put my chin up and look him dead in the eye. "No."

His face flashes to angry. "When did I ever do wrong by you?"

At his raised voice, Becky's other customers shift in their seats and glance our way.

"You haven't never," I say hastily. "But I don't want to get married, not to you, not to anybody."

"Ain't natural!"

"Seems plenty natural to me." How can people not see? A woman married is a woman with nothing of her own. Everything she's ever worked for belongs to her husband, especially if Tom's prediction proves out and California becomes a tried-and-true state.

"It ain't the Indian boy, is it?"

"What?" I am ice-cold now. Steel chilled in a mountain stream.

"We all seen him hangdogging around, you chasing him off with a stick. I figured you were just waiting for a white man, or someone older and more respectable to come along."

He's exaggerating to make his point. Still, I glance around, half hoping Jefferson isn't around to overhear, half hoping he is—because I'd sure feel safer if he were within sight. But he must have left for his claim already.

"I said no, Tug, and you need to take me at my word and walk away right now." My five-shooter is only inches from my hand. After this, I'm going to practice with it. I'm going to practice drawing quickly and shooting accurately, every single day.

Tug spits on the ground. "What the hell is wrong with you? A girl as ugly and manly as you ain't never gonna do better than me."

Everyone is watching now. Some of the men at Becky's table are giggling like schoolgirls at lunchtime. Major Craven grabs his crutch and starts hobbling over. Martin's hand drifts toward the Colt at his hip.

Bolstered by the support of my friends, I'm about to say something unforgivable about his missing teeth and his rats'-nest beard, but at the last second I remember Becky and the Major being kind when he first appeared, and I choose honey instead of vinegar.

"You are a fine, fine man, Mr. Tug," I say gravely. "Any woman would be proud to have you. But I have a fiancé back in Georgia, you see."

"Well, he ain't here."

"I shall remain true."

Old Tug's eyes narrow, like he's sussing the lie. "Well, all righty then," he says with reluctance. "I suppose it wouldn't be right."

Martin's hand relaxes.

I force a smile. "I do thank you for the offer, though, and I hope we'll see you tomorrow for breakfast."

"That you will, little lady. That you will." He plops his hat back on, then strides away as if it were all nothing.

My breath leaves in a whoosh. I'm not sure why that conversation made me so nervous, but it did, and I'm not looking forward to seeing him back in the morning.

"It isn't true, Miss Leah," Olive says, and I jump.

"I didn't see you sneak up."

"You aren't ugly, and you can do plenty better."

I laugh. "Thank you, Olive. But I don't care what that no-good son of a goat thinks of me."

"I knew he was going to ask you, after he asked Ma."

I almost drop my saddle. "He asked Becky?"

She shrugs. "Ma won't marry some stinky old man."

"Is that what she told him?"

"No, Ma was nice. Said she still loved my pa, even though he's gone, and Old Tug laughed at her and said it was just for practice anyway, and he was going to ask you."

I glare toward Becky, who is serving up a second helping of lumpy porridge to an unlucky miner. "She could have said something," I mutter. Another man proposed to me under Becky's knowing eye, back on the trail. A reverend by the name of Lowrey. Becky didn't bother giving me a warning then, either.

"That's also not true," Olive adds.

"What's not true?"

"Ma didn't love Pa."

I put the saddle down on the log and crouch to face her. "Sweet pea, what makes you say such a thing?"

"She's happy now."

Becky Joyner never speaks of her dead husband, and I haven't the foggiest notion how she felt about him. But Olive is right: Becky is happier than she used to be. She's free now. Free of a man who controlled her utterly, who owned everything she worked for. Free to make her own decisions about her day, about her children, about her *life*.

I plant a quick kiss on Olive's forehead. "I think she did love your pa. But I also think she's happier now. And that's important to understand, Olive. Even when we lose someone we love, we still have a chance at happiness."

Olive's chin trembles, but she doesn't cry. "Okay, Lee."

"Want to go for a ride with me and Peony?"

"Okay, Lee!"

Together, we head toward Hampton's makeshift corral, and I marvel at my own words, feeling their truth blossom deep inside me. I lost Mama and Daddy to my murderous snake of an uncle. I miss them every day. But I've found happiness, for sure and certain.

It scares me a little. It means I have something to lose again.

I've rubbed down Peony, and I'm heading back to camp with her tack when I hear the rumble and creak of wagon wheels. I pick up my pace and round the hill to discover the college men, back from their supply run. They left with nothing but their mounts and saddlebags, but they've returned with a cart horse and a small cart practically bursting with goods.

I run forward to help unload, but I stop when I see the long line of folks coming up the road behind the cart. Most are small-statured men, with glossy black hair tied in long braids down their backs, and each one carries a mule load's worth of equipment and supplies. They wear simple, billowy clothes, and slippers on their feet, except for one man who wears silk robes and a broad, flat hat. The man in silk carries nothing but a walking stick. He raises a hand toward the college men as he passes, and they wave back. The group continues past our camp and heads into the hills.

"Are those Indians?" I ask. "The Maidu we heard about?"

"No, those are Chinese laborers," Tom says.

I stare at their backs as they disappear over the ridge. I've never seen a Chinese person before, at least not in real life. Annabelle Smith back home boasted about encountering some in Savannah, but all I've seen are newspaper cartoons and lithographs.

"It's called a coolie gang," Tom says, frowning. "No better than slave labor."

"You talked to them?"

"To the headman," Jasper says. "His name is Henry Lee."

"For true?"

"Maybe not originally," Jasper says. "He was educated by British missionaries in the city of Canton. He speaks excellent English—with a British accent!"

"And he's well read," Henry says, lifting a bag of oats from the cart. "He was familiar with the poetry of William Wordsworth."

"You don't say." I have no idea who William Wordsworth is. "You said they're slaves?"

"Not the headman," Jasper says. "But he owns work contracts on the others. He's looking for a big mining operation or a rancher to hire the whole crew. He'll collect the wages for all of them, and probably send most of it back to China. We saw a dozen groups like this at Mormon Island. There are hundreds of Chinese here already, and more coming."

"The coolie contracts won't last long," Tom says. "Mark my words. There'll be no slavery in California, not for Negros and not for Chinese."

"Will they become American citizens? Like the Mexicans in California?"

He doesn't have the chance to answer, because Andy and Olive are tugging at our sleeves, and even though there are only two of them, it feels like we're outnumbered. "Chickens!" Olive says.

"Show us the chickens," Andy insists, dragging Jasper toward a wooden box with holes in it.

"Just pullets," Jasper says. "We didn't want grown hens until we could build a proper henhouse."

"Couldn't find a milk cow," Tom says to Becky, who comes trailing behind her children. "They're in high demand, apparently. But we brought something else for you. A present."

"Oh?" Becky peers over the cart's edge.

The Major heaves a sack of cornmeal onto his shoulder, and Jasper moves aside a barrel of beans, revealing a brand-new box stove, shining black with curved legs. Beside it is a matching flue pipe.

Becky gasps.

"That ought to help with the cooking, yes?" Jasper says with a grin. "And keep that cabin we're building warm this winter."

"But . . . how much do I owe you for this?" she asks, eyes wide.

"Not a cent," Tom says. "It's a gift. We used the gold that Lee found for us. It cost every last bit, and we're all dead broke, but we'll just get more, right?"

Gold comes hard but goes easy, Mama always said.

Whenever she worried Daddy and I were getting greedy, she'd remind us that some of the folks in Georgia who found the most gold ended up the worst off. "But they didn't have a witchy girl to help them," was how I always replied, which always made her madder than a hornet. She hated the word "witch."

"In fact," I say, "I kept filling your flour bags while you were gone. You're not dead broke. Not even close."

Andy pipes in with, "I helped!"

"Me too!" says Olive.

Tom reaches into his pocket and pulls out two pieces of hard white candy. Peppermint scent fills the air. He hands them to the little ones, saying, "For your hard work," and is answered with a chorus of thank yous.

Henry turns to me. "We got something for you too, Lee."

"You didn't need . . ." Words leave me when he pulls out a large package wrapped in paper and twine.

Henry hands it to me. "Open it!"

Jefferson peers over my shoulder as I use my knife to cut the twine, then fold back the paper to reveal beautiful calico in soft green. I lift it from the package.

It's a dress. An honest-to-God dress, with rich brown ribbon trim, a white lace collar, and the fullest, swishiest skirt I've ever seen.

At my stunned silence, Tom jumps in with, "Not saying you have to stop wearing trousers. Nothing like that. It's just . . . we recalled you once telling us how you miss dresses and that you'd like to have a nice one for special occasions."

"We had to guess at the size," Henry says. "I thought this color would be lovely on you!"

"It might be too big," Jasper adds. "But the lady at the counter assured us a dress is easier to take in than let out."

"I'm a dab at the needle myself," Henry says. "I could help you." He's practically beaming, so pleased is he to present this gift to me

I swallow hard and blink. "It's pretty," I breathe, fingering the fabric. "The prettiest thing I've seen in a long time."

Tom and Jasper share relieved smiles.

"If you don't like it, we got an extra," Henry says, reaching into his own bag. "It didn't seem right for you, but . . ."

He retrieves a lavender calico dress, shakes it out, and holds it up against his chest.

"That's big enough to fit you," I say. "No, I like this one just fine. More than fine."

He grins and folds the other dress back up.

"Two boughten dresses," I say, marveling. Seems like an overindulgence to me.

"The seamstress gave us a deal," Henry says. "It would appear there are far more dresses than women in the state at the moment, one being easier to ship west, and the other less willing. But we might be able to trade it for something later."

"Let's get all this unloaded," Jefferson says. He wears an odd expression, like he's trying to figure something out.

"We ought to find a dry spot for all that fresh ammo you brought," Major Craven says. "And we need to build a henhouse before those chickens get any bigger."

"And I guess I need to learn how to work a stove," Becky says.

Everyone stares at her. It's easy to forget she didn't cook a day in her life before hitting the trail, at which point she only cooked over an open fire. Becky gives us a sheepish shrug. "Sukey, my slave in Chattanooga, always managed the stoves."

I can't help the laugh that bubbles out of my chest. It's almost too ridiculous for words, that a grown woman could be so helpless.

But Hampton is frowning. "Don't look at me to help you with it."

"I . . . Of course not," Becky stammers.

The Major steps forward, rubbing his beard. "I've been around a woodstove or two," he says to Becky, "and I reckon you and I, we can figure this out together. If you don't mind me being in the way."

She smiles at him. "Thank you, sir."

Everyone helps unload and find places to store everything. Most of it goes into the lean-tos, a bit in our saddlebags. Barrels and sacks of foodstuffs remain in the cart, off the ground, which is rolled under a huge oak and covered in canvas.

Jefferson is the only one who goes about the work with a sour face. His look is so dark, his motions so brusque and hurried, that I finally sidle up to him and ask, "Jeff?"

"See all this stuff?" he says with a sweep of his hand. "It looks like we're rich already, and us only being here a couple of weeks."

Understanding is like a click in my brain. "Oh."

"People are going to start talking, no doubt about it. They'll talk about how prosperous Glory, California, is. Miners will come from all over to stake claims nearby. Everyone will hear about the group of folks, women and children among them, with a half Indian and a Negro besides. And when they do—"

"My uncle will come to fetch me."

He nods. "If we don't get robbed first."

I glance over toward the cart. Major Craven is using his crutch to shift some stones aside and pound out a flat area for the new box stove, his amputated leg swaying as he works. It's a marvelous feat of balance. "I can do more with one leg than most men can do with two," he always says.

"People will recognize descriptions of the Major, too," I say. "I couldn't stand it if something happened to any of them."

"I couldn't stand it if something happened to *you*," he says, his dark eyes suddenly intense on me. We stand a moment in silence, staring at each other. He has the finest face I've ever seen, with his high cheekbones and serious eyes and a wide mouth that always has a gentle curve, all surrounded by the thickest, shiniest black hair that a girl could run her fingers through.

I swallow hard. "So, what do we do?"

"Let's talk it out with everyone at supper tonight."

We sit around the campfire, which isn't as huge and roaring as usual on account of the fact that the Major and Becky have gotten the stove fired up and hotter than blazes. They made a huge pot of rabbit stew, thanks to Martin's hunting success, which is a bit watery, but still delicious with the fresh onions, turnips, potatoes, and carrots that the college men brought back.

Beside me, Jasper is showing Olive how to work stitches into the rabbit's untanned hide. "Rabbit skin is thinner and more delicate than human skin," Jasper says. "So once you've gotten the hang of it, we'll move on to something else. Maybe a deer, or better yet a boar."

Across from me, Jefferson is cleaning his rifle, but he steals glances through the wavering firelight, which I pretend not to notice.

Everyone else spoons up their stew, enjoying the rest and silence after a hard day's work.

Finally, as Becky starts gathering dishes, I clear my throat. "Jefferson and me, we think we should set a double watch tonight," I say.

"And every night," Jefferson adds.

"Not a bad idea," the Major says, bouncing the Joyner baby on his knee. "Someone on the hill near the lean-tos and the cart, another at the corral."

"Still worried about claim jumpers?" Becky asks. "We have some fine neighbors now. Well, maybe not *fine*, but they're perfectly friendly."

"People are going to start talking, friendly or not," I say. "Once they see our fancy new box stove and those chickens and that cart full of goods, they'll figure we're doing well. Maybe too well."

"I'm big now," Andy says, all seriousness. "I can stand watch."

Henry Meek rubs at his scant beard. "We should hide as many of our supplies as possible."

"At least we don't have to worry about Indians stealing our things," Becky says. "I haven't seen a single Indian since we left Mormon Island."

Jefferson glares at her, and I don't blame him for being angry. People pretend he's a white man when it suits them, erasing part of who he is. Besides, Becky shouldn't assume danger on that front, since we've had nothing but fair dealings with Indians. I guess it's hard to get past your notions about people sometimes, even when your own experience tells you otherwise.

"Hopefully," Jeff says, "the fact that we've seen so few Indians means we're not trespassing on their territory."

"They have no territory," Becky says.

Jefferson clenches his jaw, then he opens his mouth to snap back, but Hampton says, "I've seen 'em. They watch me from that big stand of oak trees sometimes, when I'm tending the oxen and horses." At Becky's gasp, he hastily adds, "They're not threatening at all. Just curious, I think."

"They're nomads," Becky says. "Here today, gone tomorrow."

"Calling them nomads," Jefferson says, "is just a fancy way of saying it's okay to squat on their land."

Becky is about to protest, but Henry interrupts. "I suspect they don't want trouble any more than we do," he says.

Hampton adds, "I went over to talk to them, but they'd disappeared. They left behind the most beautiful baskets, full of acorns." His gaze grows distant. "I've never seen anything as pretty as that weaving."

"What'd you do with them?" I ask.

"The baskets? I left them there. Weren't mine. That was somebody else's labor, and somebody else's meal."

"That was good of you," Jefferson says.

"A day later, the baskets were gone," Hampton says. "I don't think we have anything to worry about from them, that's all I'm saying."

"Doesn't mean we have nothing to worry about from others," I point out. "So far, the only people who've tried to hurt us or take our stuff is other Christians. Like those claim jumpers."

"I'll dig a cellar for our cabin," Martin says. "I'll be all day about it, if need be. We can hide our supplies there."

"Don't bother," says the Major. "Ground's too hard. Solid granite and shale, most of it."

"There's a soft, grassy spot up the creek a ways," Tom says. "Past the rapids, out of sight."

"I can pull up the sod," Martin says. "Jefferson and me'll dig it out. We'll cache some dry goods there, things the rodents won't care about." He and Jeff exchange a quick nod.

"Speaking of rodents," Tom says, "we could use a cat or two."

Olive looks up from her practice stitches. "I'll take care of her. I'll feed her and pet her all the time so she wants to stay with us."

Tom nods solemnly. "I'm sure you would do a great job at that. There probably won't be any kittens until spring, but I'll keep an eye out."

"I'm going to practice with my five-shooter, starting tomorrow," I say. "So don't be alarmed when you hear my gun going off."

"I'll join you," Jefferson says.

"Me too," Martin and Jasper chorus.

"I hate guns," says Henry.

The Major uses his crutch to stand. "If any of Mrs. Joyner's customers ask about our goods, I'm going to say we traded with things we brought from back east. No sense letting people know how much gold we've found."

We all exchange glances around the fire. It's a bold-faced lie and a sin, but no one protests.

"Heirloom jewelry," Becky offers softly. "We'll say I brought heirloom jewelry from my father's plantation in Tennessee. Traded it in Sacramento."

"Well, that was mighty generous of you!" the Major says, grinning.

Becky smiles back. She's had an awful lot of smiles for the Major lately.

It puts me in mind of Jefferson, and I look across the fire and catch him staring at me. Again.

"Lee and I will take the first watch," he says firmly.

"I've got my eye out for trouble," I mumble as I stand, but I'm not sure which way I should be looking.

Chapter Five

Our wagon train was hardly a week out of Independence before we realized that standing watch was near useless. Even on the flat prairie, there were too many dips and gullies, too many cattle, too many tents and wagons, to keep an eye on everything, especially in the dark. The Major, who was never more than a sergeant in the Missouri militia, taught us to walk the perimeter to keep attackers guessing and cover more ground. After the Major was wounded in the buffalo stampede, Frank Dilley took over leadership of the wagons. Frank was a terrible person, but a decent enough leader and guide, and he kept right on assigning perimeter watches.

So Jefferson and I make a wide, silent circuit of our camp in the dark, rifles loaded, coats buttoned tight against the night chill. Moonlight ripples across the water of our beaver pond. As we skirt the shore, a great *smack!* sounds, and we whip up our guns in reflex. Then we share a quick laugh. Just a beaver, slapping the water in warning at our approach.

We continue in silence. Being with Jefferson used to be as easy as breathing. I think of his pathetic marriage proposal, back when we were first thinking on taking to the trail west. I thought the proposal was just for show, to make traveling together easier. I didn't realize at the time that he was sweet on me.

Now everything is different. Now, being with Jefferson is both familiar and strange. Like a brand-new pair of boots from the same cobbler. Shinier, newer, maybe even nicer, but they don't fit the same until you've walked in them a spell.

"I heard about Old Tug," Jefferson says.

"He's a rascal," I say.

"You like him?"

"Not particularly."

"Good."

The smugness in his voice pleases me, for some reason. "He didn't really want to marry me. He said I was ugly and manly. Just wanted to make his friends jealous that he had a wife."

"You're not ugly."

I smile into the dark.

"And you're not manly," he adds.

"I wasn't fishing for compliments."

We walk on, giving the lean-tos and tents wide berth so as not to wake the others. In the distance, one of the horses whinnies. Just Sorry, I'd wager, bellyaching as usual.

"Olive says you don't want to get married at all."

"That girl needs to mind her own business."

"Is it true?"

My sigh is lost in the night breeze. I'm not sure what to tell him.

"Lee?"

"I don't know," I say truthfully.

"What do you mean? What's so bad about getting married?"

We've reached the edge of the corral, with its resident horses and oxen. They're mostly shapeless lumps in the dark, but I find Peony right away. I'd recognize her silhouette anywhere, as easily as I recognize my own hand. She's asleep standing up, one back leg slightly cocked.

"You see," Jefferson continues, "I was hoping you said what you did to Old Tug just because you found him objectionable."

"You mean the part about having a sweetheart back in Georgia?"

"All of it."

"You're awfully well informed for someone who was away at his claim at the time."

"Everyone was very forthcoming. Couldn't stop talking about it."

Of course they couldn't. "I *do* find him objectionable. But some of it was true."

"So you don't want to get married."

I snap, "Well, I'm not going to rush into it, that's for sure."

"But do you—"

"Once a woman gets married, she has nothing of her own. She can't own property. She can't make any decisions about her life." Now that the words are coming, they're like a burst dam, spilling so fast I can hardly catch a breath. "When Mama and Daddy died, everything went to my uncle. Everything I'd worked so hard for. I thought he'd stolen all our gold, more than a thousand dollars' worth. Our twenty acres of land. The house, the barn, our horses and tack. But it turns out it was his all along, fair and legal. Because a girl can't inherit. So here I am, all the way out in California, trying to rebuild some of what I lost. As a single girl, I can, you know. But once I get married, everything belongs to my husband. Even my own self. I have to give up the name Westfall and change it to my husband's. Don't you see? Once I get married, I lose everything all over again."

He's silent for such a long time. Maybe I've silenced him for good. We circle back toward the rapids and climb up a ways. So many of our claims lie upstream that we've worn a bit of a path. It's treacherous in the dark, but we're careful.

Finally he says, "Marriage doesn't have to be like that."

"It was like that for your mama. Your da owned her."

Jefferson doesn't like to talk about his mother. She left Georgia with the rest of the Cherokee when the Indians were forced to go to Oklahoma Territory. She could have chosen to stay, being married to a white man. Jefferson was only five years old, and she left him all alone with a no-good drunk of a man who beat her regular. No one in Dahlonega blamed her one bit, and by law, she had no right to steal a white man's son. My own daddy, who rarely spoke ill of anyone, once said that Jefferson's da was likely to kill her someday, that just because he married a Cherokee woman didn't mean he didn't hate Indians deep down.

"It wasn't like that for *your* mama," he counters.

He's sort of right. My mama and daddy were partners. Best friends. I know they loved each other. I *know* they did. But it turns out that Mama married Daddy for reasons I may never fully know. She was in love with my uncle Hiram at the time, and no one expected she'd end up with Hiram's brother instead. I never would have known, myself, if Daddy's old friend Jim hadn't found me in Independence and told me all about it.

"If I ever get married, I want it to be like that," I concede. "But Mama was a bit of a puzzle, you know. She loved Daddy, for sure and certain, but she had secrets. Even in love, she was never quite her own self."

Jefferson stops and lifts his head to gaze at the stars, and I follow his line of sight. The Big Dipper is bright above us. The Cherokee call it the Seven Brothers. Jefferson always wanted to have brothers.

"I would never take anything away from you," he whispers.

My heart cracks a little. "Not on purpose, you wouldn't. But that's how the world works. It's not something you can change just by being good."

"Can't you?"

I'm all talked out. I've got no words left in me, just a hint of sadness and a bucketful of stubbornness, and it occurs to me that maybe I'm ending up a lot like my mama.

As if sensing my thoughts, Jefferson's arms come up around my shoulders, and he pulls me tight to his wide chest. He smells of campfire smoke and fresh dirt, and there must be a bit of gold dust caught in the seam of one of his sleeves because it sets my belly to buzzing.

His head bends toward mine, and his whisper tickles my ear. "I'm going to change your mind about marriage, Leah Elizabeth Westfall. Just you wait."

And I have to consider that maybe there isn't any gold at all. Maybe it's Jefferson himself that has my skin all shivery and my breath a bit ragged.

I sleep late, finally missing a sunrise. That's the rule—if you take a watch, you get some extra shut-eye. When the scent of sizzling bacon and the clang of breakfast dishes fill my lean-to, I turn over and pull my bedroll over my ears.

I'm drifting pleasantly away when Nugget and Coney start barking their furry heads off. I groan. From the lean-to beside mine comes the sounds of stirring; Jefferson and Martin can't sleep through this god-awful racket neither.

I'm deciding whether to wait out the barking, or give in to the morning and fetch myself some breakfast, when Olive comes rushing over.

"It's Mr. Dilley and his men," she whispers, low and fast. "They've found us. Ma says you have to come quick."

My sleep fog clears like it's been whisked away by a violent wind. I throw off the bedroll and reach for my boots as Olive runs to pass the message to Jefferson.

I stumble from the lean-to and blink against the cold sunshine. I grab my rifle and start loading as I head toward the breakfast area. Nugget and Coney come trotting over and follow at my heels. I'm glad for their company.

"Well, if it isn't Mr. Lee McCauley!" says Frank Dilley from atop his dun gelding. He's clean-shaven now, except for a thick black mustache. Someone should tell him that he'll never be a gentleman, no matter how much wax he uses to make it curl and point.

Nearly a dozen men are with him, all mounted. I recognize most of the faces from our wagon train. "No skirts today, pretty boy? You know what they say; nothing like a little gold mining to put hair on your chest." He guffaws at his own joke, and his eyes drift meaningfully below my neck. Ever since everyone discovered that I'm really a girl, I haven't bothered to wrap myself with Mama's shawl. My true shape is plain as day to anyone with eyes.

"What are you doing here, Dilley?" I glance around our camp, weighing our options. Jefferson and the Major stand nearby, guns at the ready. Martin Hoffman is holding the Joyner baby, but he eyes the powder horn hanging from the corner of his lean-to. Hampton is out of sight, to my relief—Dilley and his men would surely recognize Bledsoe's former slave—and the college men are late abed, having taken second watch. Becky Joyner bustles around her breakfast table, serving miners as if nothing is amiss, but her shoulders are tense and her lips are pressed thin.

"Just thought we'd call on some old friends," Dilley says.

"Friends?" Martin exclaims, loud enough that the baby starts to fuss. "My sister . . . You left us to *die* in the desert, you good-for-nothing son of a—"

"I thought you'd be out prospecting by now," I interrupt with a warning look in Martin's direction.

The miners at Becky's table are murmuring among themselves, casting unfriendly glances toward the newcomers. Old Tug whispers something to Becky, and she whispers something back. He pulls his Colt revolver from his hip and places it on the table beside his plate.

"Only fools try to mine once the weather turns," Dilley answers. "Anybody with common sense is in Sacramento, looking for work before the rains hit. But we heard about a mixed group of folks up this way, Northerners, some Southerners, a German boy, and we figured it had to be you. Wanted to see for ourselves, didn't we, boys?"

"So you aren't mining, and you aren't working," Jefferson points out. "Who's the fool?"

"Your shirt has a bullet hole," Dilley says. "Shooting your mouth off finally get you shot?"

The Major swings forward on his crutch. "I see you've come to make friends, like always."

"Wally." Dilley acknowledges him with a tip of his hat. He spits a stream of tobacco onto the ground beside his horse, and the gelding flicks his tail in irritation. "Nice to see you up and about, even if you're not the man you used to be."

"I'm twice the man you ever were," the Major says cheerfully. "Even with half as many legs."

"Tidy little settlement you got here. Looks like you've found some color."

"Not much," the Major lies. "But we're hopeful."

"Then where'd you get all this gear?"

"I sold some heirloom jewelry," Becky pipes in, bringing a pot of porridge from the box stove to the table.

"Glad the baby turned out fine," Dilley says, with a chin lift in Martin's direction. The Hoffman boy is patting the baby's bottom to keep her quiet. "Hope he got the right number of fingers and toes."

"*She* does," Becky says, spooning lumpy porridge into Old Tug's bowl. "No thanks to you."

"You still haven't said what you're doing here, Frank Dilley," I say.

"We're following all the streams to their sources, seeing who has which claims. My boy Jonas here"—he tilts his head in the direction of Jonas Waters, his foreman—"he's recording everything, official-like."

"Official for who?"

"For somebody who knows his business. When all the placer gold plays out, and you're going hungry, he'll be ready to buy up the good claims and get to some real mining." He waves a hand dismissively at our camp. "I ain't made up my mind yet whether this claim looks like it'll amount to anything."

"That so?" I say.

"But the gentleman we're working for, a fine rich man who knows gold mining, from Georgia, he's also been asking around about his niece."

The world tilts.

"Pretty sure he means you," Dilley continues, grinning like a kitten that's snuck some cream. "Pretty sure he'll be awful glad when I tell him where you're holed up."

"I don't know what you're talking about," I whisper.

Old Tug rises from the table. Several others stand with him. "Well, sir, I expect you best get on with it," Tug says. "Lots of streams, lots of claims, lots of miles to cover."

Dilley's mustache twitches. "And who're you?"

"Name's Tuggle. Me and the rest of these boys"—he gestures around the table—"hail from Ohiya. But nowadays, we Buckeyes are neighbors to Widow Joyner and Miss Leah here, and we come to pay our respects *every day*."

Frank Dilley and Old Tug stare at each other for a spell. Dilley's eyes make a sweep of Tug's companions, noting their shiny new Colts.

Finally Dilley tips his hat. "A good day to you, Mr. McCauley. And you, too, Jefferson." He smirks at his own joke. "I won't say good-bye—I expect we'll see you again."

"I expect so," I mutter.

The Missouri men turn their horses to skirt the pond and head upstream. I gasp with the realization: when they reach the top of the rapids, there'll be a vantage point, a brief break in the trees that will allow them to see our entire camp and most of our claim land. It means they'll be able to spot Hampton.

"Andy!" I whisper. He's helping his ma take up the dishes, but he comes running. "Go to the corral and find Hampton. As fast as you can. Tell him to get out of sight and stay out of sight."

"Okay, Lee." He gestures to the dogs. "C'mon, Coney.

C'mon, Nugget." And he's off, pumping his chubby legs as fast as he can, the dogs at his heels.

A hand settles on my shoulder. "That was good thinking," says the Major.

"Frank Dilley's going to tell my uncle where I am," I say.

The Major gives my shoulder a squeeze. "We all knew he'd come looking, once he settled in."

"We'll be ready," Jefferson says, his face fierce.

Becky clears her throat. "Well, would you look at that," she calls out. "I made too many eggs today. Free seconds for everyone!"

Old Tug and his friends whoop and cheer and slap one another on the backs, and for the first time, I'm glad to have them around. Becky was right to cultivate some goodwill.

The college men tumble from their lean-to, bleary-eyed, suspenders hanging at their hips. Jasper yawns and stretches. "What'd we miss?"

Chapter Six

It's been a week since Frank Dilley's visit, and the weather has turned. Frost greets us most mornings, and panning in the creek turns my fingers and toes into icicles. Becky's customers don't thin out one bit, even though so many have headed into the valley to wait out the winter. Plenty of stubborn folk like us remain. Jefferson and I were raised in mining country, after all. We know the surface gold will play out soon enough, and we've only got this winter and the coming spring to find it before we have to start digging pit mines or diverting the creek.

Jefferson and I practice shooting our revolvers. Sometimes, Martin or Tom or Jasper joins us, but I like it best when it's just Jeff and me. We set pinecones on distant rocks and take turns trying to make them burst apart or at least fly into the air. I'm a better shot than Jefferson, even with his Colt, which has nicer action than my old five-shooter. But I can't bear to give it up in favor of a Colt of my own, even if the blasted thing is a burden to load all the time. I've precious little left of my parents and my life with them.

The college men make another supply run to Mormon Island. This time they find a cow, a milking shorthorn with a shiny red-brown coat. They name her Artemis.

Artemis's milk nearly dries up the first few days she's with us, on account of being terrified of Nugget and Coney. But one morning, Hampton finds Nugget curled up happily against Artemis's warm back, and the big, dumb-eyed cow drops plenty of milk from that day forward. I teach Olive how to use Jasper's new churn, and Becky is able to add buttered biscuits to her breakfast offerings.

Our lean-tos weren't much—just pine boughs slanted across rough-hewn wooden posts to keep out the worst of the wind and rain. We've converted them into what Old Tug calls "right, proper shanties," but they look like overgrown woodsheds to me, if woodsheds had canvas roofs.

Jefferson and Henry finish the walls of the log cabin and top it with yet more canvas, promising Becky they'll build her a real roof come spring, with shingles and all. The cabin is dark as night inside, with a single window covered in paper for now, and a dirt floor that seeps wetness at the edges whenever it rains. It's drafty—the walls need chinking badly—and it stands a bit lopsided, the peak of the roof rising slightly off-center. But it's solid, mostly dry, and warm on account of the box stove, and after six months sleeping in or under our wagons, followed by another month in tents or lean-tos, Becky announces that it feels like the finest hotel in the whole wide West.

My chest swells with warmth and pride to return each evening from a hard day's prospecting. With newcomers lending a hand, our camp has grown into a small town practically overnight, with several buildings, an awning for Becky's customers, three outhouses, and a corral and pasture—all cozied up to the clear running creek that tumbles into our wide, beautiful beaver pond.

Frank Dilley's visit with his weaselly land recorder in tow has got Tom fired up. He's already scheming on how to make the land ours, straight and legal. He says the days of informal mining claims are numbered, that we'll eventually have to file real claims at a land office, probably by next year. Once we do that, and California becomes a state, we ought to petition for a town charter.

I can hardly believe something as grand and official and permanent as a town can happen just because people settle down and make it so. But that's how it seems to work, and every evening as I wander back toward the cabin and campfire to greet my friends, it feels like coming home.

Only Jefferson seems displeased. He works as hard as anyone, but whenever Tom gets to discussing property or claim rights or town charters, he goes silent and gloomy.

My job all this time has been to find gold, and I've found plenty. Piles of it. My own claim has yielded a fair bit, but Hampton's has proved out better than anyone could dream. There, I found a small vein hidden in a big slab of slate with quartz outcroppings. It was easily accessible to our pickaxes, and both Martin and Jefferson helped us mine it out.

No one has done better than Becky Joyner, who seems to have found the mother lode by serving bad breakfasts to lonely prospectors. Now that she's hit on the idea of selling extra biscuits wrapped in kerchiefs for the miners to take along with them, she makes almost fifty dollars per day. Sometimes the men pay in gold. Sometimes they offer goods in return, like a chicken for a hankie full of biscuits, or a sack of oats for a week's worth of breakfasts. And if they don't have anything else, they pay in labor, which we make good use of, too.

Everything is going so much better than we could have hoped. We're going to be rich after a single season, every one of us. It's marvelous to think on.

And at the same time, my mind just won't take it in. I watch my flour sack fill with gold until it's bursting at the seams, and I don't believe it's actually mine. I see our camp grow, watch everyone add luxuries—like a second woodstove, an apple sapling, a large henhouse with room to grow, a feed shed beside the corral and pasture. And none of it matters. It's all temporary.

Because Frank Dilley is going to tell my uncle where I am, as soon as he finishes with his surveying job. Maybe he has already. Uncle Hiram might be on his way here right now. And this fancy little dream about a new home and a new family and more riches than a girl could imagine will meet a quick end.

It's a brisk fall night that makes us button our collars and don our gloves, but the sky is clear, showing a million sparkling stars, which means we share supper outside the cabin beside the fire pit. We sit beneath Becky's awning, which traps some of the heat, and use Becky's too-hard biscuits to mop up platefuls of beans in molasses. An oil lamp hangs from a hook beneath the awning, lighting our meal and the faces around me in soft yellow orange. Crickets chirrup in chorus, punctuated by the occasional protestation from a bullfrog.

Jefferson sits beside me. Our thighs brush occasionally, but neither of us inches away.

While the rest of us finish up, Becky is already hard at work baking for tomorrow—another batch of biscuits, along with a meat pie she's sure she can sell to someone. Martin Hoffman holds Baby Girl Joyner in one arm while he eats, occasionally giving her a taste of his beans. I suspect he misses his little sister.

Hampton sits at the table across from me. He's hardly recognizable from the half-starved Negro who followed our wagon train at a distance, gleaning scraps when he could. Regular food and water have filled him out, giving his face a healthy roundness. His strength has grown, too. I've seen him flip sheep upside down with hardly more than a thought, and he can wrestle Sorry into submission with a few tugs on her halter.

He wipes his mouth with the back of his sleeve and clears his throat. "I got something to say," he informs us, and everyone looks up expectantly. "I've found enough gold, with Lee's help here"—he indicates me with a lift of his chin—"to buy my freedom *and* that of my wife back in Arkansas."

Becky gasps. "Hampton, that's wonderful news," she says.

The Major reaches over and claps him on the back. Jasper raises his tin cup, which is purportedly filled with water, though my money's on whiskey. "To Hampton's freedom!" Jasper says, and we all lift cups or forks in echo.

"Are you going to leave us?" I ask.

Hampton shakes his head. "Not yet. Maybe never. I need to figure out how to go about this. Do it in a way that doesn't put the slave catchers after me."

He's made himself scarce the whole time we've been in California—leaving for the corral to care for the oxen and horses before the sun is up, working his claim all day, joining us only after dark for meals. Talking to folks at Mormon Island, it became clear that the general mood of California is anti-slavery, that once it joins the union, it will probably be as a free state. But I don't blame Hampton for not wanting to take any chances.

Tom Bigler sits at the rough-hewn table behind us, the one Major Craven made for Becky. He places his elbows on the surface and leans forward. "Want some help?" he asks.

Hampton shoots him a grin. "That's why I brought it up. I want everything clean and legal. Unbreakable."

"It would be an honor," Tom says. "I need to consult with one of my books first, but I think I can figure out how to draw up the sale offer without revealing your location."

"I'd appreciate that."

"After the sale's done," Becky says, "will you go for your wife?"

"I was hoping we could send somebody white for her. I don't ever want to set foot in Arkansas or any other slave state again if I can help it."

"We know some abolitionists who could help with this sort of thing," Tom says. "I'll write a letter in the morning to Reverend Sturtevant."

Hampton leans forward. "Who's that?"

"He's the president of Illinois College, and my mathematics professor. He'll know who to contact, and he'll be wholly circumspect. I won't even mention your name."

Hampton settles back with a nod, but I can see the gears spinning in his head. Sometimes when you say something out loud and ask for help with it, it becomes real in a way it never was before.

Becky's smile is soft and yearning. "I'd dearly love to have another woman around to talk to."

Jefferson chokes on his biscuit.

"Not that Lee isn't a woman," she amends hastily. To me she says, "It's just that you're always out working the claims, as God ordained for you to do."

I smile to show I take no offense. "I wouldn't mind some female company either," I tell her, with a pang for my friends Lucie and Therese. Both gone home now, one to Oregon, the other to that great beyond.

Therese's brother, Martin, is bouncing the baby on his knee, and the tiny thing babbles happily. "I need to get to Sacramento sometime this winter," Martin says. "See if I can figure out how to send some of my money home. It would be a nice surprise if it was waiting for my family when they got back to Ohio."

"I'm confident there's a way to do that," Tom assures him.

"I'm short on medical supplies," Jasper says. "I need a few things you can't find at Mormon Island. I may have to go all the way to San Francisco for them."

"Actually," Becky says, "I need to go to San Francisco, too."

"You do?" I say.

Becky drops biscuit batter into a cast-iron pan, where it sizzles and steams. "Before we left Tennessee," she explains, "Mr. Joyner had our entire house dismantled and sent to San Francisco by way of Panama."

I had forgotten about that.

"My home and everything in it—furniture, dishes, knickknacks—are all waiting for me somewhere in the harbor."

"Sounds like trips to Sacramento and San Francisco are in order," Jasper says cheerfully. "I'm keen to see the Pacific Ocean. Can you imagine it? More water than even Lake Michigan."

"It's not that easy," Becky says, wiping her hands on her apron. "Andrew passed on, God rest his soul. I have all his documentation in my trunk, but I'm just a woman. None of it belongs to me."

We all exchange looks of alarm. That she could come all this way, children in tow, nursing her sick husband for more than half the journey—only to lose everything?

"I'm thinking they might hand it over on behalf of my son,"

she continues, indicating little Andy. His face is smeared with mashed beans, and his feet knock the bench as he swings them back and forth. "As eldest son, he stands to inherit. Surely I have rights as his mother and guardian?"

Tom rubs at his chin. "Let me think about this, Mrs. Joyner. I'm sure there's a way. If we get your property released, would you have it shipped here?"

She raises a chin and primly says, "I would indeed."

"Anyone on that boat ever lay eyes on your husband?" Major Craven asks.

"I don't know. I don't think so. Everything was handled through my father's solicitor."

The Major's eyes take on a mischievous twinkle. "Then one of us can pose as Mr. Joyner."

Becky gasps. "But . . . that would be . . . I couldn't . . ."

"Just think about it," he says.

"It wouldn't be exactly legal," Tom says, and the Major glares at him. "But sometimes, the law doesn't embody justice the way we'd like," he adds.

"It's an elegant solution to a tricky problem," Jasper says.

"Maybe," she murmurs doubtfully.

"I've got no reason to go to San Francisco or Sacramento or anywhere," Jefferson declares. "So I volunteer to stay right here and watch our claims."

"If someone poses as my husband," Becky muses, "then I could stay, too. Keep feeding those miner boys."

"What about you, Lee?" Hampton says. "Staying or going?"

"I'd love to see the ocean, too," I admit. "But if Jefferson's staying, I'm staying."

My neck warms as everyone stares at me, Jefferson hardest of all. But it's true. He's the best friend I've ever had, and those months traveling all alone were some of the worst of my life. I'm not losing him again. Besides, I feel safe here, where I know the people and every hill and tree. I don't want to go someplace strange right now, where I might turn around a corner and run into Frank Dilley or my uncle.

"Blast!" Becky exclaims, and we all look up, startled. I can't remember hearing her cuss before. "Burned them again," she says, frowning down at her pan. "You know, one of these days, those miners are going to figure out that I'm a terrible cook."

No one says anything for a moment. Then Henry starts to giggle, then little Olive, and soon we're all laughing like it's the Fourth of July.

I'm snuggling down into my bedroll. From the shanty beside mine come the sounds of movement—a dropped boot, a snuffed lamp. Jefferson is settling down, too, and I close my eyes against a sudden pang of lonesomeness. We used to sleep side by side, Jefferson and me, when everyone thought we were just two friends traveling together. Sometimes we'd whisper long into the night, or at least until Becky's husband thumped the floor of his wagon to tell us to shut it. I guess I got used to the sound of Jeff's breathing, of feeling his presence beside me all through the night. Once in a while, he'd even reach out and hold my hand.

I didn't think much of it then. I thought he was sweet on Therese, that the hand-holding was just his way of showing kindness to an old friend. But I see the truth of it now. It was a declaration, maybe even a promise.

Jefferson wants a lot more from me than a little hand-holding. He wants *me*. And as I lie here all alone, feeling colder without him, I have to admit that maybe I want him right back.

I need to put it from my mind and get some shut-eye before Hampton comes to wake me for my watch shift. I close my eyes tight and try to think of pleasant things, like the way Peony's winter coat is coming in, making her look like a fuzzy cat with hooves, or the genuine mirth in Becky's face when we all laughed about her cooking.

In the distance, Coney barks. Which is nothing curious, but then Nugget joins him, and soon the two of them are caterwauling something awful. With a sigh, I throw off my bedroll and reach for my boots. Someone has to check it out, just in case something is truly amiss, and since I'm not sleeping, it might as well be me.

I stumble from my tent, rubbing at sleepy eyes. It's darker than dark, with not even a moon to light my path as I feel my way through our shanties in the direction of the corral. I grab the oil lamp from its place beneath Becky's awning and take a moment to light it.

The acrid scent of smoke pricks at my nostrils. We stomped out the fire pit hours ago, and the woodstove inside Becky's cabin sends its smoke high into the sky. Maybe it's one of our neighbors, a mile or more distant. The wind through these hills can be tricky.

Nugget's barking takes on a frenzy. A sick worry wriggles at the back of my head.

"Jefferson!" I holler, without thinking. He needs his sleep too, but something is wrong out there in the dark, I just know it, and Jeff is always the person I think of first when I'm in a predicament.

The Major barrels out of his shanty holding a lantern. He swings forward on his crutch, moving faster than I can believe. "What's going on?" he says.

"Not sure. The dogs are after something. Hampton and Martin should be walking the perimeter out there."

Jefferson comes running, rifle in one hand, ramrod in the other. The strap of his powder horn is clutched in his teeth, and the horn bangs at his chest. "Martin and Hampton still making their rounds?" he says around a mouthful of leather.

"Haven't seen either."

He starts loading his rifle. "Let's find them. Major, wake the college men and make sure they're ready for anything. Then check on the Joyners in the cabin."

"I'll join you afterward," the Major says, and heaves off in the direction of the college men's shanty. Those boys would sleep through anything if we let them.

"You got that five-shooter loaded?" Jefferson asks, with a chin lift in the direction of the gun at my hip.

"Yes, sir!" I say with a mock salute.

His glimmer of an answering grin fades quick. "It's probably nothing, but . . ."

"Better safe than sorry," I finish for him.

We head down the hill toward the corral and pasture. "With Hampton and Martin out there, we can't just shoot at any old thing," he says as we walk. My lantern barely lights our way, and we have to step carefully. "So keep your eyes open and your ears pricked."

"Always."

"Sure wish you'd consider replacing that old thing with a Colt. Better range, faster loading, and beautiful to boot." I can't see his face in the dark, but I hear the smile in his voice. He knows why I won't give up my five-shooter. "Wait." He puts up a hand. "Do you smell smoke?"

"Thought I smelled it earlier. But there are camps all through these hills. No telling where it's coming from."

"The oxen are making a bit of a racket."

"Let's hurry."

We near the bottom of the hill. The pine trees break onto a meadow, which is just a wide smear of darkness to our eyes. Hampton's fence posts enter the circle of light cast by my lantern, then the oxen, and just beyond them are the lumpy shapes of our horses. All our creatures are milling about, tossing their heads. Peony dances back and forth, stepping high.

"Hampton!" I call out. "Everything all right?"

No answer. Jefferson and I exchange a worried look.

"Maybe he walked a wide circuit tonight, to see what had the dogs all worked up."

"Maybe." The dogs' barking is distant now. "Nugget!" I call out. "Coney!"

Jefferson whistles for the dogs, a trick I haven't mastered. I climb over the log fence into the corral and make my way toward Peony. The scent of smoke grows stronger.

"How are you doing, girl?" I say soothingly. She tosses her head, but she settles and lets me plant a kiss on her nose. "I smell it, too," I say when she snorts.

Jefferson checks on Sorry, and I send a quick glance around at the other horses: the Joyners' gelding, the Major's tall mare, the cart horse. Artemis the cow is pressed up against the fence, her big eyes rolling around in her head. This corral isn't much. Hampton rigged it quick to give the animals a homey place, but it won't hold them all if they panic.

I let the scent of smoke pull me forward, through the milling animals and over the opposite fence. "Jefferson?" I call out, staring at the feed shed. Hampton built it out of the way of the animals, so they couldn't get to it at night. It looks like a wide outhouse open on one side, filled halfway to the roof with hay bales. A few bags of oats sit on shelves up high. Maybe it's the darkness, but my view of it seems fogged, and my lungs are starting to burn. "I think the shed is on fire."

He sprints toward me and clears the fence with a single leap.

"Hampton?" I call out, and it's almost a scream. Maybe he brought a lantern out here. Maybe he set it down on a hay bale and forgot about it. He's probably asleep somewhere, the fool man. He's been working too hard to keep a proper watch, I'll wager, in his eagerness to see his wife again.

Several things happen at once.

"A leg!" Jefferson says, pointing at the ground. Sure enough, a boot snakes out from behind the shed. "Hampton?" he calls out, running forward.

The shed whooshes into flame.

A gunshot cracks the air, less than fifty yards away, and something squeals—a hurt-animal sound that I feel deep in my bones.

From the opposite direction, where our camp is, comes a human scream.

I freeze, knowing I need to do something, not sure which direction to dash off to first.

"Hampton!" Jefferson says again. He squats down beside him and smacks the man's cheeks. "C'mon, wake up!"

Heat licks at my face, and I can see everything for yards now that it's washed in a firelit glow.

"Lee, don't just stand there!"

His voice jolts me to action. I heave the top log from the corral's fence and thrust it aside. Peony dashes out first. "Go on, git!" I yell, smacking the rump of the nearest ox, then Sorry, then Artemis. We'll be a day rounding them up, if we find them at all, but at least they won't hurt themselves trying to escape or, worse, get burned.

I sprint over to Jefferson and Hampton. "Is he dead?" I ask in a breathless voice, then I cough. The shed is a conflagration now. The very air feels like it's on fire.

"Not yet! Grab his legs. Help me get him away from here."

For a short man, Hampton sure is heavy. We cough and

heave our way farther into the meadow, Hampton's body swinging between us. We reach a muddy patch free of dry grass, a safe distance from the feed shed, and we lower him gently to the ground.

"What's wrong with him, Lee?" Jefferson asks, finally letting fear into his voice.

"Was he shot?" I say, remembering the gunshot moments ago.

"I don't see any blood."

"But he's breathing?"

"For now."

I jump to my feet. "I'll get Jasper. And water." I hesitate. There's no way we can bring enough water down the hill to put out that fire. "I'll bring shovels. We need to dig a break, before the trees catch fire."

Jefferson rises to come with me.

"Stay with Hampton! Someone's still out there. They might—"

"There's trouble back at camp, too."

He's right. My toes curl to think of the scream I heard. Becky, probably. No, it wasn't her voice. Henry? And something got shot, out there beyond the meadow. I'm terrified it was one of our dogs.

"Let's go."

I grab the lantern, and together we run back up the hill. My foot catches on a rock, and I nearly fall, but I don't dare slow down. The air glows, and smoke sears my lungs. We crest the top. Our camp is on fire, too.

Jefferson runs to help the Major, who has whipped off the canvas roof of his shanty and is futilely smacking at the flames licking the corner of Becky's cabin. The college men sprint back and forth from the pond with buckets of water, trying to douse the conflagration that used to be our cart. Andy and Olive stomp around, snuffing sparks and tiny flames that flutter to the ground.

"Where's Becky?" I yell. "And the baby?"

Becky barrels from the cabin, baby in her arms. She shoves her tiny daughter at me. "I'll be right back!" she says, and she turns and dashes back inside.

"No! Becky!" Smoke thickens, blurring my view of the cabin door she disappeared into.

My feet twitch to go after her, but I can't go in there with the baby in my arms. I look around for a safe place to put her so I can *do* something. She starts to wail, and tears streak the soot on her face, so I bounce her the way Martin always does.

Martin.

"Where's Martin?" I scream through the smoke. "Anyone seen Martin?"

I grab Jasper's arm as he's dashing by, water sloshing over the side of his bucket. "Hampton is hurt," I say. "Down by the corral. He's unconscious."

Jasper is wearing his long underwear, half unbuttoned. His feet and legs are drenched to the knee from fetching water in the pond. "Is he safe?"

"I don't know! There was someone out there, Jasper. Someone with a gun."

"Was Hampton shot?"

"I don't think so. Feed shed is on fire, though. Jefferson and I dragged him out of range."

"Artemis!"

"I drove her out of the corral. We'll round her up later."

"All right, fetch my kit—unless my shanty has caught fire, too. I'll meet you down by the corral once we've secured the cabin."

He turns to go, but I grab his arm again. "Have you seen Martin? He was supposed to be on watch."

The look that washes over Jasper's face sends fear stabbing into my gut. His expression becomes resigned. "Fire first, before we lose everything and put the little ones in danger."

I nod once. It's a harsh decision. An awful one. And I agree completely.

Hitching the baby onto my shoulder, I run for the college men's shanty. Mine is a wreck, the canvas roof burned to nothing, the walls caved in and sending long tongues of fire into the sky.

I can't help but think about what's left inside—my bedroll, Peony's saddle and bridle, the boughten dress the college men gave me that I will never wear.

The shanty Jefferson and Martin share is untouched, but beyond it, the college men's shanty is just starting to smoke. Fire is like that; it can leapfrog a target for no apparent reason.

I lift the door flap and peer inside, deciding whether or not to chance going in. Only the far corner is in flames. Jasper's kit is along the opposite wall, beyond their three mussed bedrolls.

Carefully I place Baby Girl Joyner on the ground. I take a moment to make sure she's not going to roll away, then I dash inside the shanty, heading straight for Jasper's medicine kit. I grab it with both handles as smoke swirls around my head. I lug it outside and place it beside the baby. Then I go back in.

Working fast, I grab the bedrolls and drag them outside. I find a saddlebag, which I throw over my shoulder, and a pair of boots—Henry's, if I don't miss my guess. A chest rests on the ground along the back wall. The flames are only inches away.

I have no idea what's inside that chest, but I have to do something, save something. I try to lift it as heat singes my eyebrows. It won't budge. I wipe a dollop of sweat from my forehead before it can pour into my eyes, then I crouch down and shove.

It slides a few inches. Working one corner and then the other, I gradually slide it across the floor and out the door.

I take a moment to gulp clean air and clear my lungs. After checking on the baby, I move to Jefferson's shanty. It's not on fire yet, but it's only a matter of time.

On the floor are two bedrolls, Martin's knapsack, and Jefferson's saddlebag. Beside the saddlebag is a small wooden box I've never seen before. A flowery design is burn-etched into the top, the latch closed with a metal clasp. I know I shouldn't pry, that I don't have time, but it's so odd that we spent months together on the trail and I never saw this box. I flick the clasp open and peer inside.

There are only a few tiny items: a small leather pouch filled with something soft, a long feather, a letter that's been unfolded and read so often that the pages are frayed and the writing is blurred, and a single gold nugget the size of my thumbnail.

I stare at the nugget. My memory is vague with the distance of both miles and months, but I'm sure of it. This is the nugget I gave him, back in Georgia, the day my uncle killed my parents. I found it on his land, so it belonged to him fair and square. He should have used it to buy supplies for the journey west, but he saved it. For some reason, even though he needed money worse than anything, he saved it.

The baby starts screaming again. I slam the box closed and dash outside. I gather all of Jefferson's and Martin's belongings into a pile where I hope they'll be safe from stray embers; then I bend to retrieve the Joyner baby.

We head toward the cabin, which is now a pillar of fire, so hot and angry I feel like the very hair on my head is in flames. I pat my scalp to make sure it isn't, even as I glance about, hoping with sick desperation that Becky made it out of the cabin. Then I see her, running toward the creek with a bucket, and I nearly fall to my knees with relief.

Olive and Andy are still stomping out embers. "Olive!" I call, and she comes running. "Hold your sister." The girl takes the baby with well-practiced hands. "You and Andy take the baby. Head down to the pond where it's safe and stay there, understand?"

"I want to help!" she protests.

I almost give in; I wouldn't want to stand by, neither. "Jasper will want your help later with some doctoring, so I need you safe."

"Okay, Lee."

She rounds up her brother and herds him toward the pond. Once the three Joyner children are safely away, I grab the Major's shovel and start heaping dirt onto the cabin fire. Jefferson yells something at me, but I can't understand because the fire is roaring, drowning out everything else.

We all work hard and fast, harder and faster than we've ever worked in our lives, but I can already tell it'll hardly matter. We're going to lose the cabin for sure, and a lot more besides. I'm grateful for the rain we've been having; otherwise all our claim land would be up in smoke by now. As it is, we have a slight chance of keeping the fire from spreading to the surrounding woods and autumn-dry meadows. Becky and the college men pour water on the edges of the fire, while the Major and Jefferson bat it down with canvas.

Sweat trickles between my shoulder blades as I shovel and shovel, until I've dug a decent trench between the cabin and the trees. The skin of my face is tight and hot as if it's been sunburned, and my hands, my clothes, everything is covered in fine gray-black dust. Every single breath is a wheeze of dry, sharp pain.

There's still no sign of Martin.

One of the nearest pine trees starts to flicker and pop. Within seconds, it's a giant torch, lighting the whole sky.

Light flares on the hill above us. A split second later the ground rumbles as a sound like a thousand trees splintering to dust pierces my head. It's our ammo exploding, in the cache Jefferson and Martin dug.

We all pause in our work, faces falling. The shovel drops from my blistered hands. I don't know what else to do.

Suddenly, figures enter the wide circle of firelight. Ten of them. No, more. At least thirty. Men, women, and children, all surrounding us. Indians.

Becky Joyner lets out a squeal, high-pitched enough to be heard over the roaring fire.

Alarm fills me, too, but for a different reason. Jefferson was right. The Indians do live here. And if the fire spreads to the trees and takes off through this dry tinder, it'll burn down their homes, maybe their food.

Most are barefoot. Some, especially the women, wear nothing but grass skirts. Thick black hair frames round faces, and long bead necklaces drape between bare breasts. Many carry huge animal-hide blankets.

The women shake off their skirts and leave them on the ground. Naked, brandishing their blankets, they step forward.

Becky flees to the pond to gather her children.

As one, the Indians rush to attack the fire—the cabin, the shanties, the tree. They beat at it like it's the devil, hides and spark flying.

My companions and I remain dumbfounded for the space

of two heartbeats. Then we leap forward to join them, fighting with renewed vigor. Now that we have help, Jasper and the Major rush down to the corral to take care of the shed and check on Hampton.

Minutes pass, or maybe an hour, as we slap and shovel and douse.

Gradually the fire succumbs to our will. The shanty flames fade, though choking black smoke still billows from hidden embers. The cabin turns to cinders. Even the tree torch is conquered, when the Indians do something I can't see that makes it topple—burning branches and all—onto the remains of the cabin, where they're able to safely beat out the fire.

The eastern horizon is hinting at dawn when a light rain begins to fall. Henry lets out a whoop of relief.

The Indians glance around at one another. They exchange a few angry words I don't understand, then they begin to leave, as swiftly and surprisingly as they came.

"Wait!" Jefferson calls out.

One of the Indians turns back, an older woman with a marked face—charcoal-colored lines stretch from her bottom lip to her chin. Her necklace is thicker and longer than any of the others.

One of the men comes up and stands behind her. He's a short but muscular man, with a beaded necklace and a pattern of dots on his bare chest. He makes no obvious threat, but it's clear he'll allow her to come to no harm.

Jefferson rushes back toward his half-burned shanty, to the pile of items I rescued. He grabs his bedroll, which is an enormous buffalo hide we acquired on a fateful hunt, months ago. He brings it back and offers it to the Indian woman.

"Thank you," he says.

Her black eyes widen. She runs a forefinger over the thick brown fur, as if considering. After a moment, she and the man nod to each other. She takes the hide in her arms, and the two of them turn away and disappear into the trees with the rest of their companions.

Chapter Seven

We are left alone in the predawn chill. The remains of our camp, of everything we've worked so hard for, smolder around us.

"All the chickens are dead," Tom says. Then he bends over, coughing.

Jasper and the Major crest the hill. Hampton is dragged between them, his arms wrapped around their shoulders for support. His head lolls, and his gaze is oddly unfocused, but his eyes are wide open and blinking. I'm so glad to see him alive that a tear leaks from my right eye and dribbles down my cheek.

"Is he . . . Will he . . ." It's Olive, slunk up beside me. I look down to see her lower lip trembling.

"He's fine," Jasper says. "Concussed, is all. Small burn on his arm. He'll have an awful headache for a few days, and he won't be keeping food down anytime soon, but he'll make it."

"Something hit me," Hampton murmurs. "Back of my head."

Jefferson's eyes find mine. Hampton wasn't the only one on watch tonight. "Martin," we both say at once.

The Major pulls his Colt from his holster. "I'm coming with you."

"Me too," says Tom.

Becky looks around at our ruined camp. Faint daylight is changing everything from black to sick gray. "I'll just . . . I guess I'll start to clean. . . ." All of a sudden she crumples to the ground, into a lump of sooty skirts. Her face falls into her hands, and her back heaves as she silently weeps.

"I'll stay with Widow Joyner," Henry says meekly.

The rest of us fan out to search. If everyone is as tuckered as I am, they can hardly lift one leg to put in front of the other, and every smoke-scarred breath feels like a major battle. That doesn't stop any of us from breaking into a jog, or from calling Martin's name at the top of our lungs.

The Major heads back toward the corral, Tom skirts the pond and veers south toward the American River. Jefferson and I climb upstream past the rapids. It's still too dark to see well. As we clamber over tumbled boulders and weave through the trees, I worry that we might pass within a few feet of Martin and never notice.

We're well past my claim now and into Jefferson's. The land is even rockier here, shale poking out of the sod, ready to trip unwary feet. The only trees able to grow in this landscape are sprawling, monstrous oaks, with their relentless roots and heavy trunks. Clumps of mistletoe hang in their highest branches, and I realize it must be getting lighter if I can make out the mistletoe.

"Martin!" Jefferson calls again. His voice is scraped, like he's swallowed a bucket of sand.

"Martin!" I echo, but my voice is too raw to carry far.

We pause at the edge of Jefferson's claim, where it borders Hampton's land. One of the stakes has been snapped in half, the splintered end sticking up from meager golden grass. We exchange an alarmed glance.

"Lee," Jefferson says in a near whisper, "I'm scared."

His words give leave for fear to come pouring into my own self. "Me too."

"I mean, after what happened to Therese . . ."

"I know." I reach out and grab his hand. It feels gritty in mine, and I wince when he squeezes back; my blisters must be enormous. But as we step forward, neither of us lets go.

The ground turns hard beneath our feet, and my gold sense goes from bees swirling a hive to raging tornado. Hampton's claim has always been the best. Even if Martin was carrying a little extra gold on his person, I wouldn't be able to find him in this maelstrom.

Jefferson stops suddenly, yanking on my hand. "Did you hear something?"

Just the usual: mountain jays joyously greet the day, while the creek rushes over the rocks and wind teases the tree branches. "There's a lot of gold here, and when I'm buzzing like this, I don't hear and see so well."

He is silent a moment, listening. Then: "This way." He drags me toward a lone digger pine, growing against all odds out of a rocky slope. Giant pinecones litter our path. We kick them aside, and they go rolling down the hill toward the creek.

I see his hand first, pale and bloody against a patch of dark shale.

"No!" Jefferson shouts, and the pain in his voice echoes my own. I rip my hand from Jefferson's grasp and run forward, then fall to my knees at Martin's side.

He lies on his back, eyes wide and blinking rapidly at the morning sky. Blood pools on the rock beneath his head; it's already sticky and dark. His right leg bends in a bad place, just below the knee, so that his foot is unnaturally canted to the side.

"I've been calling," he whispers, in a voice even rawer than mine. "Calling and calling for hours."

I grab his bloody, scraped-up hand and squeeze tight. "Go get Jasper," I order Jefferson. "As fast as you can."

Jefferson takes off at a sprint.

"Lee . . ." Martin actually smiles, and my heart hurts so bad I think it might burst. "I'm glad you're here."

"What happened?" He's not breathing enough. Just short, shallow gasps every few seconds. His hand in mine is limp and cold, like it's already dead.

"Don't know. Heard something. Mucking around in the grass. Went to check." His eyes flutter closed.

"Martin!"

He startles awake. "Something hit my head. I fell. Think my leg's broke, but I'm not sure. Can't feel it. Can't feel anything."

"Your leg's fine. Nothing Jasper can't fix."

"Liar. You got any water? Throat hurts . . ."

"No, I . . . Wait." I get to my feet. "I'll be right back."

I dash toward the creek, sliding across gravelly shale. The water runs fast and clear up here above the pond. Tiny trout dart to safety as I lean over the edge. I rip off my neckerchief and soak it, but the water that drips from it is black with soot. I wring it out, rinse again, and repeat the process two more times until the water runs clear. One last time, I dip the neckerchief and let it absorb all the water it can hold.

With it cupped in my hands, I race back to where Martin lies and crouch beside him. "Open your mouth," I command.

He does, and I let water drip from the kerchief between his cracked lips. He chokes a little but manages to swallow, so I squeeze the fabric to give him a steady stream, which he gulps eagerly.

"Want some more? I can get—"

"You think I'll see her soon?"

"Who?"

"My sister."

"Therese?"

He sighs. "*Ja.* Therese." His voice is getting fainter. "I hated her. She was so bossy. So *good*. Vater loved her best. But then she died, and I realized it wasn't true. . . . I didn't hate her at all."

His blue eyes have taken on a glazed look, like he's only half in his head anymore.

I say, "I'm sure it will be a long time before you see Therese."

"Liar. Leah the liar. Lying Lee."

I'm about to protest, but running footsteps come up behind me. It's Jefferson and Jasper, with Becky, Olive, and Henry on their heels.

Jasper drops his medicine chest on the ground beside me and grabs Martin's hand to feel the pulse in his wrist. "What happened?"

"Something hit him on the head. He fell."

"Hey, Doc," Martin says with forced cheer.

"How's that head feel?" Jasper asks. Carefully, he reaches behind Martin's head with both hands and gently palpates with his fingertips.

"Hurts."

"Sorry about this, Martin, but I have to see if your skull is intact."

"Is it?"

A pause. "No."

"Didn't think so."

Olive creeps forward and slips her hand into mine.

"Mrs. Joyner," Jasper says. "While I examine Martin, will you give him the laudanum?"

Becky wipes her hands on her soot-filthy skirt and reaches into the chest for the glass bottle. "How much?"

"All of it."

"But won't that—"

"*All* of it."

Becky straightens. "I see."

"We should have gotten here earlier," I say. "Instead of worrying about that fire. We should have—"

"Wouldn't have made a difference," Jasper whispers, for my ears only.

He doesn't even bother to examine Martin's broken leg.

Instead he unbuttons the boy's shirt and taps various places on his abdomen, occasionally pausing to put his ear to Martin's chest and listen. Meanwhile, Becky tips the bottle to Martin's lips. His face wrinkles at the taste, but he swallows.

Olive's hand slips out of mine. She takes some clean cloth from Jasper's chest, pours water from a canteen over it, and begins to bathe Martin's face.

"Jeff," Martin says, and Jefferson is beside him in an instant. "Send all my gold to Mutter, yes? And tell her I'm sorry. I'm sorry I left—"

"Don't worry about it," Jefferson says. "You'll be back to hunting rabbits with me in no time."

"Please, Jeff."

A muscle in Jefferson's jaw twitches. "All right."

"That laudanum," Martin says dreamily, eyelids fluttering. "No wonder Mr. Joyner liked it so much."

"Olive," Jasper says in a tight voice. "Bend over Martin's mouth and listen carefully to his breathing for a moment."

Her eyes are huge and bright in her face as she follows his instructions.

"You hear that?" Jasper says. "The wheeze? Can you hear how moist it is?"

Olive nods, blinking hard to keep tears back.

"Remember that," Jasper says. "We're going to talk about it later."

"Okay, Jasper."

Martin's eyes don't close, but the light leaves them. He's still breathing, though. Just a little. He's not dead.

Henry's singing voice suddenly fills the air, a high, clear tenor that echoes through the hills.

Hidden in the hollow, of His blessed hand
Never foe can follow, never traitor stand
Not a surge of worry, not a shade of care—

Martin gasps once, loud and strong, and then . . . nothing.

We all stay a moment, just staring down at him. From behind me comes the hiccupping sound of Becky Joyner's sobbing. Olive crawls into my lap and buries her face in my chest. I wrap my arms around her.

Jefferson swears softly, using a word I've never heard from his mouth before. He turns away so we can't see his face.

"Let's get him back to camp," Jasper says, his voice so tight and controlled it makes my chest ache. "Find a place to bury him."

"But what happened?" Becky practically shrieks. "I don't understand! Hampton was hit on the head and he's going to be fine. What's a little broken leg to you? You're a doctor! You could have fixed—"

"He broke his back," Jasper says gently. "His spinal cord was near severed by the fall. His organs were shutting down. If that didn't kill him, the blow to the head would have. His skull was in tatters. It's a wonder he survived as long as he did."

"Oh," Becky says. I'm glad she asked, because I had the same questions.

Jefferson turns back around. His eyes are wet. "His Colt's

missing," he says. "It wasn't enough they killed him. They robbed him, too."

Henry squeezes his shoulder. "Come on, give me a hand with him."

Henry and Jefferson lift Martin—Henry at the shoulders and Jefferson at the feet. Jeff's face is desolate. He looks so awful that I yearn to run over to him, wrap my arms around him, let him cry into my shoulder. Or maybe I want to cry into his. First Therese and now Martin. The poor Hoffmans will curse the day they decided to head west. To come all this way for nothing, except to lose two children.

But I can't let myself float down that river right now. Instead I get to my feet, heaving Olive up with me. She clings tight, so I continue to hold her as I follow everyone back to our burned-out camp.

The Major returns just as we do. He carries something on his back, wrapped around his neck.

"No!" Jefferson yells. He sets Martin's feet down and runs forward.

It's Nugget, and her golden fur is slick with blood.

"She was shot," the Major says.

Olive squirms from my grasp and I let her go, suddenly numb. I'm not sure I can stand on my own feet anymore. I've known Nugget since she was a wriggly puppy. She came all the way across the continent from Georgia with us.

Jefferson leans forward to kiss his dog's muzzle. Nugget's tail thumps once, weakly, and her pink tongue snakes out to lap clumsily at his face.

"She's alive!" Jefferson exults. "You dumb girl, what did you go and get yourself shot for?"

"It's her back leg," the Major says. "She can't walk right now, but I don't think the bone's broke."

That does it. Tears burst from me like a dam breaking. I don't know how I've held it together until now, only to lose it over a bit of happiness, but I fall to my knees and quake with sobs.

Through tears, I note the Buckeyes, led by Old Tug, start to trickle into our camp. They've worn a path up the creek and around the pond by now. I hastily wipe at my face and try to get myself under control.

"I'm so sorry," I hear Becky say in a shaky voice. "I don't have breakfast for you gentlemen today."

The Buckeyes survey our camp, faces grave. They seem to come to a silent agreement. Old Tug grabs a shovel. Another man dons his gloves. Without hesitation, without a word, they get to work cleaning up.

Olive's gaze turns fierce. She strides over to the Major and Jefferson, who are now kneeling over Nugget's prone form. "I'm going to fix you up, Nugget," she says, hand on her hips. "Just you watch and see."

We bury Martin in the meadow. The dirt is too shallow for a proper grave. Like we did for his sister months ago, we bury him as best we can, then pile rocks on top, high and thick to mark the resting place of our friend. I take the Major's ax and chop down a couple of pine branches, strip them, and lash them together to make a rickety cross, which Jefferson pounds into the ground like a claim stake.

It takes two days of light rain for the ruins to cool enough to sort through properly. The woodstoves fared the best. They are ugly now, tarnished black, and one of the door hinges is stuck, swollen and slightly melted by the heat. The Major takes a file and spends a day working it out until it opens and closes with barely more than a hiccup. All our oil's burned, so there's nothing he can do about the final little squeak.

Everything inside the cabin was lost—all the Joyners' remaining furniture, their bedding, Becky's cooking supplies and food stores, her stationery and fancy feather pen, and a whole box of ammunition. Her quick dash inside as the fire was raging wasn't for naught, though. She still has the papers proving her husband's ownership of the cargo in San Francisco, and she still has a small bag filled with coins and bits of gold—payments she received for her breakfasts.

There was another bag of gold she didn't find when she dashed inside, the one filled with dust panned by Olive and Andy, along with the occasional pinch of gold from one of the miners. But on the second day, Tom lifts up a blackened pine branch and the remains of a chair to reveal a thin, lumpy sheet of golden metal on the ground. The gold dust melted in its bag and re-formed into this flat, round thing, like one of Becky's clumsy flapjacks, except it shines in the light when the ash is brushed away.

Gold doesn't melt easily. Something made this fire extra hot.

The chest I dragged from the college men's shanty turns out to be full of odds and ends—clothes, tools, candles, pens, and ink. But it was so heavy because it also contained books from their time at Illinois College. When they realize I saved the books, Henry bursts into tears, and Tom wraps his arms around me and hugs me so tight I worry he'll never let go.

Peony, Sorry, Apollo, and Artemis wander back to their half-burned corral without being rounded up. We find the Joyners' gelding a mile away, nibbling happily on a thick patch of poison oak. He seems plenty glad to see us, though, and lets us halter him and lead him back home.

We'll likely never see the oxen or the cart horse again.

With the Buckeyes' help, we clean and salvage and sort. The children pitch in when they can, but sometimes they're so underfoot that Becky sends them off to pan for gold. She makes them stay within sight, though. No one goes anywhere alone anymore.

On the evening of the second day, we all hunker around the fire pit on logs recently cut to replace our destroyed furniture. Becky didn't much feel like cooking, and no one blamed her, so we eat cold oats soaked in water, with a bit of bacon and salt for flavor. Old Tug and a few of the Buckeyes are with us. They worked hard all day, and the least we can do is let them join us for supper.

Even Hampton has joined us. Jasper isn't comfortable letting him off alone, not until he's sure that concussion is long gone, and not while people are shooting at us and setting fire to our camp.

I watch the Buckeyes close. A few of them give Hampton measured looks.

"Didn't know you had yourselves a Negro," Old Tug says.

"Hampton is a free man," I say, and it comes out snappier than I want.

"Came west with us all the way from Missouri," Henry chimes in. "We all vouch for him."

"Glad to hear it," Old Tug says. "Being from Ohiya, most of us are of an abolitionist spirit. We don't hold with slavery." There are murmurs of agreement from the other Buckeyes, and I breathe a sigh of relief. Tug shoots a line of tobacco into the dirt, rubs any residual off his beard, and says, "Having cleared that up, me and some of my boys, we're thinking of moving our tents here."

No one says anything.

"We'll keep our claims where they are," he continues, "but we'd live here. That is, if you all don't mind. It's a mighty fine spot for a town."

"Wouldn't have to walk so far for breakfast, neither," another says.

The college men put their heads together and whisper among themselves. Becky and the Major exchange a look and a nod. Jefferson leans over and whispers, "We should think about it."

Suddenly all of my companions are looking at me, and I know why. It's my secret. And it's probably my uncle who got Martin killed.

Keeping my secret from these men will be hard with them so close. But given recent events, I'm not sure it would put us in any more danger than we're already in. In fact, having a few rough-looking men hanging around might be a mercy.

I clear my throat. "Well, Mr. Tug, I'm not sure any of us are staying. We haven't made a decision about whether or not to rebuild and keep trying at our claims."

He frowns. "Why not?"

"We just lost someone very dear to us," Becky says gently, a lot more gently than I'd manage. "I don't know that we can stand to lose even one more soul." Her voice wavers a bit with that last. She leans down and kisses her baby girl's forehead, possibly to hide tears.

"Someone set those fires on purpose," Henry says. "They knocked out the men we had on watch, shot our dog, and set those fires. We're just not sure it's safe to stay."

Old Tug chortles. "Course it ain't safe, you lily-livered pretty boy. It's *California*."

"It's *particularly* not safe for us," I say.

My companions turn to me, the big question in their eyes: Will I tell him the truth?

"Why? Because you're a bunch of soft—"

"Because . . . because these are rich claim lands, as you well know. You are your boys are doing just fine, aren't you? Able to afford a paid breakfast every single day."

Several nod agreement.

"You can't keep something like that a secret," I continue. "Everyone is going to want our land."

"If it's anyone's land," Jefferson mutters, "it's the Indians'."

My face warms. He's right, and it was a thoughtless thing to say.

Hampton stands. Jasper leans forward, ready to launch

himself to help Hampton if he needs it, but the man is steady as an oak on his feet.

"I'm not going anywhere," Hampton declares. "Just a few days ago, I had a roof to keep my wife comfortable, and a few fixings besides. Almost everything's gone now, but I'm not giving up. I'm going to get it all back. Every bit."

He sits back down.

"I'm not leaving either," Jasper says. "I've been doctoring for months now. Maybe even . . ." He shuffles his feet a bit, looking sheepish. "Maybe even saved some lives. I'm doing what I came to do. No sense giving up."

Tom says, "I haven't decided."

"Tom and I are thinking of going to San Francisco," Henry adds.

"I want to practice law," says Tom. "That's what *I* came to do. San Francisco seems like the place to do it."

Jefferson says, "I'm going where Lee's going."

"Major?" I say, mostly to divert everyone's sudden attention from Jeff and me.

The Major has a few bits of thick leather in his hand, along with a large bone awl. He's making shoes for Olive, who recently grew out of her last pair. He takes a deep breath. When he looks up, it's in Becky's direction, and his pleading heart is in his eyes.

I catch my breath. He's carrying a torch, for sure and certain. No, it's more than that. Major Wally Craven has fallen head over heels in love with Widow Joyner.

"Becky?" he says, his voice almost a whisper.

Becky blinks at him, her cheeks coloring. "I'm frightened," she admits. "Maybe I ought to go back home to Tennessee, if that's what it takes to keep my children safe. But . . ." She looks the Major straight in the eye. "I don't want to."

Old Tug rubs at his tobacco-stained whiskers. "What *do* you want, Mrs. Joyner?" His voice is kinder than I've ever heard it.

She smiles back. "I want to keep serving you breakfast, Mr. Tug. And all the rest of you Ohio boys. I want to make a home here in California for my children. I want . . ." This time, she looks at me. "I want to stay with my friends."

I swallow the sudden lump in my throat. "I want to stay, too," I say. Jasper gives me a wide, relieved smile, but I hold up a hand to forestall any celebration.

There's no getting around the fact that our very lives are in danger. My friends have gone mad, wanting to stay. Gold fever has made them take leave of their senses. Maybe it's made me take leave of my senses, too. It's amazing what a body will risk when there's a smidge of hope to be had.

"I'm staying on one condition," I tell them. "I'm going to find out who did this to us. And I'm going to end him. It's the only way we'll be safe."

Old Tug nods agreement, but I only care about the reactions of my friends. They're nodding, too, even though they know exactly who I suspect, exactly who I'm talking about. My uncle Hiram Westfall did this, as sure as the sun sets over the Pacific.

"Fine by me," Jefferson says. I look up to find his eyes alight, his face fierce.

"In that case . . ." I turn to Old Tug. "If my companions don't have any objections, I officially invite you and your boys to join us here. We'd be glad of the extra company."

The extra gunpower, I mean, and everyone knows it.

Jefferson adds, "As long as you respect our claims and don't make any trouble."

Old Tug grins, flashing his tooth. "As long as *you* respect *our* claims and don't make any trouble. We'll settle in tomorrow."

Chapter Eight

Lumber to rebuild doesn't come easy. We cut so much down for the cabin and the store of firewood—all of which was lost in the fire—that we have to hike a ways to find good trees and then use the horses to lug everything back. Our hill is now scarred black, and the autumn mud has a particular stickiness to it, being full of ash. As we fell more and more trees, even the hills around us turn barren. The wind and rain hit us harder now, and the mud never dries.

The beaver disappear from our pond, and I don't blame them. We lived in peace with them for a while on opposite ends, hearing their tails smack the water occasionally. With all the Buckeyes setting up tents, I suppose there are just too many people.

The banks of the pond and the outlet creek below lose all their grass, churned up by miners' boots. Deer that used to visit our meadow in the evenings are nowhere to be seen. Hampton, with the help of a few Ohio men, expands the corral to make room for the new horses. Within a week, the meadow is grazed out. Feed will be a lot more expensive from now on.

The world is changing around us, and we're the ones changing it. A funny feeling in my gut says we're not making it better.

I don't see a single Indian. It niggles at me that even though they're near enough to help us, they never show themselves. Becky is frightened of them, but I rather suspect they're frightened of us. Maybe Jefferson is right and this is their land we're squatting on.

I'm so tired from panning and pickaxing and chopping and carrying and keeping extra watch shifts that my very bones ache. I sleep on cold, wet ground in a threadbare blanket I got in trade for two rabbit skins. Some nights it's so cold that I take my blanket and sleep in the corral with Peony. The ground is just as churned up with mud, the air just as cold, but she stands sentry over me all night, fast asleep herself more than half the time, and she never steps on me once. It puts a warmth in my heart, if not my skin.

Becky says I can sleep in the cabin with her and the children once it's rebuilt, and I'm not going to decline. The rebuilding might take a while, though. The college men leave for Mormon Island with our leftover gold and come back with the sad news that most everyone has gone to Sacramento looking for work to wait out the winter, and everything we need is in short supply, especially canvas, hammers, and chickens.

So no shanties, no eggs, no chicken coop, and no cabin for a good long while.

They bring back plenty of oats, bacon, beans, flour, and coffee, though, and the Buckeyes don't complain one bit about getting the same breakfast almost every morning.

One day I'm late abed after a long night on watch, sleeping close to Jefferson this time, on a hard patch of rock that makes my neck ache but is relatively clean of mud. We're far away from the noise of camp; it's the morning sun, shining against my eyelids, that makes me stir. Beside me, closer than is necessarily proper, Jefferson snores as loud as a locomotive.

The camp is as clean as we can make it, and rough lean-tos are starting to replace the shanties that burned down. I've found more gold for everyone, carefully and quietly so as not to arouse the Buckeyes' suspicions. There's nothing holding me back from making good on my word. Today will be the day I start finding out who tried to burn us out.

I'll begin by heading downriver to see if those cussed claim jumpers are still there. If anyone knows what's going on, it'll be a crew of nosy good-for-nothings whose claim spot allows them to see river traffic all day long. Jefferson will put up a fuss about it. Claim jumpers are dangerous, sure, but so am I.

I blink against sleep, trying to gather the gumption to get up, but my limbs feel as heavy as lead. Maybe just a few more minutes of shut-eye. In his sleep, Jefferson rolls over, and his big arm flings across my shoulders.

I freeze.

Jefferson and I slept side by side the whole way to California, under the Joyners' wagon or beside it. But it feels different now. Every little accidental touch sets my heart to pounding and my cheeks to flushing.

His snoring abates, which I find suspicious. Maybe he's just pretending to sleep.

"Jeff?" I whisper.

"You shouldn't pester a man who's trying to rest," he grumbles.

I don't know what comes over me, but all of its own accord, my body turns over and curls up against his chest. "I'm cold," I say weakly.

His breath catches. Then his arms pull me even closer, so that our thighs press together and my nose is under his chin. His hand comes up to caress the back of my head, his fingers tangling in my hair. He's like a woodstove, for how much heat he puts out, and he smells of damp earth and campfires and the tallow he's been using to protect his saddle.

"Better?" he murmurs into my ear.

"Yes." Strange how being pressed close makes me so aware of myself. His breath on the curve of *my* neck, his arm wrapping the small of *my* back, the way his warm skin makes *my* lips buzz with the need to—

"May I kiss you?" he whispers.

One heartbeat. Two.

"Okay."

His lips press against my cheek first, a soft, gentle kiss that sets my belly on fire. He kisses me again, just as gently, but closer to my lips. He smoothens my hair from my forehead, then lets his hand linger against the side of my face, his thumb caressing my cheekbone.

He looks me boldly in the eye, leaving no doubt as to his intentions. "It's about damn time," he says. Then his lips meet mine.

They're soft at first, tentative as if filled with questions, and I wouldn't know how to answer with words, but other parts of me seem to have plenty to say, because I press into him and snake my arm around his neck so he can't get away.

He groans a little and deepens our kiss. His hand slips under my shirt to splay against the skin of my back, and just like that I'm lost, not knowing up from down from sideways. I just know Jefferson, who is familiar and strange to me all at once, and this sudden feeling that I can't get close enough to him. There's too much space between us, too much air, too many clothes, too much heartbreak.

He breaks away, leaving my lips cold, but his fingertips still caress my back. They slip lower, toward the waist of my trousers. I feel like I'm coming out of my skin, and I have to blink to make sure we're not surrounded by a cloud of gold dust.

"Leah," he whispers. "Please marry me."

It's like a bucket of cold creek water dumped over my head. "I . . ."

"Lee McCauley!" someone calls from a distance. It's a man's voice, rough and snarly. "Lee McCauley!"

Jefferson and I exchange an alarmed look. "That's Frank Dilley," he says.

I jump up and yank on my boots, heart pounding something

awful. I have no idea what he wants, but it was only a matter of time before he returned, wanting something. Maybe he's brought my uncle with him. Maybe he's come to run us out for good.

My five-shooter is in the saddlebag I'm using for a pillow, but I don't dare keep it loaded, especially with so much rain about. As Jefferson dons his boots and tends to his Colt, I load all five shots. It's a cap and ball, so I force myself to slow down and be patient, lest I drop my shot all over the ground. I buckle on my holster and slip my gun inside.

Jefferson shrugs his suspenders over his shoulders. "Let's go," he says, shoving his Colt into his own holster.

Henry meets us halfway to camp. Despite his hurried steps and panicked gaze, his hair is perfectly parted and combed, and his shirt crisp and fresh. "It's Dilley," he says. "He's here to make a bargain, but he'll only speak to you, Lee."

"Where's Hampton?" I ask.

"He already made himself scarce."

That's one less thing to worry about. "Well, let's go see what Dilley has to say."

"Reverend Lowrey is with him."

"What?" Jefferson exclaims. He never liked Reverend Lowrey, particularly because the preacher asked me to marry him, back when we were camped at Soda Springs. Jeff liked him even less when he took off with Dilley's Missouri men, leaving us in the middle of the desert with almost no supplies and Becky about to give birth. "That lousy, blasted—"

"C'mon, Jeff. Trouble doesn't need our help to make itself."

It's something Mama always said to me. As we head down the rise, my fingers find their way to her golden locket at my throat.

The camp is abuzz. Smoke curls from Becky's stove, and the air smells of firewood and cornbread. Everyone is up, breakfasts left cold on Becky's makeshift table. The Major, the college men, and the Buckeyes stand together in haphazard formation, united against the newcomers—Frank Dilley and Reverend Lowrey on horseback, eight or so riders behind them.

Andy and Olive huddle just outside the new half-built cabin, out of danger, I hope. Olive clings to a tightly wrapped bundle of baby sister.

"Mr. McCauley," Frank calls out with a tip of his hat. "And Jefferson." Frank never thought up a dumb joke he didn't want to say at least twice.

"What are you doing here again, Frank?" I ask, my hand twitching next to my holster. "Did you come to buy our claims already?"

Because if he has, I've got a mother lode of no for him.

"Came to parlay," he says. "Remember the good preacher?"

"I remember a man who left us high and dry in the desert." Looking Lowrey straight in the eye, I add, "Thought you'd be too ashamed to show your face here."

"Miss Westfall," he acknowledges, getting my name right for the first time, and somehow that sends a stab of fright into my chest. The reverend clutches his Bible to his belly; he's riding horseback, and he still carries that giant Bible. For a mean second, I imagine a snake spooking his horse, and him falling hard to the ground. "I was called to minister to miners," he says. "And I will obey the Lord, no matter how much it costs me personally."

Jasper snaps, "I'm sure it was a great sacrifice, turning your back on people in need to run away." Jasper was the one who doctored Therese, to no avail. He doesn't talk about her much, and the two never seemed like especially good friends. Still, sometimes I wonder if her death grieves him as much as it does me and Jeff.

"Get to business, Frank," the Major says. He looks fierce, his beard wild, his forearms thick with muscle, his eyes steady and smart like a wolf's. He's so kind and good-natured most of the time, I sometimes forget that many consider him a war hero.

Old Tug and the Buckeyes remain watchfully silent as Frank Dilley swings a leg over and dismounts. He approaches me, and even though I yearn to take a step back and put some distance between us, I force myself to hold my ground.

"I have an offer for all of you," he says, even though he's only looking at me. "A certain gentleman heard tell of your recent tragedy with the fire and all."

Jefferson steps up beside me, his hand very near his holster.

Dilley eyes him warily but continues on. "Being a fellow rich in both gold and compassion, he's willing to offer a tidy sum for claims in this area."

Everyone starts mumbling among themselves.

"Why this area?" I ask, even as one of the Buckeyes hollers out, "How much?"

"My employer has an eye for prospecting," Dilley explains. "He thinks there's plenty of gold to be had here, but it's deep underground. It will take money, equipment, and labor to mine it out. He's willing to invest his own wealth to make that happen."

Jefferson and I share a glance. This is not what we expected.

"In exchange, he'll offer three hundred dollars per claim, and everyone who sells will have first pick of paying jobs in his new outfit."

The mumbling grows louder. It must sound like a sweet deal to the Buckeyes, but they don't have a witchy girl helping them out. My gold sense makes our claims worth more than ten times what Dilley is offering, and only my people know it. Well, them and my uncle, who no doubt has guessed that I'd only settle my friends on the richest land available.

"Three hundred dollars is a lot of money," Old Tug says.

"It's not *that* much," Jefferson mutters, and I give him a quick kick in the leg to shut him up.

"There's one more condition," Dilley says, his eyes still keen on me.

My legs turn to rubber. Whatever's coming next, this is it. My uncle's gambit.

"My employer requires that Miss Leah Westfall accompany us back to Sacramento."

Everyone turns to me. You could hear an earthworm in the mud, for how silently they stare.

From behind everyone comes a high, feminine voice. "This employer of yours," Becky calls out. "His name wouldn't happen to be Hiram Westfall, would it?" And God bless her soul for asking the question rolling around in my head that I was unable to force out.

"Why, yes, that's his name, all right. I understand his niece ran away from him back in Georgia. Stole his horse, too." Dilley grins wide, and it feels like a steel trap closing around me. "It's comeuppance time, boy," he says.

My jaw is aching from clenching so hard, and my legs twitch as if to run. I could be on Peony's back in three minutes and halfway to Oregon before he could spit.

"Lee isn't going anywhere," Jefferson says in a dark voice.

"Now wait a minute," Old Tug says. "This is a good offer. We should consider." Several of the Buckeyes murmur agreement.

"These are probably the men who set fire to our camp," says Jasper—just loud enough for the people standing next to him to hear, but it's enough to stop the murmurs. "Lee's uncle is a double-crossing snake. You can't trust any promise he makes."

"A deal with Mr. Westfall is tantamount to a deal with the devil," Becky adds loudly.

This time, it's Reverend Lowrey who jumps in. "As part of the deal, Mr. Westfall also agrees to offer his special protection. You'll never worry about arson again."

Major Craven swings forward on his crutch. "Did you do it, Dilley? Did you set fire to our camp on Westfall's orders? You know we lost the Hoffman boy, right? You're a murderer, Frank, plain and simple." He shakes his head. "Remember when you threatened to put me out of my misery? After the buffalo stampede?"

Frank reaches up to pat the shotgun resting in his saddle holster. "The offer still stands, Wally."

"Well, I suspected you were indecent then, but I'm disappointed, Frank, deeply disappointed, at just how foul a man you are."

The reverend bristles. "Have you all turned savage?" he says. "Mr. Westfall is offering you safety. Honest pay for honest work." He shakes his head as if overcome by deep sorrow. "'For the love of money is the root of all evil—'"

"Oh, quit your sermonizing!" I holler. I've had it with thieving, self-righteous pigs. "No one wants to hear Scripture right now, especially from *you*."

He straightens in his saddle and opens his mouth to stubborn it out.

"You're not going to propose to me again, are you, preacher? Because if you do, my 'no' might be accompanied by a boot in your face."

"I think—"

"I think you should be on your way. You've said your piece."

Frank Dilley rubs at his mustache, looking around for support. "You seem like a reasonable man," he says to Old Tug.

"Reasonable *and* fine looking," Old Tug says with a wicked grin. "But I don't know you from Adam. I do know Widow Joyner, who doesn't seem to like you much, and neither does my friend *Miss* Lee, and that's enough to make me think twice about your offer."

"Well, don't think too long," Dilley says. He places his foot in the stirrup and mounts. "It would be a real shame if a terrible tragedy befalls this place before you can take advantage of Mr. Westfall's generosity."

A click echoes in the air as someone cocks a Colt.

Dilley knows it's time to retreat. "I'll be back in three days for your answer. Lee, pack up and be ready to travel when I return."

He clucks to his horse and steers him away. Reverend Lowrey and the rest of the Missouri men follow.

The murmuring starts up as soon as the trees close around their departing backs. No matter what Old Tug said, the Buckeyes are going to consider my uncle's offer. They'd be crazy not to.

"Do you really think your uncle sent his men to burn down our camp?" Jefferson asks.

"Who else?" Jasper says.

Becky has retrieved the baby and steps up to join us as she pats the tiny thing on the back. "This is California," she points out. "There's no shortage of unsavory persons here."

Old Tug and some of the others are pretending nonchalance, but their ears are pricked like a cat's. I have to choose my words carefully.

"I guess we don't have any proof he did it," I say. "But I know he killed my mama and daddy, and he stole my homestead right out from under my feet. He's capable of such a thing, for sure and certain."

The Major rubs at his beard. "I've been thinking about that fire," he says.

Jasper and the college men join our circle. It's like we're a regular town council now, with the Buckeyes whispering among themselves but staying close enough to listen.

"We know it was started on purpose," the Major continues. "Someone knocked out Hampton, while another snuck up on Martin. The fire started in at least two places at once—the feed shed and the cabin. They probably used kerosene. Or maybe even gunpowder. Because something made the fire hot enough to melt gold. And we know that whoever did it was armed, because they shot Jefferson's dog."

No new territory here. We already knew it was arson; that's why we're all so exhausted from keeping extra watch shifts.

"Where are you going with this?" Jasper asks darkly.

"Why didn't they just shoot Hampton and Martin? It would have been a lot safer for the arsonists. Wouldn't have to get close."

"Maybe it was too dark for shooting," I offer, remembering the moonless night.

The Major shrugs. "Maybe. But in my experience, there's only one reason to sneak up on someone right before a battle."

Jefferson is nodding. "To catch your enemy unaware."

"Exactly," the Major says. "Whoever did this didn't want to risk the sound of a gunshot. They wanted those fires to spread as much as possible." He pauses. "While we were still sleeping in our beds."

The world shifts. I've never been the fainting type, and I'm not going to start now, but I sidle closer to Jefferson so I have something to cling to if necessary. "You're saying that whoever did this didn't care about casualties," I whisper. "They might even have been *hoping* for casualties."

The Major doesn't answer, but his lips press thin.

"That doesn't make any sense," I protest. "My uncle wants me alive." In a voice too quiet for the Buckeyes to hear, I add, "You *know* why he wants me."

"Your uncle, yes," Becky says. Her baby gives a little hiccup, and milky spit bubbles between her lips. As Becky pats the baby's mouth with her apron, she adds, "But I wouldn't put it past Mr. Dilley to do worse than he was told, just for spite. He loathes us. I'm sure of it."

"What did we ever do to him?" Jefferson asks.

"We exist," Tom says simply. "Look at us. Look at who we are."

We're a half-Cherokee boy, a one-legged war veteran, three confirmed bachelors, and two uppity women. Little does Frank know we also have a runaway slave with us, but I'd die before I told.

"You're a dab at riding, Lee," Tom points out. "You shoot better than Frank, hunt better. You disagreed with him in front of everyone—more than once. Then you turned out to be a *girl*."

He says "girl" the way you'd say "thief" or "murderer," like it's the worst thing ever. I know Tom doesn't mean it like that, but he's right about the way Frank Dilley sees it. Dilley's the kind of fellow who feels that being a white man makes him better at everything than everyone who isn't. And if the facts prove otherwise, he'll try to destroy the facts.

"It's a good thing he doesn't know everything about me," I say.

"So what do we do?" Jefferson says.

Henry has been quiet this whole time. He looks down at his boots, shuffling them in the mud. "I'll do whatever you all decide," he says softly.

"You have no opinion at all?" the Major says.

Henry gives us a sheepish shrug. "Honestly, I'm not sure gold mining is for me. I'd like to see San Francisco someday. Maybe even Oregon. But . . ." His gaze shifts to Tom. "I don't want to leave my friends."

Jasper starts to protest, but I interrupt. "There are some things that don't add up," I tell them. "With my uncle, I mean."

"Such as?" Jasper says, squinting against the morning sun, which is full up over the mountains now.

"Dilley kept referring to him like he was a rich, powerful man. And I guess he is, a little. He was a fancy lawyer down in Milledgeville, did well enough for himself. But he didn't have *that* much money."

"He stole all your gold," Jefferson says. "Remember?" Then quieter, so the Buckeyes can't hear: "That stash you and your family had. It was worth over a thousand dollars! Then he sold your homestead, right?"

I nod. "But he spent nearly a thousand dollars just buying passage on a ship for him and Abel Topper. Besides, Frank Dilley and that weasel Jonas Waters and those Missouri fellows aren't working for free. I guess what I'm asking is this:

How can he afford to buy out all our claims? He'd need four times what he stole from me. Maybe more. Where did that money come from?"

"Maybe he's wealthier than you thought," Becky says.

"Maybe it's all a bluff," Jefferson says.

"Maybe . . ." The Major is still rubbing at his beard as his mind turns on the problem like a mill. "He's working for someone else."

Jasper's mouth forms an *O*.

"Someone with money," Becky says.

"Daddy once told me that Hiram had a problem with debt," I say. "He was impatient. Didn't want to wait around for life's finer things, so he borrowed and bought and got himself into so much debt he couldn't see straight. Daddy bailed him out once. He bailed himself out another time. And that's all I know about that."

"So maybe he's in debt again," the Major muses.

I whisper, "And he knows just the witchy girl to get him out of it."

Chapter Nine

I let the thought sink in. A shiver runs through me like Hiram's shadow is already blocking out my sun. Then someone clears his throat behind me, and I jump.

It's Old Tug. "Sorry to interrupt," he says. "I've been talking with my boys, and we ain't in no hurry to accept this deal. Seems nefarious. Besides, if we wanted to spend our lives working for a rich man, with aught to show, we'd have stayed in Ohiya."

Becky smiles bright enough to light the gloomy sky. "I'm so glad to hear that, Mr. Tug."

He blinks, caught in her brilliance, but he collects himself quickly. "We think this Dilley fellow means business, though. I'd bet my last snuff he started them fires. So if we're going to stay and prospect here, we need to do something about him."

The Major steps forward. "I could not agree more, sir."

"I'll ask again," Jefferson says. "What do we do?"

Everyone starts throwing out ideas. Old Tug wants to find

Frank Dilley and help him come to an *accidental* end, and even though the idea doesn't set right in my gut, I can't say I'd be sorry. Henry suggests we flee to Oregon Territory and give farming a go. "A good wheat crop is practically worth its weight in gold," he says. "Maybe in Oregon we'd see the Robichauds again."

Becky wants to build up the town, inviting more and more people to stay to increase our numbers. "He can't take down a whole town, isn't that right?"

The ideas come fast and fierce, but none of them are good enough.

"I'll do it," I yell, interrupting everyone. "I'll do it."

"Do what?" Becky says.

"Oh, no, you won't," Jefferson says.

"I'll go to Sacramento."

Everyone starts to protest, but I hold up a hand to forestall them.

"*Not* with Frank. I'll go of my own accord. Maybe I'll take a couple of you with me, if I get volunteers. I need to face my uncle, find out what's going on. Maybe he's working for someone else. If so, this person needs to be informed what kind of man my uncle really is. At the very least, if I leave, you'll all be safe for a spell. It'll buy us time to come up with a real plan."

"No way, Lee," says Jefferson, his voice low and furious. "Not a chance. Once your uncle has you, he'll never let you go. And I . . . You can't . . ." A muscle in his jaw twitches.

Old Tug says, "You think maybe we can go over your uncle's head to whoever is pulling his strings."

Becky frowns. "Isn't that leapfrogging a demon to make a deal with the devil?"

"I hope not," I say.

"We need you here," Jasper says. "You're—" He glances around at the Buckeyes. "Um . . . essential to our undertaking."

I glare at him. He's about as subtle as a charging buffalo.

"Lee's right," the Major says.

"What?" Becky practically shrieks, and the Major winces. "You can't possibly think—"

"He won't kill her," he insists. "And if anyone can talk to him, maybe it's his niece. But Lee . . ." He turns to me. "If you leave, and you don't come back in a reasonable amount of time, we're coming after you."

A few of the Buckeyes nod agreement, trying to look serious and fierce. But it's just bluster. They hardly know me at all.

"You saved my life," the Major continues, indicating his amputated leg. "You and Jasper. Don't think I've forgotten. So just because I think sending you to Sacramento is the right strategic decision, it doesn't mean I'm turning my back on you."

"I'm going with her," Jefferson says.

"No, absolutely not," the Major says. "Next to Lee, you're the best marksman in this outfit. We need you here."

"Jeff, I vowed I'd find out who did this to us and end him. If that means confronting my uncle, then it's something I've got to do. If I don't go, my uncle and Frank Dilley will keep hurting people I care about. And the Major is right; they need you here."

"No." He snaps out the word so hard and angry that I recoil. He takes one long stride forward and grabs my shoulders. "I'm not getting separated from you again, understand? Be as stubborn as you want; it doesn't matter. Where you go, I go."

He's a whole head taller than me now, with shoulders that block the sun and a black-eyed gaze as fierce as I've ever seen. I should feel small next to him, but I don't. I feel bigger, too, like we can do anything together.

Jeff says, "Those weeks traveling to Independence, after I left Georgia. They were a torment. I thought I'd made the worst mistake of my life, leaving my best friend behind. But then you showed up in Independence, and I got a second chance, and hell take me, but I'm never leaving you all alone again."

Everyone around us has gone silent. The Major glares at us both. Old Tug studies me, eyes narrowed beneath his bushy brows. If he has any brain in his head, he's trying to reconcile Jefferson's little speech with the fib I told him about a beau back in Georgia.

"I'm going, too," Tom says, stepping forward.

"What? No!" Henry exclaims.

"They'll need someone with knowledge of the law," Tom says, his voice gentling. "Property law, especially. Lee's uncle will try to make a claim on her. Someone needs to make sure he has no legal recourse."

We talk it out awhile longer, arguing back and forth, but in the end it's decided. Jefferson, Tom, and I will gear up and leave for Sacramento in two days.

◆ ◆ ◆

The Major sits on a log, whittling at an oak branch. I can't tell what he's making, but he goes at it with the same fervor that Nugget and Coney get digging a hole, forgetting the world around them. He's a man with busy hands, that's for sure. He's always carving, hammering, or sewing something. I've seen him create tables and benches, shoes, halters, and even a leather tie necklace for Olive, which he made by boring a hole into a bit of quartz and working the leather strap through. Afterward, he declared himself the finest jeweler in all of Glory, California.

"What do you want, Lee?" he practically growls.

"You're spitting mad at me, Major, and I ought to know why."

He sets the branch down in his lap, pointy end sticking off to the side, and looks up at me. "This trip to Sacramento," he says. "It's an awful risk. And you're taking my best man with you."

"Well, he's my best man, too."

His gaze softens. "I know, Lee. I truly do. It's just . . ." He stares off in the direction of Becky's breakfast table. She bustles around, refilling coffee, avoiding stray hands, checking on the porridge, wiping up a spill. All the while, she smiles and smiles. No power in the world can shake that smile.

"You've got the Buckeyes to help now," I remind him. "They're pulling their weight just fine. They never complain about watch shifts. They're only drunk sometimes. Some of them even help rebuild."

He sighs. "But they're doing it all for *her.* Their intentions are . . . I just don't trust them, not one bit."

Ah. So that's it.

I settle beside him on the log and stretch out my legs. "You're sweet on her," I say softly. "Aren't you."

He grabs his branch and starts whittling like the fate of all California depends on it. *Swick, swick, swick,* goes the knife.

"You mean like Jefferson's sweet on you?" His tone is accusatory, but his cheeks are burning red.

"Yes," I say honestly. "That's what I mean."

"Don't matter," he says, scowling down at his branch.

"How so?"

"She's the finest lady I ever knew. Too fine for me."

"I don't think—"

"She's beautiful and young and *so learned*. Did you know she speaks Latin? Latin! Those fine manners, that smile . . . She's bewitching every bachelor west of Indian Territory without even trying, and probably a few married men besides."

"Not the college men," I say with a smile.

He snorts. "No, not them. But Widow Joyner will never look twice at me when she can have her pick. She's had four proposals already, and those are just the ones I know about."

I almost laugh. Becky has been looking twice at the Major, all right. And three and four times besides.

It's a glorious morning, with a sky blue as cornflowers touching down on distant mountain peaks that shine white with snow. The oaks and aspens are losing their leaves, making the distant woods feel stark and barren, but it's a beautiful barrenness, all wild and thick. A giant condor circles above, and I reckon we appear tiny and insignificant to him, like ants on a hill.

After a moment, I have the courage to ask what's really on my mind. "Is it your leg? Is that why you think she won't look twice at you?"

He doesn't flinch from my question. "Of course it's my leg. And those other things I mentioned, too. But mostly my leg." He brandishes his knife at me. "Don't get me wrong, girl. You'll never hear me complain about the rocky path the good Lord has set before me. I'm lucky to be alive, and I thank God every day in my prayers." He returns to whittling, but it's more deliberate now, less hurried, like maybe he got something off his chest. "But she deserves better," he murmurs. "She deserves the best."

"You're a war hero," I protest. "A natural leader."

"That was a terrible war. Not even a war, it was just . . . running around and shooting and being bullies. There was nothing heroic about it, and it's not worth even a moment of your thoughts."

The Major fought in the Black Hawk War, according to the Missouri men. It happened around the time I was born, and I don't know anything about it but the name. The Major won't talk about it, though, and it makes me wonder what kind of horrors he was part of. The Missouri men seem to think he's violent. A killer. That's why they appointed him leader of our wagon train, until he lost his leg.

But the man I know isn't like that at all. I think of Major

Craven carrying Andy around on his shoulders or helping him catch bullfrogs in the pond, the way he made that necklace and new shoes for Olive, how hard and quietly he works to provide Becky with furniture and every other comfort he can think of. Mostly, I think of the way his eyes follow Becky everywhere she goes, like she's more precious and beautiful than all the gold in California.

"Maybe you ought to let Becky decide what she needs," I say.

He just shrugs. "She's still mourning her husband."

I laugh.

"What?"

"When we were at Mormon Island, Becky saw a dress she fancied. All black. She thought it would be proper mourning dress."

"So?"

"So, she bought a bright blue bonnet instead, and some ribbons for Olive. I guess mourning just wasn't that important to her."

"Huh." He gazes off into the distance.

"And maybe you don't want my opinion on the matter," I continue, "but I'm going to give it anyway. You *are* the best, Major. I don't see how she can do better."

A tiny grin creeps onto his face. "You'll keep this conversation to yourself, won't you?" he asks in a sheepish voice.

"Course."

He bends over and plants a kiss on the top of my head. "You're a good friend, Lee Westfall."

◆ ◆ ◆

We're up before dawn, when light barely kisses the mountain peaks and frost sparkles on fallen autumn leaves. The tree frogs chorus in the dark—I've never heard anything so small make such a large noise, not even crickets in the summer back in Georgia. Everyone rises to see us off, even the Buckeyes, and lanterns swing from more than a few hands. Becky's breakfast smells warm and wonderful; she has a loaf of bread rising in her Dutch oven by the fire, and biscuits browning atop the woodstove. I look around at everyone, at the new lean-tos, the first row of logs outlining a new cabin, the canvas tents shared by the Buckeyes—all washed in the warm glow of fire and lantern light. These people are my home, I realize in my gut. And I'm sorry to leave them.

The Major lets me borrow his knapsack, since my saddle and saddlebags burned to a crisp in the fire. I stow some jerky and hardtack, my canteen, ammunition for my revolver, my blanket, and an extra shirt and stockings. I keep the gold I've found the past few days in my pockets. I feel safer with it on my person, and I like the way the magic of it caresses my skin, making it softly buzz.

I also pack my rifle and five-shooter. The grip on the pistol was charred in the fire, but luckily it was unloaded and came through the flames otherwise unharmed. I was worried about it, but the Major took it apart, cleaned and tested it, and assured me it was fine.

One thing I don't bother taking is extra feed for Peony; we

expect good grazing as we travel, even this late in autumn. Peony tosses her head with excitement as I lead her toward one of the Major's log benches to mount up; I haven't exercised her near enough lately. She's gotten plump on meadow grass, and her winter coat is coming in thick, so she looks like ball of golden fluff.

"You okay with me riding bareback again?" I ask her. She snorts a little, which I take for assent. "That's my girl. Maybe we'll get you some new shoes in Sacramento."

The Major steps forward. "If you three aren't back in a month, we're coming after you."

"We'll make it back," Jefferson says from his seat atop Sorry. "I promise."

"It's tradition in my family to have a day of thanksgiving in the fall," Becky says, frowning. "But I'm not keen to celebrate without you."

I grin. "We'll just have another celebration when we get back."

"Twice the food!" Jefferson says, and I roll my eyes because Jefferson can eat more than any human I've ever known.

Tom has one foot in the stirrup of his gelding when Henry rushes forward. "Wait!"

Henry throws himself at Tom and buries his face in his neck. After a startled moment, Tom wraps his arms around Henry's shoulders and squeezes tight. They whisper something back and forth, and then Henry steps back, tears brimming.

Becky gives me a quick hug. "Bring back some chickens if you can," she orders, pressing a couple of cool, small items into my palm. I don't have to look at them to know they're gold nuggets. "And another butter churn."

"I'll do my best."

"And! If you find one, get yourself a new dress."

"Really?"

"A nice one," she says with a firm nod. "Christmas is coming. A lady ought to have something proper to wear. Think of it as a bonus for all your hard work along the trail. You know . . . you and Jefferson are the best hires my husband ever made." Her voice has a touch of sadness, but only a touch, and I cast my gaze in the Major's direction.

Coney runs circles around the horses' legs, certain he's about to go off on a grand adventure. Nugget does her wobbly, limping best to join her friend, but Olive grabs her and pulls her back. "No travels for you," she scolds, sounding like a woman grown. "Not until that leg has healed."

Andy hurries forward to wrap his arms around Jefferson's legs, and Jeff reaches down to give him a pat. Then the boy extricates himself to corral Coney. "Bye, Lee! Bye, Tom! Bye, Jefferson!" he calls out with a giant grin. He just lost his first tooth, and I suspect it will be days before he stops showing off the gap in his smile.

With a final wave, we turn our mounts away. We skirt the pond and follow the creek down the slope leading to the American River.

Chapter Ten

"Stop fidgeting, silly girl," I say to Peony. She's been dancing all morning as we traveled, head tossing, nostrils flaring. Maybe it's because she got so used to wearing a saddle.

"Sorry's been fretting, too," Jefferson says at my back. He rides just a few lengths behind me. I twist so I can see her. The sorrel mare's eyes roll about, and her tail twitches like her flanks are covered in flies.

Behind them, Tom and his gray gelding, Apollo, take up the rear. Apollo is as calm as a babe.

"We haven't been exercising them enough," I say to Jefferson. "And now they're as giddy as Andy with a candy jar. They'll settle."

"Hope so, or this is going to be a long trip."

But as I straighten, my neck prickles. I've known Peony her whole life, ever since she came slipping out of her mama, a bundle of wet legs. She's a good horse. The best horse. I trust her as much as I trust anyone, and right now, she thinks something is wrong.

We reach the river and head west. "Look for a ford," Tom calls to us. "It would be best to avoid those claim jumpers who attacked us. Let's go around them if we can."

"Agreed," says Jefferson.

"I want to be well past them before we make camp," I add.

A path meanders along the river now, which makes for easy riding. The prickly scent of burning pine from a nearby campfire fills the air. We pass a blackberry bramble that hugs the water's edge; a mess of fishing line is all tangled up in the branches.

Plenty of prospectors will be passing winter in this area, for sure and certain. We can't see them, but you don't have to be a dab at tracking to find marks of their passage.

We come to a flat stretch of land, where the river seems to widen and slow. We pause at the edge, sizing things up.

"We'd have to swim the horses," Jefferson says.

"At least the current doesn't look too bad," I say. "Tom, is that gelding of yours a good water horse?"

"The best," Tom says proudly.

"All right, then. Let's do this," I say, leaning down toward my boots.

We all tie the laces of our boot pairs together and hang them around our necks. Jefferson and Tom remove their saddlebags and flip them over their shoulders.

I urge Peony forward, and she splashes happily into the river, her tail whipping up as much water as possible onto her back, giving no thought to her rider's preference to stay dry.

The water is icy cold on my bare feet. I wince as it reaches my thighs, then suddenly we're swimming, bobbing downstream as much as across it, the water soaking me past my waist.

"Dear Lord in heaven, that's cold!" Tom calls out.

I hold my guns high and cluck at Peony to swim faster as the chill works its way through my whole body.

Finally we reach the opposite bank, at least a hundred yards downriver from where we entered. The horses clamber ashore over a small lip of grass and rock. Then Sorry explodes into a sudden shake that showers us all with river water.

"Blasted horse," Jefferson mumbles, wiping water from his eyes and forehead.

I'm shivering fit to burst. "We need to find a campsite and get a fire started," I say, teeth chattering.

We've hobbled the horses and laid out our blankets beside a roaring fire. I didn't bring a change of trousers, so I'll have to wear them as they dry. Our rifles are laid out and ready, all loaded, which makes me a little nervous. Daddy had a "no loaded guns in the house" rule on account of potential backfires, and it's strange to have mine heavy and full beside me, even though I'm not hunting. But this is California Territory, and we have to be prepared for anything.

"I don't like the way Sorry and Peony took to the trail," Jefferson says, poking at the fire with a stick. "They're a bundle of nerves."

"Apollo seems fine," Tom says.

We're across the river and far enough from the claim jumpers that we should be safe. But my neck is still prickling.

"I trust my horse," I tell them. "If Peony says something isn't right, I believe her."

"I'll keep first watch," Jefferson says.

"I can do it," Tom says. One of his law books lies open across his lap, and he's trying to read by the meager firelight. "I need to study up on property law before we reach Sacramento."

He'll be looking at his book more than he'll be looking out for danger. "Jeff, you do it," I say. "If I were to guess, I'd say someone has eyes on us. Horses don't like it when they can sense a critter but not see it."

"You think we're being followed?" Jefferson asks.

"I think you'd better stay extra alert tonight."

"Okay."

"I'm serious, Jeff. Someone snuck up on both Hampton and Martin, and neither of them are shirkers."

He grins. "You're worried for me, aren't you?"

"Course I am."

"Know what I think?"

I scowl at him, which only widens his grin.

He steps closer, puts a hand to my chin, and lifts it so I can't avoid his gaze. "I think you're in love with me," he says.

I stare at his lips. What comes out of my mouth is: "Jefferson McCauley Kingfisher, you have the swagger of a rooster and the swelled head of a melon." But what I'm thinking is how much I'd like to try that kissing thing again.

On the other side of the campfire, Tom is trying awfully hard to pretend to be invisible. Heat fills my cheeks, but Jefferson doesn't seem to care one whit that we're overheard. "You'll admit it soon enough," he says. "I told you I'd change your mind about . . . things. And I will." His thumb caresses the line of my jaw. He bends forward until his lips are so close to mine I can feel the warmth of his breath.

I'm about to go up on my toes to close the distance between us, to kiss him the way I want to, but he suddenly steps back, leaving me cold and off-balance. "I'll wake you when it's your turn to keep watch," he says, and the look he gives me is so smug I could spit.

True to his word, Jefferson shakes me awake in the dead of night, and I blink rapidly to clear the sleep from my mind. He's let the campfire burn low, which is why chill has worked its way into my hands and feet. A breeze rustles the branches around us, and something dark and winged swoops low overhead.

I throw off my blanket and reach for my revolver. After a good yawn and stretch, I grab my five-shooter and check for moisture.

"There's some pine-needle tea for you by the fire," Jefferson whispers. "Still hot."

"Thanks. Seen or heard anything?"

"Maybe. I'm staying up with you."

A little thrill snakes through me. Maybe it's just an excuse to kiss me again. But common sense prevails, and I shake my head. "You need your rest as much as anyone."

Nearby, Tom rolls over in his sleep, mumbling something I can't parse.

"I'm not going to sleep anyway, after hearing all that racket."

"Something big, huh? Maybe a deer."

"Maybe a catamount," he says. "There's at least one in the area. I've seen tracks."

"A catamount won't come near the fire," I say. But I decide to grab my rifle as well. She's not as easy to fire quickly, but one well-placed shot will take down anything.

"I hope you're right."

I hear what he's not saying. Something big could be worse than a catamount. It could be a person.

I shove my revolver into its holster and heft my rifle. "Going to make a quick circuit," I tell him. "Maybe I'll scare off whatever's out there."

He starts to protest but changes his mind. He knows better. "Stay within sight," he orders.

"Yes, sir!" I give him a mock salute and head into the trees.

As promised, I keep the silhouettes of our camp in sight as I work my way around. Pine needles and oak leaves crunch beneath my feet. The air is damp, but the sky is clear, the moon high and half full. It feels like a storm is coming, but with that sky so clear, it might not be here for a while yet.

I pause where the horses are hobbled, sleeping peacefully. Except Peony, who raises her head and gives it a tiny toss of greeting. She nuzzles into my shirt, looking for a treat.

"What are you doing awake, girl?" I whisper, stroking her warm neck.

A branch snaps behind me.

I whirl, bringing up my rifle.

A figure stands there, dark, tall and unidentifiable. Firelight glints off the barrel of a shiny Colt revolver, pointed right at my head. I'm furious at myself. I was worried about Tom not keeping a good watch, or Jefferson not taking it seriously enough, and I'm the one who got caught.

"Jefferson!" I holler. "We got company!"

"Don't make no difference, girl," says a familiar voice. "We got him, too."

My heart tumbles into my toes. "And *I* got *you*, Frank Dilley," I say. "Go ahead and shoot. I've got better aim than you, and you know it. Let's see who's left standing."

Dilley just grins. "If my boys hear a gun go off, Bigler and Kingfisher are dead men."

"How do I know they're not dead already? You're the kind of man who would knife someone in the back."

He turns his face toward the campsite and hollers, "Bring 'em this way. Gotta show the little lady we mean business."

The horses are awake now. Peony strains against her hobble, and I don't blame her one bit. Sorry snorts, tail swishing as booted footsteps crunch through the underbrush toward us.

It's Jefferson, all right, with a gun to his head, held by a rough-looking man I don't recognize. Tom comes up right behind him, still in his long underwear. He winces as the gun to his own head digs into his scalp, forcing him on. Behind him is Jonas Waters, Dilley's foreman.

Our meager fire provides a little bit of light, and the moon a little bit more, but it's too dark for me to see what's on Jefferson's mind, whether he's scared or angry or sorry or sad, and I want to go to him more than anything. Instead I say, "You boys are wasting your time. We're headed to Sacramento, just like my uncle asked. There's no need for any of this."

Dilley laughs. "Your uncle's not in Sacramento. Never has been."

"What?"

"Oh, don't worry, we'll take you to him. But the whole bit about Sacramento was a fib. If you knew where he really was, there'd be no convincing you to leave your flock of girl-worshipping lackeys."

"Then where is he?" Jefferson demands, and the man holding the gun knocks him in the temple so hard that Jefferson bends over, holding his head between his hands.

"If you hurt him again, I'll kill you," I say.

"Easy, Lee," Tom says. His voice is soft, almost soothing. But I know him well enough now to understand that his mind is working this problem of ours, turning and turning like a mill on a creek. "We wanted to speak with Mr. Westfall, didn't we? If these gentlemen are willing to escort us there, we'll go willingly. Isn't that right?"

He means to buy us some goodwill. With guns pointed at each of us, it's the best plan we've got.

"Yes," I say. "That's right. If you're taking us to my uncle, there's no need for all this bossing around. We're glad to go."

If I can get them to lower their guns, lower their guard, we have a chance at escape.

But while Dilley might be a mean, conniving worm who deserves the bottom of my boot, he's no fool. "Glad to hear we can expect your cooperation," he says. "But just in case, I have a special treat for you."

A fourth man comes toward me, melting from the forest like a ghost. He holds something bulky in his hand. Not a gun.

"You're going to take two big swigs of that," Dilley says.

"I'll do no such thing! If you—"

"You must want your Indun lover to die," Dilley says, and the man with Jefferson does something that makes Jeff grunt in pain.

"Stop it!" I yell. "I'll do it. Just give it here."

The ghostly man hands me a bottle. The glass is cold and hard in my hand. Fumbling in the dark, I twist the stopper open. A familiar scent wallops me in the face. Bitter and stringent.

"Drink," Dilley says. "Or your friends die."

I put the bottle neck to my lips and upend it. Cool liquid pours onto my tongue, and it's so startlingly foul that I immediately spit it out.

"Kill him," Dilley says.

"No, no, I'm sorry! I'll drink it! It just surprised me, is all."

I wait one heartbeat. They don't kill Jefferson. I tip the bottle to my lips again, and this time I'm ready for the awful taste, so bitter it almost burns. I hold it in my mouth and think desperately for a way out.

"That cost me a fair bit," Dilley says. "You do that again, and we'll knock you out the hard way." To the ghostly man, he says, "Make sure she swallows."

The ghostly man approaches. He is so huge, huger even than Mr. Hoffman, and a cowl covers his head, making it impossible for me to see his face.

I swallow. It burns going down, and I choke a little.

"One more sip," Dilley says.

Warmth fills my belly, spreads throughout my torso, into my limbs. "I think one is plenty. I feel . . . strange."

"One more sip," he repeats, and the ghostly man looms over me.

So I tip the bottle to my mouth once again, intending to take a smaller sip this time. The ghostly man's arms dart out. He grabs the bottle with one, my chin the other, and he forces the laudanum into me until I'm coughing. He pinches my nose and tilts my head back. After a few seconds, I can't help it. I have to swallow, or I'll never breathe again.

The ghostly man releases me, and I stagger back, colliding with Peony's flank. The world is starting to spin. My belly rumbles in protest, but I don't seem to care. I guess it would be good if I vomited it back up. No, no, it wouldn't be. They might kill Jeff and Tom. They might . . .

My limbs buzz, and the sky feels wide open, like it's beckoning for me to spread my arms and fly right up to that glowing moon.

"Can you sleep on horseback?" Dilley asks.

"Huh? Horse. Of course. Of course I can sleep on a horse." I giggle.

Dilley scowls. "All right, men, get some of this juice into those two. Then we'll mount up and get out of here. We're still too close to their mining camp."

"Where we going, Frank?" I ask, and it's the last thing I say before falling to my knees while a hole of blackest night sucks away the moon.

Chapter Eleven

I wake to the swaying jolt of Peony's steps. I'm bent over her neck, hands tied behind my back. My shoulders ache from the strain, like they're being pulled from their sockets. Rope digs into my thighs. I'm tied to my saddle.

Confused, I blink against the too-bright daylight. I don't have a saddle. I lost it in the fire.

Just in front of Peony and me is a large roan rump, muscles working with each step, tail flicking back and forth. The rider—dark and cloaked, maybe the ghostly man from last night—rides bareback. It must be his saddle we've borrowed.

My throat aches with the need for cool, clear water. I've lost my hat somehow, and even though the air is chilly, the sun beats down on my back and neck. Straining against the ropes, I twist as best I can, trying to spot Jefferson and Tom. There. Sorry plods along two horses back, and Jefferson is slumped over her withers. When he shifts in his seat, it feels like my heart starts beating again.

Apollo walks behind Sorry, with Tom in a similar state—bound, listless, barely awake.

Those slimy snakes drugged all three of us. I don't know much about laudanum, but I remember giving the Major a fair bit, right before we cut off his leg. He was conscious again after only a few hours, and I didn't swallow that much more than he did. Of course, I'm a slip of a girl compared to him, so maybe the laudanum would have a greater effect on me.

Even so, we can't have been traveling more than a day. We're still near enough to our camp that if we escaped, we might be able to navigate our way home.

I wriggle against my bonds to test them and instantly regret it. My skin is already raw, the rope digging a line of bright pain into my wrists, and my hands ache with cramps. Disappointment is like a rock in my gut. There'll be no escaping unless I can convince Frank to untie me, and he's already proved immune to my appeals.

Peony nickers, sensing that I'm awake.

"Everything's going to be okay, sweet girl," I whisper. "I promise."

"Look who just woke up!" Dilley crows from somewhere off to my right.

The ghostly man reigns in his horse and turns it around. Peony stops short to keep from colliding with it, and I'm jolted forward against the rope.

He clicks to his roan and trots toward me until our horses are neck to neck. His face is still shadowed by his cowl, but I can make out pale lips so full they'd be the envy of any lady if not for the wicked scar slashing diagonally across them.

"Time for some more juice," Dilley says, and the ghostly man reaches beneath his cloak and retrieves the bottle. It's already half empty, and the liquid is sickly brown in the sunlight. How much did they force into Jefferson and Tom?

"Please!" I say. "No more. I'll cooperate. I just need some water. . . ."

My pleas fall on deaf ears. The ghostly man unstoppers the bottle, grabs my face with a huge hand, and tips it to my lips.

It goes down a little easier this time, because my traitor tongue and throat don't realize it's not fit to drink, so eager are they for water.

The ghostly man grunts in satisfaction, then continues down the line to tend to Jeff and Tom.

The bright sunlight is suddenly pulsing. The air isn't chilly at all. I was wrong about that. It's as warm and fine as a summer's day.

My limbs go slack. I let myself fall back against Peony's neck. "I love you, Peony."

I don't know how long we travel. Days, I suspect, because sometimes it's dark when I wake, and I'm on the ground, tied to a tree instead of a horse. I'm always glad to wake into the dark, because it's softer on my aching eyes, which are as dry as a desert.

My belly roils with nausea, and my very bones groan with pain. Dilley feeds us hardtack and coffee, but what I need is water. One night after we've made camp, I vomit it all up into the dirt.

Dilley's solution is to force more laudanum into me, and it's glorious. I swallow it eagerly, even though I know it will be worse when I wake, even though my tongue is thick and my lips splitting from thirst. It's just like when we crossed the desert into California; if we don't get real water soon, we'll die.

It's morning. I stir long enough to realize the Missouri men are packing up camp. Jefferson and Tom are already tied to their saddles, listing sideways in their drug-induced hazes. I pretend to be asleep still, so the ghostly man won't come chasing after me with another dose so soon.

How much laudanum have I had? Too much, for sure and certain. A girl's head was not meant to feel this god-awful. My bowels cramp like everything inside is as dry as a summer gourd. My muscles ache and my wrists are rope charred and my fingers tingle with numbness.

Quietly, carefully, I take stock of my surroundings. Fewer pines, more oaks. Rolling hills smothered in golden grass. We've come west a ways, well out of the mountains. The river is nowhere to be seen.

We could be anywhere, I realize with a sinking heart. And maybe we've only traveled for a few days, but I haven't been conscious often enough to be sure. Maybe it's been a week. Maybe longer.

The ghostly man approaches. He grabs me by the armpits and yanks me up.

"Wait!" I cry out. "I need water. Jeff and Tom, too."

He ignores me, dragging me toward Peony, who is already saddled up. An arrow of panic pierces my heart. Have they been taking care of her? Have they watered and fed her properly? Rubbed her down? Checked her hooves? How do they know the new saddle isn't giving her a rub?

"Please!" I try again. "My uncle wants me alive, right?"

He pauses, and I take the opportunity to get my feet under me. My legs are so wobbly that even if I got out of these bonds, I'm not sure I could escape.

"My uncle needs me," I gasp out, suddenly grateful for this pounding headache because it cuts through the opium haze and helps my mind work. "He needs me alive and hale. If harm comes to me, there'll be hell to pay, and you know it."

The ghostly man's gaze sweeps the camp until he finds Dilley, who nods once.

All of a sudden, he lets go and strides away. My wobbly legs give out, and I drop like a stone into the dirt.

He returns moments later with a canteen, which he lifts to my lips, and sweet mother of Moses, it's the coolest, clearest, most wonderful water I ever drank in my life.

I force myself to slow down. No sense drinking it only to toss it back up again. So I take a breath. Another sip. Another breath.

"Now Jefferson and Tom."

"Your lover boys are leverage," Dilley says. "To keep you cooperative. Nothing more. So I don't give a rat's furry arse if they die of thirst."

I glare at him. "If they die, you'll have no leverage at all."

He ponders that a moment.

"She's right," says Jonas Waters, sauntering over. He looks me up and down in a way that sends a shiver spider-crawling down my spine. "Frank, she don't look so good, to be honest."

"Fine," Dilley says. "Water for Bigler and Kingfisher, too, but don't take too long about it."

I'm careful not to show even the smallest bit of relief. It's my only victory since we've been captured, and I won't risk him taking it away.

The ghostly man gives Tom and Jeff water, who gulp it down like dogs at a pond.

Then he returns to me. "Time for your breakfast, boy!" Dilley calls out, laughing.

As the ghostly man tips the laudanum to my lips, I realize that I've yet to hear him speak a single word.

The moon is a glowing orb in the velvety sky, and a lonely owls echoes low and soft as we reach our destination. My mind is fogged with laudanum, so I can't see much, just the shapes of buildings, a few tents, the whitish expanse of a steep cliff side. I should mark my surroundings better. I should look for exits, weaknesses, but I can't make myself focus, and after a moment, I don't even care. Dear Lord, I'm weary. If I could just close my eyes and sleep for a week . . .

"I told you to bring just the girl," says a low, slick voice. I know that voice. A dart of fear penetrates the fog of my mind.

"You hired me for my improvisational nature, sir," Frank

Dilley says. "We couldn't have these boys running back to everyone, telling how the girl was taken, now could we? Besides, the girl cares for them. Especially that one right there. She'll do whatever you want, so long as they're around."

"I see." A pause. I can't see the speaker in the dark. Not sure I want to.

Warm, strong fingers tip my chin up, and I roll my eyes around, trying to focus, but I can't do it for all the gold in California. It's so much easier to just close them.

"Is she drunk?" the familiar voice asks. He sounds like he's fit to smash someone's nose. I just hope it's not mine.

"We gave her some poppy juice so she wouldn't make a fuss."

"What?"

"She'll be fine."

"Laudanum is a dangerous—"

"I *know* this girl. We were six months crossing the continent together. She may be uppity and irksome, but she's clever as a fox and good with a gun. I wasn't going to take any chances."

Another pause. "If she is damaged in any way, I'll skin you alive and throw you in a bear cage."

Frank must believe it, because his voice is tremulous when he says, "We did our jobs, just as you asked. The girl is fine. I promise."

"We'll see. Tie up the boys behind the stable. Girl goes in the cabin. Second bedroom."

Peony lurches forward. After a short distance, the ropes tying me down are loosened, and strong hands grab my waist and slide me from my horse. I'm half dragged, half carried across a porch, through a doorway, and into a dark place that smells of fresh-chopped wood and linseed oil and dried tobacco.

That tobacco smell. Sweet, and a little bit spicy. Familiar.

Someone guides me to a bed and pushes me down until I'm lying on a straw tick. A bit of straw pokes at my armpit, but I don't care because it's a bed. Not hard ground or muddy ground or rocky ground. A real bed.

No one bothers to untie my wrists, which niggles at my brain. Something is wrong. And Jefferson . . . The fog takes over. I sink into the prickly mattress, and then I keep sinking, so deep it feels like darkness swallows me whole.

I wake to the smell of frying eggs and tobacco smoke. Sun shines through a single east-facing window. It's too, too bright, like a spear of light lancing my mind. In fact, my whole head feels like it's going to split open.

My belly roils with nausea. I try to sit up, and the binds on my wrist tighten, bringing more pain. Blinking to clear my vision, I stare at the rope. It leads to the footboard.

I'm tied to the bed.

Using the rope, I pull myself forward on the mattress, scanning the floor for a slop bucket, a wash bin, anything I can use to throw up in. My stomach lurches, and I pause to breathe deeply through my nose, willing things to calm down.

I'm in a small room with log walls and plank floors. Beside my small bed is a nightstand, displaying an issue of *Godey's Lady's Book* and a lantern. Along the other side of the room is a set of four empty shelves. Next to it is a doorway. A patchwork quilt hangs in the doorway like a curtain.

The quilt curtain is whisked aside, and a tiny lady in strange clothing barrels through, carrying a breakfast tray. Steam curls up from two fried eggs, a mess of bacon, a fluffy round biscuit, and a tin cup full of hot coffee.

It's too rich, too much, and I bend over and vomit onto the floor.

Frank Dilley didn't give me near enough food and water, so there's not a lot inside me, and it's over quick. My face burns, and I'm about to apologize, but the lady's hand darts out quick as a snake to mop my mouth and chin with a handkerchief.

"Thank you," I manage, looking up at her.

She's Chinese. Her eyes are different from mine, but they're not squeezed shut like in all the newspaper drawings. She has shining black hair pulled into a single thick braid down her back. The skin of her face looks as soft as a cloud. No, she's wearing some kind of powder to make it appear so. Still, her skin doesn't seem the least bit yellow to me, any more than the Indians I've seen appeared red.

"My name is Lee," I say. "Thank you for bringing me breakfast. I'm sorry I . . . made such a mess."

She gazes at me as if taking my measure, and I realize that she's just a girl, no older than I am.

She carefully skirts the puddle on the floor and sets the tray on my bed. Then she points at her chest and says, "Mary."

"Nice to meet you, Mary. Do you work for my uncle? Hiram Westfall?" Now that I'm awake and alert, the laudanum no longer swimming in my blood, I'm sure I remember his voice. His scent.

The girl's gaze drops to the rope at my wrists, or maybe the sticky, raw skin beneath. She frowns slightly. A flurry of speech comes out of her mouth, but I have no idea what she's saying.

"I'm sorry. I don't speak Chinese."

Mary points to the puddle, says something else, and walks away. Her bright blue tunic drapes softly over wide pants, and her platform shoes make a steady *clump-clump* sound as she goes. The quilt curtain swishes closed behind her.

I stare after her, wondering what to do. Eat some of this breakfast, maybe. I'm weak from my journey with Dilley and his men, and I'll need a store of strength for whatever's ahead. But the puddle on the floor smells something awful, and my belly is still churning like a fish in a trap. Maybe the coffee is a good starting place.

My bonds force me to grab the cup with both hands. I sip carefully at first, wary of putting too much in my stomach. It seems to go down okay, so I sip a little more.

Once I have some food in me, I need to think about escape. No, first I need to find out where Jefferson and Tom are. A vague memory from last night indicates they might be in a stable.

But even if we could escape, where would we go? I have no idea where Frank has taken us. I suppose fleeing in any direction is better than sticking around and waiting to see what my uncle has in store.

Just thinking about my uncle brings such a cramp to my belly that I set the cup down and clamp my hands over my mouth. This is it. The thing I've dreaded for so long. The man who killed Mama and Daddy has gotten me alone and defenseless. Maybe he's right outside that door.

The quilt is whisked aside, and I jump, almost spilling my coffee. But it's just Mary again, with some rags to mop up my puddle.

She drops the rags in front of me and makes a wiping-up gesture. When I don't do anything, she mimes it again, more vigorously. Not knowing what else to do, I strain against the ropes at my ankles and reach for the floor with my still-tied hands. I try to wipe up the puddle, but the angle is all wrong and I mostly just smear it around.

"I'm sorry," I tell her again, even though I'm not sure she understands.

She doesn't bother hiding her disgust as she gathers the soiled rags. "Eat," she says. Her voice is high and musical, and I wonder if she's even younger than I thought, maybe fifteen.

"I'll try," I say. "It's hard with . . . this." I hold up my wrists, indicating the ropes and screaming red burns on my skin beneath them.

Mary scowls, and I'm not sure what she's scowling at: that the bonds are on my wrists in the first place or that I'm complaining about them. She puts her hands together like they're tied and makes an eating gesture, as if I'm too addled to figure it out myself.

She leaves me to try it, and I give it a splendid effort, poking at the eggs, nibbling the bacon, smearing bits of biscuit around my plate. I feel better than I did before, and I manage to keep a few bites down.

I look around the room again, for my things this time, and I spot a small chest at the foot of the bed. Maybe my knapsack is inside. I suppose it would be too much to ask for my guns to be there, too.

The curtain is whisked aside again, and I look up, expecting Mary, but oh, dear Lord, it's my uncle Hiram, dressed all in fancy black, bearing down on me like a storm cloud.

I spider-crawl backward on the bed until my spine hits the wall.

"Hello, sweet pea," he says in that sleepy Milledgeville drawl.

Chapter Twelve

It's like nails on a slate, hearing my daddy's name for me out of my uncle Hiram's rotten mouth. It makes me so angry I almost forget to be afraid. "Where are Jefferson and Tom?" I demand.

He frowns. "Wasn't my plan to bring them here, but don't worry. They're fine. I expect they'll be put to work soon enough."

"Doing what?"

"I'll have Mary heat up a bath for you. I want you clean and dressed like a proper lady."

"I'll dress however I want."

"You'll dress how I tell you. Or your friend, the Cherokee boy, will regret it."

"If you hurt him, I'll kill you."

He cocks his head and folds his arms across his chest, studying me. Up close, I can see that he's not quite so fancy as he was before. The elbows of his fine jacket are wearing thin. His black leather holster is now scratched and dirty. A not-quite-matching patch is sewn into one knee of his trousers, and his boots are scuffed and flecked with mud. He had a hard journey to California, just like the rest of us.

"You have a great future here, sweet pea. With me. Reuben let you run wild as a colt, but no more." His voice turns sympathetic and soft. "I know how hard it is to change your ways. But I promise, you will be happy here. We just need to give it time."

He leans down and grasps my arms, peering at my raw, welted wrists. I try to wrench them away, but he is too strong.

"I'm sorry about this, my girl," he says. "I did not intend for any harm to come to you."

Rage makes a red curtain of my vision. "Of course you did. You've intended nothing but harm from the beginning. You killed my parents. Stole everything that was mine. And now you're worried about a few little rope burns? Go to hell."

He releases my wrists, sighing. "Not everything is as it seems."

"True. I mean, here you are, standing and talking like a human being, when the truth is you're a venomous snake worth naught but the sharp edge of a shovel."

The blow is so sudden and vicious that my neck snaps to the side and funny lights flash in my eyes. It's a moment before I can get a breath, and when I do, I realize that blood is collecting on my tongue.

I spit it out onto the quilt; it's going to stain, for sure and certain. "I thought you didn't intend harm."

"Spare the rod, spoil the child."

I hate him. God forgive me, but it's the truth.

"And now," he drawls lazily, "I'm going to give the exact same blow to your friend Jefferson. Except he'll get my fist instead of the back of my hand."

My belly heaves, and the tiny bit of breakfast I was able to get down threatens to come back up. If he's willing to wallop me, his own niece, what would he do to Jeff? "No," I gasp out. "Wait."

He cocks an eyebrow, waiting. Oh, he looks so much like my daddy it's an actual pain in my chest. Except when Daddy looked at me that way, it was because I had amused him, or made him proud.

"I'll wash up. I'll wear whatever you want."

He smiles, looking smug as a cat with a helpless rat. I've revealed too much, I realize with a sinking gut. Jefferson is my greatest weakness, and now Hiram knows it.

"Glad to hear it. Once Mary fills your washtub, I'll untie you. Don't even consider trying to run. You're to stay inside this cabin at all times, unless accompanied by me or Wilhelm. This camp is well guarded, and everyone knows you are not allowed to wander. If you try, Jefferson and the other one will be shot. Do you understand?"

I have a thousand questions—What is this camp? Where are we? Who is Wilhelm?—but more than anything, I want him away.

"I understand," I whisper.

"Good. Finish your breakfast. Mary will be back shortly."

I stare after his back as he departs.

I've killed deer, squirrels, a few pheasants, and more rabbits than I can count. Could I kill a person? The idea doesn't set right with me, but if I'm ever going to do it, I know just who to try it out on.

The breakfast tastes like grit in my mouth, but I gradually force it down. Mary drags an oval-shaped copper washtub through the doorway while I eat. She returns every few minutes with a kettle of hot water, which she dumps inside.

A bath. A real bath. Inside the finest cabin I've seen in months. Becky would trade her red-checked tablecloth for a bath like this.

True to his word, my uncle returns when the tub is full and cuts the ropes with a long knife. For an instant, the cool skin of his fingers slithers across my wrists, making bile rise in my throat.

"Now wash up," he says. "Thoroughly. I'll have Mary bring some new clothes."

I'm not too keen to undress in this place, even if I'm given my privacy. I wait until his boot steps fade. Then I shuck my clothes as fast as I can, step over the edge, and sink into the hot water. It's so hot my skin turns bright red, and there's barely enough room—I have to bring my knees to my chest to fit inside. But after days of riding tied down with little more than laudanum for sustenance, it feels like I'm absorbing the hot water into my thirsty bones.

Mary left me a bristle brush and some soap, and I get to

work scrubbing everything, paying special attention to my face and dirt-encrusted fingernails. I soap down my hair and dip beneath the water to rinse, then finger comb it as best I can. Strands of hair come away from my scalp and float like water bugs on the surface. I keep combing, and more hair comes away. Then more. I decide to leave my hair alone.

I'm scrubbing my armpits when Mary strides in again. I whip my knees to my chest and wrap my arms around them to cover myself, sloshing water over the side and onto the floor. But Mary keeps her eyes averted. In one hand is a bucket of rinse water. In another is a heavy bundle of clothing, which she dumps onto the bed.

Without a word or glance, she leaves.

As lovely as the hot water feels, I don't like being naked in this place, and I need to finish up. Carefully I wash the rope burns on my wrist. The skin is open and weeping, and soaping it up stings something fierce, so I go about it gently but quickly.

I listen to make sure no one is coming. Then I grab the rinse bucket and stand. I pour half the water over my head to get excess soap out of my hair, the rest over my neck and shoulders.

When I step from the tub, my skin turns to gooseflesh and the floor is icy cold on my feet. I stare down at the floor for a few seconds, marveling. Real plank floors instead of hard earth. A real bed instead of a bedroll. A real glass window. A copper washtub. Spare linens and clothes.

Sure, my uncle stole an awful lot of gold from me before

he left Georgia, but I can't figure how he managed to put together such a fancy place so quickly. Or how he can afford to keep a servant. Or hire men like Frank Dilley.

Something strange is going on, and I aim to find out what.

I grab the towel and wipe down, then I shake out the bundle of clothing. Everything needs to be pressed, but it looks brand-new—a clean corset and drawers, stockings, petticoats, and a dress.

The corset and drawers go on with surprising ease. I don't cinch the corset tight enough to be fashionable, but I don't give a fig for fashion right now. I do care about being able to run at a moment's notice.

The last time I put on petticoats was for Mama and Daddy's funeral, more than nine months and two thousand miles distant. I force myself not to think about it.

I lay the dress out flat to get a look at it, and my heart nearly tumbles out of my chest.

I've seen this dress before. I'm sure of it.

It's made of midnight-blue calico, with tiny yellow stars that are actually flowers when you peer close enough. The fabric is gathered at the shoulders, forming pleats that sweep down to a tiny, triangular waist. Sleeves billow out from beneath the shoulder gathers in three separate layers, each layer ending with an elaborate trim of white lace.

I plunk down on the bed, suddenly finding it hard to breathe, because it's Mama's dress.

Which is impossible. She stopped wearing it when she became heavy with my baby brother. Then he died, and instead of taking out the seams to make room for Mama's thickened waist, we cut the dress up for scraps. The quilt on my bed back in Georgia contained several patches from that dress.

I pick up a sleeve and rub it between thumb and forefinger. The fabric is crisp and bright in the way of new things that have not yet seen a summer of chores. And the lace is different; the trim is wider, with longer points.

Not the same dress, then, and I'm not sure why I'm so relieved about that, but I am.

As I stand and pull it over my head, letting the skirt settle over the petticoats, a niggling worry remains. Why would Hiram have a dress that looks so much like Mama's favorite from years ago? It has to be coincidence. It has to be.

The dress is a little large on me, which is a relief because it means I won't have to cinch this corset any further. The skirt is full enough to require better petticoats, but these will do.

There are no new shoes to go with the new dress, so I poke around the room a bit, looking for my boots. I open the chest at the foot of the bed and gasp. Daddy's boots are inside, just like I'd hoped, along with my knapsack.

I rummage through it, quick and quiet as a mouse. There's still some jerky and hardtack, my extra shirt and stockings, but no knife or ammo. What did he do with my guns?

I close the knapsack and stuff it back into the chest. It'll keep for now.

My old clothing is still piled on the floor beside the washtub. I grab it up, quick as a snake, and reach into the pocket of my trousers. My gold sense tells me my bag full of gold dust and tiny nuggets is still there, but I'm glad to wrap my fingers around it anyway.

Now, to hide it.

There's no cubbyhole, no loose floorboard. The mattress would be the obvious place. Too obvious?

My gaze alights on Daddy's boots. They've always been too big. I don't get blisters anymore, but I still stuff the toes with rags, or—like I did a few times on the trip to California—with dry grass.

I reach inside the left boot and grab the wad of dirty rags, yank it out, and replace it with the bag of gold. It'll be a tighter fit now, but that's okay.

"You finish?" comes Mary's voice from behind the door curtain.

I suppose I am, but I need a few more moments of privacy, of planning, before I face my uncle again. "Just a couple more minutes," I call out.

The single high window shines above the foot of my bed. Still in my stockinged feet, I lift my skirts and climb up onto the chest. I grasp the sill with my fingers, stand on my tiptoes, and peer outside.

It's a camp, similar to the one Jeff and Tom and I left behind, with tents and lean-tos and even a few shanties. But it's so much bigger than the camp back in Glory, so much busier. People mill about, guiding mules with carts across the hard-packed ground. A group of men with thick beards crouch around a low table at the entrance to one of the larger tents, playing cards. I recognize them as some of the Missouri men from our wagon train.

But there are also Indians, carrying bags full of ore on their stooped backs, and they're a lot thinner than the ones who helped us put out the fire in our camp. Their destination is out of the viewing range of my window, but I've no doubt they're heading to a stream to classify the ore, maybe pan it out.

A group of Chinese men are fitting lumber together—making more carts, if I don't miss my guess. They wear flowing shirts over loose trousers, and hats that look like wide, upside-down bowls. Just like the workers that passed through Glory, each one has a single long black braid swinging nearly to his waist. Maybe their headman has a British accent, too.

They work with incredible efficiency. It's as easy as flowing water, the way one man holds a plank in place while the other hammers, the gliding way they shift angles to do it again. When one turns for a new supply of nails, it's in his hand instantly.

My tiny window only shows a wedge view of this place, but I'm confident that aside from Mormon Island, this is the biggest camp I've seen yet. If I were a betting kind of girl, and I most certainly am not, I'd lay odds there's an honest-to-goodness mine here. A deep and prosperous one.

Maybe that's why my uncle has such a fancy cabin. Maybe he owns this place. Along with everyone in it.

I climb down from the trunk and slip on Daddy's boots. The gold stashed in the left one forces me to scrunch my toes, but I'm glad to have it buzzing there, close by and familiar and warm.

I've no mirror, and no pins or ribbons for my hair, so I part it down the middle and smooth it to either side as best I can. I straighten my skirt, take a deep breath, and push past the curtain into the main room.

My uncle sits in a rocking chair, reading a pamphlet by the light of a large window framed in frothy yellow curtains. His pipe rests on a table beside him, unlit. A dining table takes up the center of the room, with a bench on one side and two rickety stools on the other. Against the opposite wall is a huge woodstove, with pots and pans and cups neatly stacked on a shelf beside it. Mary is busy at the woodstove, stirring something that smells of potatoes and turnips.

A single lantern hangs from a hook in the ceiling; it's low enough that I'll have to duck slightly to walk beneath it. A door to my left is edged in daylight, which means it must lead outside. A door to my right is dark. Another bedroom maybe?

A cabin with three rooms. I haven't seen such luxury since Independence.

It's a moment before my uncle realizes I'm standing there. He looks up, startled, and sets his pamphlet aside. He takes in the dress, his eyes roving from my still-damp head to the tips of my muddy boots and back again. His face transforms. His features soften, and his eyes flare with a longing I don't understand. Finally a little smile tugs at the corners of his mouth.

"Leah," he breathes. "You are beautiful."

It feels like a snake is creeping up my throat.

"I'll get you new shoes as soon as possible," he says. "Maybe someone in camp can make you some slippers."

"I like these boots just fine."

"And you can keep them, of course. But a fine lady should have fine shoes."

"If you say so." I don't like the way he's looking at me. I don't like it one bit.

"Mary, when you're done with supper, please see to Leah's washtub and dirty clothing."

She doesn't say anything, just nods and keeps on stirring.

I take a deep breath. Time to start buttering him up to get what I need. "Thank you for the dress," I say, trying to keep the anger out of my voice. Carefully I add, "It reminds me of one Mama used to wear."

He practically beams. "I'm glad you remember! That was my favorite dress of hers. I had this one specially made."

So you can fondly remember the woman you killed? I want to scream. Instead, I fold my hands demurely. I think of Becky and the way she maintains such a ladylike composure while dealing with difficult customers, and I say, "I know I'm not supposed to leave without a chaperone, so would you be willing to accompany me to check on my friends? It would calm my nerves a great deal to see them hale."

His eyes narrow. Maybe I've gone too far. I replay the words in my head. They sound ridiculous coming from me, like make-believe at school recess.

But after a moment, he nods. "This is a reasonable request.

So long as you behave, you shall visit your friends once a day."

Once a day. Under supervision. I'll have to do a lot better than that if we're to escape.

"Thank you," I say.

We stare at each other a moment, neither certain what to say. I curl my toes against the gold in my boot, taking comfort in the warm buzz.

"I assume you'll have some . . . work . . . here for me to do?" I say finally, and I instantly wonder if it's too subtle a reference to my particular talent. I'm not sure how much Mary understands or how much my uncle takes her into his confidence, but I'd rather not say anything outright about my goldwitching ways.

"Of course," he says. "We are going to get rich together, Leah Westfall. With my experience and connections, and you to . . . help me."

"Looks like you're already richer than Midas," I mumble, briefly forgetting that I'm supposed to be buttering him up.

"What was that?"

"I mean, it looks like you've already done quite well for yourself. This is a very nice cabin."

He stands, reaching for the hat on its resident peg. Donning it, he says, "I've done well, though getting my mine up and running and hiring the right people took quite a bit of ingenuity and determination on my part."

There's nothing ingenious about starting a mine. You just find a quartz vein and start following it, and if it leads to more quartz and good ore, you keep digging. It's with a bit of a start that I realize what he really means.

"We'll pay back what you owe soon enough," I say, and it's his turn to be startled.

But then he smiles, as if proud that I sussed it out. "Come. Let's go see to your friends."

I'd give all the gold in my boot to find out more, and it's on the tip of my tongue to ask who he owes the money to and how much. But I've already won a concession from him today, and I dare not push.

I give a final glance to Mary at the dishes. Her face is hard, her eyes narrowed, as she attacks the dishes like they're an enemy in need of slaying. I suddenly get the feeling she understands everything just fine.

Hiram offers his arm, and though everything in me screams to recoil, I wrap mine in his and allow him to lead me from the cabin and into the sunshine.

Chapter Thirteen

The camp is even bigger than I realized. Another, smaller cabin faces ours. The door is wide open, revealing multiple empty bunks.

"My foremen sleep here," my uncle explains.

Up a slope is a large, rocky cliff dotted with brush and dried grass and the occasional stunted tree. At the base of the cliff is the dark opening to my uncle's mine. It's bolstered with huge wooden beams and guarded by the tallest man I've ever seen. He is cowled in black wool and carrying a rifle. The ghostly man.

In a flat space to the side of the mine opening sits a crude mill. A mule tied to a post drags a huge grindstone around a stone-lined pit. Another of Hiram's men shovels ore from a mine cart into the pit, where it's crushed again and again as the mule circles around. The gold, being a heavier metal, settles to the bottom of the pit once free of the quartz. There's not much at the moment; it feels like more of an itch than a hum. The air smells like a paste made from manure, sweat, and dust.

"Welcome home, Leah," my uncle says, and I swear he's suddenly as cocky a rooster. "What do you think of my arrastra?"

"I think it looks like a lot of work," I answer neutrally. "A grist mill for turning quartz ore into gold."

"That's industry," Hiram says. "Industry is what makes America great, and it's what will make our fortune. Most of the folks around here have already taken to calling this place Hiram's Gulch."

"You don't say."

As I study everyone around us, a few turn to stare right back. And then more and more, until the whole camp has come to a standstill. They're all dirty and thin, stooped and exhausted. Except the ghostly man. And my uncle.

"Why are they staring?" I whisper.

"Many of them haven't seen a woman in months, much less a lady."

"What about Mary?"

He shrugs. "Not the same."

That makes no sense to me—Mary seemed as mannered and beautiful as Becky Joyner on her best day—but sure enough, some of the miners' gazes are desperate, like I'm a glass of sweet tea on a hot summer day.

"Where are Tom and Jeff?" I ask.

"This way." He guides me away from the mine, past the smaller cabin to a rickety stable that's little more than a giant lean-to with four stalls. "There's a pasture to the east where we keep the mules and burros. We've plans to erect a proper barn come spring. For now, this keeps our finest stock out of the worst weather."

Sorry nickers in greeting as I approach, tossing her sorrel mane. Beside her is Tom's horse, Apollo, and next to him is my uncle's huge black gelding, whose name is Dark Wind or Black Storm or something hackneyed that I can't quite recall.

The fourth stall is empty.

"Where's Peony?" I ask, panic edging into my voice.

"Abel Topper has her."

"What?" Abel Topper is a former mine foreman from Georgia, and my uncle's lackey. He spotted me when I was fleeing home and followed me all the way to Tennessee before turning back. He's wanted my pretty palomino since the first day he laid eyes on her.

My uncle's tone is so patient and reasonable as he explains, "I promised her to Abel a long time ago, before you stole her and ran off." He puts a hand on my shoulder and looks me straight in the eye. My skin crawls. "I always keep my promises, Leah. Always."

I clench my jaw because I will not cry in front of him. I raised Peony from a foal. No one understands her better than me. I thought my uncle had taken everything, but I was wrong. There was still something left, and he found it, and he took it.

My fists curl tight. He'd never look at me this way again, so patronizing, so smug, if I turned his face into a bloody pulp and took out a few teeth.

"Where is Topper?" I manage in a tight voice.

He barks a laugh. "So you can steal her back? I think not."

Bloody pulp. Two black eyes. No teeth left. "No, I was thinking I could offer to buy her back."

His eyes narrow. "I'm not an idiot. You're up to no good."

He's right about that. "Think what you want. I'll find him later," I say, with a wave of my hand. "Anyway, you *promised* you would take me to Jefferson and Tom?"

His lips press thin, but he grabs my elbow and leads me around to the back of the stable, where a long tying post made from a tree trunk can accommodate more stock if necessary. Tied to it is a chestnut mare I don't recognize. Beside her are Tom and Jeff.

They sit on the bare earth, their arms tied overhead to the post. Tom slumps against his bonds, chin to chest, eyes closed. Jefferson looks up as we approach. "Hello, Lee," he mumbles.

I gasp. His left eye is as swollen and black as a rotten plum. His skin is blanched, his cheeks sunken. He looks at me like a drunkard, focusing on a space right in front of me, as if the real me is impossible to pinpoint.

"Oh, Jeff," I whisper. "Who did this to you?"

"Nice dress," he says.

I crouch in front of him and tip up his chin. "Who did this to you?" I repeat. "Was it Frank?"

"Yep. Said he's been wanting to box me for a long time."

Uncle Hiram jumps in with, "I didn't order them beaten. Your friend must have done something to deserve it."

I launch to my feet and get right in his face. "The only thing Jefferson ever did to antagonize Dilley was get himself born to a Cherokee mama. Frank Dilley is a bad seed, Uncle. Mark my words."

My uncle frowns. "I know you favor the boy, but . . ." I stop listening. He deserves no more of my attention. I turn back to my friends and squat down again. "Anything else hurt, Jeff?" I say. Tears pool in my eyes. So many people I care about, hurt or killed because of Hiram Westfall.

"Jaw," Jefferson says. "Can't eat. Can hardly talk. But I don't think it's broke."

I turn his chin to one side, then the other. His left side is definitely swollen. I wish Jasper was here.

"They still feeding you laudanum?"

"Yep."

"Don't worry. I'll put a stop to it." I don't know how yet, but I will. Besides, laudanum is expensive. Dilley can't keep it up forever. If I could find his stash and destroy it . . .

Strangely, my mouth is suddenly watering, my skin flushed, my heart racing.

I shake my head as if to shake it out of my mind and move over to Tom. He's so quiet and still that for a brief, awful moment, I think he's dead. When I put my hand to his still-warm face and feel his breath against my palm, I almost sing a hallelujah.

"Tom? Tom, can you hear me?"

He stirs a little but doesn't respond. His skin is hot with fever.

"He's still sleeping," Jefferson slurs. "Been sleeping a long time."

I close my eyes and take a deep breath. Then I scoot over to Jefferson, lean forward so that my forehead presses against his, and I say, so quietly that only he can hear, "Stay strong, Jeff. We'll figure this."

"Lee," he whispers. "My Leah. Best girl. My . . ."

"Hush." I press my lips to his forehead. Then I stand and face my uncle.

There's a bit of uncertainty in his eyes, or maybe I imagine it.

"Uncle Hiram," I begin. "You must treat my friends better."

"I don't know what they did to deserve this, but I'm certain—"

"I've said I'll cooperate with you, and I will. I'll make you the richest man in California. But only if you give them regular water and victuals and a place to lay their heads."

"Don't, Lee!" Jefferson pleads at my back. "Not worth it. I'll be fine. I've taken worse."

It hurts my heart that Jeff would flee his mean, drunken da only to fall into the hands of another good-for-nothing intent on using him as a punching toy. I will either get him out of here or die trying.

"And another thing," I say to my uncle. "I want them untied. They shouldn't be kept here like cattle. A true gentleman would treat them with respect."

My uncle arches a brow. "What's to keep them from running off?"

"Me," I say. "They would never leave without me."

Hiram gives me a dubious look.

"You'd be amazed," I say, "how friendship and loyalty will make a body act. Maybe you should give it a try. Maybe if anyone cared about you at all, you wouldn't have to kidnap people or knock them around to get what you want."

I instantly regret the words, because his eyes flash with more rage than I've ever seen in a man, and he steps forward, raising the back of his hand.

At the last second, just as I'm flinching away, he changes his mind and lowers his arm. "You've a saucy mouth on you, girl. Reuben's doing, no doubt."

I've a mind to tell him to shut his trap and never speak of my daddy again. Instead, I clench my teeth together.

"Very well," Hiram says in response to my silence. "I'll give orders to have these boys freed, fed, and housed. We'll make space for them in the barracks. I'll insist, though, on tying them up at night when they're not working."

Bloody pulp. Black eyes. No more teeth. "Thank you," I say aloud. "Does Hiram's Gulch have a doctor?"

"Not yet. The Chinese headman knows a little healing, more healing than English. I don't know that I'd trust him." As if knowing English is the thing that makes someone trustworthy.

Hiram leads me back to our cabin. As we walk, my mind is as busy as bees in a hive. I scan our surroundings, every shanty, tent, and lean-to, looking for cover. Places to hide. A way to escape. Unlike the area around our beautiful beaver pond, these hills are dry and mostly bare, but the north side of the cabin backs up against a thicket of cottonwood. It's wispy now, the leaves dried and fallen to the ground, but darkness might hide us if we escaped through it. The trees are too tall for me to see for sure where it leads. We could push through the cottonwoods only to find ourselves trapped against the cliff face. Sometimes, though, cottonwoods lead to a stream. And following streams or dry washes downhill would eventually point us in the direction of Sacramento and freedom.

I also keep an eye out for Abel Topper or Peony. Not many here can afford their own horses, but there are pack mules aplenty pulling carts into and out of the mine, and even a few donkeys. There's no sign of Peony, though, and when the cabin door closes behind us, leaving me in the turnip-scented gloom, I can't help the stab of despair that hits right behind my eyes.

"You have a day to rest and get your strength back," Hiram says. "Then you go to work."

Maybe he means for me to cook and clean instead of Mary, who is nowhere evident. Maybe he means for me to scour these hills looking for gold. I don't know and I don't care. But I do need to rest and get my strength back, just not for the reasons he thinks.

As politely as I can, I ask, "May I have some of that stew?"

The next morning, I take breakfast with Hiram at the dining table. I sit on the bench while he faces me on one of the stools. Mary has cooked us up a meal of soaked oats with butter and molasses, to be sopped up with biscuits, but she has since left, disappeared to wherever it is she goes. I wish she would stay. I haven't had a female friend my own age since Therese died.

"Your hair grew out a little since I last saw you," Hiram observes.

"Mm-hmm," I say around a mouthful of biscuit.

"You'll be able to put it up in a month or so," he says.

I'm not sure why it's so important to him, but I nod. Even though I don't plan on being here a month.

Becky and the Major and everyone back home expect us to be gone awhile. Past Becky's thanksgiving celebration. I either have to escape soon, or survive until they come. It's better that I escape, Jefferson and Tom in tow. Otherwise things could get deadly.

"Today, you will tour the mine," he informs me. He wipes his mouth with a napkin, folds it neatly, and sets it on the table beside his empty plate. "Our empire begins here, Leah. The mine isn't very deep yet, but it's been profitable so far. I want you to familiarize yourself with its workings and . . . well, feel it out, so to speak."

"You want me to tell you where to dig next."

"Yes."

I promised I'd help him in order to keep Tom and Jeff safe, but dear Lord in heaven, I surely don't want to.

"All right," I tell him. "Is that where you plan to set Tom and Jefferson to work?"

"Of course. They'll have to earn their keep around here, just like everyone else."

I smear oats around my plate with a biscuit, finding it hard to eat. "You could just let them go." It wouldn't be easy to convince them to leave me behind, but I'd give it a fair try.

My uncle smiles. "I think not. I have some things to attend to, so Frank Dilley will be your guide."

I spit out my biscuit. "No! Dilley is a no-good, weaselly—"

Hiram's hand darts out, snags my wrist, and gives it a shake. My skin still smarts from the rope burns. "He knows to behave." His look turns dark. "And so do you."

I say nothing, but after a moment, I'm able to snatch my wrist back. I pick up my fork and attack my breakfast with renewed vigor. I'm getting my strength back, by God.

My uncle escorts me through the camp, past the arrastra and its damp manure scent, to the mine entrance. He hands me over to Frank Dilley, who offers me his elbow like an actual gentleman instead of the filthy cur he is.

"You will treat her like a lady," my uncle warns as I take Dilley's proffered elbow.

"Of course, sir," Dilley says, with a grin and a tip of his hat. "This way, my *lady*." He pulls me toward the entrance, and several of his men—along with the tall, ghostly man—fall in line behind us. My neck prickles to know they're there, where my eyes can't mark them.

We pass into shadow, and the air instantly becomes cooler and moist. The tunnel is about three paces from wall to wall, barely wide enough for a burro and a small cart to pass. Wooden beams bolster the walls and ceiling at irregular intervals, lanterns swinging from them to light the way. The walls are rough and irregular. At one point, the tunnel widens inexplicably, revealing a table off to the side, along with a few chairs and a couple of barrels. Several of the Missouri men lounge here by lantern light, sipping from tin cups. When they see me, they all stand straight and whip off their hats.

I scowl at them. Never once on the wagon train did they show this kind of respect. Either my uncle gave them a dressing-down, or they're out of their heads because of my dressing up.

"It's break time for the foremen," Dilley explains.

Never have I seen a mine with so many foremen. "I thought Abel Topper was foreman," I say.

"Oh, he's the foremost foreman," Dilley says. "Probably down in the Drink with the Induns."

"The Drink?" Voices sound strange here, fuller and louder.

"One of the tunnels leads to a wet spot. Lots of gold there, but the Induns are up to their knees in it. Speaking of drink, show the boss's niece some hospitality, lads. A cup of sugar water for her, now."

The Missouri men fall all over themselves to comply, thrusting their own cups into the barrel and pulling them out dripping. Three are handed to me at once.

I pick the one in the middle, mumbling my thanks. They all stare at me until I take a sip. It's clear, clean water mixed with a little sugar, is all. Back home, it's what people drank when they couldn't afford decent tea, but here in California, it's as luxurious as an orange.

"This way," Dilley says. "You can take that with you." He

indicates the cup I'm holding by pointing with his chin.

Some of the others fall in behind us, including the ghostly man, and again my neck prickles that he's watching me. I remember the way he manhandled me, forced laudanum into my gullet, tossed me up on Peony and tied me down. The prickle on my neck becomes a full-blown shiver.

Enough is enough. I plant my feet and turn on him.

He's more than a head taller than I am. Taller than Jefferson, taller even than Mr. Hoffman was, and that scar on his pretty lips looks wicked and mean.

"What's your name?" I demand.

The other men with us exchanged startled glances.

"Uh, that there is Wilhelm," Frank Dilley says. "He don't say much. Actually, he don't say anything. He's a bit touched, if you ask me, but he's strong as an ox, loyal as a dog, and mean as a snake."

Wilhelm. My uncle mentioned a Wilhelm when he said I must be accompanied every time I left the cabin.

"I'd say it was nice to meet you, Wilhelm, but we've already met, and it wasn't nice at all. I don't appreciate the way you treated me and my friends, and I surely won't forget it."

I detect the faintest twitch of his lips before I turn my back on him and address Dilley. "Let's continue."

Dilley shrugs, offering his arm again. I take another sip of my sugar water, mostly to keep it from spilling as we walk, and let him lead me down the tunnel slope. My neck doesn't prickle so much now, but everything else in me starts to vibrate something fierce. It's just like when a thunderstorm is about to hit, and the air is like a buzzing blanket on your skin. Except this buzzing blanket is buzzing all the way into my insides, and I wonder if it was a disservice to my belly to accept the sugar water.

There's gold here. So much gold. A mountain of it. My vision starts to blur.

"Lee? You okay?"

It's Frank's voice, and it shakes me awake. I stopped cold in the middle of the passageway and didn't even realize it. This has happened before; gold can make me near senseless, when there's so much of it. I'll have to be more careful.

"Fine. Just . . . not used to enclosed spaces."

"Well, you better get used to it fast. Your uncle wants you paying a visit every day, though I can't imagine why he thinks it's a good idea to bring a slip of a girl to a place like this."

He never said things like that when he thought I was a boy. "This slip of girl can outride and outshoot you any day, Frank Dilley, and you know it."

"I went easy on you, thinking you just a small slip of a *lad* who talked funny. Coulda outshot you anytime."

Frank Dilley is first on the list of faces I'm going to bust before I escape this place.

We've reached a fork in the tunnel. One slopes steeper than the other.

"Which do you want to see first?" Dilley asks. "The Drink, or the Joyner?"

"The Joyner? Why'd you name it that?"

"Because it's rich and stubborn and dry as a—" Someone

smacks him on the back. "Uh, it reminded us of that persnickety widow friend of yours."

"I see." Even though I don't. "The Drink first."

"Down this way." He gestures toward the steeper tunnel. "Watch your step. It gets slippery."

He's right. Water starts leaching up out of the earth, creating a thin layer of gritty mud over slick rock that shimmers in the lantern light. Small strips of lumber have been nailed into the ground, like the ties of a train track. At first I think it's to keep the miners safe by preventing falls. But when a burro heads our way, pulling a heavy cart, I realize it's to protect the ore. The wood ties make it less likely for the carts to roll back when the poor animals become exhausted.

We all press against the cold, rocky wall to let the cart by. It's led by a skinny Indian man who's as naked as the day he was born. Another pushes the cart from behind, adding his strength to the burro's. It puts me in mind of the Joyner wagon, on a slope as steep as this one. I think of the way its rope snapped, sending the wagon tumbling, crushing everything in its path, including Becky's husband. I have to avert my eyes.

In the distance is the unmistakable echo of pickaxes battling hard rock. It's a mild *plink-plink* now, but I know from experience the sound will get louder as we get nearer. Back home in Georgia, most of the miners went home at the end of the day with splitting headaches. It's no wonder so many turned to moonshine.

"We'll be laying track and getting proper mine carts soon,"

Dilley explains. "That'll take some of the burden off these poor donkeys."

"These poor Indians, you mean," I say.

He shrugs. "Same work. To be honest, I prefer the donkeys—they're less trouble. But Induns are cheaper to come by. All you have to do is grab your guns and head out into the wilderness and round yourself up a big group."

My jaw drops open. I can't believe what he just said. But I guess all slavery starts that way, at the wrong end of a gun.

Dilley ignores me. The cart passes, and we continue our descent. The air is stuffy now, thick with dirt and moisture, making breathing difficult. Or maybe it's Frank Dilley himself who makes it hard. I take a deep breath, just to assure myself that I can.

The tunnel levels and widens onto a muddy underground pond. Lantern light gleams off the surface of the thick brown water, which is choppy and fierce with all the splashing and digging going on.

The cavern is filled with Indians hefting pickaxes. Two carts stand wheel deep in water, half filled with ore so wet it looks like cow slop. Two Indians heft a giant log into a recently dug cleft to bolster it. They push the log into place, leveraging it between muddy floor and choppy ceiling, as if a single log can hold back the earth.

"Best to stop right here, Lee," Frank says. "Any farther and you'll soil those pretty skirts."

At his voice, the Indian closest to us looks up at me, but his gaze darts back down just as fast. He's digging into the wall near the entrance, but his swings are feeble. His limbs are skinny as a colt's, his cheeks sunken, his skin covered with mud.

"Why aren't any of them wearing clothes?" I ask.

"Can't trust 'em with clothes," he says. "They'd steal the gold sooner than mine it out."

"But they're people, not—"

A whip cracks. Everyone freezes. An Indian near the far wall collapses backward into the water, which sloshes up to his armpits. A line of blood wells up on his shoulder. He ignores the wound, fishing around in the murk until he comes up with his pickax, then he gets back to work.

Nausea threatens to overwhelm me. I've never seen a man whipped before. I've heard tales, though. Some of the mine foremen back home used to whip the Negros, when the plantation owners rented them to the mines during the cold season. It's a rare Negro who hasn't felt a whip's bite at some point; Hampton has some nasty scars on his back and shoulders.

I peer into the gloom of the cavern, looking for the man doing the whipping. Lantern light doesn't penetrate the back very well, and it's hard to see how deep it goes. I'm about to ask Dilley to tell me who's responsible when a figure appears out of the shadows and wades toward us.

It's Abel Topper, the foremost foreman, the one who took Peony. A whip curls in his hand like a long, thin snake. My already low opinion of the man drops down a shaft without a bottom.

"Hello, Miss Westfall," he says, cheery as a summer's day.

"That's no way to treat people," I say.

"I ain't asking your opinion."

"How's my horse?" I ask, because I know it will needle him.

"*My* horse is doing fine. Found her a nice patch of clover, so she ain't missing you at all. Hoping she'll foal come spring."

"Peony's not a foaling horse!" I practically shout. "She's too valuable as a ride-and-train. Daddy broke two cantankerous colts to the harness with her on lead!"

Abel's grin widens. "All mares are foaling horses. If she drops a pretty palomino like herself, it'll be just like striking gold."

I couldn't stand it if something happened to Peony. I could have bred her lots of times, but never wanted to risk her. I add Abel to the list of faces to bust.

"Does my uncle know you're whipping these poor souls?" I ask.

Frank Dilley jumps in. "He knows, and he approves."

I open my mouth to protest, but something catches my eye. It's the Indian nearest the entrance, stealing glances at me. No, it's not me he's looking at. It's my tin cup. Maybe he's thirsty. There's water all around us, but it's hardly fit to drink. Or maybe it's the sugar he's desperate for.

"Lee!" calls a familiar voice. Two more figures appear in the gloom.

It's Jefferson and Tom, wearing nothing but soaked trousers. Jefferson holds a pickax, Tom a shovel. They are too pale, and bruises mark Jefferson's chest and right shoulder, but I'm so glad to see them awake and alert that tears prick at my eyes.

"Get back to work," Abel growls.

"It's all right!" I say quickly. "My uncle agreed that I could check on my friends and . . ." I enunciate my next words clearly: "And make sure they are fit and unharmed." My gaze roves Jefferson's bruised chest. He's got the muscle for mining, that's for sure. I wish I could grab a shirt and cover him up. It must be killing him to have the marks of his beating exposed for the whole world to see. "Abel, my friend Jefferson does not appear unharmed. I'll have to tell my uncle so."

Abel's eyes narrow. In the lantern gloom, they look like devil eyes. "You've gotten mighty uppity all of a sudden," he says.

I take a sip of sugar water, just to give myself something to do while my mind pokes at my problems. Somehow, I have to get Tom and Jefferson out of here. Maybe if I find a nice chunk of gold for my uncle, or a new vein, he'll listen to reason. That, or his greed will just make things worse.

The Indian nearest me continues to steal glances at my tin cup. "Here," I say, offering the cup to him. "It's yours."

His hand darts out and snatches it from mine. He's practically trembling as he tips it to his lips.

The whip cracks again. The tin cup tumbles out of the Indian's hand and splashes into the water. He dives after it, grabs it, returns it to his lips. Blood pours from his hand as his tongue reaches inside the cup to lap up the slightest remnant of sugar.

"What'd you do that for?" I bellow at Abel. Jefferson and Tom are staring aghast at him.

"A soft heart doesn't find gold," Abel says. "These lazy Induns will walk all over you if you let them."

"It was just a cup of sugar water!"

"Back to work," Abel says to the Indian, brandishing his whip.

The Indian ignores him, so intent is he on my empty cup.

So Frank Dilley pulls out his Colt and shoots the man in the head.

My mind screams agony, from the sight of murder, and from a gunshot so loud in such a small cavern. My ears ring like church bells as the man slumps into the water, leaving a huge wet stain on the rocky wall.

Abel is yelling something at Frank, and the Indians are yelling at one another, but I can't make anything out for the ringing in my head and the torment in my belly. I press my hands to my ears, trying to stop the pain. The Indian's face is half submerged. One dead eye stares up at me, accusing. My cup gradually sinks beside him.

I'm sorry, I whisper to him. Or maybe I only think the words. *I didn't mean for that to happen.*

I didn't mean for Martin to die either, or Nugget to get shot, or our camp to burn to the ground. But bad things keep happening around me.

I have to get out of this wet hole, and I have to do it now, before I crumble all to pieces. I whirl, gathering my skirts, and flee up the tunnel. I elbow men out of my way as I go, even Wilhelm, but I don't care, and maybe some of them are just as stunned as I am because they let me go. I need air and light and a kind word. I need my friends. I need Peony.

I need my guns.

Because right now, I'm fit to kill Frank Dilley. Somehow. And Abel Topper. And my uncle with them.

Chapter Fourteen

A crowd has gathered outside the mine, mostly Chinese, but a few Indians and Missouri men.

"We heard a gunshot," someone says, or at least I think so. My ears are still ringing something awful.

I turn to mark the speaker. It's one of the Indians. He's a little shorter than I am, and he's dressed the same way as the people who helped us put out the fire, with beads draped down his chest. He must be important to my uncle if he's not working in the mines with the rest of them. "Who was it? Who got shot?" His face is an agony of worry, and his English is perfect.

"Back off, Muskrat," growls one of the Missouri men, and he shoves the Indian in the chest with the butt of his rifle. "You ain't good enough to talk to her."

Muskrat staggers back, but he recovers quickly and stands his ground. "Then *you* tell me. Who was shot?"

"How the hell should I know?" the Missouri man says, and he looks at me. "Who was it, Miss Westfall?"

I blink at him. My teeth are chattering, even though I'm not cold. I see it over and over again—the man's head snapping back against the wall, his body slumping into the water, his white, dead eye staring up at me.

"I . . . It was one of the miners," I say to Muskrat. "Down in the Drink. I don't know who. Frank Dilley shot him."

"Is he alive? I should go to him." He makes as if to push past us, but the Missouri man blocks him.

"I'm sorry, Muskrat, sir," I say, my voice tremulous. "But . . . it won't do any good."

Pain fills his eyes. He lost a friend today; he just doesn't know which one.

Everyone mutters darkly, and it's possible they're talking to me, but I can't hear well enough to parse it. Wilhelm rushes out of the mine, followed by several others. When he spots me, his shoulders slump with relief.

"Where is my uncle?" I demand of everyone. I have to tell him about this. Surely he would never condone what just happened.

"He headed upstream," someone says. "To one of the other camps. Negotiating for . . ." The rest of his words are lost to the ringing in my head.

I cover my ears, as if it will help, and ram my way through the crowd toward my uncle's cabin. I have to reach it before I lose my composure completely. Or my breakfast.

But when my foot hits the stoop of the cabin porch, I hesitate. With my uncle gone, maybe this is my chance to . . . I don't know, *do* something. I'm not leaving without Jefferson and Tom, but maybe I can explore the camp, see what's behind the cabin, figure out where Abel is keeping Peony. Find a way out of this hell.

Within a split second, Wilhelm is at my side, grabbing my elbow. I try to wrench it back, but he holds tight. He drags me up the steps.

We reach the door, and when he swings it open, I'm finally able to yank my elbow away. I slip under his arm into the cabin and whirl to face him.

"You will not follow me inside. I understand you've been ordered to keep watch on me, but you will respect my privacy and . . ." I get a better idea for which tack to take. "And you will not be alone with me inside my uncle's cabin without his permission."

Wilhelm's jaw works, as if he's grinding his teeth. I can see a little more of his face now that we're in broad daylight and I'm not woozy with laudanum. His nose has a crick in it, like it's been broke a time or two, and his eyes are gray blue like slate, set deep under thick blond brows.

He stares at me. I return his stare, refusing to flinch.

All at once, he slams the door shut and whirls away.

I collapse into Hiram's rocking chair, pull my knees to my chest, and rock back and forth for a very long time.

I lie on my bed, staring up at the ceiling.

There was no chance to do any exploring today because Wilhelm stood outside the cabin like a soldier on sentry. Eventually Mary stopped by and turned a batch of soaked beans into honest-to-goodness pork and beans with molasses. She must be a quick learner, because that's a Yankee dish, one Daddy used to make on our hunting trips. I suppose it's a favorite of Hiram's, too. I ate only a few bites before retiring to my room, leaving the rest for my uncle, who finally came home as it was getting dark.

I slipped under the quilt when I heard his boot steps, and turned my back to the bedroom door. I sensed the curtain being lifted, felt his dark presence looming over me, heard his soft breathing, but I pretended to be asleep because the hate inside me was so awful that I didn't trust myself to pretend to be cooperative.

It must be past midnight now, and the moon is shimmering in the sky, casting bluish light through my single high window. It doesn't open. I checked. The only way out of this cabin is through the front door.

Something *tappity-tap*s on the window, faint like a chittering squirrel. Maybe I imagined it.

It sounds again, louder this time, and I push back the covers and get to my feet. Standing on the chest, I poke my head up over the windowsill and peer outside.

It's Jefferson, with a grin on his face and a handful of pebbles, washed in moonlight for all to see. I glance around the camp, panicked, but it's late and everyone's abed. Still, it would only take one person to see him and report to my uncle.

"Hide!" I mouth.

"Open!" he mouths back, gesturing toward the window.

I shake my head. "Can't."

His eyes turn in on themselves, and his lips press tight. It's Jefferson's thinking face, and it's so familiar and dear that my heart aches.

He steps up to the glass and stretches on his tiptoes so that his face is only inches from mine. It might be a trick of the moonlight, but his black eye is already turning sickly yellow—a good sign.

Jefferson takes a deep breath, opens his mouth into an *O*, and exhales onto the glass, forming a cloud of fog. With his forefinger, he writes:

WOЯЯOMOT

It takes me a second to parse it. *Tomorrow.* I nod.

He wipes the glass with the side of his fist, then breathes on it again. This time, he writes:

THGIИDIM

He repeats the process once more and adds:

DИIHƎB

ƎLBATƧ

My heart races. Can I do it? Can I sneak out of this cabin right under my uncle's nose?

He presses his palm to the glass. The work of the day is evident on his skin—tiny cuts filled with dirt, a blister at the base of his thumb.

Slowly I reach up with my hand and place my palm against the glass, too, fitting my fingers inside the outline of his larger ones.

Jefferson gives me a quick grin. He rubs at the window to

erase any trace of what just happened, then he ducks away and disappears.

I watch the empty camp for a while to make sure no one saw. A couple of the Chinese tents glow from within, with either candles or lanterns, but everyone else seems fast asleep.

Hiram said they would tie Jefferson up at night. How did he get free? How could he take such an awful risk to come see me?

I slip down onto the bed and sit with my back against the wall, knees to chest. Tomorrow. Midnight. Behind the stable.

The next morning, Mary shows up to make breakfast. One of her sleeves is torn, and a dark bruise swells along her left cheekbone. I know a hitting bruise when I see one; Jefferson used to have them all the time. I try to meet her eye, to gauge whether or not she's all right, but she ignores me.

Uncle Hiram doesn't seem to notice. He eats his scrambled eggs slowly, his gaze distant as if his thoughts are far away. I hate to admit it, but my uncle is a fine-looking man. Finer looking than my daddy, though he shows nothing of Daddy's warmth or kindness or joy. He's better groomed, too, with a close-shaved jaw and hair neatly parted and slicked.

Mary comes to remove our dishes from the table, which is when I finally gather the gumption to say to my uncle what's on my mind.

"Frank Dilley killed a man yesterday."

It might be my imagination, but Mary's step stutters a little before she bends to scrape the dishes.

"Yes," Hiram says casually. "I heard." He wipes his mouth with a napkin.

I gape at him. "Well, aren't you going to do something about it?"

My uncle folds the napkin neatly and places it on the table before him. "I already have."

"Oh?"

"I gave Frank a stern talking-to about being more careful. Topper tells me that Indian was well respected among the savages. A leader of sorts. He's not the one I work with, an Indian by the name of Muskrat. But the other savages looked up to him almost as much. Frank should have made an example of someone different."

I blink, trying to sort out what he just said. It's like we're having two different conversations. I might as well have asked, "Will you mend the back fence?" only to have him answer, "Sure, I'll fetch you a cup of water."

"Who's Muskrat, exactly?" I ask, remembering the man at the mine who wouldn't let himself be pushed around.

"He spent a few years in one of the Spanish missions. Got himself half civilized. Speaks English and Spanish as well as that savage gibberish, so he works as an interpreter for the foremen. I don't think Muskrat is his real name."

"It isn't?"

"They don't reveal their true names to Christians. He's been a useful creature, though."

"Will he be in charge of burying the man Frank Dilley killed?" I don't know much about Indian customs, but maybe I should go and pay my respects.

"There won't be any burial," Hiram assures me. "We'll bring in the Indian's head and collect the bounty, then we'll fetch ourselves another."

"Wait . . . bounty?"

"Don't worry. None of my men will go killing Indians just to collect that bounty themselves. I pay them too well."

"And the Indians? You pay them, too?"

"They're generously compensated with food and shelter and a chance to turn from their heathen ways and embrace the truth of our Lord. Speaking of which, Reverend Lowrey will be paying us a visit soon. He travels a circuit through the nearby camps, preaching. It's a nice break for my men."

I wouldn't mind if I never saw that uppity preacher again.

"And the Chinese? Do you pay them? I've never seen a group of folks work so well together."

"They get protection and rations like everyone else. On their own time, they're allowed to conduct trade with other members of camp. Some of them are making a tidy profit."

Mary's work at the washtub has ceased, but just as we're noticing the silence, it starts up again with a splash and clatter of dishes.

"That Indian did nothing wrong, Uncle Hiram," I say, trying to bring the conversation back to where I intended. "And Frank Dilley is a murderer."

"You're so softhearted, just like your mother." He bestows a fond smile. "It's a fine quality in a young lady."

My heart feels the opposite of soft. It feels like a hard, mean, red-hot coal.

He continues, "It's a complicated moral question, sure, and I don't think your education and gender are quite up to the task of understanding the debate's finer points. But trust me, sweet pea. It's not murder to kill an Indian."

I don't pretend to have a lot of book learning, but everything he's saying is as wrong as a fish in a tree. "I don't think you're listening—"

"Today I want you in the upper tunnel," he says, scooting his stool back. He rises to his feet and looks down at me. "We've lost the vein, and we've hit bedrock or granite or something going forward. It will save us a lot of time and expense if you . . ." He glances at Mary. "If you offer an opinion on where the gold is most like to be. Being a miner's daughter and all."

Mary is scrubbing at the dishes so hard I fear her fingers will fall off.

"I'll do my best, sir. I don't mind telling you, though, that I'd find it a real inspiration to know the Indians were treated better."

Hiram dons his hat. "I'll see to it that everyone gets an extra ration of wheat tonight, how's that?"

How many rations do they normally get? Do they get sorted wheat or the chaff, too? I've eaten raw wheat before. It has a nice, nutty taste, but it leaves grit in your molars and an ache in your belly if you eat too much.

He's still gazing at me, awaiting my response. "Thank you," I manage. And because it's what Becky would say, I add, "That's very generous."

He smiles again, and it sickens me that I've pleased him. "Wilhelm will escort you to the mine when you're done here."

He leaves, and it's just me and Mary and the clanking of dishes.

There's still a basket half filled with biscuits on the table, covered with a cloth to keep them warm and away from flies. Maybe I could grab a few. Sneak them to Jefferson and Tom in the mines.

It's a flash in my mind: the ear-piercing gunshot, the Indian splashing into the water.

I shouldn't let Frank or Abel or anyone observe me singling out anyone for special treatment. It might get them dead.

But I can do it tonight, at midnight, when no one is watching. I grab the basket. "Mary, may I take the rest of these biscuits to my room? Sometimes I get hungry at night."

She glances at me over her shoulder. "Yes. Take."

"Thank you." I turn to go, but I hesitate and turn back around. "What happened to you?"

Mary turns to face me, dripping dishcloth in her hands. "I no understand."

I gesture toward my face, mirroring the huge bruise pillowing on her cheek.

The light goes out of her eyes for the briefest instant. Then she smiles. "Is nada. The mens. Sometimes . . . what is word? Rough." She shrugs.

I frown. "Do you cook and clean for them, too?"

She laughs wickedly, like I'm the brunt of her joke. "Oh, no.

Not those mens." She returns to the dishes. "Tall man wait outside," she says, dismissing me with a wave.

I stare at her back, puzzling over our conversation. Mary reminds me of Jefferson a little, the way her face always seems deep in thought, the laughter in her eyes when I say something that has amused her somehow. But a real friendship seems miles distant, because unlike Jefferson, her demeanor is cold as a winter wind.

I run to my bedroom and stash the basket of biscuits in the chest at the foot of my bed. I lace my boots, square my shoulders, and prepare to meet Wilhelm.

Frank Dilley was right; the Joyner tunnel is a lot drier. Frank isn't at the mine today, but Abel Topper is. He and Wilhelm escort me up the tunnel, which is long and so low I have to duck to avoid hitting my head on the swinging lanterns. Tree roots poke at us occasionally, which means the slope of the land has caught up to the slope of the tunnel.

After stepping aside twice to make way for mine carts, we finally reach the end of the tunnel. Sure enough, it seems as though their pickaxes have reached a solid wall.

"The quartz vein seems to go in this direction," Abel says, pointing at the hard face of rock. "We can push through, but it's blunting our tools faster than we can smith them. Westfall headed up to Rough and Ready yesterday to get some gunpowder. We could blow a hole right through if we need to. But he said the daughter of Lucky Westfall might . . . have a special insight. Tell us where to go next."

Just how much did my uncle tell Abel? Abel Topper was a mine foreman back in Georgia, and as experienced as anyone. There's no way he buys into that bit about "special insight." Miners can be a superstitious lot, though. My uncle probably told him I'm lucky.

And what does he mean by *up* to Rough and Ready? North of here? Higher into the mountains? If I can figure out where Rough and Ready is, it will give me a clue where I am.

"Miss Westfall?"

"Er . . . let me think a moment."

Abel looks at me expectantly. Wilhelm is behind me, but even though I can't see him, his eyes on my back are like a weight bearing down.

"Shine the lantern on the wall there," I order, indicating the solid rock. Abel complies, and the light shifts away from me to the dead end ahead. Under cover of darkness, I close my eyes and reach out with my gold sense.

I find the vein right away, a bright, warm river of gold that heads off slightly to the right. If they tunneled forward, they'd miss it entirely.

My shoulder hits the wall, startling me. I moved toward the vein without realizing it, like a moth to a flame. I place my fingertips to the rough, hard dirt, letting the nearby gold vibrate my skin. It spells warmth and comfort to me. Life and hope.

It's better than peach pie. Better than autumn mornings by the box stove. I push deeper, letting my senses expand like roots in fertile soil. The buzzing intensifies until it fills me up.

I smile.

A slight tremor rocks the earth. Dirt and pebbles rain down on my head.

"What was that?" Abel says. "Did you feel that?"

I blink, coming back fully to the present. I thought it was just the gold buzzing, speaking to me like it always does, but this time Abel felt it, too.

"Maybe get some more beams in here," I say quickly. "This tunnel doesn't feel sound." And maybe that's the truth, given the twisting roots just above our heads. But maybe it was me. It was almost like the gold talked back.

Abel is frowning, the lantern light making deep hollows of his eyes. "Maybe you're right." He whips the lantern around and shines it in my face. "So, what do you think? Veer off? Move forward?"

It's so strange to me that he can't feel that vein sweeping off to the right. It's like the sun on your face, the wind in your hair. I make a swift and possibly bad decision.

"Definitely forward," I tell him. "Get that gunpowder in here and keep that tunnel growing. You're headed in the right direction."

He grins. "I knew it!"

"Need me for anything else?"

"Not just now." He waves me off absentmindedly, already contemplating the wall before him.

Wilhelm and I return to the surface, and as much as I love the feel and scent and weight of gold around me, I can't say I'm sad to leave that dark, dank hole behind.

"What now?" I ask.

He gestures toward the cabin.

"Again? All day?" I hate being cooped up, doing nothing. I've never spent an idle day in my life, and it makes me fit to burst.

He just frowns.

"Well, don't talk so fast. I can hardly understand you."

His frown deepens.

"All right, all right, if you say so. I won't make a fuss."

Something flits across his face, like a bullet whizzing by and gone. Like something hurt his feelings.

I open my mouth to josh him about his sensitive soul, but an awful thought occurs to me: Maybe he's not just quiet and stoic. Maybe he *can't* talk. If that's the case, then my funning him isn't fun at all. It's pure meanness.

We reach the cabin. The camp is lively now, with men going about their business. The arrastra grumbles and crunches as mules pull it round and round. One of the Chinese men has a small smithy going, mending pickaxes. I spot Mary sitting in the lap of one of the Missouri men, who is pausing for a smoke.

Wilhelm and I stand awkwardly a moment, him waiting for me to go inside, and me waiting for I'm not sure what.

Finally I say, "I have some leftover biscuits. You want some?"

His face freezes. Then a tiny grin tugs at those full lips, and he nods once.

"Wait here." I dash inside, retrieve two biscuits from the

stash in my chest, and hurry back to Wilhelm. "Here you go."

He takes them from me gently, then tips his hat to me and turns to stand sentry outside the cabin.

Minutes later, a *boom* cracks the air. I fling open the door. A cloud of dust and ash billows from the mine entrance, bringing the scent of gunpowder. Abel and few others stand outside, whooping and hollering and slapping their hats against their legs like they just saw Fourth of July fireworks.

They won't find that vein of gold. I sent them off in the wrong direction. If my uncle asks, I'll tell him it was a short vein, hardly worth pursing, and that they probably blew it to bits. They'll find a little gold, sure, just enough to give credence to my lie. But not enough to make my uncle rich.

I'm not sure it was the right thing to do. I'm not sure about anything.

Chapter Fifteen

I need to find my guns.

I don't know where Hiram went or when he'll be back, but I can't miss this chance. My uncle's bedroom has an actual door. If my guns are in the cabin, they'll be in his bedroom.

Even though no one else is home, I step quietly as I make my way toward the one room of the cabin I haven't been inside. My heart is as skittery as a water bug as I place my hand to the door and push it open. There's no knob; it just swings wide, squealing out a warning that I'm sure can be heard all the way to San Francisco.

The room is bigger than my own by several paces in either direction. It contains a bed big enough for two, a shelf full of books, and a beautiful cherrywood dresser beneath a wide window. The room faces north and is snugged up against the tree line, so in spite of the window, the air is murky and cool. Everything smells of tobacco and candle wax.

I check under the bed, behind the hanging clothes—

nothing. I'm tiptoeing toward the dresser to open the drawers when something catches my eye. It's a framed photograph, sitting beside a half-melted candle. It's blurry, as though it's been handled too many times. I peer closer, something niggling at my brain.

A young woman looks back at me. She's been posed primly, with her hands crossed in her lap, her chin high. She's young, maybe eighteen, with a perfect complexion and a trim figure and a firm set about her pretty mouth.

She looks like me. Except she's a lot handsomer, truth be told, with that dainty chin and skin that's never seen the sun.

I think it might be my mother.

Mama had lines around her eyes and gray at her temples, a waist thick from two pregnancies, and a perpetually sunburned nose from forgetting to wear her bonnet. Her hands were strong, not delicate, her mouth more stubborn than composed.

But those eyes. That almost-but-not-quite smile.

I ought to recognize my own mama right away. The fact that I'm not sure gives me a funny feeling. Maybe I'm already forgetting what she looked like, her not even dead a year. Or maybe life in Georgia with my daddy changed her so much it almost made her unrecognizable.

I study her dress, looking for something familiar. It's finer than anything I remember Mama wearing, but she did come from old Boston money, and her life was very different when she was a girl.

Hanging from her neck is a medallion of some kind. The

picture is too old and blurry for me to know for sure, but I'd almost swear she's wearing the same locket I wear now, the one that came all the way across the continent with me, containing a lock of my baby brother's hair. . . .

I've stood here too long lollygagging. I need to finish up and get out of here before Hiram returns.

Trying to ignore the photograph, I slide open the drawers. I ruffle the underclothes and linens inside, looking for my five-shooter or my ammunition, but there's nothing. Not a single thing I can use for a weapon. Quietly I slide the drawers closed.

I peer behind the dresser, lift Hiram's mattress, test each floorboard with my toes to see if I can lift it.

Still nothing.

Boot steps sound on the cabin steps.

No time to check and see if I've left anything in disarray. I flee from the bedroom, shut the door behind me, and drop into Hiram's rocking chair just as he pushes through the front door.

"Good afternoon, Leah," he says, all formal-like. He stares at the locket around my neck, as if it means something special to him. I cover it with my hand.

"Afternoon." I say it clear and easy, like my heart isn't stampeding in my chest and I have plenty of breath to spare.

"Abel says they blew a hole in the Joyner tunnel on your recommendation."

I shrug. "They won't find much. That vein didn't penetrate far."

His eyes narrow, but if he has suspicions, he doesn't give voice to them.

If I wasn't afraid for my life and the lives of my friends—shoot, every single person in this camp—I'd ask him straight out why he has a picture of my mama in his bedroom. Of all the keepsakes to cross an ocean with, why that one? Why does he have it placed where he can look at it every single day?

But I *am* afraid, and I'm supposed to be pretending to be cooperative, so I say, "Abel said you went to a place called Rough and Ready to fetch some gunpowder yesterday."

Hiram takes off his riding gloves and slaps them against his thigh to shake off the dust. "I did. Negotiated a fair deal. From now on, Dilley will be able to make the trip on my behalf."

"So we'll get even more?"

He removes his hat and hangs it on a peg beside the door. "Why so interested?"

"You said to familiarize myself with the workings of the mine. I'm familiarizing."

"When you were in there this morning, what did you feel?"

I know what he wants me to say. "Gold. Lots of it. The Drink is going to yield better. We might think about starting a branching tunnel down there." Nothing about that was a lie. But I might not give him the exact best direction on where to dig.

His smile is soft, and I daresay a little bit proud. "Good to know."

He fixes himself a plate from the leftovers on the woodstove, then indicates with his chin that I should move. "My chair," he says. "Up and out."

"Yes, sir." I move quickly to comply.

I'll have to search the rest of the cabin later, next time he leaves. But he doesn't leave. He sits down at his writing desk and spends the next several hours attending to correspondence. I grab *Godey's Lady's Book* from my nightstand and pretend to be absorbed by a story about a plain, unmarried woman with a heart of gold who organizes the ladies in her church to help the poor orphans of Boston.

Mary comes to make a supper of chicken and dumplings. Afterward, Hiram reads by lantern light, while I help Mary clean up. Finally he addresses me.

"Good night, sweet pea," he says. "Sleep well. See you in the morning." A dismissal, since he's making no move to leave the table himself.

"Good night," I mutter, and I retire to my bedroom.

I lie on the bed, trying to mark time. It's anxious work. I've no pocket watch, so I'll have to take my best guess about this midnight business. I try to use the moonlight as a guide, but watching it change—or not change fast enough—makes me worry even more.

What if Hiram stays up all night? What if Wilhelm is still out there, keeping watch? What if I misjudge the time?

When the moonlight through the tiny window has moved halfway across the floor, I gamble that the time is about right, and I rise from the bed. I consider leaving my boots off; it's easier to step silently in stockings. But if anyone saw my filthy, torn stockings, it would be a dead giveaway, so I pull on my boots and lace them up.

I grab the slop bucket from the corner of my room. If I'm caught, I'll just say the smell was bothering me and I'm taking it to the outhouse. It's a weak excuse, but it's the best I can come up with. At the last second, I remember the biscuits stashed in my chest. I grab as many as I can carry in one hand, squishing them badly. My hands will appear strangely lumpy if someone looks too close.

The light from Hiram's lantern winked out long ago, but I listen at the curtain for the sounds of his stirring—shifting his seat or rocking in his chair or even just breathing. Nothing.

Slowly I push the curtain aside. The main room seems empty.

There's hardly enough light to see by as I creep toward the front door. I imagine bumping into something or knocking over a chair. I don't dare light a lantern and flash my presence for all to see. The moonlight will have to suit.

I reach the door, and again I pause to listen, ear to the wood. Still nothing. This is it. If Wilhelm is outside, I've no chance at all of meeting Jefferson. If he isn't, someone else could just as easily be nearby, watching. I wouldn't put it past my uncle to make sure the cabin is watched at all times.

The door swings open with a slight squeak, and I freeze. Nothing moves outside. I slip out the door and shut it, wincing when the slop bucket hits the frame.

The camp is silent except for the wind in the grass and the rapid, trilling whistle of nighthawks in the nearby trees. The hard-packed ground is bluish in the moonlight, reminding me for a moment of the Georgia mountains, the way the trees and especially the fog seemed blue on moonlit nights.

Behind the stable, Jefferson said. All I have to do is creep past the barracks building where Frank Dilley and all the Missouri men are sleeping. You could set your pocket watch by Frank's habit of assigning a guard. So maybe I ought to take the long way around and avoid the barracks altogether. But that would mean going behind the cabin and sneaking beneath Hiram's bedroom window.

The barracks is ahead and slightly to the right. I stare at it a moment, weighing my options. A light winks on in one of the windows, making my decision for me.

I head in the opposite direction and skirt my uncle's cabin, which puts me within view of the Chinese tents. No one seems to be stirring, but I keep to the cabin's shadow as much as possible. The ground beneath my feet begins to crunch as I near the corner—detritus from the wall of cottonwoods in the back.

This would be the perfect time to figure out how far the stand of trees extends and if it leads to a creek or a dry wash as I suspect, but it's just too dark. I round the corner and creep along the rear wall. The land slopes down toward the trees a little, and a blanket of fallen leaves makes my path slippery. I'm glad I chose to don the boots.

At Hiram's window I duck down, still hugging the wall. I move forward in a half crouch, made all the more awkward by the slop bucket I'm carrying. If I bang it with my knee on accident, it will wake him for sure.

An owl calls out, soft and clear, and I'm caught for a moment in memory: hiding beneath fallen leaves on a cold night just like this while three brothers robbed me blind. I've come so far, but in some ways, I haven't gone any distance. I'm still hiding from bad men. I'm still trying to figure how to make my own way, my own fortune.

I pass Hiram's window and pause, listening, but I hear nothing. The cabin is sound, sounder than any other structure I've seen since coming to California, so it's possible he's staring out the window this very second, and I'd never know. No way to go but forward. I grit my teeth and move on.

It's with no small amount of relief that I clear the cabin. Just a hundred feet of open space until I can hide in the stable's shadow. I ponder the cottonwoods a moment. Maybe I should head down the slope and work my way parallel through the trees. But I can't risk it in the dark. A twisted ankle would be the least of my worries; a snapped twig in the night can be as startling and loud as a gunshot.

I glance around. No Wilhelm that I can see, and the barracks doesn't have a window facing this direction. I stride out into the open.

I'm a third of the way to the stable, then halfway, then—

"Lee!" comes a familiar whisper, and I can't control my fool legs, which stretch out and cover the rest of the distance in a flat-out run.

Sorry nickers when I reach her stall, but I don't have a chance to answer her greeting before a hand darts out, snags my elbow, and drags me behind the giant lean-to.

Arms wrap around my shoulders, and I'm pulled tight into a

warm chest. "Lee," Jefferson whispers into my ear. I wrap my arms around his waist and squeeze right back. My fistful of biscuits presses crumbs into his shirt.

Someone clears his throat, and I spring away from Jefferson, startled to find that we are not alone.

It's Tom, grinning fit to burst. Beside him is someone else—Muskrat, the one who spoke to me outside the mine. Still another shadow materializes out of the darkness, and I gasp. It's Mary.

I have no idea what's going on, but that doesn't stop me from launching at Tom and giving him the hug of his life. He chuckles, patting my back. "Good to see you, too, Lee," he whispers.

"Are you okay?" I say. "They been beating on you like they have Jeff? If Wilhelm is still forcing laudanum into you, I'll—"

"I'm fine, Lee. I promise. Tired and sore and hungry, but I'm fine."

He doesn't sound fine. Even whispering, his voice is weak, his words a little slurred.

I turn to Jefferson. "All right, tell me. What's going on? Why are we all here?"

Mary is the one who says, "Rebellion, Miss Westfall. Escape. For all of us."

I stare at Mary, my mind racing. "Your English is perfect," I accuse.

"My Spanish is better," she retorts.

"Then why . . ."

"Men are stupid," she says with an offhand shrug. "I get more gold when I pretend I can't speak English well. And more information."

More gold for what? Cooking and cleaning for everyone?

"Mary has been our best spy," Muskrat says. "Until you."

Realization hits like a blow to the chest. Mary is a woman of ill repute. The camp's prostitute.

"I should have made introductions," Jefferson says. "Lee, this is Muskrat of the Maidu tribe. Muskrat, this is my oldest friend, Leah."

"We've met," I say. "Sort of."

Now that a gunshot isn't ringing in my head and my belly isn't rolling from nausea, I'm able to notice how painfully thin Muskrat seems. He wears a beaded necklace, a leather breechcloth, and muddy moccasins. Dark dots on his chest are too regular and perfect to be freckles; they must be tattoos, like the dots I saw the night of the fire on one man's chest. In fact, he reminds me of that man a great deal. He's the same height, with the same sharp eyes and maybe even the same exact necklace. But that other man was strong and healthy.

"It's nice to meet you officially, sir," I say, then I add, "About your friend, I'm . . . sorry."

Muskrat remains expressionless. Finally he says, "Good."

I flinch.

"What did you bring, Lee?" Jefferson asks quickly, indicating my bucket.

"Slop bucket. In case I need an excuse to be out. But

also . . ." I hold out my hand to display the mashed biscuits. "Some food."

"Oh, sweet Lord!" Tom exclaims. He grabs one and shoves it into his mouth like a man starved.

Jefferson gobbles another just as greedily. Muskrat carefully pinches a biscuit from my fingers like a fine gentleman. Mary declines. "I'll make extra tomorrow, too," she says with a little grin.

"I don't know how much time I have," I say.

"To business, then," Tom says. "Muskrat is planning an escape for his people. He needs our help."

"Uncle Hiram isn't paying any of you, is he?" I say to Muskrat. "He's keeping you here against your will, like he is me."

"No," Muskrat says. "Not like you. You, he keeps in a fancy house and a fancy dress with fancy food and someone to cook and clean. Us, he keeps penned up like hogs, rolling in mud with only rotting leftovers to eat."

I'm glad the dark hides my burning cheeks. "I'm sorry, I didn't mean—"

Muskrat holds up his hand, and the look he gives me could wither winter wheat.

"The man Dilley killed was one of their elders," Jefferson says.

"Yes. Just because I gave . . ." My voice breaks. "Gave him some sugar water."

Tom says, "Dilley's been working himself up to kill Indians ever since we set out from Missouri. He was just looking for an excuse."

"He will kill more," Muskrat says. "If we do not first starve."

"They're getting sick," Jefferson adds. "The Missouri men are feeding the Maidu poisoned potatoes, the ones they use to absorb mercury from the gold amalgam. The Maidu know they're poison, but when a body is hungry enough, it stops caring about that sort of inconvenience."

My face is burning even more angrily now. All this time, I've been trying to figure out how to get away with Tom and Jefferson. Never once did I consider that someone else might need help, too. Even less did it occur to me that someone else might help *us*.

"I have a friend," Muskrat says. "A ranchero who will shelter us if we can just get to him. But he won't move openly against Westfall. We have to rescue ourselves."

"Mary overheard something yesterday," Tom says. "Go on, Mary. Tell Lee."

"Abel Topper was angry with Frank for killing Ezra," she says. "Ezra was very respected. He couldn't work much, but everyone else worked harder when he was around. Frank said he would just find another. That he could kill as many diggers as he liked because they had a raid planned soon to fetch more from a nearby Nisenan village. And then . . ." Her eyes widen and she leans forward. "Then he said that a fellow in Sacramento is now paying a bounty for Indian heads and that some of them, the old and weak, would be worth more dead than alive."

I'm as woozy as if I'd just gulped a gallon of laudanum.

"Lee?" says Jefferson.

"It's true," I say. "Hiram told me about the bounty just today."

"We have to get them out of here," Tom says. "They're so sick now. It's only a matter of time before Dilley kills the rest, with Hiram Westfall and Abel Topper looking on and doing nothing to stop it."

"How?" I ask. "What do you want me to do?"

"We don't know yet," Tom says.

There's a silence, and then Muskrat says, "We need a distraction. Something like one of the feast days at the mission. Like Estanislao used to make."

"Who was Estanislao?" I ask.

"A great leader of the Yokuts tribe, and an alcalde at Mission San José. When Spanish rule became cruel, he led an army and attacked the missions. The Yokuts followed him, the Chumash, others, including my own father. Because Estanislao had been an alcalde, he knew exactly when the missions would be distracted and easy to attack."

"There might be a thanksgiving celebration," Tom says. He looks at Muskrat and Mary. "It's a harvest feast. Not everyone observes it, but Hiram might. I'm pretty certain Reverend Lowrey does. He mentioned it during one of his sermons when we were on the trail."

"Hiram and my daddy were raised near Boston," I say. "It was something we always celebrated in our house. So I bet Hiram will observe it, if only because it's a chance to show off how important he is to everyone else."

"Hiram ordered extra supplies, including whiskey," Mary

said. "Very special. Locked up. We are not supposed to touch them before he orders it."

"That sounds like thanksgiving," Tom says.

"So when this harvest feast happens, we escape," Muskrat says.

"That's a when, but not a how," Jefferson says. "We still need a plan."

I nod. "We should get a message to our people in Glory. If the Major and Jasper and Becky knew we were held prisoner, they'd come after us."

"And get themselves killed or end up just like us," Jefferson says.

"He's not wrong," Tom says. "But if we don't come up with a good plan, or if things go awry, that might be our only hope."

I think of the Joyner children, sweet Andy and little Olive and the tiny baby girl who doesn't even have a name yet. I think of Hampton working so hard to buy his wife's freedom, and the Major pining for my friend Becky while doing everything he can to help. I remember Therese, her skin burning in the desert, and that gives me a flash of Martin, lying on the ground, unable to move, whispering his last words. I shiver. I don't want to put my friends in danger again. Not for anything.

"So what do you want me to do?" I ask.

"Listen," says Mary. "Watch."

"For now," Tom adds.

"And don't give anyone your water," Muskrat says, in a

scathing enough tone that I guess he figures me for a dimwit who's bound to do something stupid, no matter what. But I see his point. The first time I acted impulsively, a man died. Muskrat and Mary have been here longer, have been planning longer, and maybe the best thing I can do is trust them and listen to what they say.

"Will we meet again?" I ask. "It's not easy to sneak out—"

"It's harder for the rest of us," Mary snaps. "Trust me on that."

I clamp my mouth shut. How *did* they all manage to sneak out for this meeting? My uncle said something about Jefferson and Tom being tied up at night.

"We need to get back," Jefferson says, and Tom nods. "Working in that slimy mudhole is hard enough without a good night's sleep."

"You're sure you're both all right?" I ask. "Are they hurting you?"

Mary frowns at me, and I realize I've messed up again. The foremen are whipping the Indians, even killing them, and all I can think about is my friends. I glance at Muskrat, but he is looking away from me, into the darkness.

"Nothing we can't handle, Lee," Tom says, but his voice lacks conviction.

"Next time we are to meet," Mary says, "I'll signal by cooking cornbread biscuits with bits of apple for breakfast."

"Okay. So, in the meantime, I just watch? And listen?"

"That's our brilliant plan," Jefferson says. "For now."

"We know when we're going to do it," Tom says. "So we all sleep on it and figure out how."

"Come for a visit," Muskrat says, in a calm, quiet voice that is more of a command than an invitation. "Ask your uncle to show you. You should *see*."

He doesn't need to say what I should see. He wants me to witness the condition of his people, to understand how they are suffering. "Okay."

"Now, we leave," Mary says. "One at a time."

Muskrat gives her a quick nod and then backs away into the darkness of the trees before anyone else can move. He's in the most danger, so it makes sense for him to go first.

"My turn." Tom reaches up and clasps my shoulder. He opens his mouth to say something, but changes his mind. He leaves, creeping around the stable, in a direction opposite to Muskrat's.

"Leah, go," Mary orders.

I start to tiptoe back toward my uncle's cabin, but a hand grabs my arm and spins me around. Jefferson yanks me against him and leans down, breathing into my hair. "Stay safe, Lee," he whispers. I could stay here like this forever, his chest warming mine, his lips against my scalp.

Instead, I wrap my arms around him and squeeze tight for the barest moment before reluctantly letting go. "You too, Jeff. I . . ."

"You what?"

"Just be safe."

He regards me quizzically as I back away, and I stare at

his precious face until I'm distant enough that not even the moonlight can help me make sense of it.

I crouch down and hug the shadows, hoping I'll return as easily as I came. But my neck prickles all the while, as though spying eyes are watching my every move.

Chapter Sixteen

I make it back without incident, and I sneak inside with only the barest squeak of the door. I lower my slop bucket gently to the floor of my bedroom. Even after I've shucked my boots and pulled the quilt over my shoulders, my pulse races and my mind is too busy for sleep. It's near dawn when I finally drift off.

The sound of the bench scraping the floor awakens me, and I lurch up with a start. I've almost slept through breakfast.

My stomach growls in response to the scent of flapjacks as I hurry to dress and smooth my hair. Right before swishing aside the curtain, I pause to collect myself, straightening my spine and taking a deep breath.

My uncle looks up from his breakfast of flapjacks and honest-to-God maple syrup. "Good morning, sweet pea," he says, and his voice is as flat as the grassy plains.

"Good morning, Uncle Hiram." Mary has already set out a place for me. I sit opposite my uncle and carefully spread the napkin across my lap, trying very hard not to notice the way his eyes follow my every movement, like he's a coyote and I'm a juicy, helpless rabbit.

"You had an adventure last night," he says.

My heart stops. Every sound in the cabin is a clanging cymbal in my ear. The scrape of his knife against his plate, the sizzle of flapjacks on the stove, the creak of Hiram's bench.

At the stove, Mary is frozen like a statue, wooden spoon hanging in the air. Hiram turns toward her, a question in his eyes, and Mary becomes suddenly engrossed by the frying pan.

"An adventure?" I manage lamely.

"You were seen leaving the cabin," he says, still eyeing Mary. His voice is as dark as midnight.

"Oh, that," I say, waving my hand as if it were nothing. Surely he can hear the way my heart pounds in my throat? Surely he sees the fib making gooseflesh of my skin? "My slop bucket was full. Couldn't sleep for the stench."

He frowns.

"Oh, Uncle, I apologize!" I say. "I shouldn't mention such things at the table. Mama would tan my hide if she heard."

"You were gone a long time," he says.

Who saw me? Who told? Hiram did say I would be watched. I guess I wasn't imagining it after all, when I felt someone's gaze creeping along my neck. What else did this mysterious person see?

I force myself to breathe. What if I've gotten my co-conspirators in trouble?

"It's true," I admit, after too long a pause. "I couldn't remember exactly where the outhouse was, and I didn't want to dump it anywhere near the cabin."

Mary places a plateful of flapjacks in front of me, and I give her a grateful glance. With my fork, I spear a lump of food and shove it into my mouth, as if the conversation is over and I'm a girl with nothing to hide.

As I chew, I look anywhere but at my uncle, and my gaze rests on Mary, who is back at the stove frying up some more. But that's not a safe place to gaze either, because I can't help but compare this tiny, quiet-seeming girl to the one I met in the dark who spoke perfect English and ordered us around like she was born to it. And I can't help but think of her with all the men in camp, and what that might mean. After talking to her last night, I know her even less than I did before.

I force the next bite down, though my appetite has fled.

"Tonight, you'll be tied to the bed," Hiram says.

"What? That's not fair! You said you wouldn't hurt—"

He raises a hand to forestall argument. "My word on this is final. After a few days of good behavior, you may earn back the privilege of sleeping untied."

I'm about to protest further, but his glare deepens.

"I know you think me cruel and unreasonable," he says in a perfectly measured tone. "But know one thing: I love you. I *love* you, Leah, like you were my very own."

I fight to keep my first bites of breakfast down. It feels like worms are crawling around where my food ought to be.

Hiram smiles. "You will come to love me in return. But

don't worry; there is no hurry. I know children need time for these things, and I am a very patient man."

That's not what Mama and Daddy said about him, but I know better than to speak my piece.

He rises from the table. "Wilhelm will escort you anywhere you want to go today," he says, pulling on his gloves. He reaches for his coat and hat. "Even if it's to the outhouse to dump a slop bucket."

I remain frozen in place as he bends down and plants a kiss on my forehead that leaves a cool, wet spot on my skin.

"I'll see you later this evening, my darling girl," he says, and finally, *finally* he leaves.

I grab the napkin from my lap and rub at the spot where he kissed me, rub and rub as though he's left a poison that will burn my skin. Tears prick my eyes, and I'm still rubbing when tiny dry fingers close around my wrist, stopping me.

"We'll figure something out," Mary says softly, even though we are alone. "Don't go to pieces on me." For the first time, I sense sympathy in her gaze. Maybe a little openness.

I nod up at her.

"It always feels like that," she says. "When they touch you."

I swallow hard, not wanting to think about it too much. "Well, we're getting out of here." I say it in the tightest whisper, as though even the walls have ears. "Both of us."

"Yes," she agrees.

I straighten my shoulders, take up my fork, and doggedly force myself to down more tasteless flapjacks.

◆ ◆ ◆

I find Wilhelm standing sentry outside the cabin door.

The sky is low and dark with gray clouds, the air thick with chilled moisture. Wet mud sticks to Wilhelm's boots. It must have rained before dawn.

By way of greeting, I say, "I have some extra flapjacks. Cooked just right by Mary. You want some?"

After a pause, he nods once, sharply.

I hand him the bundle I had already prepared, wrapped in a napkin. He shoves it into his coat pocket for later.

"I'd like a tour of the camp today, Wilhelm," I tell him. "Every bit of it. Mr. Westfall wants me to continue to familiarize myself with our operation."

He doesn't wear a hood today, and I can see his eyes clearly—cold and hard as deepwater ice. His scarred lips are pulled into a frown, but he offers his arm to me.

I take it gingerly, as if I'm about to wrangle a viper, but when nothing awful happens, I clasp it a little more firmly, and together we step down from the porch.

"I'd like to see where the Indians live," I say.

He pauses, as if considering.

"They do the majority of our labor in the mines, so if I'm to familiarize myself with everything, I need to see them."

He grunts, which is downright loquacious of him, and guides me off to the left, toward the Chinese tents.

The tents are mostly empty. I figure everyone is at work, either in the mine or down by the creek, classifying all the ore being brought out and ground up by the arrastra. But a few folks remain behind. We pass a man hammering at a horseshoe; on a table beside him are more horseshoes, along with pickaxes, all in various states of wear. An older man with white hair and beautifully embroidered trim on his long shirt sits inside an open-faced tent that is filled with glass jars on shelves. Each jar holds something unfamiliar. One contains a bright red plant with spread leaves, another something soft and pink—maybe pigs' feet? He stares at me as we pass, his gaze shameless and appraising.

The older man is the only one who stares. Everyone else becomes deeply involved in their current task, clearly avoiding me.

There are no other women, and there is no sign of Mary.

Beyond the Chinese tents, the land slopes downward toward the creek edged in cottonwoods and willows. A slick, muddy path takes us through the trees and opens up onto the muckiest, sorriest, most godforsaken stretch of water I ever saw.

Thirty or so men are scattered about—Chinese, Indians, and whites—all squatting with pans at the edge or knee-deep in muck with their shovels. The water is thick brown gray, the banks devoid of vegetation. Everything is coated in mud—the miners' pants, the boulders lining the creek, forearms, pans, and even a long wooden rocker. The air smells of swamp and piss.

It's an easy mistake, to dig down into a creek bed without giving the water a place to go. It accumulates, like in a swimming hole, except churned up with dirt and mud, making it nearly impossible to see. And based on the smell, everyone is squatting to do their business in this sorry mudhole of a creek instead of taking it to an outhouse or privy trench where it belongs.

I'm deciding whether or not to have a stern talk with Hiram about this when I notice that all work has ceased. Everyone is looking at me.

"Why are they staring?" I whisper to Wilhelm, before remembering that he never answers back.

I suddenly see myself in their eyes, and I realize I stand out like a goldfinch among starlings. I'm wearing a fancy dress, for starters, with less than a quarter inch of mud on the hem. I'm the only girl in sight, and though I've worked hard my whole life, I don't have the sunken wiry limbs of these men, or wind-weathered skin like a poorly tanned hide.

A burro clatters down the bank, pulling a cart full of crushed ore from the arrastra, which shakes everyone out of their stare and sets them to working again. A strange relief fills me as Wilhelm and I continue on. It's not like I was in any danger. But something about the way they all gawked gave me the wriggles.

Downstream, the water begins to clear as it opens into a broad meadow that was probably once a field of waving golden grass but is now so grazed out it's little more than a flat of mud. They'll eventually mine this whole meadow, once they realize it's a flood plain, where the mountains have been sending the bit of gold they cough up each year during the rains.

The back of my throat buzzes with it, and my limbs tremble a little. Very few nuggets here, but there's plenty of fine dust, just waiting to be discovered. I close my eyes for a moment, savoring. It's nice to feel something so familiar and true out here. With my eyes shut and the breeze on my face and the gold tingling my skin, I can almost imagine I'm back home in Georgia, that I'll open my eyes and it will be Daddy standing next to me instead of the hulking beast of man who never speaks.

But Daddy's not here with me now, nor Mama, nor any of my friends. I'm alone, with only one thing left to me, the thing no one can take away.

I've never needed my gold sense like I need it right now. We don't have a plan to escape, and the one skill I can offer the group that Mary or Muskrat or Tom or Jefferson can't do better is sense gold. If only I could figure out a way to make a plan from that.

I listen with it now, searching. Something lies off to the right. The tiniest nugget, barely the size of my pinky fingernail. It sings to me, clear as a bell, and something in me responds, reaches out to it.

The earth tilts.

My eyes fly open, and I'm suddenly breathless. Something happened just then, though I'm not sure what.

Wilhelm has halted—or maybe I was the one who stopped—and he glares down at me, a question in his eyes.

Did I lose time again? How long was I standing there? I nearly lost my balance, I think. Another moment and I would have tumbled to the ground. It felt like the earth tried to toss me away.

No, it's like the gold feels my need and is trying to answer me. My magic is changing. Becoming more sensitive.

Or maybe I'm imagining things. Wishing, because nothing else is working.

I've never been a fanciful sort of girl, though, and if my daddy were here, I would tell him straight out what happened, and he would listen. Suddenly, more than anything, I want to see Jefferson. No, I *need* to see him, like I need water and air. I need his warm, sympathetic gaze, his softly smiling mouth, his sharp and interesting mind. Together we could figure this, for sure and certain.

Wilhelm tugs on my arm.

"Sorry," I mumble. "My heel caught in the mud."

I yank him forward. Wilhelm's step hitches, but he catches himself quickly. I give him a sidelong glance; I didn't yank that hard.

His scarred lips are pressed thin, his eyes cast determinedly forward, as a blush of pink spreads on his cheeks. Something pains him, and he's embarrassed that I noticed.

We press on toward a large stockade made of logs sticking upright out of the ground and lashed together. It's the sturdiest structure I've seen aside from my uncle's cabin, and my heart quickens. Maybe Peony is there. Maybe I'll finally see my horse.

The log fence is tall, taller even than Wilhelm. We reach a swinging gate, guarded by two sentries with bayoneted rifles. One of them is Jonas Waters, who was Dilley's second-in-command on our journey to California. Jonas ignores me, but he nods to Wilhelm, and he reaches up to unlatch the gate and swing it wide. He smells strongly of rotgut, which is no surprise; Jonas always did love his moonshine.

But the stink of moonshine is nothing compared to the air from inside, which hits my nostrils, forcing me to step back. It's like a stable that hasn't been mucked in months, mixed with the scent of rancid vegetables.

I cover my nose with my hand, though it does little good. My belly quivers.

Wilhelm pulls me forward into the reeking stockade.

Ahead are a few crooked lean-tos, mixed in with some small buildings that seem to be made of mud. There are no horses anywhere, which makes me glad. I don't know what I'd do if I saw Peony being housed in this awful place.

To the right is a trough, filled with muddy rainwater and a few bobbing lumps—potatoes, maybe? At the other end, across the expanse of mud and slop, is a roofed tower. A man stands looking down at us, rifle at the ready.

"Where are the animals?" I say to Wilhelm. "There's no feed here. The lean-tos would only house the smallest burros, and the . . ."

Something catches my eye beside one of the lean-tos. A bit of paleness against the dark mud. I peer closer.

It's flesh colored and scaly, like a molting snake. I step toward it, and tiny flies lift from the ground as my boots squish through the mud. Something is wrong; my belly knows it.

Another step, and suddenly I recognize what I'm looking at. It's a leg, sticking out from behind the lean-to, the foot burrowed in mud.

Why would someone lie down in this muck?

I'm lifting my skirts and running forward, my limbs understanding what my mind is struggling to accept, and sure enough, I round the corner of the lean-to and there's the body, lying on its side, naked and muddy and scaly. It's a young man, though his limp black hair is half fallen out, leaving ragged patches of scalp. A cloud of flies lifts from his face, exposing a pale, open mouth and a filmed-over eye, sunken way too far beneath a delicate brow.

I whirl and make it two strides before all my flapjacks come rushing up my throat and pour out onto the fetid mud. I choke and cough, my eyes tearing from the acid in my throat.

Someone thrusts a kerchief in front of my face. No, it's the napkin, Wilhelm's napkin, the one that contained the flapjacks I gave him.

I grab it and wipe my mouth, spitting once or twice to clear it. "Thank you," I manage. Then I wince at my words because it seems like the deepest, nastiest wrong to thank an awful man for a napkin when an innocent person lies dead beside us, probably poisoned and starved to death.

Jonas Waters has followed us inside. He's as bearded and sun blasted as any of my uncle's men, and he has nothing but frowns for me.

"Why haven't you removed that body?" I demand. "Why haven't you seen to his burial?"

Jonas shrugs. "It'll keep."

I gape at him.

"Tonight, when they get back from the mines, we'll let 'em tidy up a bit."

I glance around the stockade, seeing it with new eyes. So this is where the Indians live. I didn't think I had any more breakfast to give up, but suddenly I'm not so sure. It's more like a giant pigpen. A pigpen for humans.

Along the far wall are a few huddled lumps. I didn't notice them before because they're covered in mud, possibly on purpose for warmth and protection, because not one has a stitch of clothing. One is a very old woman. Another is a younger woman nursing a baby. A few children crouch beside her.

"No one should live like this," I say.

"We give 'em food," Jonas says with another shrug. "Safety. It's more than they'd get on their own."

I peer at his bushy face. He can't be serious. The Indians we saw near Glory seemed perfectly healthy and safe, much better off than the ones here. "What will they do with the body?" I ask.

"There's a pit outside. Every two or three days, we let 'em dump their trash there."

I open my mouth to protest, but nothing comes out. It's too awful for words.

This is what Muskrat wanted me to see. This is the kind of man my uncle is.

One of the tiny children shifts listlessly, and a cloud of bugs lifts away, swirls a bit, and settles back down on his muddy skin.

Suddenly my feet are pounding through the mud toward the entrance and I'm banging, banging, banging on the huge swinging doors and yelling at the sentry to let me out and finally he does and I half run, half fall out of the stockade into cleaner air.

Chapter Seventeen

I bend over, my hands on my knees, and suck in breaths, trying not to vomit again. My skirt is filthy now, at least six inches deep in mud. Which terrifies me. What will my uncle do when he sees that I've ruined the hem of the dress he so painstakingly created to remind him of my mama?

A tiny whimper bleeds from my lips. I'm a horrible person. More horrible than Frank Dilley. Because after seeing that awful pigpen for people, I'm still terrified for myself.

Peony. I need my horse. Or Jefferson, but he's working in the mines right now. So Peony it is.

I stand up straight and take a deep breath as the stockade doors swing shut behind me. I hear the latch slide home as I face Wilhelm and say, "Thank you for bringing me here. Next, I'd like to see where we keep all our stock."

Once again, Wilhelm offers me his arm, and this time I take it without hesitation. He leads me beyond the stockade, past a large pit I choose not to look at, toward a large stand of cottonwoods hugging a steep slope. With a start, I realize exactly where we are. Up that slope beyond the cottonwoods is my uncle's cabin, and we've circled around behind it.

If I ever tried to escape through those trees, this is where I'd end up. I remember thinking the cottonwoods and steep slope might indicate water, and sure enough, a few steps later we come across the creek again, which has curved back into the meadow before disappearing into a tree line of scrub oak and stunted pines.

That creek might be our way out. It leads into California's big valley, for sure and certain.

We follow the creek a ways. The earth here is a little less churned up, with clumps of stubborn grass poking up here and there. Deer visit this creek to drink at night; I see pebbly scat and forked hoofprints at regular intervals.

The land slopes sharply downward, and there it is. A large, muddy corral stretching across both creek banks. It's guarded by several rough-looking men, and inside are a few mules, a handful of burros, and even some horses.

"Peony?" I call out, wrenching my arm away from Wilhelm. I lift my skirts and dash forward. "Peony!"

"Whoa, there, little lady, just where are you going?" someone says, but I don't care because there she is, standing tall and proud, ears pricked forward at the sound of my voice.

I climb over the low fence, and my skirt or petticoats catch on something, but I rip right through, and for a split second I think, *My uncle is going to kill me,* but then it doesn't matter because Peony has closed the distance between us. I throw my arms around her neck, my fingers snagging in her bright blond mane. She whuffles into my hair, and then she's head butting my ear and snorting and swishing her tail like she's being attacked by flies.

She's madder than a hornet and glad to see me all at once, and I don't blame her one bit.

"I'm so sorry, girl," I tell her. "It wasn't my choice for them to take you away."

"Hey, that's Topper's horse!" someone says as a hand grabs my elbow with the hardness and strength of a farrier's tongs.

Peony is my horse, and she always will be, and somehow, we're going to get away from this awful place together. But I know better than to say so aloud.

"She was my horse before she belonged to Topper," I say to the man on watch. "Just wanted to check on her. Make sure Topper was treating her right."

The man adjusts his holster. He carries a Colt, like everyone else, and it was half drawn before he realized I meant no harm. "Abel Topper treats that pretty palomino like she's the Queen of England," he says. "Comes by regular to give her treats and brush her down. Tried to get her housed in the stable with the rest of our finer stock, but Mr. Westfall wouldn't have it."

My shoulders slump a little with relief. I miss Peony something fierce, but maybe I don't need to worry about her. I know why my uncle refused to stable her, though. The stable is too close to the cabin. It would be easy for me to sneak out and ride off into the night. In fact, now that I look around, I recognize Sorry and Apollo, too. My uncle must have moved them here for the same reason.

I stroke Peony's neck and murmur at her until she calms. Then I run my hands down her legs, testing for soundness, pick up her hooves and scoop out the mud with a forefinger so I can check the frogs of her feet.

"Her front shoes are getting worn," I point out.

The man with the Colt gives me a strange look. "Never seen a wee gal so taken with a horse," he says. "You're willing to get muddied up for her and everything."

"Not a lot of wee gals in these parts for comparison," I point out.

"That's God's truth," he says with a despairing sigh.

"You'll mention the worn shoes to Topper?" I say.

"I'll mention it."

"Say you noticed all by yourself," I tell him. "Please. He won't listen if knew it came from a wee gal."

He chews on this a moment, but then he says, "All right."

I linger over Peony as long as they'll let me, but all too soon Wilhelm tugs on my arm. "Good-bye, sweet girl. I'll try to visit again soon."

This time I don't have to climb over the fence. Wilhelm and the guard lift a post so I can step over easily, then we head back toward the camp.

My mind churns over everything I just learned. The Indians are kept in the worst squalor I've ever seen, and I have to confront my uncle about it. I have to. Otherwise they won't live long enough for Muskrat to help them escape.

Making plans, escaping, all of it will be near impossible if

Hiram keeps me tied up at night. Either I need to convince him to trust me again—and quickly—or I need to find a knife to smuggle into my bedroom.

Wouldn't hurt to figure out what he did with my guns, too. Or maybe I can steal one. It seems everyone is carrying a Colt these days. I'm not well practiced with a Colt, but I've shot Jefferson's a few times. It's its own beast, but maybe it's familiar enough that I could be dangerous at close range.

And once I do escape, Peony will be right here, down the slope from my uncle's cabin and through the trees, waiting for me. She might even be freshly shod.

How well guarded is this corral? I glance back over my shoulder as Wilhelm and I walk away. I see the man who promised to tell Abel Topper about Peony's shoes, along with three others, all evenly spread. Each one carries at least one gun. Two carry both a revolver and a rifle.

I have to assume the place will be equally well guarded at night.

Someone saw me leave the cabin when I snuck out to meet Jefferson. Which means that even when Wilhelm is not outside standing sentry, the cabin is watched. It's probably watched by a lot of people. My uncle may be a no-good son of a hairy goat, but he's not stupid.

So that's why Mary and Muskrat are trying to come up with a distraction for the thanksgiving celebration. Something so huge that no one will be watching the cabin or the stockade or the corral.

You should see, Muskrat said.

I've seen just as much as a body can take today, but somehow,

I have to do more. I need to find out where Jefferson and Tom sleep at night and learn exactly how they managed to sneak off. I need to start saving food for a journey; maybe Mary can help with this. And we need to figure out some sort of distraction.

A long, loud distraction. If the Indians I saw in the mine and in the stockade are any indication, none of them are fit for making a run for it. So we'll need mounts. Lots of mounts. And maybe something to slow down pursuers.

I stumble in my tracks as the thought hits, but Wilhelm's iron grip keeps me from falling.

Escaping won't be enough.

My uncle will try again. He'll either hunt us all down and round us up, or he'll just find more people to work his mine. I swore to end him after Dilley burned Glory to the ground, but bluster won't get the job done. We have to destroy him for real, and soon.

I'm back inside the cabin, having a bit of much-needed dinner. After vomiting up all my breakfast, I'm hungry as a bear. Fortunately Mary left some buttermilk biscuits on the table, along with a jar of apple butter, and I eat three biscuits in quick succession, thinking about anything except what I saw in the stockade.

When my belly is full, I want nothing more than to curl up on my bed, quilt over my head, but I know it for a foolishness at once. As if a quilt could keep the world out or make my mind stop churning.

So I wipe my mouth with a napkin and sit up straight on my stool and think harder than I've ever thought.

To destroy my uncle, I probably have to kill him.

The thought has crossed my mind before. About him, Frank Dilley, Abel Topper. But that was just impulse. This is cold calculation.

It would be murder, plain and simple. I've killed plenty of living creatures, sure, and every single one would have preferred to go on living, thank you very much. But I've never killed a man. And I've never killed something just because it was hateful and dangerous.

My daddy did, once. Not a man, but a bear. It was prowling the hills around Dahlonega, breaking into cabins and making a horrible mess of things. It had developed a taste for salted pork, apparently, but one day it burst into a cabin and suddenly developed a taste for old Benjamin Dalton, too. The bear had to die. It was a menace. So my daddy shot him.

I'm not sure whether killing my uncle is the same as putting down that bear, or not. Hiram is a menace, for sure and certain. What would my daddy say if he knew what I was thinking now? That his own daughter was contemplating coldblooded murder?

He'd probably be shocked and appalled. *No daughter of mine is a murderer. You're a smart girl. You can figure this. Find another solution.*

But maybe he'd cheer me on.

Take him out, sweet pea. He killed me first.

If I were to do this awful thing, I'd need a weapon. A gun

would bring everyone running so fast I'd never get away. But maybe getting away isn't my priority. Stopping my uncle is.

A knife is a quieter way. And a more intimate one. I'd have to get close. Close enough that he could hurt me if I wasn't swift and silent.

Maybe I could steal some laudanum. Frank Dilley still has some, and maybe Wilhelm. Could I sneak it into my uncle's food? The taste is strong. I'd have to be very careful.

I lurch up from the table and start pacing out of frustration.

None of these options is a good one, but even if they were, there's still the problem of getting my hands on one of these items.

Then again, jumping into the fray without knowing the whole plan might just muck everything up. Muskrat and Mary seem pretty capable. Maybe I should sit tight and trust them to figure everything out.

But I can't help feeling that Hiram Westfall is my responsibility. And it's up to me to make sure he doesn't hurt anyone else ever again.

Chapter Eighteen

The door creaks open, and I freeze midstep. My uncle enters with a rush of cold air.

"Hello, sweet pea," he says. He carries a large package wrapped in twine beneath one arm, which he sets down just inside the door.

"Uncle."

He whips off his gloves and places them on top of the package. "Have you been to the mine yet today?"

"Not yet." I hide my hands behind my back, the ones that have been contemplating murder, as if hiding them can hide my intentions.

"I want you to visit *every day*. Make sure the boys are going in the right dir—" His gaze drifts down to my muddy, ragged hem, and his face becomes so dark it puts a chill in my throat. "What happened to your dress?"

I swallow. "I had Wilhelm take me on a tour of the south fields. It was very muddy."

"That's not a place for a young lady."

"You said to familiarize myself with our operation. I'm still familiarizing. It's a big, complicated place, and you can't expect me to take it all in at one go."

He removes his hat and hangs it on its peg by the door. "You wanted to see that horse."

No sense lying about that. "Well, yes, that too. I raised her from a foal. Wanted to make sure Abel Topper was taking care of her."

"And if he wasn't? What then, Leah?"

I would have gutted that worthless worm. "Well, I suppose I would have told you about it, hoping you'd have a word with him."

"A man doesn't interfere with how another man handles what's his."

"Seems to me men don't always do a good job handling what's theirs."

His eyes flash with anger, and I almost take a step back. "That's his business," he says. "A man ought to be sovereign in his house, even if his house is only a horse, a woman, and a gun."

My molars grind together so hard it makes my jaw ache. Jefferson got beaten by his da all the time because no one would interfere. Mrs. Lowrey died giving birth because everyone refused to interfere. And no one in Dahlonega dared interfere when my parents were murdered and a strange man rode into town claiming their homestead and me along with it.

Well, I'm going to interfere. I'm going to interfere plenty.

"Visit the mine," my uncle orders. "The gold's not coming up fast enough. We need more, and soon."

"All right."

"Speaking of . . . odd thing happened."

My heart pounds a little faster, even though I'm not sure what he's going to say. "The foremen blasted forward into the rock, like you suggested. They found almost nothing. But the blast impact carved out a bit more than expected of the west wall. And wouldn't you know but the vein picked up right there, exactly where you *didn't* tell them to go."

My heart is pounding in earnest now. "I . . . well . . . sometimes my sense of things is foggy where there's so much gold to be had."

Two swift strides is all it takes for him to close the distance between us. His hand darts out and cups my chin, raising my face to meet his gaze. His thumb and forefinger bore into my jaw as he says, "Don't ever do that again."

"I . . . Okay."

"Your friends Bigler and McCauley are going to be mighty hungry tonight on account of missing supper. A second time, and hunger will be the least of their worries."

His grip on my jaw is so tight and my frustration and anger so great that a single blasted tear leaks from my right eye. Judas tear, betrayer tear. "I'll . . . I'll do better."

Hiram releases me all at once, and I stumble backward. "That's my girl," he says. "I have some more errands to run, but I'll be back later to make sure you visited the mine. Also, there will be no visiting your friends today. You may see them again after you've been on good behavior."

My back is against the cabin wall now, and I take a bit of strength in its solidness. "Where did you go this morning?" I ask. He's always off on some errand or other, but it doesn't seem like there's all that much business to attend to in this wilderness.

"Why do you ask?"

"I'm showing an interest." I swallow hard, but I'm not sure if it's my pride or my reservations. "I'm trying to be the young lady you expect me to be."

"In that case, I visited Don Antonio de Solá, a ranchero just west of here. He owns one of the largest ranchos in California. We need financing to expand our operation, and he needs more able-bodied laborers. We might come to an agreement."

I chew on that a moment. If this ranchero has so much money and needs able-bodied laborers, why doesn't he just hire more?

"You don't have laborers to spare," I point out. "Not if you want to expand operations."

"We don't. We'd have to fetch some more."

"How would we . . . Oh." He's talking about the Indians. He plans to send Dilley and his men to round them up. *No,* I correct myself. He plans to send Dilley and his men to *kidnap* them.

I suspect I *do* know what my daddy would say. *It's okay to put down a bear if it's a man-eater.*

"That package is for you," my uncle says, pointing to the bundle at the door. "You'll begin wearing them immediately.

And after you visit the mine today, you will launder that dress."

"Yes, Uncle," I say meekly.

I can't stand to be in his company a moment more. I grab the package and take it to my bedroom.

I'm not surprised to open it and find a new pair of lady's boots. They are elegant and beautiful, with shiny brass eyelets, silk laces in soft blue, and a tiny rosette sculpted in leather at each toe. I am surprised, however, at how practical and sturdy they seem. They're made of stiff black leather, polished to shine, and the heel is a little less dainty than necessarily fashionable. They're the farthest thing from the perfect, flimsy silk things Annabelle Smith back home used to wear. In fact, they're perfect for a girl who might encounter a little mud or even hop onto a horse.

It's a thoughtful and wonderful gift, and my skin crawls to think of donning them.

I've worn nothing but Daddy's too-large boots for almost a year now. It's the only thing of his I have left. I won't give them up. I won't.

But there's no telling what my uncle will do if I don't wear the new ones.

A smile tugs at my mouth. I know just what to do.

Quickly I shuck Daddy's boots and retrieve the small bag of gold stashed in the toe. I shove it under my mattress. Not the best hiding place, but it will keep for a short while.

I slip on the new boots. They're stiff, and they pinch my toes together, but I've no doubt they'll fit perfectly once broken in.

Strange how my uncle could estimate my shoe size so easily. Did he measure me in my sleep? I don't remember him ever staring at my feet.

I lace up the boots and head back into the main room. Hiram is sitting at the table, eating dinner while penning a note. He looks up when I enter.

"Thank you for the boots," I say.

His smile is as wide and kind and generous as I've ever seen. "They're perfect on you!" he says. "Once you get that hem cleaned up, you'll be as proper as they come."

I can't stand to play at niceness even one second more. "I'm off to the mine," I tell him, heading for the door. "See you later." And I swing the door wide, dart outside, and shut it behind me before he can respond.

Wilhelm is standing sentry as usual.

"Mr. Westfall wishes me to pay a visit to the mine," I say.

It's possible I'm mistaken, but the look he gives me seems commiserative. He offers his arm, and off we go.

Frank Dilley and several of his men are sitting in the alcove near the barrels of sugar water, playing cards. I frown. Seems to me that if we need to bring more gold out of this mine, there are plenty of able-bodied men right here who could get to work.

"Miss Westfall," Frank says, with a tip of his hat, and the deference startles me. I can't remember the last time he addressed me without making fun of me for dressing like a boy.

But his jaw is tight and his eyes mean. He doesn't like being forced to pay me any respect.

"Dilley," I say. "My uncle wants me to have a look at the Drink today."

I don't want to go back down there. Just stepping inside this dark, musty place makes me think of that poor man, the one who practically got his head blown off right before my eyes. But I have to do this. I have to.

Frank Dilley shrugs. "Whatever the boss says."

But he doesn't want to leave his card game, so Wilhelm and I continue alone.

This time, I know the way, so I lead us down the dank, slippery passage. The air moves constantly, almost like a breeze, and the lanterns lining the low ceiling sway and bob, making moving patterns of light along the walls and floor.

The sounds of splashing and clanging pickaxes grow louder as we near the tunnel's end. We skirt a cart, half full with sopping-wet ore, and its bored burro whose ears twitch irritably at every sound, and then the tunnel opens wide into the hollowed-out cavern. I stop when the toes of my new boots meet the water's edge.

I glance around for Jefferson or Tom or Muskrat. There are people everywhere, soaked and naked. Abel Topper stands shadowed in an alcove, whip held ready. "My uncle wishes me to do a thorough inspection," I call out to him, and he nods.

And I don't even bother to lift my skirts before I wade right into the muck, new boots and all.

I make a show of examining everything—the ceiling, the walls, a lone pickax leaning against a rock, its wooden haft split from so much constant moisture. Gold tingles in the back of my throat. There's plenty of it down here, but they'll have to do something about this water to reach it.

Wilhelm has waded in after me; in this gloomy place, his giant form feels like a huge shadow looming over my shoulder. I have to figure out a way to distract him.

I let my witchy sense pull me forward, toward the westernmost wall. At least I think it's the westernmost; it's so easy to get turned around down here. It's an area of the mine that's been much neglected—Topper seems to be focusing the miners in a different direction—and only one man is working it, doggedly attacking it with a pickax. His strikes are strong and quick, even though his body is thinner than a deer in a drought.

He hears me sloshing through the water and turns. It's Muskrat.

I thought he didn't work in the mines. Something has changed. Maybe my uncle has become suspicious. But I dare not ask my questions in front of Wilhelm.

Pretending nothing is amiss, I put my hand to the wall and close my eyes.

This bit of rock was laid down by flooding water, maybe over thousands of years, and it's riddled with gold—it glitters bright in my mind, like endless stars against a dark velvet night. But beyond that is a vein, a river of honey sweetness, singing as loud and clear as an oriole.

It's the first nice thing I've felt all day, and I wrap my thoughts around it, embrace it, let its shiver flow deep inside me.

The wall vibrates, fast and soft like hummingbird wings.

I lurch back as if bitten, and I hold up the palm of my hand and stare at it. The meager lantern light casts yellow warmth onto my skin, with occasional shifting shadows, so that it almost appears my hand is on fire.

What just happened? It's like I placed my hand on the wall, and when the gold spoke to me, I spoke back. It wasn't my witchy senses making it *seem* like the wall vibrated. It really moved.

I made the wall move.

Behind me, Wilhelm grunts. Muskrat waits, patient and tense. If Topper catches him idle, he might be whipped, even though he's just being courteous to me.

I've stood here too long, and I need to get moving. I'll figure out this gold business later.

"Wilhelm," I say.

He regards me expectantly. The shadows snag on his scar, making it seem as though he sneers.

"Fetch Abel Topper for me, please. We need to discuss this section of the mine."

Wilhelm frowns.

"And please hurry," I say brazenly. "I need to get him back on track." I return my hand to the wall and pretend to continue my inspection, peering at the rough rock as though my eyes could possibly tell me something I don't already know.

This time, when the siren call of gold invades my senses, I ignore it, tamp it down, tell it to go drown itself in a creek. Because I have other things to focus on right now.

Wilhelm hesitates only a moment more, then reluctantly backs away, splashing through the water toward Topper and his whip.

Once he's a safe distance, I whisper, "Muskrat, you were right. I saw. And I will do everything I can."

He says nothing.

"Why are you here?" I ask. "I thought you were an interpreter."

He hammers at the wall with his pickax. "Westfall," he says between blows. "Insists I take Ezra's place. The man who was killed."

"Ezra," I whisper, because I want to lodge the name in my mind forever.

A tiny nod, almost imperceptible. "We met at the mission. He helped teach me English. He . . ." A chunk of rock falls from the wall and splashes into the water. Muskrat reaches for it and heaves it dripping into a nearby cart, where it clatters around loudly before settling. "And now, I will make sure Ezra's grandchildren leave this place alive."

"Do you have a plan yet?"

"Almost. Do whatever Mary tells you."

I'm about to ask Muskrat if he has a family, too, but Topper and Wilhelm come splashing toward me. Their movement waves the water above my knees. My dress—and my new boots—are well and truly ruined.

"Miss Westfall, I've work to do down here," Topper says as Muskrat attacks the wall with his pickax, ignoring us. "We haven't met quota yet and—"

"There's gold to be had here," I say, indicating the wall. "This is the spot my daddy would have picked." Everyone from Lumpkin County back home has heard of my daddy—Reuben "Lucky" Westfall—and his uncanny ability to find gold where there was none. Of course, hardly anyone knew it was really me doing the finding.

"You being sure, girl?" Topper says with a frown.

"I'd bet my mare on it."

"*My* mare."

"I'd bet your mare on it, too."

Topper rubs at his gray-brown beard, gone curly now with a bit of length. Like just about everyone I know, the trip west aged him about ten years. "All right," he says finally. "We'll give it a try. But if we don't find anything, your uncle will hear tell."

I smile. "No worries on that account, Mr. Topper. I'm going to tell him at supper tonight that you changed direction on my orders. There'll be no one to blame but me." And no one to take credit but me, when they find a whole heap of gold.

Topper blinks. "Your *orders*?"

"This is a Westfall mine, is it not?"

"I guess."

"Then you'd better get to work. I'll return tomorrow to check your progress."

Before he can say another word, I gather my sopping skirts, gesture at Wilhelm to follow, and wade through the mine toward the exit tunnel.

My limbs are shaky as we head up the steep slope. I hope

I've done the right thing. Creating urgency might encourage Topper to use that whip. But finding gold makes me valuable. Someone who might be listened to. Someone who might be able to help Mary and Muskrat with their mysterious plan.

When we've climbed high enough to reach the fork, I gaze into the dark Joyner tunnel. Jefferson and Tom are probably there, since I didn't see them down in the Drink, and I'd just about give my left pinky to pay them a visit, if only to assure myself that they're okay. But I've already pushed my luck today. If I went against my uncle's orders and visited my friends, there'd be hell to pay.

Reluctantly I turn my back on the upper tunnel and continue, past Frank and the foremen in their break area, and out into the sunshine.

I pause a moment, breathing deep of the cold, fresh air. This mine is tiny compared to the mines in Dahlonega, too new to be deeply excavated. How did people do it? How did they spend day in and day out, so deep inside an earth that could swallow them whole at any moment?

My legs take on a chill as a breeze flutters my soaked skirt and my drenched boots. We near the arrastra, and my heart leaps. Jefferson is there, dumping ore from a cart so it can be ground up.

His sleeves are filthy and rolled up to the elbows, and his forehead is streaked from constantly wiping his growing hair from his brow. In spite of the autumn cold, sweat sheens his forehead, and his hair sticks curled to the nape of his neck.

I study him carefully, looking for any kind of hurt, but there are no new visible wounds. I've taken a step toward him without realizing it, and he looks up. Our eyes meet, and his face breaks into a smile that's like the sun rising over the Sierras.

I can't help it; I pick up my water-heavy skirts and hurry toward him. Wilhelm's heavy boot steps pound to keep up, but I don't care. I have to see Jefferson. I have to talk to him.

Jefferson is not alone. There's no sign of Tom, but two Chinese men coax the burros along as they go round and round, crushing ore. Another is shoveling the crushed ore into a different cart, to be hauled down to the creek for classifying and panning. Standing on a crate overlooking the whole process is a dark-skinned man with black hair, a mean rifle, and the widest-brimmed hat I've ever seen. Borrowed from the rancho my uncle mentioned, if I don't miss my guess.

"Hello, Miss Westfall," Jefferson says as I approach. He doesn't pause in his shoveling, but a smile still quirks his mouth.

"Mr. Kingfisher," I reply, just as formally. I stop well short, keeping a solid distance between us. "My uncle has asked me to familiarize myself with our operation." I say it too loudly, for the benefit of whoever is watching and listening.

"In that case, are there any questions I can answer for you?" Jefferson says as the foreman steps down from his crate and ambles toward us, hefting his rifle.

All the things I shouldn't ask in front of everyone else tumble through my mind. *Did they hurt you again? Are they treating you right? Where is Tom? How did you sneak out last night?*

When will we meet next? Do you have any idea how much I miss seeing you and talking to you all day long?

"I thought you were working the mine," I say finally.

"Dilley didn't want me fraternizing with the diggers. So I got reassigned." He says it like he's spitting venom. Jefferson hates Dilley worse than anyone, even me.

I'm about to say I'm glad he's out of that awful place, absorbing fresh air and sunshine, but I realize that maybe Jefferson wanted to work the mine. Maybe Dilley is smarter than I've been giving him credit for, and he knows that to keep people in line, he has to prevent them from talking to each other.

"Wilhelm here took me on a tour of the entire camp this morning," I say carefully. "I learned a great deal about this venture, as my uncle requested."

Jefferson's shoveling hitches a little. It's not quite a pause, but I know he takes my meaning.

"That's good," he says, his voice flat as a flapjack. "Mr. Westfall will be happy to know you've taken his desires to heart."

"I think so."

"He cares for you, in his way. That's important." This time he does pause, his shovel hovering in the air. "A man will do just about anything for the woman he cares about."

The foreman closes the distance between us. "Señorita Westfall," he says with a soft Spanish accent, tipping his wide hat. "These men must be to doing their work."

I force a smile. "Of course, sir. I just wanted to observe for a moment."

Leaving Jefferson is the last thing I want to do, but I must. I give him one long last look, my eyes roving him from head to toe. I save it up in my mind, the way he stands so strong in spite of everything that's happened, the determined way he attacks the ore with his shovel.

I grab Wilhelm's arm. Walking away feels like scooping out my heart with a shovel and dumping it in the arrastra to be crushed into dust.

Chapter Nineteen

Hiram has not left yet; he's at his desk, still working on correspondence, when I return. He looks up as I enter. A smear of ink streaks his cheek.

"I ran into Jefferson!" I blurt. "It was an accident. But I kept my distance and left almost immediately. I didn't mean to disobey."

"Leah . . ." His gaze falls to my ruined skirt. He shoots up from the chair and covers the distance in two strides. He grabs my upper arms and shakes me so that my teeth rattle. He can't stop staring at the skirt. Anguish pulls at his features. "What have you done?"

"I went to the Drink, and—"

He shakes me again. "The dress. My . . . Your dress. And . . ." He grabs my skirts and lifts them, which makes me feel like I'm naked before him. "Your new shoes are ruined."

His eyes on my exposed stockings make my skin crawl.

"I had to," I say. "I *had* to. I sensed gold, and I had to wade through the Drink to find it. To be sure."

Hiram's jaw twitches. He drops my skirt, to my great relief, and his grip on my upper arm relaxes a fraction. He takes a deep breath. "You found gold?" he manages. His voice is shaky, and I can't believe a ruined dress would cause him such pain.

"Uncle, I suspect I found a great deal."

Finally he lets my arm go. He takes a step back, rubs at his jaw, the back of his head. "Good. That's good."

"I told Topper where to dig next. They'll see a little bit of color today, but by evening tomorrow, they'll find a large vein."

He is silent in the space before me. Then: "I hope so. For your sake."

And suddenly I'm doubting myself. What if there's nothing? What if I imagined it? Will he hurt the Indians if the vein doesn't pan out? Or me? Or worst of all, Jefferson?

No, I know what I sensed. I know it. And I didn't just sense it. I talked to it. I commanded the gold to move, and it did. It was almost like a dog on a leash, straining toward me.

"You'll see," I tell him, chin lifted high. "You're going to be a very rich man."

And I must have chosen the exact, most perfect words, because his shoulders relax and his gaze softens. "I'm glad to hear it, sweet pea."

I think I've pleased him, but that night, after supper, he keeps to his word. He takes up a rope with one hand, grabs me by the wrist with the other, and drags me into my bedroom.

"What are you doing?"

He pushes me down on the bed. "It's just temporary, sweet pea. Until I know I can trust you."

"You can trust me!"

He ties my wrists to the bedpost. Everything in me wants to kick out at him, to scream and thrash, but I think of how he threatened Jefferson, and I submit meekly. It feels like the worst thing I've ever done.

He ties my ankles to the other end so that I'm forced to remain stretched out on the bed. It's a clever bit of work. There's no way I can reach the ropes to untie myself.

He leans down, his neatly trimmed beard tickling my neck.

"Good night, love," he says, and he kisses my cheek, near to my earlobe.

Somehow, this kiss is the worst of all. I watch him depart, staring daggers of hate at his back. I won't complain, though. Other folks in this camp are a lot worse off than me.

The gold buzzes at me from its hiding place beneath my mattress. I'll put it back in the toe of my boot as soon as I'm able, but for now, I let it surround me, comfort me. By morning, my tears have dried. My neck is cricked, my flesh rubbed raw with rope burn, and my heart determined.

I've spent the last week being on my best behavior. I worked hard to launder my dress, and though the hem is well and truly ruined, I succeeded in getting out the worst stains and making it somewhat presentable for daily work. I've visited the mine every day, giving advice on exactly where to dig. The miners have brought up more gold in the past few days than in the entire previous two months combined. Dilley, Topper, and the other foremen think I'm lucky.

I haven't complained once about how thin Jefferson is becoming, how badly my wrists smart from the rope burns, or that the foremen laze around all day, watching the starving, mercury-sick Indians do all the work. I haven't once mentioned the fact that Dilley's men are polite to my face, even friendly, but they ogle me as soon as my back is turned, and I feel their eyes crawling all over my body like flies.

I itch to *do* something, anything, but I know that biding my time is the right thing. Destroying my uncle is a long hunt, with lots of tiny, quiet moves leading up to the big kill.

I know long hunts. I am patient. I am a ghost.

A ghost who sees things. My angelic behavior has earned me knowledge. *Listen,* Muskrat said. *Watch.* And that's exactly what I've done.

I've learned that all the guns are kept in the foremen's barracks, which makes sense. Aside from my uncle's cabin, it's the driest place in camp. I bet my guns are there, too.

I see Mary every day in Hiram's cabin, and sometimes I pass Muskrat on his way to the mines, but I say nothing to either of them. A hunting ghost takes no chances.

I look for Tom, who is absent from the camp, and discover that he has been assigned to the creek, along with most of the Chinese workers and several of the Indian women. He pans for gold from sunup until sundown, and I know from experience how that makes for a brutal day, but not so brutal as hefting a pickax in the cold, wet dark. Knowing Tom, he smoothly talked himself into such a prime assignment.

Muskrat said things are coming together. And I have faith in him and Mary and the others; I do. Still, I know I'll feel a lot better if I have my own weapon to use against Uncle Hiram.

So, one morning after my uncle leaves, I tiptoe over to his writing desk. The drawer slides open with a scraping noise so loud I'm sure it can be heard east of the Mississippi. I hope to find his letter opener, or something sharp, but he's too smart to leave something like that lying around. All I find are several folded letters and a small book bound in leather.

The leather book is a ledger, containing rows of numbers and notations. Mathematics has never been my strong suit, so it takes a while for me to makes sense of the mess. We're bringing out a lot of gold, if this ledger is any indication. But there are too many entries in the expenses column: more materials for a proper cart track for the tunnels, more gunpowder, more pickaxes, more burros—even a few luxury items like the washtub I bathed in on that first day, an extra box stove, a set of fine dishes.

There's a number on the bottom right of each page that changes with that page's entries. On the first page, it's eight thousand dollars. A month later, that number has shrunk to three thousand. But lately, it has crept back up to more than four thousand dollars.

I was right. Uncle Hiram owes someone money. A whole heap of it.

Hiram's only focus—no, obsession—is to bring out more gold. And he'll spend whatever he must in order to do it. Mama used to say that the fever made idiots of grown men, and she always said it like she knew from experience.

I rifle through the letters. Most are from Sacramento and San Francisco. Many of them have to do with supplies; turns out Hiram does a good deal of negotiation by correspondence. But one name crops up over and over again, and I skim all the letters from this one man as quickly as I can, until I find the most recent.

Thank you for the detailed notes on your progress. Your request is granted, and I've instructed my attorney to amend your note. It shall come due on Christmas Eve. This is the last extension I will approve. If your debt is not paid in full on that day, the mine, its surrounding acreage, and all its assets will be repossessed.

Yours truly,

James Henry Hardwick

I stare at it a long moment. This is not the weapon I was looking for, but it is definitely a weapon. I finally have a name. I say it over and over in my mind so I won't forget. *James Henry Hardwick. James Henry Hardwick.* This is the man my uncle owes. This is a man who has power over Hiram Westfall.

Chapter Twenty

Later, I return from the mine and discover my uncle waiting for me in the cabin. The air smells sweetly of tobacco, and he blows smoke from his pipe as I enter. On the dining table are two large packages.

"For you," he says with a soft smile.

My hackles instantly go up, but I sound as cool as ever when I say, "There's nothing I need, Uncle."

"Allow me to spoil you, sweet pea."

He needs to be paying down his debt, not buying presents. I approach the table slowly, like the packages are animals caught in a trap, waiting for me to come within range of their teeth.

Gingerly, I open the smallest. I gasp.

My uncle grins around his pipe, but my gasp was not a happy one. Inside the package is another dress. Another dress exactly like the one I'm wearing, with blue calico and lace-trimmed sleeves.

"You should continue to wear the old one when you visit the mine and the creek," he says in a perfectly reasonable tone. "But I want you to look well-groomed and lovely at all other times."

My stomach curls in on itself. "Why?" I whisper.

"Because any girl of mine will be dressed properly, as befits her status as a—"

"No. I mean, why this dress? Why do you want me to look just like my mother?"

I know it's a mistake as soon as the words leave my mouth, because his eyes are suddenly as dark and threatening as storm clouds. "Your mother was a lovely woman," he says coldly. "You should be proud to look like her."

"Why do you have a picture of her on your dresser?"

Another mistake, and I wish I could put up a dam to keep the words I'm thinking from flowing out of my mouth, but a strange, desperate fear has gripped me so hard that I don't think I could do it for all the gold in California.

He slams his pipe down on the table. "You've been in my room."

"Just . . . once . . . to clean. I was sweeping that day. I haven't gone back in since." That last part, at least, is true.

He says nothing. We stare at each other a long moment.

"Open the other package," he says.

My fingers tremble as I untie the twine and fold aside the paper to reveal another pair of women's boots, even fancier than the last, with little cuffs of lace folding over the ankles.

"I've commissioned a gown also," he adds. "It will take time to finish, but there will be a Christmas ball in Sacramento, the first ball to be held in the goldfields. It's imperative that you look your best, for I expect it to be well attended. I plan on making several good connections there."

I stare down at the shoes. They are the silliest things I've ever seen. I couldn't make it from here to the outhouse without ruining them.

"Leah?"

"You didn't answer my question. About my mother."

Hiram pauses, as if deciding something. Finally he slides onto the bench and gestures me to sit.

I do, folding my hands carefully in my lap to hide their trembling.

"Your mother was very special to me," he begins.

"I know," I admit. "Free Jim told me you were sweet on her. Everyone was surprised when she went and married my daddy instead of you."

His fist comes down hard on the table. "We were sweet on *each other*!"

I flinch back. "Yes. Of course. That's what I meant."

Some of the fight bleeds out of him, and he says, "No one was more surprised than I. Elizabeth and I were engaged. Then one morning I went into town and learned that she and Reuben had tied the knot, all secretive."

His gaze becomes distant. "That was the worst time of my life, you know. I've never felt so betrayed. So . . ." He swallows hard. "So lonely. My brother stole the woman I loved right out from under me."

This part I knew, but it still doesn't explain why he's dressing me to look like her. Or why he killed them both. I keep my voice neutral when I ask, "Why did Daddy do it, do you think?"

He frowns. "I wish you'd stop talking about him."

"Why? So you'll stop feeling guilty for murdering him?"

He stares at me, neither in shock nor rage, but like a bookkeeper adding up a column of numbers. He retrieves his pipe and takes a good long puff. I expect he's working himself up to deny everything, but what he says is: "He deserved it."

I gape at him.

The vision appears unbidden in my head: my daddy lying on the steps, his blood staining the wood, his face frozen in surprise.

"He took everything from me," my uncle continues. "Everything!" His fist pounds the table again, and the corner of his mouth gleams with wetness.

"Just because Mama chose to marry him—"

"He took my woman, my land, and you. Even you."

"What in tarnation are you going on about?" Tears are leaking from my eyes now. They're born of anger and frustration and a whole heap of grief that I mistakenly thought had faded to a tiny tickle in the back of my head. But in this moment, facing down my deranged uncle, I miss Mama and Daddy more than anything.

"Don't you see, Leah? Haven't you figured it out? Reuben always said you were a smart girl, but—"

"For heaven's sake, Uncle Hiram, just spit out whatever's on your mind."

"You're mine. My very own girl. Born of the love shared between Elizabeth and me."

My face prickles with sudden heat, and my breath feels thin and forced. "You're mistaken."

"Have you ever looked in a mirror, my Leah? You're my spitting image. Your jaw, your chin, the shape of your mouth . . ." His eyes rove my face, searching, desperate to see.

"It's not unusual for a niece and her uncle to share a passing resemblance."

"Anyone with eyes to see knows it's more than that," he insists. "I'm your father, no doubt about it."

I'm shaking my head against the possibility. It's too horrible to bear. "Mama and Daddy were years married by the time I came along."

"Yes. We were . . . This is not a proper conversation to have with a young lady."

"Fine. Don't tell me anything, and I'll persist in never believing you."

He sighs. Reaches forward and fingers the lace of my new boots. "We were intimate. Once. Several years after she married Reuben. I came upon her in the barn, and . . . well, something came over us, and . . . we were true with each other at last."

His gaze is shifty, refusing to light on any one thing. And I know, as sure as I know the sky is blue, that his story stinks to high heaven. My hands tremble.

"That's impossible," I tell him, my hand going to the locket at my heart. "My mother would never . . ." He coils in on himself, like a viper about to strike, so I let my words hang in the air, unsaid.

He's still touching the lace, rubbing it gently between thumb and forefinger. He says, "She had boots just like this."

The boiled oats and molasses I ate for breakfast churn in my belly. I breathe deep through my nose, afraid of what might happen if I vomit up my meal all over my new clothes.

"I'd appreciate it if you put on the new boots," he says.

"Right now?" I practically squeak.

"Now," he says firmly. "To check their fit."

"All right," I manage. Keeping one eye on him, I bend down to unlace Daddy's boots. They make my feet look huge, but they're his, and they've held up through miles of mud and rock, of sun and rain, of happiness and heartbreak.

I give a quick thought to the small bag of gold shoved down inside the toe of one, but I doubt Uncle Hiram will think to check, and I plan on putting these boots back on at my soonest opportunity.

Reluctantly, I slide them from my feet. Uncle Hiram's eyes are wide as I slip on the new ones, with mania or fever or something I don't quite understand. He is not my father. He's *not.*

I lace them up and stand. They feel funny on my feet—pinched and tiny and fragile. "Perfect fit," I say with a forced smile. "Thank you."

He beams. "You're welcome." He stands and circles the table to get a better view. "They are lovely on you."

Then, faster than a swooping hawk, he scoops up Daddy's boots from the floor where I left them.

"What are you doing?" I demand.

"You don't need these anymore."

"Of course I do. All the mud and—"

He opens the door to the box stove and thrusts them inside, slams the door shut, latches it.

"No!" I reach for the stove, but he blocks me, batting my hands away. "Daddy?" I whisper. I try once more to lunge past him, but Hiram grabs me by the throat and shoves me away. I collide with the table, scooting it back several inches.

While I struggle to rise, he stands sentry before the stove, arms crossed, face resolute. "You'll wear the other boots I gave you, the ones you ruined, when you visit the mine. These you will save for special occasions."

I should say something back, but if I open my mouth, all that will come out is a scream.

"Leah, never mention Reuben again, do you hear me? *Never.*"

I give up trying to stand and fall to my knees instead, sobs quaking in my chest, tears free falling down my cheeks. Grief is a whipping whirlwind inside me, like gold gone sour. Because my daddy was the best person I knew, and I've lost him all over again.

Something pops inside the stove. Burning leather has a peculiar smell, different from wood.

A minute passes. Two. Then Hiram's footsteps stomp across the room and he slams the door as he leaves.

I jump up and use the tongs to pull Daddy's ruined boots from the stove. They're stiff and shrunken and blackened, the edges crumbled to ash. I leave a nasty soot mark on the table when I set them down, but I'll worry about that later.

I allow them to cool awhile, then carefully peel back the charred leather tongue and find what I'm looking for, still lodged in the toe. Some of the tiny nuggets stick to one another, the result of impurities melting a little, but the gold is intact. I upend the boot and shake the gold out onto a napkin, but my sense tells me there's still some stuck inside, so I take a finger and sweep around until I've recovered every possible speck.

My finger smarts from the still too-hot leather as I ponder a moment. If I save these boots, my uncle—I refuse to think on him as my father—will find them and throw them away again. So I can't hide the gold inside them. Maybe the best place is the box stove, after all. It's rare for a fire to get hot enough to melt gold.

Then again, I don't know how often the stove is cleaned out. And what if I need to grab the gold fast, someday soon? There'll be no time to let it cool, no way to carry what would amount to a burning coal.

Under my mattress will have to do for a hiding place again, though I wouldn't put it past Hiram to search my bedroom on occasion. Inside the mattress would be better, but I've no knife to cut with. Hiram has been careful—there is not a single knife in this cabin that I can see, not even to cut food. He tidies up his desk and takes his letter opener with him every time he leaves.

But maybe not this time. I upset him quite a bit.

My gaze falls upon Hiram's writing desk. I dash toward it and fling open the single drawer. Sure enough, a bronze letter opener gleams at me from inside. The handle is shaped like a sword hilt, so that it looks like a tiny dagger. I grab it and run my finger down its length.

A tiny, *dull* dagger. But it's hard and pointy, and I bet I can make do.

I run to my bedroom, fling off the quilt, and lift the mattress. I stab into the ticking with the letter opener, then poke my finger into the hole and pull and yank until it's large enough for my napkin-wrapped gold.

I work the tiny bundle through the hole, then smooth out the fabric as best I can before letting the mattress fall back into place. I flip the quilt over the bed and stand back.

Perfect. Without my witchy sense, I'd never know what treasure lay hidden inside.

I return to the writing desk. Before replacing the letter opener, I hold it up for a moment, staring at it. It's too dull to cut with, but a strong girl like me could still do a lot of damage with its hard point. If I don't find my guns or a proper knife, this might end up my weapon of choice.

It was lying to the right of the papers when I found it, cocked at a slight diagonal. I put the letter opener in the drawer, hoping I'm remembering correctly, and slide the drawer home.

I grab Daddy's boots from the table, and I close my mind, my heart, as I toss them back into the box stove, then close and latch the door. Using one of Mary's dishrags, I wipe the soot from the table, dampening with water and scrubbing to get it all up.

There. I have done something. Something that is not wallowing in despair.

The next day passes as though nothing happened. Wilhelm and I visit the mine, and I wear the ruined boots just like Hiram ordered. I wave to Jefferson as we pass the arrastra on our way back. It's a casual wave, a wave of nothingness, as if every fiber of my being is not yearning to close the distance between us.

Mary comes by to make supper—a chicken soup with raw egg drizzled into it and cooked. Hiram and I eat in silence while the box stove sizzles and pops, continuing to burn my daddy's boots to cinders.

When he's finished eating, Hiram wipes his mouth with a napkin, folds it neatly in front of him, and says, "Take a walk with me."

"All right," I say meekly.

"Change into your new dress first."

My blood boils, but I say, "Yes, sir."

I change quickly, and it's a bit odd to remove one dress and replace it with its identical copy. But the fabric is brighter, the hem clean and perfect, and Hiram is beaming when I take his proffered arm.

"You look beautiful," he says, reaching up to touch a lock of my hair.

I don't trust myself to open my mouth without screaming,

so I say nothing as he pushes through the door and leads me into the late-evening darkness.

Several of the foremen sit outside their barracks at a table, playing cards and drinking from mugs and laughing. Mary is sitting in someone's lap again. She wears his too-large hat on her head, and her fingers are tangled in his hair.

To our left, the Chinese area of camp is equally busy. The clang of metal indicates the blacksmith is working into the night. Several sit around his tent, probably taking advantage of the warmth of his bellows, including the old man from the tent full of jars. He studies me as we walk, sizing me up like I'm a prize heifer.

The air heralds winter with its bitter cold, and everyone's breath frosts in the lantern light. Campfire brightness keeps the stars from view, but a half-moon hovers over us all.

There is no sign of Jefferson or Tom.

"Where are we going?" I dare to ask.

"Nowhere in particular," Hiram says. "But a father and his daughter ought to spend some time together, don't you think?"

It takes everything I have to not rip my hand from his grip.

Abel Topper approaches. His eyes widen when he takes in my new dress and shoes, and he removes his hat, crumpling it to his chest. "Good evening, Mr. Westfall," he says. "And Miss Westfall."

I don't respond, but Hiram says, "Mr. Topper."

Topper's gaze hasn't left me. "You look fetching tonight," he says.

When I remain silent, Hiram gives my arm a firm squeeze. "This gentleman has paid you a compliment," he says.

"Thank you," I choke out.

"It's you I have to thank," Topper says. "You've a nose for gold, no doubt about it. It's no wonder your daddy was so lucky."

Hiram stiffens in the space beside me.

Topper continues blithely. "We've met or exceeded quota all week, thanks to you."

"I'm glad," I manage.

"Thanks to *you*," Hiram says to him. "You're a hardworking man, Abel Topper. It has not gone unnoticed."

It's impossible to keep the frown from my face. Topper is an experienced foreman, sure, and capable enough. But far as I can tell, it's the Indians and the Chinese who do all the actual work. Unless you count whipping starving people as hard labor.

"Thank you, sir," Topper says with a dip of his head. "Thank you kindly."

Hiram begins to lead me away, but Topper says, "Excuse me, sir. Sorry to be a bother, sir, but there's a small matter."

"Oh?" I know my uncle well enough to tell that his impatience is piqued.

"It's the Indians, sir. See, they're wearing out. Not working as hard as they should. I'll need more stock soon, if I'm to keep making quota. Either that, or . . . would it be too much trouble to give them an extra ration now and again?" His hat twists and twists in his hands. "I know we're trying to be frugal and such, but the biggest ones, the strongest ones . . . well, they could sure use a little more fuel for their labors."

I peer closely at him, not sure what he just said. Is he trying to *help* the Indians? He called them *stock*. Though I've never seen cattle stock treated as poorly as everyone here treats these people.

"I agree with Topper," I say before I can change my mind. "I think they'll all work a little harder with more food in their bellies."

"Do you now?" Hiram says, one eyebrow raised.

"I know you've done gentleman's work your whole life, but those of us who have had to labor with our hands and arms and backs need full stomachs to keep us going."

It's an insult doing a poor job of dressing up as a compliment, but Hiram considers. He actually considers. "It would be easier and cheaper to just fetch more. I've been planning to send Dilley and Wilhelm anyway."

That's been his plan all along. To work the Indians to death, collect on their bounties, and enslave more as needed.

"Well," I say in as cool a voice as possible. "In the meantime, we have to keep the ones we already have working to potential, don't we?"

My uncle's gaze on me turns soft. "Would it make you happy?" he says.

"Yes."

"In that case . . ." He turns to Topper. "An extra ration of wheat for the Indians tomorrow and every Saturday.

Additionally we will close the mine for Thanksgiving. Everyone will have a day of rest."

One extra ration per week? That's the best he can do?

My heart is sinking as Hiram looks to me, waiting for some kind of approval.

"That's . . . very generous of you."

"Thank you, Mr. Westfall," Topper says, but his face is hard. He knows it won't be enough.

Hiram and I continue our circuit of the camp. I'm greeted by such deference when seen on my uncle's arm, but my gut knows it's all rotten. By the time we return to the cabin, I'm full up on *Good evening, Miss Westfalls* and well-meaning hat tips, and I want nothing more than to be with people I love and trust again.

I miss Becky Joyner and the kids so badly it's an ache in my chest. I hope little Andy has caught bucketsful of frogs, that Olive is learning good doctoring from Jasper, and that the Major has made the finest furniture for Becky this side of the Mississippi. I bet Hampton has enough gold now to bring his wife out, and Henry has composed a magnificent ode to the beauty of the Sierras.

I need someone to talk to soon, or I'll take leave of my senses. I wish I could talk to Mary, get to know her a little, but Hiram is always hovering when she's nearby.

Mainly, I miss Jefferson. These fancy new dresses that look just like what Mama used to wear, Hiram's impossible claim that's he's my father, the way he refuses any sympathy for the Indians . . . I could figure it all, if Jefferson were here to talk to.

Most of all, this daft idea that maybe I ought to kill Hiram, probably sooner rather than later, is a decision that no one ought to have to make alone. Jefferson could help me figure it. We've always been a team, that way. Even just looking into his calm face, feeling his arms around me, and letting his strength seep into my body might help me understand it all.

Maybe it's my perfect meek behavior. Maybe it's the dress I'm wearing. Or maybe burning Daddy's boots got something off his chest. Whatever the reason, when we return to the cabin and say our good-nights, Hiram leaves me untied.

Chapter Twenty-One

After breakfast, while Mary is washing up, Hiram leaves without dismissing her or saying a word to me. Maybe he's gone to run more mysterious errands, but maybe to use the outhouse. So I have to make this quick.

"Mary," I whisper, soft but fierce, as she towels a plate dry.

Her hands freeze.

"He didn't tie me up last night." I resist the urge to rub my red, stinging wrists.

She resumes toweling, slowly now.

"I need to talk to someone soon," I add. "I'm trying to figure out a way to . . . help." To kill my own uncle, is what I don't say.

"Don't be stupid," she snaps. "You could ruin everything for me."

"For the Maidu, you mean."

"Them too."

We are silent a long moment, and her back is still to me when she says, "Thanksgiving. Everything will be ready by then."

It's a great comfort to confirm that they *have* been busy planning. "That's less than two weeks," I say.

"Muskrat's people won't last any longer than that."

"I see." How many more bodies have they pulled from the stockade since the day I saw it? "What can I do?"

Mary finishes the dishes. "Tonight. Look to your window." And she walks out the door.

I do my duty. I tidy up the cabin after Mary leaves, then meet Wilhelm outside. I offer him a few leftover biscuits, which he gulps down so fast I almost miss it. Together we visit the mine, and I've no advice to give except to keep going in the same direction. Abel Topper practically falls all over himself to be polite to me, and I allow him to waste my time in a useless, boring conversation about weather and statehood and our upcoming thanksgiving celebration, because it wastes *his* time and keeps his attention away from the working Indians.

Wilhelm escorts me back to the cabin, and I turn to him before going inside.

"Why do you work for my uncle?"

His face is stony, which is exactly the response I expected.

"He's a bad man, Wilhelm. Maybe the worst person I know. Well, I suppose it's a toss-up between him and Frank Dilley. Did you know that Dilley once offered to shoot my friend in the head just because his leg got busted?"

Wilhelm's blue eyes narrow.

"That was *your* laudanum he forced into me, wasn't it?" A guess, but a good one. I've seen pain flash across his face occasionally, the way his step hitches once in a while. Something bad happened to this man, maybe the same thing that took his voice.

He gives me a single curt nod, which is so unexpected I almost take a step back.

"That's expensive stuff, isn't it?" I press on. "I wonder how much it cost you, to hand over so much of it."

His perpetual scowl deepens.

"You're a bad man, too, Wilhelm. And maybe you think you're not, because you only do what others order you to do. Maybe you're in a prison, like me."

Wilhelm's eyes rove my face, and I'm not sure what he's looking for. He might have been a fine-looking man once, before that scar slashed across his face.

"I suppose I could be wrong about that," I tell him. "Maybe you're not doing anything you don't want to do. Maybe you like kidnapping innocent people and enslaving them."

A muscle in his jaw twitches.

"I guess it doesn't matter. Whether you love what you do, or you just don't have the gumption to do the right thing—either way, you're a bad man."

I turn my back on him and go inside.

Hiram has returned already, and he sits at his writing desk as usual.

"Uncle Hiram?" I say.

He continues to make careful loops with his pen. "I'm not your uncle."

He's not my father, either. His story about Mama doesn't set right, in a way that makes me not want to think about it too much. But even if it were true, there was more than just blood between Reuben Westfall and me. He raised me, taught me, loved me.

"Well, that was a lot of knowledge to dump on a girl all at once," I say in a perfectly reasonable voice. "It's going to take me some time to get used to it all."

When did I become such a lying, manipulative Delilah? When did I become like *him*?

He turns in his seat to face me, and a soft smile graces his lips. "I understand, sweet pea. What can I do for you?"

"I was wondering if I could borrow some paper and a pen."

"For what purpose?"

For talking to someone through the window tonight. "There are folks back home I'd love to write to," I say brightly. "Judge Smith and his family, to let them know I arrived safely in California."

His eyes narrow. I suspect he doesn't care for judges unless he owns them.

"Mama and I used to write our correspondence together once a week. She always said a proper girl ought to have beautiful penmanship. I practiced by writing letters to Annabelle Smith, and she'd write to me. We exchanged them at school."

It's another rotten lie, mostly, on a whole heap of rotten lies I've been telling lately. Mama loved her lettering, sure, and she always kept pretty stationery on hand. But I never gave a rat's eyeball for handwriting.

Which might be a problem. If Hiram sees my awful

penmanship, he might suspect I'm pulling his leg, so I add, "To be honest, my penmanship is terrible. But I was getting better at it! And I just . . . well, I suppose I miss it."

He considers, tapping the end of his pen to his top lip. "It's true that all the fine young ladies I knew in Milledgeville were accomplished in the art of correspondence," he says.

I hold my breath.

"And at the Christmas ball in Sacramento, I expect you will establish some female connections, which you will wish to properly maintain."

"I reckon so."

"You must promise to show me your letters before sealing them," he says.

Blast. "Of course."

"In that case, I will be glad to share my stationery with you. I'm planning a trip to Sacramento right after Thanksgiving. I can take your letters and post them for you."

"That would be wonderful. Thank you."

"Would you like to get started right now?" he asks. A shy, hopeful smile graces his lips. "We could . . . write together. Like you and Elizabeth used to."

Caught in my own trap. Now I'll have to pretend to write letters to people I pretend to care about. Annabelle Smith feels so far away and part of such a different world that I don't know if we'd recognize each other in the street. I suppose I'd write to Jim Boisclair if I could. But I have no idea where he is. I last saw him in Independence, before he headed west for California. I'd surely love to run into him someday, though I know my chances are small, this being such a huge territory.

"It's been a very long time since I've written anything," I say. "I'd like to start by practicing my letters, if you've pen and paper to spare."

"I do," he says.

I sit at the table and roll up my sleeves to keep them out of the ink while he rummages through his desk for paper, pen, and inkwell. He opens the back of the pen and pours several drops of ink inside before closing it back up

"This is costly," he says, setting everything on the table beside me. "So write small. And that is my only spare pen, so be gentle. I'll pick up more stationery when I can, along with extra nibs and more ink. But this will have to do for now."

"I wouldn't mind a slate," I say. "To practice with until my penmanship is no longer a disgrace."

"That's a good idea," he says.

It's a fabulous idea. One of my best. I could write messages and simply erase them, if I had a slate and some chalk. That would give me a much better way to communicate with Jefferson.

"Go ahead and get started. I'll check with the headman. He just might have a slate in stock. Lots of miners use slates for signage."

"The headman?"

"The leader of the Chinese. He acts as a peddler here in camp. Has a tent full of oddities. Surely you've seen him?"

"Yes, sir."

He leaves the cabin, and I set to work pretending to care

about penmanship. The ink is slow to reach the nib, and I scratch a tiny hole in the paper with my first few attempts. I lick my fingers and pinch the resulting moisture against the nib, and a few tries later the ink flows nice as you please.

Starting at the very corner of the sheet and writing small, I begin scripting the uppercase alphabet. I do a terrible job of it, smearing my *B* and my *H* badly. I press on doggedly, but it's hard to concentrate. *A slate! Please, please let the headman have a slate in stock.*

Writing has always seemed a useless task to me. It's hardly something that puts food on the table or a roof over your head, and it requires the kind of stilled focus I'd rather save for bagging a nice fat deer. But now that I've spoken the lie, I have to live with it.

I'm finishing off my *X* with a swirling loop—which looks too much like an accidental blot—when Hiram returns.

In his hand is a dark green slate inside an oak frame and several pieces of chalk. "Look what I found!" he says.

I don't have to fake my smile. "Thank you so much."

He glances down at my sloppy alphabet and gets a pained expression.

"I told you my penmanship is a disgrace, and it's worse for lack of practice. But I'll get better, I promise."

"I know you will," he says, and his gaze on me is so fond and proud, you'd think he actually cared.

Hiram takes up the paper, pen, and ink and puts the slate and chalk in their place on the table.

I start my alphabet over again, writing as slow as I can to

preserve my chalk, because I'll need all of it for tonight. It's going to be a long, long day.

I lie in bed forever, listening to the night noise of camp—a few distant conversations, some laughter, a snorting burro, a crackling fire. Gradually it all fades. It's too late in the season for crickets and frogs, and I find the silence odd. Maybe even frightening. I like knowing there's some kind of life outside these walls.

I listen, too, for my uncle. The scratch of his pen, the scrape of his chair. He always stays up late, and the light from his lantern edges my quilt-covered doorway.

I hold the slate to my chest. Hiram didn't put up a fight when I brought it to my bedroom, didn't even raise an eyebrow. And now I'll use it to talk to someone. Maybe even Jefferson.

Please, let it be Jefferson.

Then again, talking to him might put him at risk. It would be best if he stayed far away from me right now.

My uncle's lantern goes dark. The floor creaks. I slide my slate beneath my bed quilt and close my eyes tight. Air whispers across my face when he lifts the quilt in the doorway and stands there awhile, staring. I will my muscles to stillness, to keeping my breath regular.

The floor creaks again when he walks away, and I hear the soft *clunk* of his bedroom door as he finally retires for the night.

I lie awake a long time, hoping I'll see Jefferson, hoping I won't see Jefferson, wondering what I'll say to whoever shows up.

A light tap sounds at my window.

I lurch up off the bed before I can tell myself to be slow and silent. I grab the slate, step onto the chest, peer outside, and all the breath leaves my body—from both relief and dread, because it *is* Jefferson, grinning like a madman.

The moon is barely a thumbnail sliver, and a single lantern sways from one of the Chinese tents, giving shape to his silhouette. My legs twitch with the need to run outside and throw my arms around him and have a real conversation, but last time I sneaked out, someone saw me.

Instead, I write on my slate: *How did you get out?* And I put it up to the window.

His eyes widen at the sight of my slate. Then he fogs the window with his breath and uses his forefinger to write:

FOREMAN

I gape at the word, spending a precious moment making sure I'm parsing it true. To the slate, I add: *A foreman is helping you?*

Jefferson nods.

Why?

He hesitates a moment, then writes:

NOT ALL BAD

And I guess that's part of the problem. Bad men are never all bad, and good men are never all good, and it makes it hard to know up from down. I erase the slate with the side of my hand and write: *Is it a trap? Is he a spy?*

Jefferson shakes his head emphatically no.

What's the plan?

He makes an *O* with his lips and leans toward the window. I want to lean forward and kiss him through the glass. Then it becomes clouded, and his fingertip scrawls a new word.

THNKSGIV

I nod. I knew this already. *What do you want me to do?*

LAUD

W

Get laudanum from Wilhelm?

He nods.

GUNPWDR

My heart races. *How?*

He shakes his head and gestures with his hands, a giving motion, from him to me.

I erase the first half of my board and start writing: *You give me gunpwdr?*

He nods.

That'll be a distraction, for sure. *Why me?*

SEARCH

That makes sense. I'm not searched. In fact, I might be the *only* person who leaves the mine without being searched. *What do I do with it?*

HIDE

I've seen the barrels of gunpowder just outside the mine, protected from the rain by canvas. Another barrel sits in the foremen's break area. Muskrat and Mary must be planning on using some of it for their distraction, but I have no idea how someone will pass it to me without being seen. In a jar? A folded-up handkerchief? Where could I possibly hide it?

I write: *Where?*

He shrugs. Then he gives a little start, and he writes:

SLOP

I'm about to protest, but I remember how Mary empties the bucket every morning when she comes to make us breakfast, sometimes even before I'm awake.

I write: *Smart.*

We stare at each other through the glass. I suppose he's said what he came to say, but I don't want him to leave. I don't ever want him to leave again.

Quickly I write: *Hiram burned Daddy's boots.*

Tears leak from my eyes as I raise the slate back up to the window.

Jefferson's face turns angry and fierce, and just being able to tell him, watching him be furious on my behalf, is the greatest comfort I've had in a long while.

He writes:

I'M SORRY

I erase and write: *He says he's my real father.*

Jefferson gapes. Then he shakes his head. He writes:

NO

His lips move: *Never*

I put my fingertips to the window, and he reaches up and mirrors me, finger for finger. Even though it's dark, even though his black eyes are lost in shadow, I sense his agony. It's in the set of his shoulders, his lips pressed tight. What are they doing to him? If they've hurt Jefferson . . .

One last time, he fogs the window and writes:

ƎM YЯЯAM

My heart races. I wipe off my slate, but then I stare at it, not sure what to write.

Jefferson answers my hesitation with a lightning grin that could brighten a whole dark night. He wipes off the window, erasing all traces of our conversation. He's still grinning as he dashes away.

If he can find something to grin about in our situation, then maybe there's reason to hope, after all. I only wish I felt it, too.

Chapter Twenty-Two

"You got chalk on your dress," Hiram says with a frown.

We're sitting at the breakfast table, eating fried eggs and buttermilk biscuits with honey.

"Sorry," I mumble around a mouthful of eggs.

His frown deepens.

I mentally kick myself. I know better than to talk with my mouth full in my uncle's presence. I swallow quickly and add, "I'll wash up better before heading to the mine today."

"See that you do."

I nod as I take another bite.

"You're developing a reputation as a fine young lady with proper airs and grooming. I want to keep it that way."

I almost choke. "I am?"

"Indeed." His smile makes my very toes shiver. "In fact, I've received two offers for your hand." I'm not sure what that means at first. Does someone want my help with something? Finally it dawns on me. My hand in marriage.

"Who?" I squeak out.

"The Chinese headman," he says. "He sent another man to suggest a wedding date and negotiate a bride price. Offered a tea set, can you imagine? Naturally I declined."

"Naturally," I say in a thin voice.

"Don't worry, sweet pea. You're young for marriage, but when I do consent to give you away, it will be to an upstanding American citizen with good breeding."

I frown. I suppose my uncle would consider Jefferson to have terrible "breeding," even though he can recite all the presidents backward and do long division in his head.

"You said two offers," I remind him.

"The other was from Abel Topper."

"What?" Is there anyone in this whole blasted territory who isn't consumed with acquiring a woman?

My uncle grins. "Well, he asked to court you, with the intention of eventual marriage. Said you had grown into a fine, handsome lady, against everyone's expectations. He was very clumsy about the whole thing. It made me shudder. I told him I'd think about it."

"First you give my horse to him, and now—"

"Now, now, control your nerves, Leah. I have no intention of giving you to one of my foremen. We can make a much more advantageous match for ourselves than that. I expect you'll meet far more eligible men at the Christmas ball."

The eggs are like sawdust in my mouth. Hiram talks like I'm a prime breeding mare, to be dispensed with at auction to the best bidder. And why not? Hiram considers me his property.

"In the meantime," he continues, "I'd appreciate it if you would be very polite to Mr. Topper. Even solicitous. We need to make quota every day until the ball, so I need him working hard."

"You want me to string him along."

He blinks. "Well, that's a vulgar way of putting it."

"Does your note come due soon? Is that why quota is so important right now?" I know this already, of course, but I want to see if he'll tell me.

His gaze slides away from my face, and he becomes absorbed by the half-eaten biscuit on his plate. "Yes," he admits.

"Who do we owe the money to?" I hate using "we" to discuss the mine, this camp, Hiram's debt, but I'm hoping the gesture will make him trust me.

"No one you know. A very successful man who made his fortune, first with gold, then by selling land plots in Sacramento. He's contending for California's first governorship, though I expect he won't get it."

"I see." *James Henry Hardwick. James Henry Hardwick.* "Will I meet him at the Christmas ball?"

"It's very likely."

I intend to be long gone by then, but I say, "I promise I'll do my best to charm him utterly."

Hiram gives me such a wide, warm, genuine smile that it takes me aback. "That's my girl," he says.

He excuses himself to run errands, making me promise to practice my penmanship. I breathe deep as soon as the cabin door shuts behind him. It always seems like the air is a little lighter, a little fresher, after he is gone.

"Mary," I begin cautiously. There's no one to overhear us that I know of, but she's always so careful when she's inside this cabin, and I follow her lead.

She turns to face me.

"May I take the extra biscuits today? My escort will enjoy them."

It's the only thing I can think of to bribe Wilhelm with. There is no reaction in her lovely features that I can see, but she takes a basket from the shelf in front of her and plops it onto the table before me.

I peel back the linen to find a whole mess of warm biscuits. More importantly, my gold sense sharpens, becomes a harsh prickle in my throat.

Following the sense, I reach inside, tunneling through the biscuits. Something cool, flat, and round jumps into my hand.

I pull it out. It's a gold eagle coin, worth five dollars. It should be enough to tempt Wilhelm away from some of his laudanum. This is better than anything I would have come up with. Once again, I feel like I'm running behind and trying to catch up.

"Thank you for the biscuits," I say. Mary gives me nothing but silence in response and returns to her chores.

I have money and biscuits to buy laudanum. Now I need to figure out a way to smuggle gunpowder out of the mine.

This dress Hiram insists I wear has no pockets. Maybe Mary has an apron or pinafore I could borrow. Then again, it would seem very suspicious if I suddenly started wearing a pinafore. Also, I have a feeling that covering up this dress in any way would anger my uncle beyond reason.

My new, dainty boots are too tiny and tight to slip anything inside. The dress's high collar prevents me from sneaking anything down my bodice.

Perhaps these sleeves . . . I consider them a moment. The lace might disguise any bulges, especially in the murk of the mine. Daylight, however, would be another thing entirely. And it would have to be a very small package of gunpowder to fit under a sleeve.

I sigh. I don't even know exactly what I'll be smuggling out of there.

The air in the cabin is colder than usual, so I open the box stove and toss in some fresh wood. It hisses and pops a little—the wood wasn't quite cured—as I close the door to the stove and begin to pace.

Frost edges the glass of the front window. Winter will be here soon. The Indians in the stockade will be in even worse trouble then. Our thanksgiving plan, whatever it is, has to work. So I need to do my part.

If I had a needle and thread, I could cut a piece of fabric from the old blue dress and create a pocket for the new one. I'm not a proficient seamstress, but Mama taught me the basics, and I'm sure I could wrangle something.

Maybe I can get sewing supplies from the Chinese headman, though my belly churns to imagine talking to a stranger who offered my uncle a bride price for me. Would it bother my uncle if I acquired a needle? He won't even let a butter knife into the house.

I continue pacing, to my bedroom and back, over the small braid rug, past the writing desk. Something above the writing desk catches my eye.

It's a small pelt, stretched along the wall for decoration. It was taken from a snowshoe rabbit with winter-white fur.

Annabelle Smith back home always wore a rabbit-fur muff in winter. It was one of her prize possessions.

Could my solution possibly be so easy?

I step onto my uncle's writing chair and reach for the pelt. It's nailed to the wall, but with patience and care, I'm able to work it off the nails without tearing larger holes.

I'm taking a big risk, grabbing the pelt without asking permission first. Surely my uncle won't deny me a warm muff for my hands? A lovely rabbit-fur muff is fashionable. A white one, even more so. I will simply tell him that my hands were cold, and I thought the bright fur would be beautiful against my blue calico dress.

Better yet, I'll tell him that Mama used to wear a white rabbit-fur muff.

Guilt twinges in my chest. I've become a no-good liar, and I'm using my parents' good names to do it. It doesn't set right.

But what other choice do I have?

I can't make a proper muff of it without needle, thread, and batting. I'd need a nail or awl too, to punch the leather, and I can't imagine my uncle granting me these things. For now, I'll have to be content with simply letting it drape over my hands.

It will be more than enough to conceal a bit of gunpowder.

Before donning the makeshift muff, I step outside the door with the basket of biscuits in one hand, my golden half eagle in the other. Wilhelm stands there as always, his breath frosting in the air.

"Good morning, Wilhelm," I say, offering a biscuit.

He grabs it with a quick nod of thanks. Do they never feed this huge man? Maybe he just really loves biscuits.

"I'm sorry you have to stand out here in the cold," I tell him. "I'd invite you inside, but Mr. Westfall would probably whip me if I did."

Wilhelm gives me a tiny, sheepish shrug.

I'm putting off the inevitable, and there's no easy way to ask what I must. I just have to do it. Before I can think about it a moment more, I blurt, "Do you have any laudanum to spare?"

His lips part in surprise.

"I'm having a terrible time sleeping," I add quickly. "It's all the noise of camp. That and my uncle always stays up so late. When he finally goes to sleep, he snores like a rumbling locomotive, and now I'm exhausted every morning. I could pay you. I have five dollars. It's all the money I have, but it's yours. Also, biscuits. I'll bring you biscuits every morning."

His eyes narrow, and he studies my face. I wish I had even the tiniest clue what he's thinking.

"Biscuits with honey?" I add.

Of course he says nothing, just stares steadily, breathing in and out through his nose.

"Please, Wilhelm. I don't know who else to turn to."

He looks away, as if the answer to my problem lies in the distant, snowy peaks of the Sierra Nevada. His scarred lips twist in thought.

Five dollars is enough to buy several bottles of laudanum. At least it would have been back east. I know from visiting Mormon Island that everything is more expensive out here, but it still should be enough to buy at least two.

I reach out with the half eagle. It flashes in the morning light. "I only need . . ." I almost say one bottle, but I don't know what Jefferson and the others have planned. "Two bottles. You can keep the rest of the money for yourself."

Finally his gaze returns to me, and he snatches the coin from my hand. There's something strange in his eyes. I'd mark it for gold fever, had we been discussing gold.

"Thank you," I say, more than a little relieved. I hand him the basket of biscuits. "Take as many as you like. I'll be back in a moment."

I go inside, just long enough to grab my rabbit pelt and screw up my courage. I've successfully negotiated for laudanum. I can do this next thing, too.

But as I offer my fur-wrapped arm to Wilhelm, I'm plagued with doubt. What if he tells my uncle? He's never shown the smallest inclination for talking, but I suppose he can write. He has to report to my uncle somehow.

If Hiram asks about it, I'll give him the same lie I gave Wilhelm. *I'm tired. I need to sleep to do my job.* Maybe I'll even embellish a little. *My gold sense goes weak on me when I'm tired,* is what I'll say.

I'm not sure how the gunpowder is going to be smuggled to me, so I try to be ready for anything. Fortunately I don't worry about it long. I'm halfway down the Joyner tunnel when I feel something round and cool pressed against my elbow. Quickly I grab it and hide it under my rabbit fur. A moment later, when I casually turn to see who it was, no one remains. They have slipped away as silently as falling snow.

Just like with Mary and the biscuits. I don't know what the plan is yet, but I can feel the pieces in motion. Other people are doing their part. I must do mine.

I go through my daily motions of assuring Dilley he's mining in the right direction and pay quick visits to the Drink and to the foreman break area. I take a sip of sugar water, just to make the men happy, and then finally Wilhelm and I leave the mine and return to the cabin.

My uncle is still gone, to my great relief.

Only when I'm in the relative privacy of my bedroom, with the quilt blocking the doorway, do I pull out the object I'm holding.

It's an inkwell. Not as nice as my uncle's. Filled to the rim with gunpowder.

As planned, I set it inside the slop bucket. When I wake in the morning, it is gone.

As I hoped he would, Hiram approves of the way I've used the rabbit fur. He even brings me an awl and thread so I can fashion it into a proper muff. I spend the entire evening working on the muff by candlelight while he manages correspondence.

I've never been a dab at sewing, but it's a nice change from pretending to practice my penmanship. After I'm finished, he declares my muff to be the height of fashion, and immediately confiscates my awl.

Somehow, Muskrat has arranged for a bit of gunpowder to come my way every single day. Each time, I receive it in a different container, from a different pair of hands. Once, it's no more than a double layer of worn calico, like a quilt square, tied with twine. Another day, I get a small but bulging leather bag. Each morning, the gunpowder is gone from the bucket when I wake.

A few days after speaking to Wilhelm about the laudanum, he greets me at the doorway with two bottles. I glance around to make sure no one is looking, then I grab the bottles, in exchange for several biscuits.

That night, I put both gunpowder and laudanum in the slop bucket. I lie awake a long time, wondering if I'll know when Mary—or whoever—sneaks into my bedroom to retrieve it. Truth be told, I hate all this sneaking around, and I especially hate that I can't feel alone and safe even in my own bedroom. How often do people come in here when I'm not aware?

Naturally my thoughts move to the gold stashed in my mattress. I'm like the princess and the pea—no matter how many layers between it and me, I'll always be able to sense whether or not it's there. It hasn't been discovered yet, and I wrap my mind around it, enjoying the buzz in my throat.

My mattress jerks beneath me, and I sit up straight in bed.

Once I assure myself that I'm truly alone, and that no rats

or mice or stray cats or people have invaded my bedroom, I reach out with my gold sense again, gently this time.

Gradually a pressure makes itself known against the back of my leg. It's the bag of gold, poking up through the mattress, trying to come as I call.

Is such a thing possible? Can I call the gold to myself? It seems outrageous, but so does the idea of a witchy girl who can divine the stuff in the first place. Why did I never discover this trick back in Georgia? Maybe it's the sheer amount of gold here in California. I've suspected for a while that my sense was growing, changing.

I practice for hours. Calling the gold, releasing it. Calling it again. Gradually I drift off to sleep, a hard, uncomfortable but not unwelcome lump pressing into my spine.

Hiram and I are taking breakfast and Mary is cleaning up when someone pounds on the door.

I glance at my uncle, alarmed, and he gives me a quick shrug before rising to open it.

Cold air rushes in as a shadow fills the doorway. It's Frank Dilley. "There's been an incident," he says.

"Oh?" my uncle says, reaching for his hat.

"Jonas Waters is dead," Dilley says.

I gasp.

"What happened?" Hiram asks.

"He was killed in the stockade."

"The Indians?"

"Maybe. He fell off the guard tower and broke his neck. My

men are grumbling about foul play, and I admit it's awfully suspicious."

"It's not suspicious at all," I say, skidding my chair back and gaining my feet.

"Leah," Hiram warns, but I pay him no mind.

"Jonas loved his moonshine," I insist, "and he never saw a watch shift that couldn't be improved by the liberal application of rotgut."

"That's enough, Leah."

"You know it's true, Dilley. Tell him."

Dilley's hat is in his hand, and his eyes are stricken. I suppose even a man like Dilley has friends, people he cares about, and Jonas's death is hard for him to take. He considers my words a few moments, but I see the exact moment his grief hardens into something else.

"Indians did this," Dilley spits out. "Mark my words."

Hiram dons his hat. "We must deal with this at once," he says, and he steps toward the door.

I grab the fabric at his elbow. "Wait. What are you going to do?"

He yanks his arm away. "Practice your penmanship while I'm gone," he says, and he shuts the door in my face.

"It wasn't the Indians," Mary whispers, her voice tremulous. A dishrag dangles uselessly from her hands.

"I know."

"They all know Muskrat's plan. They wouldn't risk it. Not now."

"I know."

"What will your uncle do?"

"I don't know."

"Leah," she says to the wall. "I'm worried."

Something about her voice, as unguarded as I've ever heard it, makes me reach up with my hand and grab hers. "Me too," I whisper.

She squeezes my hand back, but then she shakes it off and brusquely resumes her work with the dishes.

A few minutes later, she leaves me to stew in my own worries. No one returns to tell me what's happening, so I determine to find out for myself. But when it's time to make my daily visit to the mine, Wilhelm blocks the doorway, shaking his head.

"I have to go to the mine," I insist. "Every day. My uncle's orders."

Again he shakes his head.

I frown. "Not today, huh?"

He nods, once.

In the distance, a single rifle shot rips the air. Wilhelm winces.

I go back inside.

To make the time pass more quickly, I practice my penmanship and think of all the things I could write that would destroy Hiram's reputation. I pace. I sweep the entire cabin, save for my uncle's bedroom, and shake out all the rugs.

It's hours later when my uncle returns.

"What happened?" I ask. "What did you do?"

He hangs his hat on its peg. "I dealt with it."

"How?"

He collapses into his rocking chair and lifts one foot toward me. "Help me with my boots?"

I swallow against nausea as I approach and kneel before him. My fingers squelch in muck as I grab the bottom of his boot. "How?" I repeat.

"Dilley shot an Indian as reparation for his friend."

My hands on his boot freeze. "Even though the Indians are innocent?"

"That's your opinion."

I pull off the boot and set it beside me on the floor. "Which one?"

"What do you mean?"

"Which man did Dilley kill?"

"How should I know? A younger fellow. I'm letting Dilley turn in the head for the bounty. Hopefully that will help keep him cooled off."

He stares down at me as I pull off the other boot, and it feels like spiders are crawling all over my skin.

"Leah, I want you to stay inside this cabin for a few days. Just until everyone's settled down. No visits to the mines."

"Please—"

"You will obey me in this, Leah. No arguments. I couldn't stand it if something happened to you."

But I need to keep fetching gunpowder. The plan depends on me. Or maybe I've smuggled out enough by now. I just don't know, and I hate not knowing.

"Surely by tomorrow—"

"You will spend the days practicing your penmanship. If your slop bucket fills, Mary or Wilhelm will dispose of it. You are not to leave the cabin for any reason. Do you understand?"

My hands are shaking now, my heart pounding. I blink fast to keep tears from pooling. I hate feeling so helpless. I hate that he controls every hour of my every day. I hate him.

"I can take care of myself!" I say. "You said you want me to familiarize myself with—"

The backhand is so sudden it's like a thunderclap to my face. I fall back onto the floor as my vision blurs and tears pour down my face. My cheek starts to sting and then throb in earnest. I put my fingers to my cheekbone. I'm going to have a mean bruise, for sure and certain.

"I don't want to tie you up during the day," he says, almost kindly. "But I will if I have to."

I don't trust myself to say anything. Still cupping my cheek with my hand, I just nod.

Chapter Twenty-Three

That night he ties me up again, tighter than ever, and my illusions of freedom are over. I hardly sleep for the ache in my shoulders and the gnawing pain in my wrists. It's a relief when morning comes. When Hiram unties me, he bends to press his lips to my forehead and says, "I hope you slept well, sweet pea."

We eat breakfast in silence. Only once does my uncle speak, and only to say, "Remember, you are not to leave the cabin. Wilhelm will be keeping guard outside the door. For your protection."

I shove a biscuit in my mouth to excuse my lack of response.

After he leaves, I open the door to find Wilhelm on alert, his hand on his holster. He fills the space with his huge body, a barrier to the outside world.

"Don't worry. I won't try to leave. I just wanted to give you this." I hand him a basket full of biscuits.

Slowly he takes it from me, his eyes lingering on my face.

No, it's my cheek that's caught his attention, and the huge bruise pillowing there. Wilhelm frowns.

"Knock on the door if you get thirsty," I say. "We have plenty of leftover coffee, still warm on the stove."

He just stares at my cheek.

I'm cooped up in the cabin for days. I have no idea what's going on, but I can make some guesses. The laudanum could be added to the sugar-water barrels, or someone's canteen. The gunpowder could create a thunderstorm of chaos. Maybe the plan is to blow up the fort wall, so Muskrat's people can escape. Or blow up the foremen's shack and destroy all the weapons. Or just blow up the thanksgiving dinner itself and get rid of the whole Missouri gang. In that case, the laudanum would be used to drug the poor saps stuck with guard duty, and that's how Muskrat's people will escape the fort.

Several possibilities. Any of them might work.

But is Muskrat's plan going forward? Did we get enough gunpowder out of the mine? Are Jeff and Tom all right? I've lost track of the days, but surely the celebration of thanksgiving is fast approaching.

Mary ignores me when she comes to cook, won't even meet my eye. I spend the days listening through the walls for any sound, any clues. I practice my penmanship endlessly. It's a strange thing, being bored and scared all at once. I think I might die of it.

One morning, as we sit down to breakfast, Uncle Hiram says, "I want you to bathe today. Mary will help you fill the tub. Press your dress. The new one. I want you looking your best tonight." His voice is stern, almost angry, though I'm not sure why.

"Why?" I'm breathless with hope. Maybe he means to let me out.

"Reverend Lowrey is here. There's to be a tent meeting, and you shall attend. Fitting, don't you think, to have some church the night before our Thanksgiving? It will get everyone into the proper state of somber gratitude." He frowns as he says it, staring off at nothing.

"Sure. If you say so."

"These oats are runny," he growls in Mary's direction.

Mary doesn't even flinch. She just keeps toweling the dishes dry.

"They seem delicious to me," I say.

"Don't contradict," he snaps.

"You're in a foul mood," I say. "Even for you."

He starts to protest but changes his mind, his shoulders slumping over his bowl. "You're right. I am. And I've no right to take it out on you."

The apology startles me nearly as much as his backhand a few mornings ago.

"What's wrong?" I say, in as gentle a voice as I can muster.

He sighs. "It's the Chinese," he says.

Mary has started a new batch of biscuits, and her stirring hitches before continuing on, faster and more determined than before.

"What do you mean?" I ask.

"The headman is demanding higher pay for everyone. He insists they could make more if they went elsewhere and kept the gold they panned, instead of handing it over. Doesn't seem to matter to him that they're panning ore brought out of *my* mine."

"You pay them a flat rate?"

He nods. "The blacksmith raised his prices, too. And the other day, Dilley tried to buy a barrel of salt pork from the headman and was charged double what he'd paid before."

I shrug. "Everything is expensive in California, and it's only getting more so."

"The Chinese are greedy," Hiram insists. "Here they have steady pay, a place to do business, and my personal protection. I'm glad tomorrow is Thanksgiving. If anyone needs to learn a little gratitude, it's the Chinese."

The air sizzles as Mary drops biscuits onto a hot griddle.

"Seems to me the Chinese work plenty hard," I say. "I can't remember seeing even one of them idle."

"Appearances can be deceiving," Hiram says.

Well, that's for sure. Hiram, for instance, appears to be a rich man and a fine gentleman.

"My foremen are feeling the injustice of it," my uncle continues. "They work so hard all day, but here come the Chinese, set to steal California right out from underneath them."

I'm not sure how you can have something stolen that didn't belong to you in the first place, but I'm afraid if I say as much, Hiram won't let me out for the camp meeting tonight.

"I'm sure you'll handle everything appropriately," is what I say, and even though I feel dirty and deceitful, Hiram gives me a fond smile.

"Yes, I suspect I will," he says.

The sun is long gone when we finally step out into the cold autumn air. Even though my arm is firmly lodged in the crook of Hiram's elbow, I breathe deep of this tiny taste of freedom.

Our camp looks like it's ready for a dance. Lanterns hang from every shanty and post, and candles surround a wagon turned into a makeshift stage. All this light is an enormous expense, but my uncle's face shines like he's a man with no regrets.

I think about the regrets he'll have when James Henry Hardwick discovers that he can't pay on time. Every additional extravagance is my uncle shooting himself in the foot again.

Chairs and stools surround the wagon. One log lies across two stumps in a fair approximation of a church pew. Even though the pew is empty, several Indians sit in the mud in front of it, their backs straight, eyes wary. They're dressed in threadbare shirts and pants, and my step hitches a little. It's the first time I've seen them allowed to wear clothes.

"You made the Indians come," I observe.

"Muskrat advised against it, but Reverend Lowrey suggested that a sermon about gratitude might go some way toward correcting their poor behavior lately," he says. "It's the same reason we sent slaves to church in Georgia."

"They're wearing clothes. You're not afraid they'll steal from the collection plate?" If Hiram detects the sourness in my voice, he doesn't let on.

"I'm paying Lowrey a generous fee tonight, to support his missionary work among the miners and the Indians, so there won't be a collection plate," he says. "And a church meeting demands modesty."

He guides me to a pair of chairs and we settle down, side by side. Everyone else is trickling in, too—Chinese, foremen, and several more Indians, herded by watchful guards. I'm delighted to glimpse Jefferson, who gives me a quick tip of his chin. Beside him is Tom, who seems awful thin to me, but his eyes are bright, and when he sees me, he gives me a forced smile.

I twist in my chair and spot Mary. Beside her is Muskrat, dressed in someone's threadbare long johns. My first feeling is relief—Muskrat is alive!—followed by hope. He and Mary exchange a quick word, and then they look up, as if sensing my gaze. Muskrat meets my eye with a confident, determined gaze and a slight nod of his head. I hope that means the plan is moving forward, that tomorrow will be the day.

Muskrat moves past Mary and joins his own people. They settle on the ground together and talk among themselves. Something makes Muskrat laugh.

Behind everyone stand several other foremen, including Frank Dilley and Wilhelm. All have rifles or revolvers held at the ready. Abel Topper carries his whip.

"Why all the guns?" I ask. Another expense. The night is damp, and most of those guns will have to be discharged of their gunpowder after Lowrey's sermon.

"A precaution. Topper got word the Indians might be planning something."

My breath is suddenly icy in my chest. "Then why allow them to attend at all?"

"For the sake of their immortal souls, of course," Hiram says. "We cannot neglect God's work even as we seek after industry."

"How decent of you."

Hiram gives me a warning look, and his grip on my arm tightens, but I'm spared any scolding because Reverend Lowrey climbs up into the wagon, straightens and smoothens his suit, and opens his huge Bible.

A hush descends, and Lowrey says, "As we prepare to celebrate Thanksgiving, there is one thing we ought to be thankful for above all things: God's saving grace." And he launches into a sermon about the most fiery, awful, painful fate imaginable, and how we can avoid it by simply putting our faith and trust in the savior of man.

Lowrey isn't remarkable as preachers go; I've seen better. But his hand-waving tirade about fire and brimstone is the most entertaining thing to happen to this camp since I arrived, and everyone sits rapt as Lowrey works himself into a lather.

The whip cracks behind me.

I launch from my chair and turn, just quick enough to see one of the Indians, eyes glazed with golden lantern light, as he topples face-first into the mud. Abel Topper stands behind him, whip hanging limp.

Everyone is as silent as rabbits in their burrows.

Finally Lowrey hollers, "What is the meaning of this?"

"Beg your pardon, Reverend," Topper says. "But this man was disrespecting the word of God."

No one says anything. The Indians beside the toppled man are frozen like statues.

"He was muttering some heathen nonsense to himself," he insists. "Swaying back and forth. I told him to shut it, but he didn't listen."

"Let's have no more interruptions, yes?" Hiram says.

My uncle grabs my arm and pulls me back down into my chair. I give one last glance to the fallen man. He remains crumpled in the mud, as still as the grave.

Muskrat catches my eye, and I shake my head slightly. *Please don't do anything,* I warn silently. Not here, not now, not with all the guns and the foremen wary. Everything inside me tenses up, like I'm bracing to take a beating, as Lowrey picks right up where he left off.

Will no one tend to the fallen man? To my right, Jefferson leans over and whispers something to Tom, who nods. Then they turn to find me, and the look on Jefferson's face makes my throat tighten. He's angry and worried sick that something awful's going to happen, or I don't know him at all.

Lowrey drones on, with considerably less fire than he started with. He quotes Scripture from the Apostle Paul, enjoining slaves to be obedient and to please their masters in all things.

Gradually I become aware of a hubbub growing around the fallen man. I risk Hiram's wrath to twist in my seat and take a look.

His companions are whispering and gesturing among

themselves. One shakes the fallen man's shoulders, but he doesn't respond.

Hiram's hand goes to the Colt at his hip. Lowrey's singsong sermon dribbles away. One of the Indians begins to keen, high and loud.

Topper's whips snaps toward the keening man.

But he misses, snagging the cheek of a Chinese man sitting nearby, opening a line of bright crimson across his cheek.

So Topper tries again, and this time his whip lances across the Indian's shoulder.

Everyone starts yelling. The Chinese are yelling at the foremen, and the foremen are yelling at Topper, and Muskrat is suddenly beside the other Indians, talking low and fast.

The man who was whipped shakes his head at Muskrat, yelling something back. Muskrat pleads with him.

The mood is like water twitching toward a rolling boil. Everyone has a breaking point. You think you can endure anything, you can take just one more day, and then suddenly you can't. The smooth surface bubbles over all at once, and fear makes you do something desperate just to escape.

"We need to get you back to the cabin," my uncle says in my ear.

"They're scared!" I say. Take the kettle off the fire and the water doesn't boil. "They want a way out, they don't want to get hurt. If we just back off, it'll settle—"

A gunshot pierces the night.

Everyone freezes. Frank Dilley stands there, Colt pointed toward the sky. A warning shot only.

Suddenly a man lurches up, hands aiming for Frank Dilley's throat. A foreman jumps to Dilley's defense, knife raised. He stabs the man in the back.

A cry of rage and grief tears into my soul as more leap toward Dilley and the foreman, who disappear beneath a blur of flailing limbs. I can't tell whether people are attacking, or just trying to climb over to escape.

Everyone is out of their chairs now, the Chinese fleeing in all directions. Hiram yanks at my elbow. "Let's go," he commands.

I am sick with fear, with rage, with disgust, but I recognize an opportunity. "You have to stop this!" I yell. Muskrat's people don't have a chance if Hiram doesn't intervene. He hesitates. "Please, Father!"

It's the "Father" that does it.

"Get to the cabin and lock yourself inside," Hiram says. He yanks his gun from his holster and rushes forward. He's a big coward, though, because he stops short of the fray, refusing to get into the thick of things.

Slowly I begin to back away, glancing around for Jefferson or Tom, Mary or Muskrat, anyone who can give me an indication of what I should do.

Another gun goes off. Someone screams. A ragged thunder of gunshots follows.

I stand frozen, covering my ears.

This was not the plan.

Chapter Twenty-Four

Jefferson is suddenly at my side. He pulls a hand away from my ear and says, "We have to find cover."

I'm only too happy to comply. He yanks me out of the light and into the shadows. Guns continue to fire. My head pounds with them, and my ears ring.

We reach the Chinese tents. "No one will look for us here," he says, and he ducks into the headman's tent, pulling me down behind shelves filled with sundries. In the dark, the jars look like black blobs that occasionally spark with reflected lantern light.

After a moment, my heart calms and my head clears enough to say, "Was this how the plan was supposed to go?"

"No," he says, his voice fierce. "But it's the way it's going now. Same plan, just a day early."

More shots ring out.

"We have to get to the stockade," I say, yanking on his sleeve. "The ones who are left, the women and children . . .

Frank and Hiram might go for them next. And we have to . . . Oh, God, Jefferson, what's happening?"

It's too terrible. A mind is not meant to see these things, or even think of them. But I'll see them forever. I'll remember the way that Indian was whipped during the sermon. The knife in the back of the other man. People going down like sacks of wheat, screams of pain. The dead body lying limp in the mud of the stockade. The way the man's head snapped back when Frank Dilley shot him in the mine, and how his blood sprayed the nearest lantern, casting mottled shadows all over the walls.

Jefferson's arms wrap around me, and I'm snugged tight to his chest. He smells terrible—of sweat and gunpowder and dirty creek water—but I don't care. It seems like I've wanted his arms around me forever.

He says, "We'll have to be silent and quick if we're to get there before Frank and his men."

I start to rise. "Then let's go!"

He yanks me back down. "We wait for Tom. We agreed to meet here if things went bad."

"What if he's . . ." I can't finish my own question.

"We'll give him a chance."

"And the rest of the plan?"

"Gunpowder is already in place outside the barracks, near the shanty where they stash the rotgut. Someone will set it off. We didn't get as much powder from you as we wanted, so once it got dark, Muskrat grabbed a couple of the lamps that were lying around for tonight's meeting and doused the back wall of the barracks with oil. For days, Tom and I have been gradually stacking firewood and blankets and such—anything that catches fire—against the back wall on the inside. Should burn long and hot now."

"Our guns are in the barracks!"

"Yep. In a chest near the door. We hoped to retrieve a few in the confusion. Might not be able to, if the fire gets out of hand. Either way, I expect Mary will scream her head off about the Indians trying to burn the camp. She'll convince everyone she saw a whole bunch heading toward the tents with more gunpowder."

Everything is so much clearer, so much less impossible, when Jefferson is here. "And that will give us time to get to the stockade."

"Yes."

"It will be guarded."

"That's our biggest problem. Mary was going to take them some moonshine tomorrow, laced with laudanum. Tell them it was on Dilley's orders, being the thanksgiving day and all, and just because they drew the watch shift didn't mean they shouldn't celebrate. It wouldn't have been enough to knock them out, but it would have made them sleepy and slow."

Slow enough that they couldn't aim their guns, especially in the dark.

"It was a good plan," I say.

"It was Muskrat's plan," Jefferson says. "That man is one of the smartest people I've had the pleasure to know." High praise, coming from Jefferson. "But now I don't know how we'll get the stockade open," he adds.

"We'll think of something. But . . . Jeff? You could have told me everything."

The bitterness must be plain in my voice because his "How?" comes out sharp and angry.

"I don't know. Somehow. Mary sees me every morning."

"Do you have any idea how closely your cabin is watched?"

"I . . . No, I guess not."

"In order for me to visit your window, we had to count watch shifts, make several bribes, and Mary had to—"

"I'm sorry. You're right."

Footsteps sound at the tent's entrance, and a shadow blocks the night sky. I freeze in Jefferson's arms, which tighten around me.

Then a voice comes. "Jeff?"

"Tom!" I whisper, launching to my feet and barreling toward him.

He hugs me right back, but only for a second. "We have to reach that stockade and then get out of here."

"But what do we do about the guards?" I ask.

"Maybe we ask the guards for help?" Jefferson suggests. "Tell them a riot is happening, and Westfall has ordered every able-bodied man to the fight?"

"That might work," I say.

Tom rubs at his jaw. "Maybe. Especially if it comes from you. Everybody knows you've got special status around here. Hiram calls you his lady."

The thought makes me see red. But if it helps us out now, then I'm glad for it.

"If we're escaping tonight, we could use our guns. Also, my pack. I have some gold hidden in my mattress. It could pay for our journey back."

"No time," Tom says.

"I don't mind saying good-bye to the gold," I say, "but my guns . . ."

"We do need that gold," Jefferson says. "We're days from home. Maybe weeks. We'll need supplies on the way, and we've got nothing to trade."

"I won't be able to stop long enough to find gold along the way," I add. "Not if we're pursued."

The three of us stare at each other.

"We split up," I say at last.

"No!" Jefferson says. "I'm not letting you out of my sight. Never ag—"

"I can get the guards to leave the stockade. I'm *Miss Westfall*, right?" I say it bitterly. "They'll take orders from me. But not if I have you and Tom in tow."

"She's right," Tom says. "Jefferson, you hurry back to the barracks and fetch our guns. Unless it's too dangerous; use your own judgment there. Meet us at the corral. Lee, you run to the stockade and tell them they're needed at the mine. Sound a little panicked if you can. Tell them to hurry."

"What will you do?" Jefferson asks.

"I guess it's up to me to sneak into the cabin and get Lee's gold."

"Absolutely not," I say. "That cabin is too near the camp meeting. You'll be seen."

"Not if Mary has done her job," he says. "Everyone will be racing to the mine soon enough."

I hate this idea. I don't want to let either one out of my sight, but I'm not sure there's any help for it.

"All right," I say with no small amount of reluctance. "Tom, the gold is hidden in my mattress. Lift it to find the hole underneath. My bedroom is the one with the quilt hanging in the doorway, along the east side of the cabin. There's a pack in the chest at the foot of my bed. I'd dearly love it, but it's not as important as that gold."

"Got it," Tom says.

"Both of you, promise me that if you can't get inside quick and easy, you'll let it go and head to the corral. Don't take any unnecessary risks."

"Agreed," Tom says.

"Agreed," Jefferson says. "But I don't want you to lose that five-shooter."

"Better it than you," I say in a wavery voice. I'd rather lose a dozen guns than lose Jeff.

An explosion shakes the earth, rattling my very bones.

"That's our signal," Tom says. "It's a fair bet that barracks is on fire now."

Even though I can hardly see a thing, my gold sense prickles all over, as though the air is filled with sparkling dust. Then comes yelling. Beating footsteps. A female voice screaming—Mary, no doubt.

The golden motes in the air demand to be acknowledged. I know I should make my feet run toward the stockade, but

I'm caught by their glory, their warmth. I reach out with my mind in greeting. And the gold comes at me like a swarm of hornets.

Suddenly I'm choking on dust. My companions are, too. We hunch over, coughing.

"Must have been some explosion," Tom says hoarsely.

Jefferson spits to clear his mouth.

I just stand there, hardly able to breathe, my heart racing. What just happened?

"We've got to get moving!" Tom says.

My feet unstick from the ground, and I run from the tent, Tom and Jefferson at my heels.

"Meet you all at the corral," Tom says, and he dashes off in the direction of the cabin.

Jefferson's hand on my shoulder spins me around. "Lee," he says. "I . . ." And he cups my face in his hands and kisses me quick but hard.

Then he's off running too, toward the barracks, and it takes all my focus to get my feet moving downhill toward the stockade, because I'm terrified and I can't see hardly anything and I also know with sudden clarity that someday soon I want to start kissing Jefferson and not have to stop.

I skid down the hill in my useless dainty boots, trying to figure out what to say to the guards. What if they don't believe me? What will I do then?

The pasture area is dark like ink. I'm forced to slow down, lest the trampled, lumpy sod rise up to trip me. I'm not even sure I'm going the right direction.

A light blinks just ahead. It's high up, like a star falling from the sky. I almost miss it when it blinks again.

It's a lantern, hanging in the stockade tower, shifting and spinning with the breeze, and it becomes my beacon as I press forward.

I reach the log wall. If my sense of direction has not led me astray, I can follow the wall left and turn the corner to reach the entrance. Time to start making a ruckus.

"Help!" I yell, waving my hands. I run along the base of the wall, yelling as I go. "Help us, please!"

My voice sounds about as convincing as a peddler selling a map to the mother lode, but I keep at it with gusto. "Somebody, help!"

I round the corner just as boot steps start pounding my way. Another lantern hangs at the barred entrance. One guard stands sentry, his rifle held ready. The other is dashing toward me.

"Miss Westfall?" he says. "We heard guns. A big boom. What's going on?"

"It's a revolt!" I say, and I don't have to fake the terror and sickness in my voice. "My uncle . . . Mr. Westfall, he's alive but hurt. He needs your help."

Together, we head toward the entrance, where the other guard stands. "I'm not sure we ought to leave our posts," the guard says.

I yank on his sleeve and allow a sob to escape my throat. "Please, I beg you. Dilley sent me to get you. Said he needs every able-bodied man. Oh, Lord help me, but I don't know what I'd do if something happened to my uncle. You have to help him! Promise me you'll help him!"

A rough hand pats my back. "There, there, little lady. If Mr. Westfall demands our aid, of course he shall have it."

That's right, you no-good snake. I'm just a hysterical female. "Oh, thank you! Thank you so much!"

Three knocks sound from behind the gate. "Boggs?" comes a voice. "Shelby? What's going on?"

The guard at the gate—Boggs—lifts the latch and cracks it open. A third man slips out, rifle in hand. Quickly the gate is closed and latched behind him, but not before a wave of stench—feces and rotting vegetables and vomit—almost knocks me over.

It's the guard from the tower, come to see what's going on. I've got all of them now.

"Miss Westfall says there's trouble back in camp," Boggs says. "They need our guns."

"Please hurry!" I say. "You have to help. If my uncle . . . I don't know what will become of me . . ." I allow my face to fall into my hands so they don't see how deeply I disgust myself with my own words.

"All right, come along then," says the third man. "Let's go." His arm descends to my shoulder.

"No!" I say, wrenching away. "My uncle ordered me away to safety. Said to fetch you all and then stay out of sight."

The men hesitate, exchanging glances.

"I'll stay right here," I say. "I'll stand guard for you. Leave me one of the guns in case I must defend myself."

Maybe I've pushed things too far. I shouldn't have mentioned a gun—the Missouri men know all about me and guns—but Shelby grabs his Colt from his holster and hands it to me. "You know how to use this?"

I grab it from him. "Point and pull the trigger, right?" Something about the guns niggles at me. In the light of the swinging lantern, the shiny walnut hilt fairly blazes with newness. My thumb passes over a rough patch, and I peer closer, heart pounding.

The fellow Boggs, from Missouri, snorts. "This lass could outshoot us all. You should have seen her on the trail coming out to California."

I'm about to insist that I'm out of practice, but then I recognize something and my breath catches. The rough patch is actually a tiny *H*, scratched into the hilt. An *H* for Hoffman.

"Don't worry, Shelby," Boggs adds. "Your gun is in good hands."

It's Martin's gun. The one that disappeared the night he died. "Thank you, sir," I say, my voice as dark as the grave. "Now, please. Go find my uncle before it's too late."

More gunshots ring from the camp above. After a quick tip of their hats, they start running.

I watch their fleeing backs, rage boiling inside me. I could shoot them right now if I wanted to. Maybe I should.

Instead, I allow them to fade into darkness as they start climbing uphill toward the camp and the mine. I force myself to wait, to give them a few moments to get well and truly out of sight. Just because I can't see them doesn't mean they can't see me. I'm the one with the gate lantern swinging over my head.

In case they take it upon themselves to look back, I stand straight, feet slightly apart, gun cocked and ready, like I'm proudly standing sentry. I hope Jefferson is okay. I hope Tom got inside the cabin unseen. How many people lie dead up there? By the time Jefferson yanked me away, it was clearly about to become a massacre.

More gunshots echo. The horizon lights up, showing the trees in sharp relief, just like that awful night we lost Martin, when Dilley and his men set fire to our camp. *Please hurry, Jeff and Tom. Please be okay.* I send a little prayer heavenward for Muskrat and Mary, too. Then I turn toward the gate.

The latch is huge and heavy, an enormous beam held in place by brackets. It takes two tries for me to lift it, and I don't have the strength to set it down gently, so I let it drop with a loud *thunk*.

I push the gate open.

"Hello?" I call out. "You need to leave," I say. "Quickly."

What if no one inside this stockade speaks English? And suddenly I realize that even if they did, they might not listen. I'm Hiram's niece, who wears fancy clothes and sleeps in a fancy cabin and eats three fine meals per day. They have no reason to trust me. Not one.

"Please!" I say louder. "The Indians at the camp meeting, they were attacked. They fought back. It's bad up there, real bad. My uncle's men might come here next."

A woman steps into the lantern light—black eyes and thin

hair and mottled skin. Her breasts sag halfway down her belly, which is sunken and bony.

"You have to leave," I insist. "Or you might be killed."

"Muskrat?" she says.

I shake my head. "I don't know where he is. I didn't see what happened to him."

She frowns. "He has everything. For leaving. He's been saving it for weeks."

I'm so relieved to be able to communicate with her. Gradually others come toward me. More women, children, a few young men, until there are close to fifteen. I'm betting there are even more, waiting in darkness.

"I don't know if Muskrat is coming. I'm sorry. But if you don't leave now, you will probably die."

"If we don't get food soon, we die," she says. "We have no weapons for hunting, no baskets for gathering."

Oh, God. Why did I not think of this? "Maybe I can get you some supplies. Maybe . . ." But where? How? There might be some foodstuffs in Hiram's cabin, but I can't possibly round up enough to feed all these people. I couldn't even carry everything they'll need.

"Here," I say, thrusting Martin's revolver at her. She lurches back, eyes wide, but her posture eases when she understands what I intend. "Take it. It's a good gun." Tears prick at my eyes. "A really good gun. Shoots straight. Almost new. It will buy a lot of food."

She grabs it, eyeing me warily. "And this, too." I slip my white rabbit-fur muff from my left arm and offer it. A young man steps up and grabs the muff from my hand before I can change my mind. "Please hurry," I say.

The woman turns around and confers with her companions. She speaks first, fast and low in a language I don't recognize. Two other older women speak. All at once everyone is nodding, as if they've come to an agreement.

She faces me and says, "We go." Then, with a steady glare, she adds, "Do not expect us to thank you."

"I . . . No, of course not."

She gestures toward the others, and they fall in behind her. She leads them from the stockade in a neat single-file line, as though they've been practicing.

I hope they make it, but this does not seem like a good night for hope.

Chapter Twenty-Five

The line of women and children gradually disappears into darkness. My uncle did this. He and his men. And even after Tom and Jefferson and I escape—if we escape—Hiram will still be here. I know he's not the only one responsible for the misery of the Indians in California, but he's the one I could have done something to stop. If only I'd had the means—and the courage—to kill him.

But right now Tom and Jeff are waiting at the corral. I think I know which direction to go. I stare at the lamp swinging from the gate. It could light my way. It would also be a beacon, giving away my position to anyone who might be looking for me.

Lifting my muddy skirts, I turn my back on the stinking stockade and push into the dark. I listen as I walk, hoping for the sound of nickering horses and complaining cattle, worried that instead I'll hear footsteps or angry voices. The corral is large, but I could easily miss it in the dark. I suppose if

I encounter the cottonwoods or a steep slope, I'll know I've gone the wrong way.

"Lee!" comes a whispered voice. "Over here!"

My feet aim me in the voice's direction a split second before my ears identify Tom's baritone.

"Tom!" I whisper, rushing forward. The corral's low fence comes into view just in time to keep me from crashing into it. I lift my skirts and climb over to meet him.

He thrusts my pack toward me. "I put the gold inside."

"Did anyone see you?"

"Yes. The big blond fellow."

"Wilhelm?"

"That's his name. Saw me, didn't even bat an eye. He stayed clear of the fighting. Just stood a few paces from the cabin, arms crossed, watching everything."

I'm not sure what to make of that. "Wilhelm might be able to write or gesture to someone that he saw you, but he can't talk, so maybe we still have some time. What about Jefferson?"

"Haven't seen him. Let's find the horses. We'll have them gathered up by the time he gets here."

He doesn't have to tell me twice. I heave the pack over one shoulder and start weaving through burros and milk cows and even a couple of oxen, looking for my mare. "Peony!" I whisper. "Where are you, sweet girl?"

Hot breath whuffs at my neck. I spin and fling my arms around her, but she's hard to hold on to. She raises and lowers her head, over and over, nostrils flaring.

"I'm sorry, Peony. You've always been a vengeful critter, but if you let me ride you out of here tonight, everything is going to be okay."

I've become so awful that now I'm even lying to my horse. Things will not be okay. Not until my uncle no longer threatens me or my friends. Or anyone else in California. But one thing at a time.

Gradually Peony settles. Tom appears before me, pulling Sorry by her halter.

"Where's Apollo?" I whisper.

"I'll get him next."

"Will he let you ride bareback? We've not a lick of tack between us, except their halters."

"I guess we'll see," Tom says with forced brightness. "Wait here for Jefferson. I'll be right back."

I finger the gold inside the pack, just for comfort. I'm terrible at waiting. Always have been. I tell myself it's like being on a hunt, when the slightest bit of recklessness can ruin everything. *Be patient, Lee. Be a ghost.*

Something squishes in the mud nearby. Probably one of the animals, but instinct makes me crouch beside Peony's shoulder. Two shapes appear against the darkness, and my hand goes to the empty space at my waist where my gun used to be.

"Lee?" someone whispers. "Tom?"

It's Jefferson's voice, and gladness fills me like sunshine on a rainy day.

"Jeff!" I surge forward, my boots squelching in the paddock's churned-up mud, and I throw my arms around him.

He gives me a squeeze but pushes me away quick. "We've got company," he says.

Only now do I realize it's Mary who stands beside him. She carries a small rucksack in one hand, a revolver in the other.

"I'm coming with you," she says.

"I have no problem with that," Jefferson says firmly.

"Glad to have you along, Mary," I say.

Tom creeps up, Apollo in tow. "Hello, Mary," he says, unsurprised.

"Things are bad up there, Tom," she says. "When they ran out of Maidu, they started killing the Chinese. The headman . . . he . . ." Her voice trembles.

"They killed *all* of them?" I say. "Everyone?" I suspected that was where things were headed when Jefferson and I ran off, but hearing it is another thing entirely.

"I wanted . . ." Her voice stumbles, as though it's full of tears. "I just wanted to get away. Doesn't mean I wanted anyone to die."

"Muskrat?" Tom asks.

"I lost track of him," Mary says.

"Did you get the women and children out of the stockade?" Jefferson asks me.

"Yes. But, Jeff, they're in terrible shape."

"At least they're out," Tom says. "They might be the only ones who escape if we don't get moving."

"Here," Jefferson says, handing me my rifle. "It's not loaded. We'll have to buy ammo somewhere along the way."

I caress the length of the barrel. It used to belong to Becky's husband, but it became mine when he was killed. Now it's as familiar to me as my own hand.

"I have your five-shooter, too," he says, rummaging in his pack.

"Hurry," Tom says. "Any moment now, Dilley's men will come for the Indians they think are in the stockade."

Jefferson hands me the revolver, and I shove it inside my own pack. "Let's go," I say. "Mary, can you ride?"

"No," she says. "But I can run. I once ran all day without stopping."

"You'll have to tell us about that sometime," Tom says. "For now, you'll take turns riding double with each of us."

Jefferson gives me a boost onto Peony, who dances beneath me with excitement. Then he boosts Tom onto Apollo, and Mary right behind Tom. He pulls up the top rung of fencing and tosses it aside, then he rushes around the corral, smacking horses on their rumps and herding them out.

There are still a few horses stabled by the cabin—like my uncle's—but the rest of the men will have to round up their mounts before chasing after us. Jefferson has given us a nice head start.

He vaults onto Sorry's back. "We follow the creek west and downhill as much as possible," he says.

"Agreed," I say. "We ride until daylight, no matter what."

Jefferson leads, and Tom and I fall in behind. In the distance, a volley of gunshots pierces the night sky, echoing through the hills. More than anything, I want to urge Peony into a gallop, but it's too dark to risk it.

Our horses splash into the creek, which will take us far away from this blasted place. Quietly and slowly—too slowly—we follow it around the pasture and into the trees. Branches close over our heads, blocking what little moonlight and starlight we had to guide us, and we are forced to slow even further.

I comfort myself with the thought that even though the darkness makes our path difficult, it also makes us hard to pursue. If we just keep going, slow and steady, we'll be safe.

Then why am I not full of gladness? Why am I not rejoicing at our escape? Instead, as we clomp and splash along in darkness, my heart grows heavier and heavier.

Finally, when I can stand it no more, I pull Peony up short. "Wait," I whisper, too loudly. "Stop!"

"What is it? What's wrong?" Jefferson says as he and Tom rein in their mounts.

"I have to go back."

"What?"

"We're not escaping. Not really. I mean, maybe you are, but not me. Never me."

"You think Westfall will come after you again," Tom says.

"I know he will."

"Maybe he's dead," Mary says. "Maybe he got killed in the fighting."

"That would save me a heap of trouble," I admit. "But I've got to go back and make sure. You three go on without me."

"Like hell," Jefferson says. He's turned his horse around, and he and Sorry splash toward us. "Listen, Lee, we *have* to go. This is our one chance. We'll get back to our friends, and we'll tell everyone what happened, and then we'll make a plan."

"No."

"Lee—"

"That sounds wonderful. In fact, it might be the most tempting thing I've ever heard. But he'll come after me again, no doubt about it. Maybe the next time he tries to burn us out we'll lose *everyone*. What if something happened to Olive or Andy? I'd never forgive myself."

Peony fidgets beneath me, impatient after being stuck in that corral for so long.

"We should go," Mary says, her voice urgent. "If Lee wants to be daft, let her stay."

"If I stay," I add, "he won't come after you. You'll be free."

"Not true," Tom says, and he cuts off Mary's protest by saying, "He'll figure on us coming back for you. And eventually he'll realize the gorgeous spot you picked for us by that beaver pond is richer with gold than Midas."

Tom is right. My uncle knows I'd use my witchy senses to find the best spot in all the Sierras. He'll want it for himself, for sure and certain.

Jefferson sighs. "And he'll keep killing the Maidu. He'll find more. Enslave them. Work them to death."

"No one will be safe," I say hollowly. "Not ever. Until my uncle is taken care of."

A pause. Apollo dances nervously.

Finally Jefferson says, "You mean to do murder."

"Yes."

"That's not you."

"It has to be someone."

"Lee, it's a slaughter up there. You're just as like to get killed by accident."

"I'll chance it."

"I'm not going back," Mary says. "No matter what. You can drop me off right here, and I'll run all the way to San Francisco if I have to."

Using knees and hands, I direct Peony to circle around back the way we came, and she's such a dab at bareback riding that she responds to the slightest touch.

"Wait, Lee," Jefferson says. "I'm going with you."

"Me too," Tom says. "Or we'll never be free of this man."

Mary begins to cry softly.

"You don't have to come, Mary," Jefferson says.

"We can give you some of our supplies and wish you Godspeed," Tom agrees.

Mary lets go of Tom's waist long enough to wipe her face. "It was all just bluster. Truth is, I have nowhere to go."

We face one another in the dark, wasting precious moments as thoughts chase themselves around in my head. At last I say, "I have an idea."

The rise leading toward the mine is awash with firelight, and the scent of burning wood fills the air. Things are awful up there, and if I have my way, they'll get even worse.

"There's a way to ruin my uncle completely without doing murder," I add.

"Oh?" Tom says.

"He's done most of the work himself already. We just need to help him along." I pull everyone close. "This is what we're going to do."

Chapter Twenty-Six

The uprising is over, and the mining camp is littered with bodies—limbs pale against dark earth made muddy with blood. It's impossible to identify the fallen, but based on what I see of the living, the dead are mostly Indians and Chinese.

Jefferson and I crouch in shadow behind the arrastra. We've circled around, sticking to the trees, until we reached a good hiding place. From here, we have a perfect view of the entire camp—the mine is to our immediate right, and stretching below us are the barracks, the stables, my uncle's cabin, and the Chinese tents. The barracks are a raging inferno. Heat washes my face.

"Glad you grabbed the guns when you did," I whisper.

Boggs and the stockade guards are nowhere to be seen. They're either dead, or on their way back to the stockade, or out trying to round up the horses we let loose. There's no sign of Frank Dilley, whom I suspect did not survive, but several foremen remain, trying to put out the fire. Abel Topper works his way through the dead bodies with an ax. He aims for someone's neck, then raises the ax. I have to look away, but I can't avoid the sound of the blade crushing flesh and bone.

There's no sign of my uncle or Muskrat.

"There," Jefferson whispers, pointing. "Look."

I follow the direction of his finger and discover Reverend Lowrey. His back is turned to me and he's covered in mud, but there's no mistaking the huge Bible under his arm. Pity he survived the uprising.

That thought sets my belly to twitching, though, because even if Lowrey is a self-righteous son of a goat, he doesn't deserve to die. I need to finish this business quick and get back to the good people I care about. Otherwise, I'm on my way to becoming as mean-spirited as Frank Dilley.

Reverend Lowrey is speaking to someone. He shifts to the left, revealing his companion, and it's like a rock sticking in my chest, because there's my uncle, looking as prim and perfect as you please, with nary a scratch or even a smear of mud.

"Blast," Jefferson mutters, echoing my own thought, because my uncle being a special case, I'm not sure it exactly qualifies as mean-spirited to wish death upon *him*.

We wait in silence. To our right, between us and the mine, are three stacked barrels beneath a canvas awning, which are nearly full of gunpowder, fresh from one of Hiram's trading errands. I rummage through my pack and pull out the dress—the first one Hiram got for me. I put the skirt hem in my teeth and tear until I have a nice rip going. While I rip up the skirt, Jefferson retrieves his tinderbox.

Now we just need the signal.

Jefferson whispers, "How much longer do you think—"

Someone screams, distant but forceful.

Everyone in camp stops what they're doing and stares in the direction of the stockade, even though it's way out of sight. My uncle's hand goes to the gun at his hip.

The scream comes again, louder and drawn out. "Wow," Jefferson mutters. "Nice work, Mary."

Hiram shouts some orders that I can't quite hear over the raging fire of the barracks, but several men check their guns and start making their way through the Chinese tents toward the creek and the pasture.

"Still too many left," I say.

"The gunshot might take care of that," Jefferson says.

Hardly a moment later, a single rifle shot rings out.

"It's the Indian camp!" Topper hollers. He gestures for everyone left to follow him. "Leave the barracks; it's lost to us. We need every gun, every able-bodied man."

They obey without hesitation, and there's murder in their eyes as they weave through the bodies, toward the creek and away from the mine. Everyone, that is, except Hiram.

Another shot cracks the air. We were right to give Jefferson's rifle to Mary, figuring it would boom louder than a revolver. Everyone heading away breaks into a run. This time, my uncle turns to follow, though at a leisurely pace.

"Mary was slow to reload," Jefferson observes.

"If she sticks with us, we'll teach her true," I say.

I watch my uncle's dallying back. He plans to arrive at the

stockade after all the dirty work is done. That's why his vest and jacket are as clean as the morning. He gets people to do his killing for him. My mama and daddy were an exception.

Hiram's men are going to be awful surprised when they find the stockade empty, which means Jefferson and I have to work fast.

"Now!" I say, as soon as my uncle is out of sight.

Jefferson grabs a flake of flint and strikes it against an old busted horseshoe. A shower of sparks rains down on his char cloth, but it doesn't ignite. Neither does it catch fire on the second try.

"Might be a little damp," he says, and he reaches for the powder horn at his hip to measure out a tiny pinch of gunpowder, which he sprinkles onto the cloth.

His next strike ignites the char cloth in several places. He grabs some tinder, places it carefully on the tiny flames, and begins to blow and coax it into a decent fire, adding small sticks as he goes.

While he does that, I find a nice rock about half again the size of my fist and wrap my torn rag around it. I tie it off so it looks like a ball with a tiny waving flag on the end.

"I guess we could have just borrowed from the fire at the barracks," I say.

"It's better this way," Jefferson says. "If someone is still hanging around, and they see us running for the barracks, it's all over. Okay, this fire is good for now. Time to move those barrels."

He stands to go, and I grab his hand. "Be careful," I tell him.

Jefferson grins. "You'd be heartsick if something happened to me, wouldn't you?"

I glare at him.

"Back soon. Keep that fire going."

My pulse is in my throat, now that he mentioned the possibility of someone hanging around. What if he's seen?

Jefferson reaches the barrels and yanks off the top one. All that work to steal little bits of gunpowder, and now in the chaos we can take as much as we want. He pulls the plug, and gunpowder streams out. It keeps right on streaming as he drags the barrel into the mine.

This is the most dangerous part of my plan. If anyone sees us, we're done for. If gunpowder gets anywhere near the lanterns inside the mine, we're done for. And once my uncle's men realize they've been tricked, they'll come rushing back. If we're not finished with our work by then, we're done for.

The barracks fire is burning itself out. The camp is still washed in firelight, but shadows hug the edges now, and maybe that's a good thing. I'm staring past the barracks toward my uncle's cabin, gladdened with the thought that I'll never see the inside of that awful place again, when something flickers in the shadows. A shadowier shadow, moving with purpose.

I should warn Jefferson that we are not alone. I can't call out to him. I'll have to sneak into the mine myself.

Leaving the fire where it is, I gather my legs and quietly stand. I make it two steps before I glimpse the shadow again. This time, I recognize the tall, skinny form.

It's Tom. He's supposed to be hiding in the trees at our

rendezvous point, keeping an eye on our mounts so we can flee as soon as possible. Dawn is still hours away, and firelight makes the darkness hard to parse, but God bless the man, because he's done our plan one better. Instead of doing what he was told, he's freeing the horses from the stable—they're near panicked already, from the scents of fire and blood—and grabbing their extra tack.

After he smacks the rump of the last horse, a dark, beautiful animal that is surely Hiram's, he looks up toward the arrastra where I'm hiding and flashes a wide white grin against the black night. He waves once, and I wave back, and then he and the gear he's stolen melt back into the darkness.

"That's one barrel in position."

I jump out of my skin at Jefferson's voice.

"Just let me roll the others inside," he says. "See if we can't bring the whole mountain down."

"I'll help. Let's be quick."

We rush over and each grab a barrel. Mine is heavier than heavy, and rolling it even the tiniest bit uphill almost proves too much, because it keeps wanting to roll back over my toes.

"How did you get that first barrel inside so easy?" I say between huffing breaths.

"It was hardly three-quarters full," Jefferson admits.

We're running out of time. So I think about Hiram and how this is my one shot to completely ruin him without doing murder, and I push a little harder, and bit by bit, we manage to get the barrels farther inside the entrance.

My uncle's men have surely reached the stockade by now.

They've seen the place is empty. It might take them a moment or two to figure out what's really happening; a few will undoubtedly take off into the trees in pursuit of Indians—who are hopefully long gone. But not my uncle. He'll turn around and come right back. He might be walking up the hill this very moment.

Inside the mine, Jefferson's thick trail of gunpowder twists like a black snake down the tunnel. "I put a whole pile of it at the edge of the Drink, right up against the supports," he says. "Another pile near the end of the Joyner. I don't have a lot of experience with gunpowder other than for shooting guns, but it should do its work."

We settle our barrels, each one against a beam bolstering the entrance. As we start to leave, I grab his arm. "Thank you," I tell him.

His hand comes up to mine, and he squeezes.

We exit the mine together and head toward the arrastra and our tiny fire. As I bend to pick up my rag-covered rock, drops of water splatter onto my face.

"No," I whisper. "No, no, please no."

"Rain!" Jefferson says. "We have to move fast."

I dip the flag of fabric into the fire until it ignites, then hold it gingerly as it creeps up toward my hand.

"I'll do it," Jefferson says. "You should be a safe distance away."

I think of Frank Dilley shooting that Indian in the head, of Hiram burning my daddy's boots, of scaly, mercury-sick skin and the picture of Mama on Hiram's dresser and the rawness of my wrists that will show scars for a long time. I think of the broken bodies littering my uncle's camp. "No, I need to do it."

I step toward the line of gunpowder. It stretches out of the mine for several paces, but once I light it, we'll have to run like demons are chasing us. And maybe they will be.

"Hurry!" Jefferson says. "Someone's coming."

I touch the flame to the gunpowder. It sizzles and sparks as a tiny lick of fire races away from me toward the mine.

Voices carry now, men's voices, coming toward us.

"Lee!" Jefferson pleads.

I turn to flee, but in that moment, heaven opens up and dumps all the water of the world atop our heads. My racing lick of fire winks out, two paces short of the mine entrance.

This can't be happening. My one shot, lost to a stupid storm.

Figures move just beyond the firelight. Hiram's men have returned.

The gunpowder is soaked. Ruined. But I can't make my feet move.

"Here," Jefferson says. "Give me the rock."

A growing flame still licks the end, partly sheltered from the deluge by my own body. The bundle is warm in my hand. Shielding it as best I can, I give it to Jefferson.

"I'm going to throw it. With luck it will hit one of the barrels inside."

"That will never work!"

"Get ready to run, just in case." And with that, he sends it sailing in a long arc.

By some miracle, the flame survives, and Jeff's throw is a bull's-eye, landing just inside the entrance.

The explosion shakes the ground all around us, and dust chokes the air as something flies out and hits my cheek hard enough to draw blood.

I wipe at my cheek as Jefferson grabs my hand and pulls me away. "Let's go!" he says. But we're too late, because an enormous shadow bears down on us—an impossibly tall, broad man in a hood.

Wilhelm.

The sudden flood of rain has all but put out the fire in the barracks, so I can hardly see his face, but he stands strong before us, arms crossed, as if daring us to pass. From behind him come the sounds of approaching men—angry voices, boots scrunching through mud, someone yelling orders.

"Oh, Lee," Jefferson says, despair in his voice, and at first I think it's Wilhelm he's worried about, but then I realize he's looking toward the mine. "The entrance is only half collapsed," he says. "The other barrel didn't ignite."

Water must have rushed into the mine as soon as the storm hit. My plan didn't work at all. And now we're caught.

Jefferson and Tom will be whipped and beaten. I'll be tied to the bedposts again. Hiram will find himself a new batch of Indians to work until death. It was all for nothing.

I fall to my knees in the mud. Rain streams through my hair and down my face, blurring my vision. Thunder claps overhead.

My hands form fists that beat at the ground, splashing mud

and water everywhere, but I'm so angry I can't seem to stop, and it's impossible to tell where the rain ends and my rage tears begin.

"Leah? What happened? What did you do?" It's my uncle's voice. He's coming for me. He always comes for me. My fingers burrow into the mud, as if by clenching the earth I can keep from being dragged away.

Gold tingles in my fingertips. Spreads up my hands and arms like liquid sunshine flowing through my veins. My chest swells with the sense of gold, my legs shiver with it, my mouth and throat practically hum.

I sense it all now. The whole of the earth glitters with gold, interspersed with tiny veins weaving everywhere. It's like the earth is alive, and gold is its lifeblood.

I stretch out with my senses, taking it all in. I want this one thing, this one, beautiful, shining moment before I'm my uncle's forever.

The ground trembles.

"What was that?" yells someone, Abel Topper maybe, but I'm too far gone to care.

I reach farther, coaxing, caressing, apologizing. *I'm so sorry. You deserve better than my uncle.*

The earth shakes again, dropping someone to his knees beside me.

Wind whips my hair, and tiny flecks of mud swirl around me, sticking to my arms, my face, even my dress, until I am covered in the stuff. The tiny bits of mud are like a blanket wrapping me tight, warming me.

Shakily, I gain my feet. Someone nearby holds up a lantern. "Miss Westfall? What in tarnation . . ."

The lantern glints against the skin of my hands, the lace at my sleeves. It's not mud swirling about, sticking to me like a long-lost friend.

It's gold. I'm covered in the stuff.

Its light courses through my blood, and its warmth washes the air around me. A mere thought is all it takes to sense a tiny nugget nearby and bring it flying toward me.

Someone screams. The nugget drops into my palm, but it's smeared with blood.

The gold is my servant, obeying my every whim. It comes when I call. I could do anything with it. I could move mountains.

I turn and face the mine.

"Jefferson," I say, my voice dark and deep even to my own ears. "Take cover."

I send my witchy sense inside the deep cavern. Our failed explosion didn't wholly collapse the entrance, but it did notable damage. Ore lies in chunks along the path—the gold inside it gives me a decent understanding of their shapes and sizes. A new vein is exposed on the north wall.

I reach and reach, sending tendrils of thought through every vein, every nugget, every bit of dust in the mountain.

"Come to me," I whisper.

The earth trembles as the gold struggles to reach me. People around me start yelling—no, screaming—but I pay them no mind.

Come.

The gold strains toward me like a dog on a leash, trying, trying, trying, and though my witchy powers could easily make a bit of gold worm through dirt or water or something soft like flesh, granite and quartz and shale are another matter.

The mine shakes. Clouds of dust pour from the entrance, only to be immediately tamped down by pouring rain. So I pull harder. More gold coats my arms and legs. I don't have to look to know I am a golden statue, shining like the daughter of Midas. Except the gold is mine. I'm the one in control.

Come.

The mountain vibrates. A pine tree beside the entrance topples over, crashing into the arrastra, leaving its gnarled roots reaching for the air. I sense everyone around me fleeing as the earth heaves and bucks like a colt with its first saddle.

I close my eyes, reaching one last time for every bit of gold inside Hiram's mine. I imagine I'm gripping it all in my fist. I imagine I give it all a *twist*.

The earth shakes violently, and the mountain crumples in on itself, so suddenly that it seems the very air gets sucked away. I open my eyes just in time to watch the land cave in, tossing rocks and trees in all directions. Then the rain finally succeeds in dousing the barracks fire completely, and I can see no more.

I am wrung out. Spent.

My knees are wobbly and my heart is like hummingbird wings in my chest as I turn about, peering through the rain and the dark for Jefferson. Now that I'm no longer calling the gold to me, streams of it wash from my dress, my arms, my boots, swirling into the mud. It mixes and washes away, mixes and washes away until it's no more. It would take a witchy girl to know the gold was ever there.

Something cracks my cheekbone. Pain explodes through my eye.

Chapter Twenty-Seven

"What have you done?" someone screams.

Another blow rattles my teeth and splits my lip. Blood dribbles down my chin.

My uncle is going to kill me. I have ruined him, and he's finally going to kill me. I just hope Jefferson got away in all the chaos.

I struggle to remain standing. I sense another blow coming, and I try to dodge, but I'm not fast enough, and it glances against my temple. My vision turns starry, and I drop to my knees.

"Hiram," I manage through my busted, swelling lip.

My voice stops him. He crouches down, gets right in my face. His eyes are wide and bereft, his cheeks smeared with mud. Traces of gold cling to his sopping coat, though I'm sure he has no idea.

He grabs my upper arms, and he shakes and shakes. "Why, Leah? How could you? Your very own father! And after everything I've done for you."

"You mean steal my home, destroy my family, kidnap me, and box my face?"

"I just wanted us to be together, to be family. Now, I'll have to . . . I'll never . . ."

"You'll never be able to borrow money again," I say. "No one will agree to work for you. You've lost everything. You're ruined."

He gapes at me.

"And my father," I add, "is Reuben Westfall. He always has been. He always will be. Doesn't matter who I was born to. He's the man I'd pick for my daddy, no matter what, and that counts way more than blood, to my way of thinking."

Even in the darkness, I feel Hiram's features harden. I feel the rage growing inside him like a storm cloud, and I know, for sure and certain, that I have yet to understand the violence this man is capable of.

So I don't know why my next words come out of my mouth, but they do. "And you are nothing to me. Less than nothing. You are a viper to be stepped on. You are not worthy of my love, or my time, or even my words. From this day forward, I shall not speak to you again."

He yells something unintelligible, raising his arm to give me the beating of all beatings. This is it. The moment he kills me.

Like lightning, another hand comes up, catches Hiram's wrist as it descends toward my face. And the blow does not come.

I blink through the rain, trying to make sense of it.

Jefferson stands over me, fierceness in his face. He is like a mama bear, protecting her cub. Blood streams from his temple, like he fell and struck his head on a rock, but it doesn't seem to be slowing him down now. With his other hand, he grabs Hiram by the throat and shoves him back. My uncle falls onto his rear, squishing up mud. He tries to get up, and suddenly Wilhelm is there too, pushing him back down.

Wilhelm's hand reaches inside his coat. He draws out a bottle of laudanum.

I should tell him to stop. I know I should. Instead, I watch, somewhat horrified, somewhat glad, as he yanks the stopper, puts the bottle to Hiram's lips, and forces him to drink.

Hiram tries to scuttle back like a crab, but Jefferson has his shoulders in a firm grip, and Hiram can only guzzle helplessly as Wilhelm forces any remaining laudanum in the bottle down his gullet.

Jefferson rises, reaches for my hand. "Tom and Mary are waiting," he says, trying to lead me away, but I resist.

"Wait," I say. I step forward and tug on the sleeve of Wilhelm's coat.

My uncle has clasped his arms around his knees, and now he's rocking back and forth in the mud, rocking, rocking.

Wilhelm turns to stare at me, an apology in his face, though in this darkness I could be mistaken.

"Wilhelm, we're leaving. You coming?"

His eyes widen. I've well and truly surprised him. His mouth opens and an odd sound comes out. He's trying to talk.

I wait for the sounds to form words in my ears, to make any

kind of sense, but they don't. He sounds like a baby babbling. He tries once more, but frustration clouds his features and he goes silent. Finally he nods once, firmly.

"Let's go, then."

I'm not sure where Abel Topper is, or Reverend Lowrey, or who else might have survived. I decide I don't care. I just want to be away from this place.

"This way," Jefferson says, with a wary look in Wilhelm's direction.

We follow after. The air smells of mud and wet soot and something else, something tangy. Blood, maybe. Though the dark and the rain make seeing nearly impossible, Jefferson leads us unerringly past the burned-out barracks, down to the pasture, and across the creek into the trees.

By the time we find Tom and Mary and the horses, I'm shivering with cold. Tom has rounded up an extra mount for Mary, but when he sees Wilhelm, he just shrugs and hands over the reins.

Jefferson boosts me up onto Peony, and everyone else mounts, with Mary riding double with Tom again. Jefferson clucks to Sorry, and together they lead us toward the great valley and eventually home.

We follow the creek downstream all through the night, wanting to be as far from Hiram's Gulch as possible before dawn breaks. The rain and darkness force us to travel with agonizing slowness. We trust Jefferson to lead; when we hunted together as children, he always tracked and I always shot, partly because his sense of direction is so good it's almost like magic.

As the sky begins to brighten, casting the golden hills with their twisted oaks in a gray, rainy haze, we urge our mounts to go faster. After less than an hour, Apollo begins to protest, and we're forced to stop and rest lest he turn up lame.

"Mary can ride with me and Peony next," I say as we stretch our legs and grab a quick bite of jerky.

"I don't have much in the way of supplies," Jefferson says. "I wasn't prepared. I thought we'd be leaving tonight."

"We'll make do," Tom says. "By the way, happy thanksgiving, everyone."

"Happy thanksgiving," everyone returns, somewhat glumly. Wilhelm says nothing, of course, but he raises his canteen with the rest of us, and I'm shocked to discover a hint of a smile on his face.

"Thanksgiving is a stupid celebration," Mary says.

We all turn to stare at her.

"You're grateful enough to have a holiday, but then you go and slaughter Indians and steal their land. It makes no sense."

I start to protest, "*We* didn't slaughter them. Not all—"

Mary mutters something in Chinese, and even though I have no idea what she's saying, I'd bet my witchy powers it's something unseemly. Then she adds, "Your people. You. There's no difference."

"Giving thanks is not stupid," Tom says. "Killing Indians is."

Jefferson says nothing, but he looks back and forth between us, his mind obviously busy.

"Well, I don't know if the holiday is stupid or not," I say. "But I'm thankful for all of you just the same. And I'm thankful for Muskrat. We wouldn't have escaped without his help."

"Hear! Hear!" Tom says, raising his canteen once more, and we all follow suit, even Mary.

We drink for a moment in silence. Then Jefferson says, "I didn't see Muskrat go down."

Mary looks back over the path we've been traveling. "It's not right," she murmurs. "That he should be the one to make the plan, but we should be the ones to get away."

"Maybe he did get away," Tom says.

"I hope so," I say, but my voice lacks sureness

"Break's over," Jefferson says. We mount up, sobered, and it doesn't feel like a holiday at all.

We're too far west to encounter more mining camps, but the creek eventually reaches a river—which turns out to be the Yuba—and at their conjunction is a small trading post. We ask directions, trade my gold for supplies, and follow the river until it joins up with the Feather, which leads us due south, exactly the way we want to go.

With the mine a total ruin, any of Dilley's men who survived will winter in Sacramento, looking for work. So we skirt Sacramento to avoid them, instead of visiting the town. There's probably a better, shorter way to go, but we surely don't know it, and it takes more than a week just to reach the American River.

The American is well traveled, with little paths and roads

worn all along its banks, and we pick up our pace. I'm so eager to see Becky and the kids, the Major, Jasper and Henry, Hampton, even Old Tug and the Buckeyes. I hope Nugget has made a full recovery, that Olive has nursed her back to perfect health. I hope everyone has found mountains of gold.

When we find the tributary creek that leads to our beaver pond, the horses recognize home, and it becomes difficult to keep them to a wise, leisurely pace. And when the trees break onto our beautiful pond and the tiny town growing on the hill above it, my heart is so full of happiness I think I might burst.

There are more tents and shanties than when we left, more people. A wide path winds around the pond and straight up the hill to what almost looks like a town square. In the middle of the square, a tall sign post has been pounded into the ground. On the sign are the burn-etched words: WELCOME TO GLORY, CALIFORNIA.

Becky's cabin seems to be Glory's cornerstone, and it has a temporary canvas roof now. Attached to the west wall is a wide awning that stretches far enough to shade several tables and benches.

Even though it's midday, a few miners sit on the benches drinking from tin cups. Becky bursts from the cabin carrying a tray piled with biscuits. She rushes to the miners, serving each one with a growl and a frown, and I'm so happy to see her I can hardly stand it. I dismount, and Mary slides down behind me.

Beside us, Jefferson chuckles. "Looks like Widow Joyner has finally had enough of smiling and being nice," he says.

Just then, Becky wags her finger at the nose of a particularly gnarled-looking fellow, and I can't hear what she's saying, but it's clear she's giving him a piece of her mind. The gnarled fellow just grins in response.

"Indeed," Tom says. "It seems she is embracing her true nature." He gestures toward a sign hanging from the awning.

I stop short. The sign's large black letters read THE WORST TAVERN IN CALIFORNIA. And below it, in smaller letters: BAD FOOD, BAD SERVICE.

Jefferson bends over laughing, and I'm trying very hard not to laugh, too, when Becky finally turns and sees us.

The men at the table are caught in the sudden sunbeam of her smile, and they don't care one whit when she drops her tray beside them, sending biscuits flying everywhere, and starts running toward us.

"Olive!" she calls. "Fetch the Major. Lee and Jeff and Tom are back!"

Becky throws her arms around me, and I hug her right back. We cling to each other for a moment, and then she steps back, smoothing her apron and otherwise collecting herself.

Looking primly toward Wilhelm and Mary, she says, "I see we have company." Then her gaze roves Jefferson and Tom, and her eyes narrow. "You all look terrible. Worse than terrible."

"It was a rough time," I tell her. "Becky Joyner, this is Wilhelm." Wilhelm nods. "And this is Mary."

"Hello," Mary says, and suddenly it occurs to me that Mary can't possibly be her real name. Later, when we're alone, I'll ask her if there's something else she'd like us to call her. A Chinese name.

Becky frowns. "Pleased to meet you," she says, though I'm not sure it's true. "I've been sick with worry, Lee. Jasper and the Major were hatching a plan to go after you. What happened?"

I sigh loudly and follow it with a deep breath, as if by doing so I can purge all the bad things that happened and fill myself with clean air and friendly faces and safety. "We have a lot to tell you."

The news of our return flows through Glory like wildfire. Henry and Jasper come running first, and Henry is so happy to see Tom that he hugs him like he'll never let go while tears stream from his eyes. We repeat the story to the college men; then Olive returns with the Major and Hampton in tow, and we tell the story a third time. We're about to launch into a fourth telling for Old Tug and a few of his Buckeyes, but Becky intercedes.

"Food and rest," she insists. "There'll be time for the telling later. Lee, you and your friend Mary can share the cabin with me and the children for a while." She looks pointedly at Mary. "I could use an extra hand running the tavern, if you're not afraid of rough men and rougher work."

Mary nods. "Hard work and I are old friends, ma'am. I have a different trade in mind for myself, but tavern work will do for now, if you'll have me."

"Good. I just hope you're a terrible cook. This establishment has a reputation to maintain." To Jefferson, Becky says, "I'm afraid your shanty was taken over by a couple of boys come south from Oregon; you'll have to build a new one, but I know just the place. And you." She peers up at Wilhelm, frowning. "You look like you could do the work of ten men. We've a new blacksmith in town who has more orders than he can handle, and he needs an assistant."

And just like that, we are folded back into the community as if we never left.

Becky serves us a meal of half-baked bread topped with lumpy gravy, and no poorly cooked food ever tasted so fine. Afterward, I fall into a bedroll and sleep like the dead.

In the morning, the Major comes by carrying a new pair of boots. "I made these for you last night," he says. "To replace the ones your uncle burned."

He must have been up all night. Tears of gratitude fill my eyes, and my lips tremble so badly I almost can't force the thank you from my mouth. Because they look just like Daddy's boots, with laces, low heels, and the shiny curve of steel at their tips. Except they're smaller and newer, and they fit just right.

Later, I help Jefferson build his shanty, which for now will be a large tent stretched over a wooden frame. We work mostly in silence, just glad to be together and safe. First we level out the area a bit with shovels, then I hold the posts steady while he pounds them into the ground. I love watching him work—the play of muscles in his forearms, the look of intense focus in his eyes, the way he laughs when a post snaps in two, instead of getting angry and swearing the way his father would have.

At one point, he looks up from digging a post hole, his face full of mischief. He says, "You know, Lee, this shanty will be big enough for two."

My heart is suddenly racing. "Only if they don't mind getting cozy," I manage.

"Oh, trust me. I don't mind."

"In that case," I say, and it's my turn to tease, "I bet Wilhelm would join you if you asked."

Speak of the devil and you summon him, because movement catches my eye and I turn to find Wilhelm trudging up the rise, carrying something. It's a slate, and he clutches it tight with both huge hands.

"Hello, Wilhelm," I say. "Did you and the blacksmith come to an arrangement?"

He nods, but he won't meet my gaze.

"I'm glad," I say, only to fill the silence.

Wilhelm stares at the slate. Then his feet. His scarred lips press together firmly. *Clank, clank, clank* goes Jefferson's hammer.

Finally Wilhelm raises the slate toward me, indicating with his chin that I ought to take it, along with a bit of chalk.

I do, and I turn the slate over to discover that he has written something.

I am not a bad man.

I stare at the words a long moment. I can talk just fine, thank you very much, but it seems right not to. So beneath his words, I write, *Then you've come to the right place.*

I hand it back, and he offers me a hesitant grin. Then he turns away and heads back down the hill toward the blacksmith's stall.

Only two days after our return, a courier rides into camp, his saddlebags bursting with letters. Everyone gathers around, hoping for a bit of correspondence or even just news. He calls out a few names I don't recognize, and various miners step forward to claim their letters. Then he hollers, "Leah Westfall!"

I'm so taken aback that I freeze. After a heart-pounding silence, I step forward on wary feet. I've no family back home. The only people who know me, know where I am, are my uncle and his men.

The courier hands me the letter and moves on to the next bit of correspondence as I step away. Suddenly my friends are surrounding me—Jefferson, Becky, Jasper, Hampton, Mary.

"Who's it from?" Hampton asks.

"Aren't you going to open it?" Mary says.

It's addressed to me in flowing, beautiful script. Not my uncle's handwriting, I note with relief. I turn it over, and I nearly drop it when I see the wax seal. It says OFFICE OF THE TERRITORIAL CIVILIAN GOVERNOR OF CALIFORNIA.

"Well, aren't you fancy!" Jasper says, delighted.

I use my thumb to break the seal and unfold the letter. I read quickly. "It's an invitation," I say. "A formal invitation to the Christmas ball in Sacramento, on behalf of the new governor, Burnett himself."

"Oh, my," Becky breathes.

"It says I'm to select a contingent from the thriving American settlement of Glory, California, to accompany me."

We all stare at the invitation in wonder.

"You'll have to leave in the next few days if you're to make it on time," Jasper says.

Jefferson is the first person to ask, "But why?"

And with that single question, my brief pleasure at feeling flattered evaporates.

"People have been talking about Miss Leah," Old Tug says.

I blink. "Really?"

"Folks say you destroyed Hiram's Gulch with nothing but gunpowder and grit."

"Gossip spreads awful fast for an unsettled territory," Jefferson grumbles, but I can't help feeling gratified. It's a whole heap better than everyone knowing the truth, that I crushed the mine to smithereens using my witchy powers.

"That's what we get for going around Sacramento," Mary says. "News traveled ahead of us. Now people want to meet you, Lee. Take your measure."

Tug says, "The peddler who stopped by two days back said the mine exploded in a cloud of gold dust. He called you the Golden Goddess."

I groan, but Tom laughs. "That's ridiculous."

"Course it ain't nothing but tall tales," Tug says.

"Course," I agree quickly.

"But it's enough to make a bunch of rich, uppity men curious, don't you think?"

"It's probably a legal matter," Tom says. "Hiram Westfall

owed these men a lot of money. He also had a lot of property in his name. You're his only relative. If something happened to him, they might need your signature on some papers."

"What if I ignore it?" I ask. "Just because they send me an invitation doesn't mean I have to attend."

"I like that plan," Jefferson says.

Tom shakes his head. "Lee, you must take this seriously. I wouldn't be surprised if your uncle's patron, the one to whom he owed thousands of dollars, will insist you make good on your uncle's debt. If you don't go to him, he could come to us. The law regarding property is still unsettled here, and he could find a way to take everything we've built. *Everything.*"

I look around at their anxious faces. "I won't let that happen."

Becky Joyner reaches over and squeezes my hand gratefully.

James Henry Hardwick, I say to myself. I frown at the invitation. It's not from Hardwick officially, but it might as well be.

"It feels like a trap," Jefferson says, echoing my thoughts.

"Whatever you decide, be wary," Jasper says, and there's a murmured chorus of agreement.

And that gets me thinking.

Maybe I'm the one they should be wary of. Maybe I'm the one who will spring a trap. And maybe being surrounded by friends is making me brash, but an idea has come knocking, and I know I have to try. All I need is money. Lots of money. Money is no trouble for a witchy girl, right? But even a witchy girl needs time, and I have none.

I lift my head from the letter and look at everyone in the group, meeting them eye to eye, and I make up my mind.

I say, "I'm going to need your help."

We spend all of the next day feverishly preparing. Everyone wants to come with me, except Becky, who doesn't want to leave her children or her thriving business, and Hampton, who has no time for "dancing and frippery." It turns out, he's going to go broke buying his wife's freedom and paying for her passage on a steamship. Her name is Adelaide, and Tom thinks he can arrange to get her here by next year. Hampton wants to have his stake built back up by then.

Becky gives me a gown she brought west for a special occasion. "I'm glad I saved it from the fire, but it's no good to me now," she says, holding it up against me to eyeball the fit. It's the most beautiful thing I've ever seen, made of sheened yellow silk, with a tiny pointed waist and a full swishing skirt. It will practically shimmer by lantern light, almost golden.

"You might need it someday," I insist. "We still have to make that trip to San Francisco, remember? To get your home out of impound."

She smiles. "I *am* home."

The way she looks at me, her eyes shining but a little bit shy, her smile questioning, it's like she *needs* me to take this dress from her. I wonder if it's a bit of an apology, for everything that happened along the trail. "In that case, I thank you, Becky."

"Maybe I'll go to the ball next year, when Olive and Andy

are a bit older and I don't have a baby who wants to nurse every waking moment."

"I'd love that," I say, giving her arm a squeeze.

Her face grows serious. "Let's just hope this gown helps you do your business."

Together we take in the dress a smidge at the waist, and take up the hem an inch. We work in silence, each of us too aware of all that is at stake.

Jefferson, Jasper, and the Major are in charge of taking up a collection. They visit every single person with a nearby claim to tell them the plan and ask for a donation. The town seems to have acquired a few folks not interested in gold at all, like a dentist and the new blacksmith. Almost everyone cheerfully donates, but I can't imagine it will be nearly enough.

But we don't have any other choice. It will have to do.

I will have to do.

Chapter Twenty-Eight

In the afternoon, as the sun is arching down toward the big valley, Jefferson and I steal away to our claims. We make sure no one is around to see, then we sit down together beside the creek.

"You don't need to do this, Lee," Jefferson says, and he has a smile on his face, like he knows something I don't.

"I do," I insist. "I need the money. Badly. And I have to know whether or not I can control it. I can't let anyone else get hurt."

"If you say so."

I close my eyes and call to the gold. I'm careful this time, selective. I don't rumble the gold in the ground under my legs or in the cliffs to our left. Instead, I reach for surface gold—powder and specks and a few tiny nuggets.

"It's working," Jefferson says, his voice full of wonder. "You're covered in gold again."

I open my eyes. Gold coats my arms, my skirt, everything. "I didn't hurt you, did I?" I ask, peering into his face. Last time, I'm sure I injured people as the gold flew through the air, impacting or maybe even piercing skin.

"Not even a little. But look." He points to the grassy creek bank. It's no longer a smooth, round hill, but rather a series of smaller hillocks, as though the mud tried to ripple toward me. "You'll get better with practice," he says.

Together we scrape the gold from my skin and shake it from my hair. We lose a bit in the process, but it's no matter. We'll just mark the spot and pan it out later. I suppose we could retrieve it with mercury, but truth be told, after what happened to the Indians, I may never use mercury again.

"How much do you think we got?" Jefferson asks.

I heft the bag of gold dust in my hand, reaching with my witchy sense to get a feel for its purity and weight. "About three hundred dollars' worth," I guess.

Jefferson whistles. "In just one day!"

"I might have to witch up some more along the way," I say glumly.

He laughs.

"What?" I say, frowning.

"You don't need it."

"What are you talking about?"

"Our collection. The good people of Glory donated everything you need. And more."

I gape at him.

"Becky herself gave five hundred dollars. Said she'll earn it back in a week. Turns out, people are coming from far and wide to visit the Worst Tavern."

I can hardly breathe. "That's so much money," I choke out.

"Old Tug and the Buckeyes put together about six hundred between them. The college men each gave a hundred. The Major gave a bunch, even Hampton. And then all these strangers, people who wandered into town after we left, well, they gave us a heap of money and gold, too. Lee, we raised more than four thousand dollars. At least I think so. I'm not as good at estimating gold value as you are."

My legs don't seem to work right, and I'm forced to plop back down onto the ground. I let my face fall into my hands, and I just concentrate on trying to breathe. Four thousand dollars. And people just *gave* to us.

"Lee, what's wrong? I thought you'd be happy!"

"I'm fine! It's just . . ." Another deep breath. "I've spent my whole life witching up gold. It's how I fed my family. It's how I was supposed to become rich. I thought . . ." My voice turns sheepish as I admit this. "I thought my magic would save us all. But it turns out, all the magic in the world is rubbish compared to good people who take care of their own."

Jefferson has this maddening grin that make my toes feel funny. "Well, that sounds like wisdom to me." He reaches a hand for me. "Come on. Let's head over to the Worst Tavern for supper."

I allow him to drag me to my feet and lead me back toward town. We're almost there when Jefferson grabs my arm. "Wait. Lee, there's something I've got to say."

My eyes are level with his shirt. He's finally patched up that bullet hole, with clumsy black stitches. And he desperately needs a new pair of suspenders. He deserves a nice, new set of boughten clothes. Maybe he'll let me buy it for him.

"Lee?"

I look up. He's gazing down at me with such pleading, such yearning, and it feels like I'm not getting enough air, because if he asks me to marry him again, I'm not sure what I ought to say.

"I know I've asked you to marry me a few times," he begins.

"Just a few."

"And that offer is still on the table; don't think it's not."

"All right."

"It's just . . . you should know . . . all this talk about California becoming a state soon and us getting a proper town charter and all . . ."

I reach for his hand and squeeze it tight. "Go on."

"I'm not sure I want anything to do with it."

"What?" Is he saying he'll leave me? How could he not want to be part of our town?

As if reading my mind, he says, "I mean, I'm not going anywhere. But . . . My mother's people were forced to leave Georgia so white men could get rich. And when we left to head west, I thought it would finally be my turn. *I* would be the one getting rich for a change. I deserved it, right?"

"You do deserve it, Jeff."

"I don't. No one does. Not that way. And now, after what I saw at Hiram's Gulch, I'm not sure what to do."

"So what are you saying? You won't mine? You won't be part of the town?"

He frowns. "I don't know what I'm saying exactly. I'm still figuring it. I'll probably do some mining, I'll hunt, a lot of the things I did back home. But I don't think I'll ever own property. It's not my land, Lee. And it wouldn't be right to just . . . take it. Maybe it doesn't matter. Maybe I can't own land free and legal, anyway, being half-Cherokee. But I thought you should know, on the off chance that you're considering becoming my wife. I mean, maybe you're not. But if you are . . . I may never own land. I'll probably never be rich."

I'm not sure how to respond, or if I should. It's too much to think on to let any old thing come out of my mouth. I settle for squeezing his hand again and saying, "Thank you for telling me."

Chapter Twenty-Nine

Tom, Henry, Jefferson, Mary, and I ride into Sacramento on Christmas Eve. It's a muddy, busy town, and even though it's new, it's already bigger than Dahlonega. It snugs up against the water, just south of the convergence of the Sacramento and American Rivers, which creates a wide, watery highway that isn't nearly as awe-inspiring as the Mississippi, but respectable just the same.

The river is muddy brown with autumn flooding, filled with detritus and boats. Most are sailboats of various sizes, but a few are large paddle steamers, and for the life of me, I can't figure how they can all maneuver without crashing into one another.

"Town's built too close to the river," Jefferson observes.

"Yep," Tom agrees. "If we'd built Glory this near the creek, it'd flood come spring for sure."

"It's bigger than I expected," I say. Though regular two-story buildings make up the heart of town, tents and shanties extend east almost as far as the eye can see.

"They say San Francisco is even bigger," Henry says. "Four or five times bigger."

We all turn to stare at him.

"Cross my heart!" he says.

"We ought to find a hotel," Tom says, so we follow his lead and urge our horses forward.

The hotels are all booked full for the holiday, and we are forced to try a saloon, but Tom comes back outside with a frown, saying, "No place for young ladies." Finally a kind soul points us in the direction of a boardinghouse one block off the main square. The gentleman running the place insists we pay for two separate rooms—one for the men, one for Mary and me—which is a ridiculous expense, since we've all been sleeping side by side on the trail for days. But now that we're in a city, I guess we have to start behaving in city ways.

Becky's gown, along with a corset and petticoat, has been folded up in my saddlebag. I don't have an iron, and I'm not sure how to take care of silk, anyway, so I just shake everything out and hang it on a peg to air, hoping it will be suitable enough.

In the evening, we begin to get ready. My hair is almost long enough to put up, but not quite. I settle for parting it down the middle and pinning it smooth over my ears. Becky gave me a little bauble of lace and yellow rosettes, and once I pin it in place, it almost looks like I have a proper bun.

The gown is still a bit wrinkled, but not too badly. It slips over my corset and petticoats with ease. Mary helps me lace up the back and ties a perfect bow.

"You sure you don't want to go to the ball?" I ask her as I give the skirt an experimental swish. I'm delighted with the way it moves around my ankles, like flowing water. "I'd love to have your company."

"I'm sure. It's bad for business, to show up at these sorts of things."

I have no idea what that means, so I just shrug. Then I remember something else.

"Is Mary your real name?" I blurt clumsily.

Her eyes narrow.

"I mean, is there another name you'd like me to call you? A Chinese name?"

Maybe I've overstepped my bounds. Maybe, where Mary comes from, a name is an important thing, like it is among the Maidu. A meaningful thing not blithely shared.

But her gaze softens, and she says, "When I was in China, my name was Chan Suk Yee, or Suk Yee Chan, in the backward way you do names here. But I'm not sure that girl even exists anymore."

"Oh." I think I know what she means. The Leah Westfall of Lumpkin County, Georgia, feels like another life, another girl.

"How did you get here? To California, I mean."

"I walked across the ocean. On water, like your Jesus."

It takes a split second to realize she's funning me.

"On a ship, you dolt. In the hold, actually. I stowed away. But I was caught a week before we hit San Francisco."

My eyes widen. "That sounds terrifying."

"Maybe I'll tell you about it someday." She gives the ribbon at my back a finishing flick and shoves me out the door before I can ask any more questions. I vow silently to ask them soon, though. After what happened to Therese, I won't waste an opportunity to have a friend.

I haven't been this dressed up since Mama and Daddy's funeral, except this time, I'm wearing a bright, happy color. It feels right, like I'm finally in my own skin. Which is not to say I'd wear this getup to bag a deer; Lee-in-trousers is an important part of me, too. But for tonight, I like the way I feel in a fancy dress.

We convene outside the boardinghouse before walking to the hotel together. Sure enough, Becky's gown ripples like liquid gold in the light of the gas lamps. Jefferson eyes widen when he sees me. "Oh, Lee," is all he says, but it makes my skin warm all over.

Jefferson stands tall in a new suit he bought at Mormon Island, and with his hair combed back and his fancy lace cuffs, he is as handsome as I've ever seen him.

"You look very nice," I tell him.

He grins wider than the Mississippi. "You never give compliments," he says.

"Only when they're well deserved."

Tom also wears a nice suit, a little less fine perhaps, but he looks every inch the college-educated lawyer.

Henry is the last to join us, and I gasp a little because he wears the finest black vest and trousers I've ever seen, set off by a bright blue silk cravat. His face is cleanly shaved, and his scant hair is covered by a shining black top hat. He beams with such delight that I say, "That's a lovely color for you, Henry. Your eyes are as blue as I've ever seen them."

Henry beams. "Truth is, I love to dance," he says. "I never run out of partners, so long as I'm dressed like a duke."

"You can take all of my partners," I say.

"You have the invitation?" Tom asks me, but his eyes are on Henry so I wave it in front of his face. "Let's go, then."

Each of us carries a fair bit of gold—we decided it would be safer to divvy it up—so as we walk the single block toward the hotel, stepping carefully to avoid mud, I feel as though I'm surrounded by a miasma of light and buzzing warmth.

We arrive at the City Hotel—built brand-new just last summer—at precisely seven o'clock in the evening. Before we enter, I pause to take a deep breath.

"You can do this, Lee," Jefferson whispers as others pass us, waving their invitations to be let inside.

"I can," I say. "And I will." I have one goal. Find the man who loaned my uncle so much money. James Henry Hardwick. He's sure to be here. He might even find me first.

The doorman lets us pass, and we wander through a large carpeted lobby that smells of tangy pine boughs and the giant Christmas tree at its center, decorated in gold ribbons. Beyond it are double doors leading to the ballroom. There, another doorman asks our names. I tell him, and he turns to announce us.

My heart pounds as he booms, "From Glory, California. Miss Leah Westfall! Mr. Jefferson Kingfisher! Mr. Thomas Bigler! Mr. Henry Meek!"

I hold my head high and sweep inside as if I belong. The ballroom is packed, and all eyes turn toward me. Perhaps they've all heard of the Golden Goddess and her motley friends. I expect hostility toward us. Suspicion. Maybe even anger.

Instead, the gazes leveled at us are friendly and curious. Some are openly smiling. I force myself to smile back as we drift farther into the room.

Chandeliers bright with candles hang from the ceiling. Tables heaped with food line the walls. There's even a sparkling glass punch bowl. In the far corner a small orchestra plays "Greensleeves." I'm one of the few women in the room. I count three others, all much older, one of whom is a beautiful Mexican woman with gray streaks in her glossy black hair and a ruffled, multicolored skirt. She hangs on the arm of a man who wears a tight, high-waisted red vest with shining rows of brass buttons.

She gives me a smile and a wave, even though I'm a total stranger to her, and the gesture fills me with warmth.

Two men wear dresses. One sports an enormous beard and mustache. Both are already dancing with partners, and by all appearances having a grand time of it. It's a sight I'd never see in Georgia, and it puts to mind what a strange and marvelous place California is.

"I should have worn a dress," Henry says, his voice full of wonder.

Suddenly men are approaching me from all directions, congregating into an eager gaggle, but a stocky fellow with long brown sideburns reaches me first. "You look ravishing, Miss Westfall," he says. "Are you . . . unattached?"

Well, he sure didn't waste time getting to the point. "I am unmarried," I say, before I can think better of it. I resist the urge to step back, a little closer to Jefferson and Tom and Henry.

He grins, revealing tobacco-stained teeth. "I'm delighted to hear it. I'm Matthew Jannison, carpenter by trade. May I have this dance?" And he extends his hand to me.

I've never been much for dancing, much less with strangers, but it's better than standing around growing increasingly nervous about meeting my uncle's patron, so I place my hand in his sweaty one and allow him to lead me onto the floor. I feel Jefferson's eyes on my back as we step away.

"Where are you from, Miss Westfall?" he asks as we fall into time with the orchestra. His hand remains acceptably high on my waist, and he maintains a proper distance between us, so I relax enough to tell him the truth.

"Lumpkin County, Georgia. And you, Mr. Jannison?"

"Boston. You came by ship, I assume?"

"No, sir. Wagon train."

His eyes widen. "But you're so . . ."

"I'm not at all a proper lady, and don't you dare imply that I am." I say it with a smile, hoping he understands my mood.

"I wouldn't dream of making such a gauche insinuation!" he declares with mock affront. "Did you arrive with your parents?"

"I came alone. But I'm not alone anymore."

"But you said you are unmarried."

Beside us, Henry is now dancing with a strange man, chatting at him with as much comfort and animation as I've ever seen.

"I have many friends," I say, smiling.

"I see." But I can tell he doesn't, and this conversation is growing tiresome.

"Mr. Jannison," I say, "do you happen to know a Mr. James Henry Hardwick? He's a business partner of my uncle's, and I'd dearly love to make his acquaintance."

Mr. Jannison's cheeks are already bright red with the exertion of dancing. "All of Sacramento knows Mr. Hardwick!" he says. "He's a member of the city council, and he owns more acreage than—"

"Oh, I'd be so delighted if you could introduce me!"

"Of course! He is a personal friend, you know. Right this way, my dear."

Well, that was easy. I allow him to lead me away, but I quickly cast around the ballroom for my friends. Henry sees me first, and when I nod to him, he makes apologies to his dancing partner and moves to follow. Jefferson stands beside one of the food tables, staring glumly into a cup full of punch as if trying to augur something. My gesture to get his attention is less than subtle, and he sets down his cup and follows too.

I sense the two of them falling in line behind me as we make our way to a curved stair with a shiny banister wrapped in garlands. I don't see Tom anywhere nearby, but hopefully he'll notice us and join soon.

Several smartly dressed men cluster together on the steps. It seems as though they are deep in counsel, purposely posed in a spot from which they can survey their domain—and easily be seen, as well. I feel my hackles go up, and I'm not sure why, except maybe that they remind me of my uncle. Even the way they stand, the way they talk and carry themselves, speaks of power and a deep sense of their personal place in the world.

"Excuse me, good sirs," Mr. Jannison says. "Please forgive the interruption."

The men cease their discussion to turn as one and stare at us.

"This young lady would like to make the acquaintance of Councilman Hardwick," he continues blithely. "Naturally I thought to bring her over before her dance card filled."

"How gracious of you," a man with white hair says dryly. He has harsh cheekbones and sideburns as fluffy as rabbit cottontails.

Mr. Jannison beams, but it occurs to me that Mr. Jannison's assertion of personal friendship might be much exaggerated.

"You are Miss Westfall, I presume?" the white-haired man says. "I heard you announced as you entered."

"Yes. Are you Mr. Hardwick?"

"I am he."

"Then I believe we have some business to attend to."

He smiles down at me as though I'm a favorite hound. "I'm attending to business right now, with these gentleman. I can make some time for you tomorrow."

The gazes of his companions are apprising rather than

friendly; calculated and prim. They are so like my uncle that I almost walk away, defeated.

"You will treat with me now, sir," I say in as firm a voice as I can muster. "I'm in Sacramento today only. Surely these gentlemen would not begrudge a lady in need this small bit of your time?"

One of the other men laughs. "We'll continue this later, James," he says, placing a companionable hand on Hardwick's shoulder.

Hardwick frowns. "Thank you, Governor Burnett."

My eyes widen. The governor?

Governor Burnett turns to me. "It's nice to finally see you in the flesh. Though you are markedly less golden than advertised."

I force a smile and wave nonchalantly. "You know these miners and their tall tales."

"Indeed." And with a look of dismissal, the governor steps down the stairs and onto the dance floor, the other men following in his wake.

Now it's just me and a flustered Mr. Jannison, Jefferson and Henry at our backs, gazing up at my uncle's patron. I don't like having him look down on me from the stairs, so I step up beside him, bringing us closer to eye level. He frowns.

"I understand you blew up my mine," he says for an opening sally.

"My uncle told me it was *his* mine," I say. "And it collapsed in a bad storm."

Mr. Jannison looks back and forth between us, eyes wide,

then beats a hasty retreat. Were I a betting woman, I'd lay odds he'll never invite me to dance again.

"With the help of a little gunpowder, they say," Hardwick insists. I don't contradict him. Better for everyone to blame gunpowder than magic. "I could have you jailed for the destruction of my property. I've been considering it."

"I'd like to see you try," Jefferson mutters.

"I have a much better idea," I say quickly, before Jefferson gets us in trouble.

Hardwick raises an eyebrow. "Oh?"

"I understand my uncle still owed you four thousand dollars."

"He did. But he'll be unable to pay. Apparently your sabotage has ruined him. Besides that, I'm not certain he's in his right mind anymore."

I guess that means he survived Wilhelm's laudanum. I'm not sure how I feel about that.

"He was never in his right mind," Tom says, and I'm so relieved that he has finally joined us. "Hiram Westfall is a thief and a murderer. I'm sorry you got taken in by such a wicked fellow."

Hardwick glares. "And who are you?"

"Thomas Bigler, attorney, of Illinois College," he says proudly. It's the first time I've heard him own up to being a real lawyer, and I can't help my smile.

"I see," Hardwick says. "Well, I must say I'm not surprised to hear that. He seemed polished and intelligent when we met, and he claimed a great deal of mining experience. But he was in terrible shape when I fetched him."

"You fetched him?" I glance around the ballroom, suddenly wary. Is he here? I had hoped never to see him again.

"Of course I fetched him. I figured he could work off his debt to me over time, but he is not fit for work."

"Where is he?"

"Locked up on one of the prison ships, the *Stirling*, until I decide what to do with him."

My stomach turns over. Hardwick won't be able to do things like that if California becomes a state; it's a crime in this country to lock someone up over a debt. My uncle deserves jail and worse, but not for that. It's badness upon badness upon badness.

But I can't help the relief that swells inside me at the thought of my uncle locked up. Maybe that makes me bad, too.

I'm silent for so long that Tom has to jump in. "We would like to make a deal with you, sir."

Hardwick's gaze surveys the four of us—me in my almost-golden gown; Jefferson, whose skin is as sun burnished and Cherokee as ever; Tom in his smart but inexpensive suit; Henry in his finery. "I assume you've come to beg for clemency," Hardwick says.

I laugh, loudly and genuinely, and several people on the floor below us turn to stare.

"Mr. Hardwick," I say, "we've come to help you."

His lips part with surprise.

"You can't imprison this young lady for destroying your mine," Tom says. "You have no proof."

"I have my word," Hardwick says.

"Who would believe you?" Tom counters. "A sweet, small lass like this? Collapsing a whole mine?"

Hardwick's frown deepens.

"And you can't hold me responsible for my uncle's debt," I add.

"It's true," Tom says. "She was not in Hiram Westfall's custody when he incurred it. If anyone could take on the debt, it would be Westfall's heir, but he has named none that I know of, and as I'm sure you know, women cannot inherit."

If women could inherit property, I'd still be in Georgia, working my family's homestead. Funny how the thing that made me flee my home will be the thing that saves me now.

Hardwick's gaze on me is frank and appraising. He is reconsidering his notions about me; I can see it in his eyes. After a long moment, he says, "Seems I partnered with the wrong Westfall."

I waste no time pressing my advantage. "I'm prepared to pay my uncle's debt, anyway, if you agree to my conditions."

He raises an eyebrow. "How will you come up with so much money? You expect to succeed where your uncle failed? Let me guess: You wish to reopen the mine. You think you can—"

Another laugh bubbles from my throat. "No, no, nothing like that. I already have the money, sir. California has been very good to me."

He contemplates us for a long moment. Then, "Follow me. All of you."

Hardwick leads us up the stairs and down a hallway of doors. He opens one and ushers us inside. It's one of the guest rooms, simply but cleanly furnished with a bed, a dressing table, and two oil lamps. The music of the orchestra and the buzz of conversation dim as he closes the door behind us.

Immediately, he turns to me and says, "What are your conditions?"

"Hiram Westfall must leave California, along with a man by the name of Frank Dilley."

"Ah, yes, Westfall's foreman. He's dead."

"Oh." I had suspected, but I hadn't known for sure. "Just my uncle, then."

"And how do you propose I do that?"

"I don't much care," I tell him. "Just ship him somewhere far away. I'm sure a smart man like you with resources can make it happen."

He rubs his chin with one hand, considering me. "Hmm, maybe Australia. You will pay in advance?"

I almost say yes, but Tom jumps in. "Half now, half when we see a passenger manifest, independently witnessed, with Westfall's name."

"Yes, half now," I say.

"In addition," Tom says, "we want your word as a gentleman and council member that when California becomes a state, you will use every means at your disposal to ensure that Glory is granted a proper town charter."

Hardwick rubs at his chin. "I think I can manage that. Tell

me, Miss Westfall, how did you come up with so much? Dare I ask if you stole it from your uncle?"

"Well, I can speak for four of us in this room and say that we are not thieves."

He actually smiles. "How *did* you come by it?"

"Hard work and charity," I tell him. "Glory is a thriving, wonderful place brimming with people full of good will. They *gave* us the money."

Now he seems genuinely surprised. "That's hardly what I've come to expect from miners."

"Well, pardon my saying, sir, but maybe you ought to broaden your expectations."

Tom steps in. "To be perfectly frank, California has been a somewhat lawless place this past year, but with statehood coming, that's going to change. People who've prospered from their hard work and sacrifice thus far—like our neighbors in Glory—will sacrifice even more for the guarantee that they can continue to prosper under the new laws."

"But why come to me instead of going to the governor-elect?"

Tom smiles with tight lips. "I presume that's a rhetorical question."

"Do we have a deal?" I ask impatiently.

"Self-interest rules us all," Hardwick says. He turns back to me. "Yes, you have a deal, young lady. My man will draw up the papers tonight for you to sign."

"I'm glad to hear it, Mr. Hardwick. We will *all* sign," I say, indicating my friends. "In case you had any notion of later voiding the contract on account of its being signed by a woman."

A slight widening of his eyes indicates I might have guessed right.

I spit into my palm and hold it out to him. "To our new arrangement," I say.

After a moment's hesitation, he spits into his own palm and grasps mine. "To our new arrangement."

Chapter Thirty

It's not a complex agreement, so his attorney is able to draft something quickly. Jefferson, Tom, Henry, and I each read it over carefully and sign it, then Hardwick does the same. We insist the attorney scribe a second copy that we can take back to Glory and show around, and we hand Hardwick two thousand dollars as a down payment, and that's that.

We're done, and my friends and I are, finally, truly safe.

"Weather permitting," Hardwick says as we head back downstairs, "there will be fireworks along the riverfront tonight. I encourage you to view them."

We reach the dance floor. "Thank you, Mr. Hardwick. That sounds like just the thing."

"I might pay a visit to Glory this spring," he says. "Can't miss the opportunity to see such a blessed place full of earthen angels."

His tone is mocking, but I choose to take his words at face value. "You would surely be welcome, sir," I tell him.

From the corner of my eye, I see a throng of hopeful men approaching, full of purpose, each angling to reach me first. In a panic, I look to Jefferson. "Help?" I squeak out.

With that lightning grin I love so much, he grabs my hand and pulls me into the dancing fray. Jefferson is a terrible dancer, and so am I, and after a while I'm fairly sure the new boots the Major made for me are ruined from being stepped on so much. But it doesn't matter, because I'm so breathless with relief and laughter and the wonderful familiarity of being with my best friend in the whole world.

Someone taps Jefferson on the shoulder to cut in, and he is about to comply, but I grab his hand and pull him close. "I only want to dance with you tonight," I say.

His smile disappears. As we dance and dance and dance, he stares down at me with so much hope in his eyes that my heart hurts.

The music stops, and the governor steps onto the stage and announces that everyone is invited to head toward the docks to see the fireworks. Jefferson's hand stays clasped in mine as we leave the ballroom, skirt the giant Christmas tree, and step into the night.

We follow everyone else across the street and between buildings, toward the river and its network of hasty, haphazard docks. "Jefferson," I whisper, yanking on his arm. "Look. It's the *Stirling*."

It's a schooner devoid of sails, anchored permanently just offshore. In the dark, it seems a great hulking beast, a leviathan waiting to leap out of the water.

"That's where your uncle is," Jefferson says.

"Yes." It's odd to be so close to him just now. Does he have a window? Could he look out and see me?

"Do you want to visit him before he leaves?" Jefferson asks. "I'm sure we can arrange it, if that's what you want."

I stare at the ship. The water laps peacefully against its hull—along with the hulls of dozens of other ships that look abandoned and half salvaged for building materials.

"No. I told him I'd never speak to him again, and I meant it." And I turn my back on the *Stirling* and Hiram Westfall and follow all the other ball attendees to a long dock lined with candles.

Violins take up a hymn, and I recognize it as the one Olive hums while she helps her ma serve miners, the same one Henry sang as Martin lay dying. Several people around us begin to sing along:

Like a river glorious, is God's perfect peace
Over all victorious, in its bright increase . . .

"We were victorious today," Jefferson whispers in my ear.

I smile. "We were."

Beside us, Tom has an arm around Henry as the two gaze toward the sky.

The first fireworks shoot across the night, reflecting sparks of color on the surface of the river. More and more shoot up, higher and higher, so that it seems we're surrounded by glittering light.

"This is what it's like, Jeff!" I say. "When I call the gold to me. Do you see? Isn't it fine?"

"I see."

But I get the sense he's not looking at the sky at all.

"Lee—" he begins, but I interrupt.

"Don't ask me to marry you again," I say. "Not even one more time."

"I . . . Okay." His voice is suddenly small.

"Because I'm going to ask you."

His breath catches.

I turn to face him. "Remember when we left for Sacramento the first time? Before Dilley and his men found us? You told me I was in love with you."

"I remember."

"Well, I reckon you were right."

"Oh, Lee." He wraps his arms around me and pulls me close, nuzzling my hair.

"So, is that a yes?" I say, though it comes out muffled against his chest.

"You haven't asked me anything yet."

"Oh. Right."

I step away just so I can take in his face—his black eyes that have so much kindness in them. His perfect mouth. The way his hair curls at the nape, just so. "Jefferson McCauley Kingfisher, will you do me the honor of becoming my husband?"

Finally his grin is back. "Even though I won't ever own property?"

"Especially because of that. Jeff, all this time I thought I was coming to California so I could finally have something of my own. But I had it all along. I had you. And now I have Jasper and Tom and Henry, Becky and her kids, the Major, Hampton, maybe even Mary. My home is not a place; it's people."

He tips up my chin with a forefinger. "It's about blasted time you came to your fool senses," he murmurs, then he bends down and kisses me, and it's better than fireworks, better even than sparkling gold.

Reluctantly I break away to say, "So is *that* a yes?"

"That's a hell yes."

"What a relief. I was afraid that after everything I'd put you through, you'd say no."

Jefferson laughs. "Leah, surely you know? You've been the only girl for me since we were five years old."

Tom and Henry sidle over, and I can tell they're curious about what just happened, but neither Jefferson nor I offer them anything yet. I want to keep this moment precious, just between us, for a little longer.

The fireworks swell to a climactic finale, as the violins play "O Christmas Tree." Then the lights and the music cease, and everyone begins to drift away. "Let's go, Golden Goddess," Jefferson says. "Time to go home."

I punch him in the shoulder. "Never call me that again."

Author's Note

Historical fiction—even when it has a touch of magic—requires a delicate balancing act between fact and fantasy, and to best tell Lee's story, I took some minor historical liberties. For instance, Hiram Westfall establishes a tunnel mine in 1849, even though hard rock mining for gold quartz isn't recorded on this scale until 1851. Likewise, Thanksgiving did not become a national holiday until 1863, but it was widely celebrated in New England before then, and I thought that Hiram, being from Massachusetts, might have grown up with it. Also, Hiram discusses collecting bounties on Indian scalps, even though California's governor Peter Burnett did not call for "a war of extermination" against the Indians until 1851, and the state did not begin paying bounties until after that . . . but I would have felt remiss to ignore this atrocity.

I chose to place some political wrangling in Sacramento, because doing so eased logistical plot burdens and because

Sacramento was a geographic and political center long before it became the official state capital in 1854. The first ball in gold country took place on December 25, 1849, at Mormon Island, not in Sacramento as portrayed in this book; Mormon Island is largely submerged beneath Lake Folsom now, although parts of it have reappeared due to the recent drought. I don't know how prevalent cross-dressing was at formal dances like these, but numerous written Gold Rush accounts and contemporary illustrations show men dressed as women when dancing. Without hearing those accounts in their own voices, I could only speculate about their orientations and intentions.

The plight of Muskrat and his friends was drawn from the fact that the Gold Rush happened at the expense of California's indigenous population, through enslavement, the confiscation of their tribal lands, and destruction of their traditional ways of life. In 1845, more than 150,000 Native Americans lived in California. By 1870, that population had been reduced through starvation, disease, and murder to less than 30,000. It is entirely appropriate to refer to this as genocide. To learn more, I recommend reading Albert L. Hurtado's *Indian Survival on the California Frontier* (Yale University Press, 1990 edition).

Even so, it's important to acknowledge the active, vibrant communities of Native Americans still living in California. For the perspective of California's indigenous people, given in their own voices, I also recommend *The Way We Lived: California Indian Stories, Songs & Reminiscences*, edited by

Malcolm Margolin (Heyday Books, published in conjunction with the California Historical Society, 1992).

In creating the character of Mary, I hoped to honor the thousands of women like her, many of whom found ways to escape their situations and invent different lives for themselves. Because the oversexualization of Asian American women in modern media and culture has such deep and unpleasant roots in history—by the 1870s, 70 percent of all Chinese women in San Francisco were prostitutes—I strove to acknowledge this aspect of the Gold Rush era without perpetuating harmful stereotypes. This means I may have erred on the side of caution, insufficiently addressing the atrocities and indignities Mary likely would have suffered. A hard-hitting academic history on this subject is *Unsubmissive Women: Chinese Prostitutes in Nineteenth-Century San Francisco*, by Benson Tong (University of Oklahoma Press, 1994).

California entered the Union as a free state on September 9, 1850, but slavery and the treatment of free African Americans as slaves continued. Despite this, many African Americans—both freemen who rushed west like James "Free Jim" Boisclair, as well as escaped slaves like Hampton who worked to buy their freedom—played key roles in the Gold Rush and used it to create opportunities for themselves and their families. I recommend *The Negro Trail Blazers of California*, by Delilah L. Beasley, originally published in 1919 but reprinted several times recently, as an important resource and collection of primary documents.

In 1849, only 3 percent of Gold Rush immigrants to California identified as female. To capture the experiences of women like Lee and Mrs. Joyner, I relied heavily on *They Saw the Elephant: Women in the California Gold Rush*, by JoAnn Levy (University of Oklahoma Press, 1990). For general background on this period of California history, I frequently found myself thumbing through the pages of *The Age of Gold: The California Gold Rush and the New American Dream*, by H. W. Brands (Doubleday, 2002).

Like a River Glorious has been improved by the contributions of numerous people. I want to thank the librarians, curators, and docents of the following institutions, where I did much of my research:

- The California Historical Society (http://www.californiahistoricalsociety.org) in San Francisco
- The Chinese Historical Society of America (http://chsa.org) in San Francisco
- Sutter's Fort State Historic Park (http://www.suttersfort.org) in Sacramento
- The Sacramento History Museum (http://sachistorymuseum.org), especially the permanent exhibits "Coming to California and the Lure of Gold" and "Gold, Greed, & Speculation: The Beginnings of Sacramento City"
- Though not focused on Gold Rush history, the Heard Museum of American Indian Art & History (http://heard.org) in Phoenix is a valuable resource in general

◆ ◆ ◆

I'm also deeply grateful to the following readers for their contributions: My agent, Holly Root, was an endless source of encouragement and guidance in navigating the path of this novel. My editor, Martha Mihalick, exhibited patience, humor, and intelligence through multiple drafts. Marlette Grant Jackson of the Yurok tribe of Northern California holds a degree in Native American Studies and works in the Indian Teacher Education Personnel Program at Humboldt State University; her feedback was invaluable. Albert L. Hurtado, formerly the Paul H. and Doris Eaton Travis Chair in Modern American History at the University of Oklahoma and a leading expert on Native Americans and the history of the western frontier, read the manuscript for historical accuracy. Jay Cravath, PhD, applied his expertise in curriculum and cultural research to the text. Erika Gee, M.S. Ed., of the Chinatown Community Development Center, and my friends and fellow authors Samantha Ling and Heidi Heilig all offered essential insights into the perspectives of Chinese American women and their connections to the Gold Rush.

This is a better book for all their contributions. Any remaining errors of fact or perspective are my own.

If you decide to write historical fiction, I recommend being married to someone who is both an editor and a historian. My husband, C. C. Finlay, was endlessly supportive, whether we were researching, visiting museums and historical sites, or doing the backbreaking work of panning for gold in the Sierra foothills.

My uncle David "Jericho" Yarbrough is the one who took us gold mining and taught us how to pan and sluice using traditional methods. I owe him, not just for that but for sharing his love of California and the outdoors throughout my childhood. Uncle Jericho, this one is for you.